THE
HAUNTING
OF
H. G. WELLS

ALSO BY ROBERT MASELLO

FICTION

The Night Crossing
The Jekyll Revelation
The Einstein Prophecy
The Romanov Cross
The Medusa Amulet
Blood and Ice
Vigil
Bestiary
Black Horizon
Private Demons
The Spirit Wood

NONFICTION

Robert's Rules of Writing
A Friend in the Business
Writer Tells All
The Things Your Father Never Taught You
What Do Men Want from Women?
Fallen Angels and Spirits of the Dark
Raising Hell: A Concise History of the Black Arts

THE
HAUNTING
OF
H. G. WELLS

ROBERT MASELLO

Published by 47North, Seattle

www.apub.com

Amazon, the Amazon logo, and 47North are trademarks of Amazon.com, Inc., or its affiliates.

ISBN-13: 9781542093781
ISBN-10: 1542093783

Cover design by Damon Freeman

Printed in the United States of America

For my brother David,
always my most enthusiastic and supportive reader.
Thanks, Da.

PROLOGUE

Mons, Belgium, the Western Front, August 23, 1914

"Hold the line!" the captain shouted. "Hold the damned line!"

But the German onslaught was simply too overwhelming, the line of British soldiers holding them off too thin. Already the trench was littered with the dead, and Captain Mills was certain that he would soon be lying among them. If this rear guard action failed, then the entire British Expeditionary Force, now in retreat, could be overrun and annihilated by the advancing horde.

Right now that annihilation looked inevitable.

A hand grenade, hurled by one of the advancing Huns, arced above the last tattered line of barbed wire, looking oddly like a blackbird swooping down to earth. It landed on top of one of the few remaining Vickers machine guns, blowing the gunners to smithereens. Mud and blood, flesh and bones, rained down on the soldiers still clinging to their rifles and firing as rapidly as they could.

As Mills hunkered down to reload, the clatter of exploding shells grew deafening. When he dared raise his head again above the lip of the trench, he saw what looked like another great gray wave of soldiers, bayonets extended, marching implacably forward. My God, how many could there be? They'd been coming all morning—mown down like grass—but there were always more, and more, and more.

He fired a shot and a man went down, instantly replaced by another stepping over the fallen body, and a dozen others behind him. They were only fifty or sixty yards off, and Mills knew that the soldiers left in his battalion could no more hold them at bay than they could turn back an ocean tide.

Nothing but a miracle could save them now.

Wiping the sweat from his eyes—there was so much dirt and debris in the air that Mills could barely see what he was shooting at—he prayed for just that: a miracle. There was a plaque to St. George, the patron saint of England, which had once hung on the schoolroom wall where he taught mathematics. Its motto, which he now murmured under his breath, read *Adsit Anglis Sanctus Georgius*. May St. George be a present help to the English. That was all the Latin he'd ever mastered, but he had no sooner uttered the words than a cold shudder went down his spine. He felt an icy tingling in his fingertips, and for a second, he thought he must have been shot.

The cloud of smoke that clung to the no man's land before him seemed to thicken, obscuring the oncoming Huns. Damn, now he wouldn't even be able to spot the bastards before they were close enough to stick him with their bayonets.

"Where are they?" Foster shouted from down the line. "I can't see a bloody thing anymore!"

And yet, the battlefield had not grown darker, but lighter. There were shapes coalescing in the fog, shapes that seemed to be somehow . . . radiant. What was going on?

To the constant rattle of machine gun fire and blasts of artillery, another sound was added—a strange whistling noise, a whishing like wind through the rushes . . . and archaic cries of "Array! Array!" They seemed to be coming from all around.

And then, Mills thought he saw something equally impossible.

Archers, wearing the leather doublets and round helmets worn by the English bowmen who had won the Battle of Agincourt hundreds of years before . . . they were standing, ranks of them, in front of the fragile English lines, dispatching volley after volley of arrows at the approaching horde.

He heard the sound of galloping hooves, and glimpsed a knight in armor riding a white horse, rallying his ghostly troops with a raised sword, before being swallowed up in the mist.

Again, Mills wondered if he was still alive. None of this could be real. Maybe he had been shot, after all, and this was all the dream of a dying man.

But his prayer to St. George kept repeating in his head. He could hear the *thwang* of the bowstrings, letting fly another shot. Before long the onslaught had abated and the shining archers were gradually enveloped in the fog. The Germans fell back, the battlefield saturated with their blood, and even their artillery fire let up.

Thunderstruck, Mills lowered his rifle, resting the barrel on a sandbag, and glanced over at Foster, who had done the same, as had all the others left defending the trench.

"Did you see that?" Foster said.

Mills nodded, speechless, glad that someone else could attest to it.

"Because I still don't believe that I did," Foster added. A butcher in civilian life, he was not one to engage in flights of fancy. "I thought we were all goners for sure."

So had Mills. So had every man still peering in disbelief out over the barren wasteland.

When the glowing fog lifted, Captain Mills stood up on the firing step and raised his binoculars, but there was no sign of the golden bowmen, nor of the knight on the white horse, anywhere.

"Well, I'll be damned," he murmured.

There was no reason to believe that the phantoms had ever been there at all . . . were it not for the inexplicable arrow wounds found in so many of the enemy corpses examined the next day.

CHAPTER ONE

Easton Glebe, Essex, England, February 1915

Although he usually did most of his writing earlier in the day, tonight H. G. Wells was at it long past dark, his head bent low over the desk tucked away in the sitting area off his bedroom. His pen scratched quickly across the pages, in an idiosyncratic handwriting that his wife, Jane, could read—and then transcribe on her typewriter—even when no one else could. Sometimes, she even took the liberty of improving some of his hastily written prose, finding a more precise word, or recasting a bit of dialogue altogether, and though he liked to chide her for her gall, secretly he appreciated it. She was his best reader, most capable editor, and, if the occasion called for it, bluntest critic.

So absorbed was he in his work that he must not have heard her footstep on the stairs, or the sound of the bedroom door opening. Ensconced in the warm nimbus of light from the banker's lamp on the desk, he was startled when he heard her say, "H. G.? Don't you think you've done enough for tonight?"

"What?" he muttered, his pen still flying across the page before the words escaped him.

"Dr. Gruber said you needed to take it easy. You're not out of the woods quite yet."

"I feel fine," he said, still not raising his head. "Gruber worries too much." He finished a sentence, pressing the period home. "And so do you."

"It's my job."

"Right you are," he said, shifting the completed page to the stack on his left. "And I am grateful beyond measure." Looking up with a smile, he said, "But you may cease worrying now."

She was a compact woman, no nonsense about her, brown hair tidily gathered in a bun.

"You have an early day tomorrow," she added. "Time you got into bed."

She was probably right. He was feeling a cramp in his neck, and his shoulders were stiff. When he was a young man, he'd been able to write all night long if the deadline called for it, but now—at forty-nine—even writing required a stamina he could not always muster. He put the pen, one of a dozen kept at the ready, back in its brass holder, and stretched his arms out in the silk dressing gown. Perhaps he *was* written out for the day; better to start fresh in the morning.

"By the way, I've had a telegram from the War Office, asking me to come in next week to confer about something," he said, pushing his chair back from the desk. "Not the worst idea to show the colors in London now and then, anyway."

"I wish you wouldn't go."

He knew why she was saying that. "Despite any present infirmities, I'm still nimble enough to dodge the occasional bomb," he replied. "And it might be a good idea to make sure that one hasn't dropped right through the roof of our place on St. James's Court."

"The neighbors would have alerted us."

"What if it had landed *on* the neighbors?"

"Don't even joke about such things."

The war made Jane surly; Wells was accustomed to that. It was one of the many idiocies, as unforgivable as it was destructive, that Jane felt men, with their ungovernable urge to aggression, inflicted on the rest of the human race. Wells, a man who had long championed in his essays a socialist and utopian future, had no cause to argue with that; in fact, he quite agreed. But once the war had begun, he'd felt in his bosom an undeniable patriotic stirring. So many of his books—*The War of the Worlds*, *The War in the Air*, even *The Time Machine*—had focused on the violence that men do, and the ingenious ways in which they do it (why, he'd even predicted the invention of armored tanks and the scourge of poison gas), but once the Germans had invaded Belgium and France, once the reports of their atrocities had started to filter home, his mind had begun to change. And once their airships had crossed the Channel to drop their bombs and incendiary devices on the civilian populations of England, he had reverted to this more traditional stance. Now was not the moment for the pacifism he had once preached; now was the time to repel the barbarians at the gates, and in so doing, perhaps put a stop to this monstrous behavior once and for all. This cataclysm, already dubbed the Great War, with its dreadful death tolls and no immediate end in sight, might prove to be the one to end all wars forever. He had put that very sentiment in writing, and if it turned out to be true, then this war was well worth fighting.

Maybe that was why, when he heard the bugle call off in the distance, he thought for a moment that he had imagined it. The look on Jane's face told him otherwise. She ran to the window, and yanked the curtains back with both hands; across a sloping lawn lay a country road, and beyond that, on the other side, were cornfields lying fallow in the moonlight. The bugle was coming closer, and as Wells watched over her shoulder, he saw the Boy Scout on his bicycle pedaling past, blowing his lungs out, heading toward the village.

"Here?" Jane murmured. They were forty-five miles from London, in the middle of nowhere, a stretch of nothing but fields and farms and ancient forest.

Wells scanned the sky, but he could see only a sliver from this vantage point. "Come on!" he said, racing toward the door, his slippers scuffing on the carpet. At the bottom of the stairs, he kicked them off his feet, pulled on a pair of rubber boots, and with his overcoat thrown over his robe and pajamas, darted out onto the lawn.

The moon—bright silver, dotted with its familiar craters, and as usual quite stationary—had a rival in the sky that night, a *moving* rival. Pewter-colored, shaped like a cucumber, and drifting just below the clouds . . . a zeppelin—called a "baby-killer" by the British public because of its indiscriminate attacks on the innocent civilians of London—whose engines could be heard thrumming.

"What could they want to target here?" Jane said, coming to his side, clutching the collar of her own coat against the cold night wind.

"It's probably been blown off course."

There was something both malignant and magnificent about the great lumbering beast in the sky, a machine measuring as much as six hundred feet long, kept aloft by hydrogen gasbags, and carrying a crew of perhaps a dozen or more, along with a load of thermite bombs bound with tar. Although it appeared from below to be moving at a glacial pace, Wells knew that it was actually cruising at perhaps fifty miles per hour, and was well defended by gunners in glass gondolas at both ends.

"Will it just move on?"

One could only hope so, Wells thought, although there was something that gave him pause. Why was it flying so low? The great advantage to the German airships was that they could travel at altitudes high enough to be out of range of anti-aircraft fire from the ground, as well as attacks from British fighter planes. This one was descending even lower, its nose tilting down, and it was only then that Wells spotted a lick of flame from its rear.

"I think it's been hit," he said.

"By what?"

That he could not know. But some damage had been done, and now it was even more evident—the fire was spreading its livid fingers across the duralumin fuselage, like a tracery of red veins, and the thrumming of its engines became louder and more high-pitched, the cry of a wounded animal.

"My God," Jane said, her breath fogging the air, "it's going to crash!"

Though its propellers were still whirring, its rounded ribs were already showing in the spots where the outer fabric skin had been burnt away. Something fell—jumped?—from the burning shell, and was lost once it dropped below the treetops. Wells started running.

"What are you doing?" Jane cried. "You must come back inside!"

But he was already across the road.

"H. G.!"

As best he could judge, the zeppelin would crash in the open meadows surrounding Lady Warwick's extensive property. Maybe the pilot, in one last desperate attempt to save himself and his crew, had even been trying to land there. With his open coattails flapping around his pajama bottoms, Wells picked his way across the barren earth matted with corn husks. He tried to keep one eye on the ground to keep from tripping, and the other on the airship, its metal struts popping loose as the flames coursed toward its bow. He was dimly aware of other people, here and there, racing along in the same direction, pointing at the sky and shouting to each other.

Breaking through a copse of trees and scrambling over a low stone wall, he saw the zeppelin turn on one side and then the other, as if writhing in pain, before its nose nudged the ground . . . gently at first, but then crumpling as the rest of its massive frame plowed deeper into the earth with a great grinding noise. There was a series of explosions, like fireworks going off, and a shudder went through the entire craft; its front gun turret was squashed against the ground and the propellers threw up a last massive gout of soil, a geyser of dirt and dead grass, before stopping dead. The carcass settled on the ground, crackling with orange flames from one long end to the other.

He heard villagers' voices—"It's down!" and "We got it!" and "Fetch the fire brigade before the sparks catch the trees!"—and then he was close enough that he could feel the heat. He slowed down, his breath labored by the run, and plodded toward the blaze. Impregnable as it had looked in the sky, it was now just an immense pile of twisted wreckage, reeking of chemicals and canvas and oil . . . and burning flesh. When Wells saw several of his neighbors getting too close, he warned them to stay back: "There might yet be a hydrogen pocket, or a bomb, that hasn't exploded yet."

Slattery, who ran the town livery service, used a pitchfork he was carrying to draw a line in the dirt and warned a couple of children not to cross it. Mrs. Willoughby, who helped Jane with the household chores, was wringing her hands and muttering something to the tobacconist, Mr. Spool. The Boy Scout was sitting astride his bicycle, his duty done, bugle dangling from one hand.

"You'll catch your death all over again," Wells heard, as Jane came up behind him, squashing a hat onto his head and wrapping a woolen scarf around his neck. It was all oddly like a harvest bonfire, though the festive note was entirely replaced by one of alarm.

And then, like a worm wriggling up out of the earth, Wells saw something emerge from the shattered remnants of the rear gun turret. An arm was flung out, and then another, followed by a head scorched as black as ink, except for the whites of the eyes, wide with fear.

The bugle boy cried, "Look there!"

"One of 'em's still alive!" Mrs. Willoughby shouted.

The gunner slithered on his belly away from the wreck, smoke and even a touch of fire still smoldering from his leather pants. His fingers were digging in the sod to pull himself along, a few inches at a time. His legs looked broken. Goggles hung down from his neck.

How on earth could he have survived the fire, and the crash? Wells wondered.

Slattery stepped over his own line, and strode to where the man was now panting on a tiny patch of grass and weed. Wells assumed—though why?—that he was about to pull him farther away from the flames.

"Bitte," the gunner said, too injured even to lift his head. *"Bitte."*

But Slattery didn't say anything. He simply straddled him, one foot on either side, raised his pitchfork with both hands, then plunged it into the gunner's shoulders, pinning him to the ground like a butterfly to a mat. Still leaning down hard on the handle, and putting his full weight on it, he muttered, "Baby-killer."

CHAPTER TWO

The next day, the downed zeppelin was not only the talk of the town, but of the whole country. The late edition of the London papers made space for it on their front pages. At the tobacconist's shop, Wells picked up a sheaf of the newspapers, along with his usual haul of whatever magazines, pamphlets, and tabloids caught his eye. One on the rack was new—the *Freewoman*, which billed itself as a monthly journal aimed at the free-thinking (read "suffragette") women of England. He added a copy of that to his pile on the counter—he always liked to keep up with current opinion of every stripe—and as Mr. Spool toted them all up, Wells asked, "Has your business been up today, what with all the national attention?"

"Oh, yes," Spool said, making change from the fiver Wells had handed him. "Lots of folks stopping for directions to the site."

"That doesn't do you much good," Wells said. "Directions." His own parents had owned a small and unsuccessful shop, and he remained sensitive to the plight of shopkeepers.

"Oh, I manage to sell them a packet of Woodbines or a good cigar before they go." With a stringy finger stained yellow from nicotine, Spool pushed his glasses back onto the bridge of his nose. "Not that they get to see much. The army's pretty well got the whole field roped off."

Wells had seen some signs of it before coming into town; two or three military cars and a pair of lorries, with a half dozen soldiers in each, had bucketed past him as he'd walked along the road.

By the time he was heading back home, it was dark out, but on the far field he could see that lights had been set up and he could hear some commotion. Jane would worry that he was late for dinner, but he couldn't resist, and detoured toward the meadow. He was still a few hundred yards off when a sentry stepped into his path.

"Sorry, sir, but this is as far as you can go."

"Saw it all last night."

"Must have been quite a show."

Was that what it had been? Hard to think of it that way at all, especially as the one moment that had come back to him all night—and all that day as he'd attempted to work on his new manuscript—had been the livery driver finishing off the German gunner.

"Were there any survivors?" Wells asked.

"From the zepp? Not very likely. Why?"

"I thought I might have seen someone fall, or jump, before the crash."

This appeared to give the soldier pause. The question was above his pay grade. "Can you wait here? I'll have to get my CO." He started to turn away, then said, "Oh, and may I ask your name, sir?"

"Wells. H. G."

The soldier nodded quickly, starting to turn again, when the name struck him. "The author?"

"I like to think so."

The soldier loped off toward the wreckage in the distance, but not without one backward glance at the famous writer. Wells was used to it, but still enjoyed the recognition. God knows he'd spent enough time at his desk to have earned it.

When a Lieutenant Talbot arrived, looking just as young and callow as the sentry, he began by burbling about Wells's books and how much he had enjoyed them as a boy, before getting to the matter at hand. "We've found the remains of perhaps a dozen men inside and around the wreckage," he said, "but the fire was so intense it's hard to know for sure if we've found them all. You say you think you saw someone escape before the crash?"

"Off behind that copse of trees, to the south, there."

The lieutenant looked that way and said, yes, they'd searched there. "And at least a quarter mile in every direction," he added.

"Were any parachutes found?"

"None. And judging from the trajectory and speed of the descent, there wouldn't have been time to deploy one properly."

Maybe he'd been mistaken, Wells thought. Either way, it was out of his hands now. "Would it be possible," he said, "for me to get a look at what's left of the zeppelin before you haul it all away?"

The lieutenant wrestled with it. "Orders are very strict about that; no civilians are to be—"

"For my writing," Wells said, playing his ace. "The *Evening Standard* has requested anything I can give them." Not strictly true in this instance, but if it helped . . .

The lieutenant folded like a house of cards; how could he refuse such a request from the most famous writer in the world? Nodding at the sentry, as if to warn him to keep mum about this breach, he escorted Wells the few hundred yards between where they'd been conferring and the sodden pile of bent metal and scorched fabric, all thoroughly drenched by the fire brigade, and now bathed in the harsh glare of arc lights powered by two rumbling field generators. While soldiers kept up a wide perimeter around the site, a few experts were still picking over the remains, looking for all the world like men exploring the innards of a beached and eviscerated whale. The rounded struts rose up like broken ribs above their heads; the propellers resembled wounded tail fins. The twin Daimler engines, the beating heart of the beast, had already been removed and were lashed to platforms tied to the back of the lorries.

A dozen canvas body bags were discreetly being loaded into a pair of hearses.

Wells was standing on the very spot where the gunner had been dispatched with the pitchfork. He could still see the divots torn in the soil by its prongs, and perhaps the lieutenant had noticed them, too.

"We found a crewman here," he said, "who'd managed to crawl away. He'd made it this far, but he was pretty well burnt and had a number of wounds, and no one has been able to tell us if he was able to say anything."

Wells remained silent.

"Standard military protocol dictates that enemy combatants, when captured, be treated with decency."

Wells nodded thoughtfully.

"Did you observe anything that would not conform to such a view?"

Had the puncture marks been so evident? "No, but then I was not among the first on the scene."

"It appears," the lieutenant said dryly, "that no one was."

There was nothing Wells could say without indicting Slattery. And he knew for a fact that the livery man had had a special reason for what he did. His sister and her family had been killed in Sheringham, in one of the very first zeppelin raids. Not an excuse necessarily . . . but under the circumstances understandable. Wells would not be the one to bring down further calamity on the man's head, especially as the German gunner had looked only moments away from death, anyway.

"Would you mind if I just poked around a bit on my own?"

"I guess it would be all right," the lieutenant replied, "so long as you don't get in the way of the inspectors."

Wells deposited the bundle of newspapers he was carrying on the hood of one of the army cars, and gingerly approached the carcass of the airship. Hard to believe that just the night before it had been a mighty behemoth, ruler of the sky, dealer of death and destruction. Now look at it. Bits of glass ground under his shoes. He was thankful that the corpses of the crew had already been removed; indeed, he could hear the hearses starting up and slowly driving from the field back toward the road, their headlights briefly sweeping across the scene and adding to the unnatural glare. Wells had to hold his arm up in front of his eyes until they had passed.

The bodies might be gone, but there was still a lingering odor of death. A fiery one at that.

Wells dug in the pocket of his coat and removed his pad and pencil—no writer worth his salt went anywhere without one—and a nearby inspector, kneeling among some metal bits, gave him a quizzical look. "Just a few notes for the War Office," Wells said, in a jaunty yet authoritative tone. "Memory's not what it used to be."

The inspector went back to his task, and Wells began not only jotting down notes, but making quick sketches of the scene—the twisted fuselage, the long trail of wreckage, the flattened gondolas where the gunners had crouched. He'd always been a quick hand at drawing—the only part of the draper's trade, to which he had once been apprenticed, at which he'd excelled; even in his private correspondence, he often relied on what he jokingly called his "picshuas" to recapture certain scenes. These hasty sketches would no doubt prove useful in the construction of some future novel or story.

When he was done, he looked up again at the night sky. The stars were out and the moon had no rival tonight. Then he turned his gaze toward the distant copse of towering oaks and elms where he had thought he'd seen something fall. Perhaps his eyes had been strained from overwork . . . it would not be the first time.

Thanking the lieutenant, he picked up his parcel of newspapers and trudged the rest of the way home. Jane, popping her head out of the kitchen, said, "I don't even need to ask where you've been."

He plopped the papers on the hall table, then hung his coat and hat on the rack by the door.

"But if you catch pneumonia," she said, "don't come to me for tea and sympathy."

After a dinner of hot roast beef and burnt potatoes, followed by a good Stilton, Wells and Jane retired to their usual armchairs on either side of the fireplace. He had a glass of Scotch on the table at his elbow, she had a cup of chamomile tea. The haul of newspapers from the tobacconist's shop had been duly divided, and each was reading through his or her allotment.

Wells's latest novel, entitled *Marriage*, had come out the week before, and the reviews were starting to appear. The *Daily News* had already praised the book for its "almost vicious gaiety," and the *Sphere* had claimed it was "alive with flashes of the most perfect insight at every turn." All the reviews so far had been laudatory; he hadn't had such a uniformly good reception for a novel since *The War of the Worlds*—his terrifying tale of a Martian invasion, replete with three-legged mechanical monsters brought down in the end by Earth's humblest organisms. And that had been, what, nineteen years before? He had published a trove of other books of a similar ilk. *The Invisible Man*, where a mad scientist discovered the secret of invisibility, but not its cure. *The Island of Dr. Moreau*, in which a ruthless vivisectionist had relegated to himself the powers of God, hewing humanoid creatures from tortured beasts. *The First Men in the Moon*, in which a pair of explorers landed on the moon and encountered a race of insect-like creatures. Not to mention *The Time Machine*, the book that had launched his career, featuring a gentleman inventor who traveled into a far future where cannibalistic Morlocks preyed upon the helpless Eloi who lived above ground.

No, this new book had been an attempt, hardly his first, to put his epic tales of science-inflected fiction behind him and broaden his audience. He had begun to write more domestic and contemporary stories, ones in which he could explore and explain his views on social mores and issues of the day. He had a lot to say on such matters, especially those pertaining to love and sex, and books like this one, and *Ann Veronica* before it, were his way of doing so.

"Here's a good notice," Jane said, without looking up from the paper in her lap. "'Mr. Wells has put all his cleverness into this long story of an engagement and marriage between two attractive and, we may add, perfectly moral young people.' From the *Spectator*."

Wells harrumphed. "Not sure I like that morality bit."

"You can't have it both ways," Jane said, carefully tearing the review from the paper for Wells's later and full perusal.

There was nothing in the next two papers, but in the third Wells struck gold again. "From the *Daily Chronicle*," he announced. "'A book that thrills with the life, the questioning, of to-day. Whatever the publishing season may produce, it is not likely to bring us anything more vital, more significant, than *Marriage*.'"

"And they never like anything," Jane said.

Wells had just finished reading the whole review and put it to one side, when he noticed Jane's now furrowed brow.

"What," he said, "a dissenting voice?"

But she didn't answer immediately. He craned his neck to see what she was reading, and saw that it was that new journal he'd never read before, the *Freewoman*.

"How bad is it?"

"You won't be happy."

"I'm braced."

"You'd better be. 'Mr. Wells's mannerisms are more infuriating than ever. One knows at once that Marjorie is speaking in a crisis of wedded chastity when she says at regular intervals, "Oh, my dear . . . Oh, my dear!" or at moments of ecstasy, "Oh, my dear! Oh, my dear!" For Mr. Wells's heroines who are loving under legal difficulties say "My Man!" or "Master!" Of course he is the old maid among novelists; even the sex obsession that lay clotted on *Ann Veronica* and *The New Machiavelli* like cold white sauce was merely old maid's mania, the reaction toward the flesh of a mind too long absorbed in airships and colloids.'"

There was more where that came from, and when she was done reading, Jane did not immediately look up. She knew that the reviewer had pricked his vanity—and precisely where it would hurt the most—but Wells was determined not to let on. He took a sip of his whiskey, smacked his lips, and asked, "Who wrote it?"

Jane flipped back to the previous page and said, "Someone named Rebecca West."

"Never heard of her. Have you?"

"No, but I suspect it's a nom de plume, anyway. It's the name of the heroine in Ibsen's play, *Rosmersholm*."

Wells mulled it over. "At least she writes well." That joke about the ladies' ardent exclamations in his books . . .

"I think that's enough for one night," Jane said, tactfully closing the *Freewoman* without excising the review.

"I'm going to read for a bit," Wells said, setting the papers aside and picking up a copy of the latest book by Henry James, a collection of his late short fictions, sent to him by the author himself. "This one ought to make me sleepy."

"Your friend Henry can be relied on for that," Jane said, trailing a hand lightly across his shoulder as she went upstairs to her bedroom. They had kept separate sleeping quarters almost since the day they were married. "Just don't fall asleep in your chair again."

Wells removed his bookmark—that telegram from the War Office asking him to stop by at his discretion for a private conference—opened the book again, but had more trouble than usual focusing on the words. Good God, why couldn't James ever just say something in plain English? Why did everything have to be so belabored, so drawn out? But it really wasn't James. That wasn't what was bothering him. It was that damned Rebecca West, whoever she really was, and her pointed pen. He was both annoyed and intrigued by her nerve. He felt like a bear who'd been stung by a bee.

He picked up the *Freewoman* and read the entire review, and by the time he was done, he had resolved to invite her to his house and see if she was willing to stand in front of him and stick by what she had written. Yes, he would invite her to lunch at Easton Glebe and see what this young woman—and she had to be young or he would have heard of her already—was made of.

CHAPTER THREE

Cicily Fairfield boarded the train at Liverpool Street Station, and found a seat in a compartment occupied only by an elderly woman and her lap dog. Although Bishop's Stortford was the closest station on the regular schedule, she had advised the conductor that, per the instructions Wells had sent her, she would need to be dropped off at a private halt a mile or so on, reserved for visitors to the estate of Lady Frances Warwick.

She had fretted for hours over what to wear, attended by her two older sisters and her mother, who had at first refused to believe that she had been summoned to meet the great man at all. They had studied his invitation as if decoding Sanskrit. But her mother, who had often wondered what would become of her willful daughter—until the year before, she'd aspired to become an actress—was openly encouraged by this sign. Perhaps the girl, whose essays and reviews had begun to appear quite regularly in small presses and publications, had real talent after all. But it was of paramount importance, her mother insisted, that she make the right first impression, and so she was wearing a dark green woolen suit and matching hat, with a starchy white blouse fastened high at the throat by a cameo broach Mrs. Fairfield's mother had once worn to Ascot. Cicily's dark brown hair, thick and lustrous, was tamed as best it could be, but there was nothing to diminish the flashing brilliance of her big dark brown eyes.

In her purse, she carried a copy of the *Freewoman* in which she had written the blistering review of *Marriage*. She'd been so proud of it at the time—the boldness of attacking a popular novel by an acknowledged master of the craft, a book unanimously praised elsewhere—but now she was mortified at her hubris, and the invective of the prose. It had never dawned on her that she might one day have to beard the lion in his den. Although the invitation had been mildly worded, simply suggesting that as the author of the book in question Wells would be interested in a candid exchange of views, she wondered if, when it came to it, he might not thunder down at her like Zeus from Olympus. As a very pretty young woman, she had learned from experience that men's vanity could be so easily pricked.

The lap dog on the seat opposite studied her with an unwavering gaze. Could it tell how nervous she was? And when the train made a special stop at the estate station, even the dog's owner looked up with undisguised curiosity as Cicily stood.

"Do you know Lady Warwick?" she asked.

"No. But I know H. G. Wells, who leases the rectory on her property."

This left the woman even more slack-jawed, as Cicily stepped onto the platform and looked around. No one else had disembarked, and no one else was waiting there except for a slight, middle-aged man with a wispy brown mustache, the sort who might have been mistaken for a second-tier solicitor. He was wearing a long brown overcoat, a bowler hat, and muddied walking boots.

"Miss Rebecca West, I presume?" he said, coming forward with a bright smile and an outstretched hand.

"Cicily Fairfield, actually."

"Ah, at last. I'd had to address the telegram to your pseudonym at the magazine office. Nice to know the true identity of my closest reader."

"And one of your greatest admirers," she said, "really. I'm so sorry about the tone of that review. I don't know what got into me that day. I was—"

But he stopped her with another smile and an upraised palm.

"No need to defend yourself, or the review. I'm a big boy. I've weathered worse."

She had sworn to herself that she wouldn't burble, that she wouldn't recant her views, that she wouldn't melt in the glare of Wells's celebrity, and here she'd done all three in a matter of seconds. She had to get a hold of herself, especially as he was hardly a formidable figure—he was not much taller than she was, twice her age, and if it weren't for his kind eyes, which took her in with evident delight and interest, he might have been someone she passed on the street without a second glance.

"Do you mind if we walk to the house?" he suggested. "It's not far."

"I'd like that," she said. "My legs are cramped from the train."

Why had she said that about her legs? It was inappropriate, particularly on first meeting someone. A gentleman yet. Sometimes she wondered if she was really the firebrand she liked to imagine herself—and that her mother worried that she had become—or just another conventional young woman brought up to be a proper lady. Was she the dutiful Cicily Fairfield . . . or the radical, yet devious, heroine Rebecca West, whose name she had appropriated?

On the way to the house, a stately redbrick Georgian positioned at the top of a hill—before what was no doubt a very green lawn in spring and summer, but sere now—Wells told her a little bit about the countryside, the reason he'd taken the house there. "I have a place in London, of course, but here there are so few intrusions on my time and my writing, and no clanging trolleys or crowds to contend with." And then there was his landlady, the grand benefactress who had "so generously" given him a long lease on the old rectory.

"It does seem the ideal getaway," she said. "A sleepy little village like this."

"Yes, well, it is, except when a zeppelin crashes at your front door. The town is still all abuzz with it."

"That's right. Was it far from your house?"

He turned to point across some barren fields. "You can still see the scorch marks on the earth."

Indeed she could. A long black trail seared into the ground. The war was everywhere these days.

At the house, he scraped his boots clean, then ushered her into a spacious square reception hall, with wainscoted walls and a large chandelier looming overhead, and called out, "Jane! Our Ibsen girl is here!"

It was a clever play on words—the Gibson Girl was once a popular American icon, an ethereal beauty with delicate features and upswept hair, an image that could no longer hold its place in the horrors of a war-torn world—and Wells's wife answered with a welcoming, "Show the dear girl into the drawing room. I'll be right down just as soon as I've finished cleaning up your mess. Do you know that you spilled a bottle of ink last night?"

"Leave it for the housekeeper."

"She's in town getting the groceries."

Wells shrugged guiltily—"I sometimes work quite late," he whispered—before beckoning her into the next room. Here, the walls were lined with bookshelves, and Rebecca couldn't resist going straight to them, to see what the great author himself was reading. Conrad, Galsworthy, Chesterton, Gissing, Kipling, along with a number of less expected books from the likes of Marx, Engels, Henry George, and other socialists and utopians. There were also dozens of Wells's own books, many in their foreign editions. What must this be like? To see so many of your own works bound in leather, with beautifully embossed covers, and translated into a dozen different tongues? Would she ever be able to see such a display of her own works?

Perhaps Wells had been reading her mind. "Someday," he said, "if you keep at your writing, you may have the pleasure of surveying your own oeuvre. How old are you now, if I may ask?"

Blushing, she replied, "Nearly twenty," and he laughed.

"All of that, are you? Well, then, you'd better get cracking."

When Jane came down, she had a warm smile, but did not extend a hand. "My skin's stained blue from the ink."

"I'm sorry, dear, I must have fallen asleep at the switch," Wells apologized.

"Wouldn't be the first time," Jane said good-naturedly, motioning for them all to be seated. Rebecca took a wingback chair to one side of the fireplace, and Wells sat directly opposite. Jane sat on a well-worn loveseat, and picked up a bit of knitting from the side table. Rebecca suspected that she was glimpsing them in their accustomed spots, and felt all the more like an intruder. How in the world had she wound up here?

To put her at her ease, Jane asked several questions about her journey up from London, and Rebecca was only too happy to fill in the trivial details. Then the conversation moved on to her family—her absent father, who had simply vanished six years before, her two sisters, her attempts to be an actress. "My mother was dead set against it, but that only made me more determined than ever."

"But you've dropped those plans?" Wells asked.

"They were dropped for me," she replied, with a smile. "I enrolled at the Academy of Dramatic Art, and after giving several performances there that were, shall we say, less than well received, I saw the writing on the wall."

"But you did take away something from your stage career," Jane prompted her, and Rebecca laughed.

"If you mean my new name, yes—Cicily Fairfield was retired forever, in favor of Rebecca West, the last part I played."

Tea was served by Mrs. Willoughby, now returned from the market, and when that was done, Jane excused herself to attend to some correspondence. "I'll leave you two to discuss literary matters."

And that was when Rebecca felt, for the first time, the full force and effect of Wells's personality and his undivided attention. Although he had struck her as rather ordinary when she had first seen him on the train platform, now she was entranced by the blue-gray eyes that looked at her with such penetration—she was used to male attention, but not from someone so deeply interested in who she truly was—and even more so by the ungovernable tide of his conversation. She had never heard one man throw off so many brilliant ideas, so many casual aperçus, with such ease, or ask her—a young woman most noted up until now for her good looks—for her own opinions and views. With some of them, he was in agreement—women's suffrage, for example—but with others, even when he disagreed, he did so with such respect and intelligence that she never felt the least bit slighted or condescended to. Before she knew it, she had missed the last train connection back to London, and was invited by Jane to stay for dinner and the night.

After the last of the wine and cheese, Jane ushered her to a bedroom upstairs, and provided her with everything she might need, including a voluminous white flannel nightgown. "You'll look like an angel once you've put that on," Jane said, and with a chuckle Rebecca replied, "If only my mother could hear you say that."

Before turning in, she looked out the window at a freshly painted barn, quite white in the moonlight, and a boxed herb garden under a winter screen; a covered stone well that might have served as an illustration in a children's book stood beside it. She could also just discern some croquet wickets, and the rough borders of a tennis court, with a drooping net.

It was like a little paradise that Wells and his wife had constructed here, she reflected, before banishing the very thought, because if that was true, then that left only one role for her. It was a meaty role indeed, playing the serpent—the kind of role that actresses vied for—but hadn't she given up on such dramatics?

She heard the soft patter of slippered feet outside her door, and Wells's muted voice, saying, "Good night. Sleep well."

"Thank you, and good night, Mr. Wells."

There was a short pause. Was this exchange meant to continue?

But then the footfalls receded . . . and she was left to wonder what might have happened if—and not as the proper Cicily Fairfield, but as the bold Rebecca West—she had opened that door.

CHAPTER FOUR

Kurt pressed his eye to the peephole he had whittled into the wall of the hayloft—it hadn't been easy, using only his jackknife—and looked out at the back of the big brick house. In the three days that he had been hiding in the barn, he had become accustomed to the rhythms of the house and the comings and goings of its inhabitants. A middle-aged couple, an occasional housekeeper, a gardener now and then. But tonight, something was different—another light was on in one of the upstairs rooms, and he caught a glimpse of a woman, younger and trimmer than the other women, standing at the window in a white nightgown. Then she drew the curtains, and moments later extinguished the light.

He lay back on the hay, exhaling slowly, trying to ignore the ache in his rib cage and the throbbing pain in his broken ankle. He had been lucky to survive at all; he knew that. When the flames in the fuselage had come charging at him, he had strapped on his parachute and leapt from the zeppelin, but too late, and too low, for the canopy to open properly. He had been buffeted wildly in the wind from the failing rotors, and then hurled into the top of a grove of trees, which had probably saved his life but done considerable collateral damage. Winded and hurt, he had still had the sense to gather in the shredded chute and clutch it to his chest. It had provided him with the warmth to make it through the worst night of his life, hidden among the uppermost boughs.

The zeppelin died a minute later, nosing into the ground like an enormous pig hunting for truffles, engulfed in flames. From what he could see through the thick tangle of branches and dead leaves, it was soon surrounded by English people, running across the fields. He thought he had heard a bugle. He'd started to wipe away the black smudge of oil on his face before thinking better of it and spreading it around for camouflage instead.

Inside that inferno, his fellow crewmen were all already incinerated, except, as it turned out, for one. He could never be sure but for some reason he thought it was the rear gunner, Otto, whom he saw crawling away from the wreckage, writhing like a worm on the ground. A few of the English had looked on as one of them—a burly bearded man—had stood over him and then stabbed a pitchfork through his back. Kurt had felt the pain as if it had been his own body.

But wasn't this exactly what he had always been told about the barbaric English people? Wasn't it one of them—a man he would never be able to know, or to exact his revenge upon—who had killed his brother Caspar in some Belgian battlefield? And an English pilot who had shot down his brother Albert's plane over the Channel? The night he'd been told about Albert, while sweeping up the factory floor in Stuttgart, he had sworn to make the English pay, and the next day, sneaking out of the house so that his parents would not stop him, he had fudged his real age and enlisted in the air corps.

Propping himself up on one elbow, he looked out again at the house. All was silent and dark. His stomach growled from hunger, and he licked his chapped lips. He wondered what time it was. Late enough that everyone would be safely asleep? Inching his way across the loft, his feet felt for the rickety wooden ladder. Climbing down, he was careful not to put too much weight on the broken ankle, or to do anything to disturb the barn's only other occupant—a gray owl with a baleful glare.

He cracked open the barn door, waited several seconds after the creaking had subsided, then poked his head out and looked all around. A light wind was making the bucket swing above the well. He went to it, lowered it quickly, and drew it up half-filled. He gulped the cold water down, feeling it run down his chin, onto his chest, under his torn shirt and scorched leather flying jacket. Bending his head, he poured the rest over his bristly blond hair and scrubbed the remaining oil from his face. Then his hunger couldn't wait any longer, and he limped around the side of the house to the scullery door, where a refuse bin was kept. Inside it, he found a veritable treasure chest—scraps of fatty beef, potato skins, bones from which the marrow had not yet been sucked, the hard rind from a very aromatic cheese. He stuffed some in his mouth, the rest in his pockets, and made sure to leave the lid off the bin; that way, if they noticed that the bin had been pillaged, they'd attribute it to animals.

After another quick survey of the yard—the only thing stirring was a rabbit, foraging in the herb garden—he scurried back to the barn. The owl, perched on a beam overhead, fluttered its wings and hooted three or four times. *"Schlafen,"* Kurt said softly, *"schlafen sie gut"*—then clambered up the ladder to his hiding place. He flopped back onto the hay, his ankle throbbing from the exertion, and he clutched his leg hard, just above the knee, to keep the pain from traveling. Staring up at the rafters, he wondered, how long could this last? How long could he stay undetected? How long would it be before the English people, whose savagery he had read about in all the German newspapers and had now seen firsthand, found him and finished him off, just as they had the rear gunner Otto?

One thing he knew—he could expect no quarter, and should give none in return.

CHAPTER FIVE

"And where will you be off to now?" Wells asked, as he helped Rebecca off the train at Charing Cross Station.

"The office of the magazine, I think."

"Have you got a piece to turn in?"

"Much better than that!" she exclaimed with a wide grin. "I've had a personal interview with none other than Herbert George Wells himself."

"What?" he protested. How had he forgotten that she was a journalist? "You are not going to attempt to capitalize on a personal encounter, are you? Everything said at the rectory was strictly off the record."

She laid a hand playfully on his sleeve—a gesture whose intimacy was not lost on him—and said, "Oh, I'll honor that. But may I not at least boast of having been invited to your house and even spending a night under your roof?"

"You might be wise," he said, mulling it over, "to leave out the part about spending the night." He already had a reputation that he was trying to live down, nor did he wish to see her inadvertently do any damage to her own. "But I give you permission to admit the rest. Just make me out to be madly dashing."

"That won't be hard at all."

With a quick peck on his cheek, she turned away, and he stood still to watch her go. She was small in stature, but carried herself with a winning assurance as she made her way toward Trafalgar Square and its bustling crowds. He noticed young men turning their heads as she passed, and just when he was ready to move on himself—his appointment was in ten minutes—she swiveled her head, caught him staring, and wagged a finger. He blushed, despite himself. When would he learn?

Although the building that housed the War Office had been built in 1906, it was a vast neo-baroque affair, trapezoidal in shape and punctuated by dozens of spires, with over a thousand rooms and probably twice as many windows. He made several wrong turns and went up and then down a couple of wrong staircases, before finding the Ministry of Military Information. But even then he thought he must have gotten it wrong, because slouched in an armchair by the desk was his brash, outspoken friend Winston Churchill.

"What on earth are you doing here?" Wells said, shaking his hand enthusiastically. "Has the Admiralty office thrown you out for insubordination?"

"No, no, I am what you might call on loan. To Colonel Bryce," Churchill said, indicating the tall, lean man standing stiff as a ramrod, his khaki uniform adorned with a neat row of medals, behind the desk.

Wells greeted him, too, and took the remaining chair. The office was a perfunctory affair, with wooden filing cabinets along one wall, a scuffed linoleum floor, and glaring overhead lights—as ordinary as the outside of the building was not.

"In fact," Churchill said, "it was my idea to bring you in."

"Should I be pleased?"

"You shall soon find out," Churchill said, deferring to Bryce, who cleared his throat, and passed to Wells a yellow copy of the *Evening News*, a halfpenny London paper whose color distinguished it from its more respectable full penny competitors. "I'm sure you saw this at the time it was first published."

Wells glanced at the section outlined in red pen and said, "Yes, of course." It was a piece entitled "The Bowmen," by Arthur Machen, a popular journalist and author of gothic tales. It told the incredible tale of some British soldiers, fighting a rear guard action at a key salient in the line, who were about to be overrun by a German assault. Just when they thought all was lost, one of them had called upon St. George, who had descended with a heavenly host of angelic archers, dressed in medieval garb, to come to their defense. Wells had thought it a workmanlike piece, though its placement in the paper had puzzled him; instead of appearing on the page where short stories and imaginative items were printed, it had shown up in the news section.

When he mentioned that now, Colonel Bryce nodded his head purposefully, and Churchill said, "Precisely. The editor has since printed a retraction, but no one seems to notice, or care."

"It was all a mix-up at the paper," the colonel put in, "but with unintended consequences."

"Such as?" Wells said.

"A great upswelling of national pride. I don't think we've seen anything like it since Shackleton set sail for the Antarctic, just days before this war was declared."

It had been months now since any further word had been received from that expedition. Wells, like many, often wondered if the *Endurance* and its crew were still plowing through the icy seas, or had foundered on some barren shore. It was a pity that such a grand adventure should be subordinated to the exigencies of war.

"This story of the bowmen has instilled a new sense of confidence," Churchill added. "Preachers are assuring their flock that God is on our side. Children are clamoring for toy archers. St. George sausage rolls are being sold in Piccadilly."

Wells was still unsure about where all this was going or what it had to do with him.

"To be blunt," Bryce said, steepling his hands on the desk before him, "the British Expeditionary Force in Belgium was no match for the German war machine. We were out trained, out supplied, out gunned, and out maneuvered. Needless to say, that assessment goes no further than this room."

Wells nodded.

"But that story, misplaced as it was," Churchill said, leaning forward in his chair, "snatched victory from the jaws of defeat. What was an ignominious rout—to be even more blunt about it than the colonel here—became a story of steadfast English bravery, and something else even more important."

"An endorsement from on high," Bryce said, finishing the thought. "Seven months ago, at a critical moment in the opening days of this war, when things were looking very bleak indeed, that story convinced a large part of the public that the patron saint of England would intervene, if necessary, in human affairs."

"But surely people realized it was just a story," Wells said, "that it was simply a bit of folderol, however inspiring."

"Some did, but many did not."

"Which is what gave me the thought of publishing something real, but along similar lines," Churchill said. "It's not as if we're out of the woods, after all. This war could go on for years."

That was a prognosis seldom heard; everyone had gone into the war thinking it would be a matter of weeks or months before the whole ugly episode was resolved and Europe could return to the status quo. Even Wells, a man whose work was characterized by its ability to see and predict the future, had thought so at first. He'd been beguiled by all the happy jingoistic fervor and the patriotic clamor in the streets; his heart had been rent by the propaganda depicting the systematic rape of their ally, Belgium. He had not foreseen, no one had, the trenches that would be dug—hundreds of miles of them already—or the scale of the carnage inflicted by modern weaponry. But sitting in the War Office now, looking at a scrap of blue sky through a smudged windowpane, he caught a glimmer of why he'd been summoned here.

"What exactly is it that you'd like me to write?"

Churchill and Bryce exchanged a look.

"Something to lift the national spirit," Churchill said.

"Something to confirm what Mr. Machen's story has already suggested," the colonel said.

"That God is our ally?"

"That the English soldier is endowed with a nobility of spirit, and the English army with a moral purpose, which will assure us of victory in the end."

"You're the only man who can do it," Churchill urged.

"I should think that Machen was. He got this ball rolling, after all."

"No, he's too played out, too compromised."

"And he writes a lot of stories filled with occult mumbo jumbo," the colonel said dismissively.

"The Admiralty office thought I was overstepping my bounds," Churchill said, "and that it was out of my official purview. That's why I took the idea here."

"If you are willing," Bryce said, gathering together some papers on his desk, "we would want you to travel to the Front—ideally somewhere near Mons, in the Ypres salient—and billet, for perhaps a week or two, with the officers of the regiment."

"The Front?" Wells had imagined concocting a story out of whole cloth, from the comfort and safe remove of his study.

"Yes. It's important that any dispatches or stories you send back have the seal of authenticity, that they come from the front lines. We want the country to know that our soldiers are in good spirits, and we want our soldiers to know that the country is foursquare behind them, every step of the way."

"We want fact from you, H. G., not fiction," Churchill pointed out. "Make no mistake about that. But we want it told with your unmistakable flair for story and invention."

Could he do it? Wells thought. He was forty-nine years old, for God's sake, and even in his prime had not been an especially vigorous specimen; he had always put it down to growing up in straitened circumstances, with a diet sorely lacking in wholesome foods. And he could only imagine the howls from Jane at the very thought of his placing himself so deliberately in harm's way.

"So what do you think, H. G.?" Churchill said. "Are you ready to do your bit for king and country?"

Bryce gently slid the papers—official-looking documents, including a map—across the desk toward him. Wells could spot the empty signature line at the bottom of the form with the heading, all in red capitals, "TOP SECRET."

He drew the papers into his lap, and thought, How could he ever face his own young sons, both of them away at boarding school, if he shirked his duty now? How, for that matter, could he face himself?

"I only wish I could accompany you," Churchill said, and Wells knew that he meant it. Winston had always been one for derring-do.

Finally, what would posterity make of it if he failed to come up to the mark? "May I borrow this?" he asked, taking the pen from the stand on Bryce's desk. The colonel sat back in his chair, hands folded across his abdomen, and Churchill clapped Wells on the back the moment he had finished scrawling his name on the empty line at the bottom of the page.

"Drinks at the club," Churchill exclaimed, "and I won't take no for an answer," as Wells replaced the pen and wondered, *What have I just done?*

CHAPTER SIX

"You didn't!" Winnie exclaimed.

"The whole night?" Lettie asked.

Rebecca nodded, watching her mother out of the corner of her eye; she was still sitting on the piano bench, where she'd been playing Mendelssohn's *Songs without Words*—something she played whenever most perturbed—as Rebecca had come up the walk to the cottage.

"And what was he like?" Lettie, her oldest sister, said. "Was he tall?"

"No."

"Thin?" Winnie, the middle one, asked.

"No."

"Fat?"

"No, not that either. He looks rather like an unassuming, middle-aged solicitor." She was aware that she was disappointing her audience. "But his eyes—they positively sparkle with intelligence and insight. They look as if they see farther, and more deeply, than anyone else's." She certainly felt as if they had peered more deeply into her than anyone else's had ever done.

Her sisters beamed, even as her mother's scowl remained unchanged.

"And his conversation is the most inspiring and surprising of any I have ever heard. You just want to remember every word of it. He throws off ideas like a pinwheel, until your head spins."

"I hope he didn't turn your head too much," her mother said. "The man has a reputation for doing just that with silly young girls."

Rebecca knew that she was referring to the scandal with Amber Reeves, an idealistic young Fabian with whom Wells had reputedly had an out-of-wedlock child. But she bridled at the word "silly."

"Nothing untoward occurred, I can assure you of that, Mother."

"Where was his wife?"

"In the house, all night long. She was very kind and hospitable to me."

"And he accompanied you back to the city?"

"He even paid the surcharge to make mine a first-class ticket."

"No doubt so you could sit together."

"There were others in the carriage. He behaved like a perfect gentleman."

"But did you behave like a perfect lady, Cissie?"

It was her mother's way of reminding her that she was Cicily in this house, and Rebecca only when she was swanning about in literary London, or getting herself into trouble at some street demonstration for the suffragette movement.

"And now I'm not sure why you were summoned there in the first place," Mrs. Fairfield continued. "Was it really to do with your work?"

"First of all, I wasn't summoned—I was invited—and yes, he had read my review of his novel and simply wanted to discuss it."

"No doubt a gushing review."

"Hardly, Mother. In fact, it was quite the opposite."

"Oh, yes, I read it, too," Lettie put in, to draw off some of the fire. "And when I showed it to several of the women at the clinic, and admitted that its author was my little sister, they marveled at her audacity, taking on the great H. G. Wells."

"So long as this is the end of it," Mrs. Fairfield declared. "I do not trust his motives."

"Then perhaps you should trust mine," Rebecca replied. "I'm not some flibbertigibbet schoolgirl."

"Then be sure you don't act like one."

Rebecca was about to retort when Winnie, always the peacemaker, put a hand on her arm and gave her a look that said, *Let it go.* She was right; Rebecca knew there was nothing to be gained from bickering. Her mother would never understand her. When their father had abandoned them all years before—for a mythical employment opportunity in Sierra Leone—it had fallen to her mother to somehow keep the household together and to provide for her three daughters. She had managed, but just barely, and her only dream ever since had been for security—for a solid base, and rectitude, and conformity to all the social norms that might provide protection for a female household of limited means. Rebecca wanted none of it; she wanted to break free and live her life exactly as she saw fit.

"I'm going upstairs to change," she said.

"I'll come, too," her sisters said in unison.

Rebecca knew that they wanted to hear more about her encounter with Wells. Their curiosity was only exceeded by that of her fellow writers and editors at the *Freewoman*, where Rebecca had perched on the edge of a desk, regaling them with details of the Wells household and, mindful of Wells's admonition that their conversation remain off the record, an expurgated version of what had been said. When the editor in chief, Mrs. Marsden, had pressed her to write a piece about it, she had had to demur.

"Are you mad?" Marsden had said, pushing the glasses back up to the bridge of her very long nose. "A private interview with H. G. Wells and you don't wish to exploit it?"

Rebecca knew it would be a great scoop and garner a lot of attention, but she felt already that this was one bridge she did not want to burn. Although Wells had entered her life unexpectedly, she was oddly confident that it would be some time before he exited it.

"What did you have for dinner there?" Winnie asked now, trailing her up the stairs.

"What was his library like?" Lettie asked, bringing up the rear.

They continued to pepper her with questions as she changed out of her workaday clothes and into something more comfortable, and she did her best to recall every detail, from the books on the shelves to the herb garden in the yard. But all the while she felt something strange stirring within her, a kind of power that up until now she had allowed to remain latent, something for which she had never found a suitable outlet, or worthy counterpart.

Now, she had. In Wells, she had more than met her match, and she was not about to wait another nineteen years for a similar opportunity to present itself.

CHAPTER SEVEN

Wells stopped in front of the dilapidated lodging house in Notting Hill and consulted the paper in his hand again. Could this be the right address? But there it was, just as the young copy boy at the *Evening News*, to which Arthur Machen was a regular contributor, had written it: 23 Clarendon Road. "He's all the way at the top," the boy had said. "You'll smell his flat long before you get there."

Wells hadn't known exactly what he meant by that, but if this crumbling stoop and dirty brown brick facade were any indication, it did not bode well. The front door, though it had a lock, was propped open with a worn boot, and Wells started up the stairs with one hand on the rickety banister and the other holding the portfolio of material he'd received from the War Office. The only light came from small dirty windows on each landing, and the boy was right about the smell. Halfway up, Wells detected a strange and unpleasant aroma—a mixture of everything from incense to spoiled fish. At the top, the smell was much worse, and behind the scarred wooden door with a brass 8 hanging askew, he heard a low mumbling—chanting?—sound.

Perhaps this was not such a good idea after all; he could simply leave word for Machen at the newspaper office and arrange for a meeting in some more congenial spot, like his club, for another day. But then, Wells had never been a man to put off till tomorrow what could just as easily be done today.

He knocked on the door.

The noise from within abruptly stopped, and a voice called out, "Just leave it!"

Who did he take him for? "I'm afraid there's nothing to leave."

Footsteps approached the door, which opened a crack. "Who's that?" Machen said, peering out onto the gloomy landing. "You're not the copy boy. What do you want?"

"I wanted to talk to you, if I might. I'm sorry for the intrusion, but I was in London for the day, and—"

"Good Christ, is that you, Wells?"

"It is." They had met once or twice, briefly, at literary events, and written, twenty years before, for a magazine called the *Unicorn*.

"What in God's name are you doing here?"

"It's not easy to explain through this crack in the door."

"Oh," Machen said, "yes, of course." The door swung wider, but not to its full extent. "The cats," Machen said, toeing one back with the tip of his shoe, "can't let them get out."

Wells slipped inside, where the full impact of the sandalwood mingled with the scent of sour milk and stale cigarettes. The room was hard to take in at first, with a cluttered desk at one end and what might have been an altar to some saint at the other, where candles still burned in pewter dishes in front of a five-pointed iron star mounted on the wall.

"Caught me performing one of my rituals," Machen said, hastily moving to extinguish the candles, and throwing open the long red drapes to let what was left of the winter daylight into the room. "My God, I never expected to see you here."

The flat was in total disarray, with five or six cats roaming freely about—one languished on the mantelpiece, licking its paws, another was rubbing itself back and forth against Wells's trouser leg—and it struck him, as it sometimes did, how truly fortunate he had been in his own career. This was how most writers, even ones as talented as Machen, wound up—living hand-to-mouth, in rented quarters, cranking out essays, articles, stories, whimsical columns, anything that might bring in a few pounds. Of course, Machen had had a couple of notable successes—his occult novel, *The Great God Pan,* had achieved a certain notoriety with its frank depiction of sex and magic and religion—but the kind of gothic fiction he had been known for had gone out of style in the 1890s, and anything otherwise controversial had suffered a setback after Oscar Wilde's conviction for gross indecency. These days, with the war on, the nation was in no mood for such decadent tomfoolery. Wells made sure to cloak any of his own revolutionary sentiments in a sufficiently acceptable tale.

"What can I get you? Tea?"

"Oh, no, please don't go to the trouble."

"A glass of sherry, then?" Machen said, ushering him to the office end of the room, where he whisked a cat off the sagging armchair that faced the desk. "I'm eager to know what's brought you here."

Wells accepted the sherry out of courtesy, and once Machen had sat down behind the desk, said, "I was just at the War Office." He indicated the portfolio, loosely tied, that he held in his lap.

Before he could say another word, Machen snorted, and said, "Colonel Bryce?"

"Yes, in fact."

"Are they still banging on then about the bowmen at Mons?"

"They are."

"How many times have I had to tell them? I made the whole thing up. It never happened. Some incompetent typesetter stuck it in the paper in the wrong place, and ever since I've had entreaties from earnest ministers in every parish in the land, asking me to elaborate on the appearance of the so-called angels—which, let me say, was a word that never so much as appeared in the tale—and requesting further proofs to bolster their arguments. The Society for Psychical Research has gone so far as to undertake its own study." He ran a hand in exasperation over the vast expanse of his pallid forehead, his lank gray hair beginning only halfway back on his skull. Although he'd lived in London for years, his speech still carried a strong flavor of his Welsh upbringing. "But the more I deny it, the more I declare it nothing more than a wild taradiddle, the more firmly people seem to believe in it."

"As a fellow practitioner, what *was* the wellspring of the piece, then?"

"It was *that*," Machen said, gesturing widely with one arm at the window. "There's a newsstand across the street, and the paper boy for the *Weekly Dispatch* was bellowing about our headlong retreat toward Paris. My heart sank into my boots, as did everyone's. The war had barely begun and already we were running for our lives from the German hordes. I wrote it, I suppose, to buck myself up."

"So there was no actual sighting, or reporting, involved in it?"

"I haven't even been to the Front."

"And the valiant Captain Mills, and his compatriot Foster?"

"Purely characters. Sprung from the Olympian brow," he said, tapping his own forehead.

Wells nodded, and sipped the sherry—better than he'd expected it to be—from the chipped glass.

"But what do they want from you?" Machen asked. "Did they send you to persuade me to come around in the interest of national unity? To get me to affirm that yes, every word was God's own truth?"

"Not exactly. But they do want me to tour the Front, and come back with heart-lifting news of some kind, something to offset the endless rolls of carnage."

"No easy task, that. On some nights, when the wind is right, I swear I can hear the endless thunder of the guns, all the way from France." Machen's weary eyes turned to the window. "And oh, how I pity the poor blokes huddling under that relentless barrage. It goes on for hours on end."

Soon, Wells reflected, he would be one of those blokes himself.

"But don't tell me you're going to take them up on it? Risk getting your head blown off for a bit of propaganda?"

"I am."

"You're a better man than I, Wells, though that's not saying much. If there is anything I can do to help—anything at all—you have only to ask. I may know the bowmen are a figment of my own imagination, but I at least believe in the possibility of these things. I suspect you don't."

"It's true," Wells conceded, "that I extrapolate more from the seen than the unseen. My science background, you know."

"But that's only because you're not looking at things properly. You can't see an atom, after all, but you know it exists."

"True enough, but one day we'll have the means of doing so."

"Maybe, maybe not. The problem is, people can't see what's right in front of them even now. There's a veil that stands between us and true reality. I believe that we perceive, with our limited senses, only the slightest portion of all that surrounds us. We're the proverbial blind men, with groping fingers, trying to feel our way around an elephant and gather some description of it. It is only by means of other avenues—introspection and meditation, ancient rites and hypnagogic states—that we can access otherwise underutilized parts of the mind—"

Wells had heard it all before.

"—and thereby explore the universe. Incidentally, a properly ingested substance can help immeasurably in that regard."

What substance? Wells wondered, casting a suspicious glance at his sherry. As the author of many groundbreaking books of scientific speculation, he had long been considered a ripe recruit for every paranormal society and occult group in Britain, ranging from the Theosophists to the Order of the Golden Dawn, to which he knew Machen—not to mention the Great Satan himself, Aleister Crowley—belonged. But he preferred to keep his own speculations firmly rooted in science, in empirical facts rather than woolly conjecture, and as a consequence he made a practice of declining their overtures.

"You wouldn't care to join me," Machen said, as Wells might have expected, "for a symposium on the Eleusinian Mysteries tonight, would you?"

"I'm afraid I must get back home on the next train."

"Ah, another time, then . . ."

"But before I go, is there anything else you can tell me about the origins, or the composition, of that very original and timely story?"

"I can only tell you that credulity, wedded to desire, cannot be denied. The world wants that story to be true, and so it shall be."

Without warning, a black cat leapt up onto Wells's lap, smack on top of the portfolio.

"That one's Beelzebub. He loves to have the groove between his ears stroked."

Wells, a cat fancier himself, ran a finger back and forth, and the cat closed its eyes and purred.

"You've made a friend," Machen said.

"It's never wise to make an enemy of Beelzebub," Wells replied, before gently lifting the cat onto the edge of the desk and rising from his chair. Taking his card from his wallet, he laid it down and said, "Should anything else occur to you, I've taken a flat in town. You may always reach me there."

The moment Wells stepped out of the flat, the air became slightly less fetid, but he had barely rounded the landing when a man in full Scottish garb, his face concealed beneath a hat, barged past him on his way up. Another man, a hulking brute with a square head and a thatch of dirty blond hair, followed close on his heels. Making no allowance for anyone else, he brushed Wells's shoulder roughly enough that the portfolio of papers was dislodged and fell on the stairs, the pages scattering loose.

"Excuse me," Wells protested, "but are you blind?"

The man didn't so much as pause, his only reply a cold sneer as he continued on his way.

The Scotsman, if that was what he was, was banging on the door above and Wells heard Machen call out, "Did you forget something, Wells?" before opening the door. "Oh, it's you, Crowley."

"Who's Wells?" the man boomed, in a voice that bore no Scots accent.

"H. G."

"That's who we just passed on the stairs?"

Wells, scrunched down and picking up the papers, stayed silent.

"Yes."

"Then you'll have to tell me what business such an eminence had to conduct with the likes of you," Crowley said, his voice becoming less audible as he and his cohort entered the flat, and the door slammed shut behind them.

Wells waited, gathering up the last of the papers and wondering precisely the same thing. What business had Aleister Crowley, the most controversial figure in all of England, the grand master of magic and devilry, come here to conduct with Machen?

CHAPTER EIGHT

Since Jane was at the back of the house, peering into the ash can, she did not hear her husband, home from London, until he poked his head out the door and said, "Reading the tea leaves?"

"Something like that."

He stepped outside, still in his coat and hat.

"How was your appointment at the War Office?" she asked, putting the lid back on the can and jamming it down hard.

"Badgers?"

"Must be. Or a local vagabond who's become partial to our kitchen scraps." She raised her eyes and looked around at the empty back lawn, herb garden, and barn. "If I knew it was a person, I'd be inclined to leave something more substantial."

"Come inside," Wells said. "It's cold out here."

Once in the front parlor, and settled into their usual places, Wells started in on a very roundabout account of his day, which was Jane's first clue that he was withholding something that he knew she would not be pleased to hear. Whenever he did not come straight to the heart of the matter, he was prevaricating.

"But Machen's situation must be far more dire than anyone knows," he was saying. "I would have thought his fortunes had improved, what with the popularity of that story about Mons. In fact, I daresay—"

"Enough about Arthur Machen," Jane interrupted, putting down her knitting. "And Colonel Bryce. Or your old friend Winston. What is it about that meeting that you are still not telling me? Surely, they didn't have you come to London just to congratulate you on your latest novel. It's the War Office, after all."

"Yes, well, we did talk about what's going on at the Western Front."

"And?"

"They'd like me to write something about it."

"You've already written several pieces about the war. Haven't they seen them?"

"They have. Only in this instance, they would like me to write something more immediate, something more visceral . . . something from the Front itself."

Ah, so that was it. "I hope you told them that a man of your age, and one who is not, I might add, in the best of health, was a poor candidate for open warfare?"

Wells didn't reply, which answered her question. "H. G., you cannot do this."

"And why can't I?" Now his back was up.

"Because you are too old."

"I resent that."

"And because the best use of your talents is in writing the sort of pieces you've already been doing, pieces assuring the public that one day soon this terrible war will end, and that when it's done, it will be the last of its kind. The war to end all wars, as you've so deftly put it. You don't need to put your own head up, like some target in a shooting gallery, to prove the point. What was the War Office thinking?"

"They were thinking that every man has his duty these days, and that this might be mine."

"Winston was behind it, wasn't he?"

"What makes you say that?"

So she'd scored another direct hit. "Because Winston approaches war as if it were a game, and a game he can't wait to play."

"I'm the one who wrote the books on that, *Little Wars* and such."

"And those were books for children playing with tin soldiers and tiny wooden ships and planes. Churchill is playing with real lives and real artillery and real casualties, and I won't have you be one of them. No, and that's an end of it."

Now he was fuming; she could see that. Jane seldom laid down the law—Wells could be as stubborn as a mule and as proud as a prima donna—but this was one time she saw no other course. He was forty-nine years old, he had two children (three, if you counted the illegitimate child with Amber Reeves), and the most exercise he normally got was a walk in the woods or a round of croquet on the back lawn. But she had pricked—no, pierced—his vanity, and she feared that he would go forward with the plan now at least as much out of spite as patriotism. "H. G." she said, in a more mollifying tone, "you have supported the war effort in the best way possible. No one could ever fault you. And if you wish to put aside some of your more literary work and devote yourself to working in some capacity in Whitehall—where I am quite sure they would be delighted to have you—I would back you to the hilt. We have the flat on St. James's Court now; you could live there during the week, and come up here on weekends, or I could come down sometimes and—"

"I'm going to the Front," he blurted, rising from his chair and leaving the parlor in a huff, "and *that's* an end of it."

Undressing in her room later that night, Jane conceded that she had mishandled it. She still wasn't sure what else she could have done, how else she could have persuaded him of the folly of this, but what she *had* done had backfired in spectacular fashion, and Wells had stormed up to his bedroom, where she had heard him scrounging about in the closet, no doubt to unearth his best boots and warmest woolen vests to withstand the hardships of life in the trenches.

Pulling the nightgown down over her head, she did think of one thing that she had failed to say, one thing that she had neglected to include in her argument—and that was her overwhelming love for him, coupled with an equally overwhelming fear for his safety. For all its shortcomings—most notably his extramarital affairs, or "passades," as he liked to call them to diminish their importance—theirs was a marriage of intellectual equals, of soul mates whose lives, for twenty years now, had been bound together by mutual respect and interests and regard. She could not imagine going on without him.

Turning off the bedside lamp, she went to draw the curtains, but sat instead on the window seat, her knees drawn up to her chest—just as she had sat and read in her bedroom when she was a little girl. It was a dark night, the stars obscured by banks of clouds, and she could barely make out anything more than the outline of the barn and the covered well.

It was a good life they led—far better than most people were able to enjoy, that much she freely acknowledged—but that didn't diminish the sense of loss she felt, too. H. G. had been married to his first wife when they met, and so it had taken some time before they had embarked on their own love affair—but once they had, it had been the greatest adventure of her life. Passionate, intense, sensual. She could still remember those days (though sometimes she wished she could not), and she often wondered what had happened to all that. Gradually, it had just dissipated, his interest had waned, until one night he had taken the bull by the horns and explained that he was not constitutionally capable of remaining monogamous. He was and would always be attracted to other women, in need of their vitality and freshness, the way that they sparked his curiosity and reinvigorated his imagination. For him sex could even be a purely recreational experience, but one that he was unwilling to give up.

"Are you saying that you want to leave me?" she had finally asked, the words barely able to escape her lips.

And he had rushed in to make the case—as strongly as he had made the case for his own infidelities—to reassure her that she was his Gibraltar, his lodestar, his boon companion, the one woman on whose judgment he relied, on whose care he counted, and whose affection he most prized. He could no sooner imagine his life without her than he could imagine life on the moon.

"But you *did* imagine life on the moon," she had said, referring to his novel about the first men to travel there, and, catching himself, he had laughed.

"A bad analogy," he'd conceded, before gathering her in his arms and consoling her. "Will you be able to accommodate yourself to such an unorthodox modus vivendi? Can you allow me these trifling passades, secure in the conviction that you are the one immutable constant in my life? The only one without whom my life would surely founder on the rocks?"

It had not been easy, but she had done so. They slept in separate bedrooms, but that did not mean she didn't wait for those rare occasions when she heard a gentle rapping on her door . . . to which she always acquiesced. And by now, they had come to the point where he would speak openly of some of his transgressions, even going so far as to ask her advice and counsel—which, to her own astonishment, she gave. If history was her guide, she would soon be hearing more of that young Rebecca West.

There was a squeaking from the yard, and though the tree branches betrayed no sign of wind, the wooden bucket was swinging on its chain. She cracked open the casement window, to see outside better, but if she had hoped to spot some enterprising badger or hungry vagrant, she was disappointed. Everything else remained still.

Leaving the window ajar, she slipped into bed, piling the coverlet high around her shoulders, and fell into a troubled sleep, filled with images of lines of men, gaunt and gloomy, in matching brown suits, with rifles tucked under their arms as if they were furled umbrellas, crowding into an underground station from which a suspiciously infernal glow emanated. Wells was among them, and she was trying to give him something important, something precious, but when she finally spotted him and waved wildly, he looked at her with no recognition. His eyes were glassy and vacant, and on his lapel there was a circular stain that she at first took for a shiny medal, before she realized it was wet like blood.

CHAPTER NINE

For a man of science, whose books had explored everything from space travel to bacterial warfare, Wells was inordinately averse to needles.

"Come now," Colonel Bryce scoffed, "the nurse's time is valuable, and your typhoid inoculation is mandatory. Get that jacket off."

Wells had come by the Ministry Office to pick up the last of his official papers, in preparation for his departure for France the next day, and to receive his final instructions. It seemed he was to be stationed close to the site where Machen's short story had been set, and would be entrusted to the protective custody of the Northumberland Fusiliers and a Captain Gerald Lillyfield.

"We haven't advanced from that spot?" Wells asked.

"We have since lost that ground, and then recaptured it. Even now our grip on it is tenuous. The line has extended in a lateral direction for close to five hundred miles, from the Channel to Switzerland."

In other words, stalemate, Wells thought. If you insist on fighting a new war with the same old strategies and armaments, this was bound to happen. He had already written about it—about the need to concentrate on the newer weapons of war, from armored land vehicles to a system of overhead cables and poles, capable of transporting everything from rations to ammunition far more swiftly and effectively than mules and muddy roads could do—but most of his proposals fell on deaf ears.

In fact, it was only Churchill who had taken up the pulley idea, and tried to promote it, "but they're as deaf at the Admiralty as they appear to be at the army," he'd grumbled. Churchill had also floated, unsuccessfully, Wells's suggestion that the nation build fewer battleships, which would only be sunk by the other side's battleships, and more airplanes, loaded down with bombs that the pilot could fling from the cockpit instead.

"Here, just hand it to me," Bryce said, when he saw that Wells was not sure where to deposit his jacket.

"And are you right- or left-handed?" the nurse inquired.

"Left."

"Then roll up your right sleeve, please, above the bicep."

Wells did so, all the while trying not to see the waiting syringe. Still, he caught a glimpse of it, its evil tip gleaming and wet, just before the nurse wiped a spot on his upper arm with iodine, gripped his elbow firmly, and jabbed the needle in. It seemed to Wells that she left it there, depressing the plunger, for far longer than was necessary, before withdrawing it, swabbing the spot once more, and flattening a bandage across the injection site. "You might experience some soreness or redness in the muscle for a day or two, but that should pass," she said, before gathering up her medical kit and leaving the office.

"Normally, you'd have had to line up in the barracks with a hundred other half-naked men for that," the colonel said, as Wells rolled his sleeve back down and retrieved his jacket.

"I'm forever in your debt."

Together, they went over his itinerary for the next day, along with his orders to report and, finally, the issuance of his uniform. Bryce opened a cabinet, the same one where he'd hung Wells's overcoat, and took from a top shelf a neatly folded khaki uniform—wool tunic and riding breeches and peaked cap—and then a pair of regulation brown leather boots, which he plunked down on the edge of the desk with a thump. "All in the sizes you gave us."

"Thank you," Wells said, the mission taking on greater reality with the arrival of each item. "Helmet?" he asked.

Bryce laughed. "We're outfitting you as a line officer, but good God, Wells, we're not expecting you to lead a charge across no man's land." Then he grew serious. "Besides, when and if you need one, there are always plenty of them lying about."

Plenty of them lying about. Wells wondered if he would have to pry it literally from a dead man's skull.

"But you will have this," Bryce said, returning to the cabinet to remove a webbed canvas belt with holster and gun attached. "Have you ever fired a Webley Mk?"

"No."

"Chances are, you won't have to," he said, laying the revolver more gently on the pile of clothing. "But once you get there, have one of the men run through it with you. It's got a bit of a jump when fired, but at close range, you'll find it's quite reliable."

Wells hoped to make no such discovery. He had no more use for the Boche than the next Englishman, but up until now he had never killed, or even tried to kill, a German, and wasn't at all sure, should the occasion arise, if he would be capable of it.

"You'll be leaving from Waterloo Station at seven thirty tomorrow morning, accompanied by a Sergeant Stubb. He was supposed to be here today, but he had a medical appointment of his own. He'll get you all the way to the Front, get you settled, and remain your liaison. So, any questions?"

"I'm sure many will arise."

"Hence, Sergeant Stubb."

Bryce let a pause fall, before asking, "Now, is there anything you wish to tell me?"

"Tell you?"

"About your meeting with Mr. Machen?"

"You know about that?"

"We *are* the War Office, and we *do* have a branch called Military Intelligence."

Wells was suddenly made uncomfortable at the notion that he might have been trailed.

"What did you make of him?" Bryce asked.

"We've met before. A good-hearted chap, but admittedly on the eccentric side."

"To say the least," Bryce said, with a chuckle. "He's quite round the bend, if you ask me."

"But he did extend his help, and he meant it."

"That's the kind of help we do not need," the colonel said, laughing again. "No, not from that sort." Wells suddenly took a disliking to him. *That sort.* Bryce reminded him of the upper-form boys at school, the hearty lads who mocked the less athletic and more scholarly boys, of which Wells had been one.

"Well, then," Bryce said, sticking out his hand, "it's been an honor to know you, Mr. Wells, and I wish you much luck."

"Thank you," Wells said, shaking his hand nonetheless and packing all his gear into the Gladstone bag he had been advised to bring.

As he left, Bryce called out, "Oh, and do give my best to Captain Lillyfield—a capital fellow. We were at Harrow together."

Of course you were, Wells thought. *Of course you were.*

On the way to St. James's Court, Wells's shoulder already began to ache, but he knew he would never be able to complain about it to Jane. She had seen him off tenderly the night before, but without taking back her strong disapproval of this entire enterprise.

"If you get yourself killed, I will never forgive you," she'd said, trying, without much success, to make light of the situation.

"I'll be quite peeved myself if that happens."

Tonight, he would stay at the flat, alone, and simply try to get a good night's sleep. There was no telling when he'd get another. After failing to hail any available cab—at dusk, there was always a shortage— he elected to take the tube instead, where he happened to be seated across from a gawky young man, no more than seventeen or eighteen years old, so absorbed in a book that he was biting his fingernails while reading. Like any author, Wells was curious to know more about the book—could it be one of his own, or something by one of his many literary friends? At the next station, several passengers got off, but among those who got on were a pair of attractive girls, about the same age as the boy. They were laughing and talking to each other, and he noticed one of them, in the wide-brimmed hat, call her friend's attention to the reader. Still standing as the train took off, they bent their heads together conspiratorially, and then approached the boy. Ah, Wells thought, the eternal and unchanging mating dance; if the fellow didn't look up from his seat soon, he'd miss his chance!

Although their backs were to him, and the roar from the train too loud for him to make out what they were saying, Wells could tell that they had asked him what he was reading, as he bashfully turned the book over to show them the cover. It was *Ivanhoe*, nothing Wells would ever have guessed. The classics endured. The boy, whose complexion was spotty to begin with, was blushing with confusion—two pretty girls hovering over him like this! Wells hoped he would not muff it. The girl in the fancy hat chuckled at something he said, and squeezed her friend's arm. The boy looked as if he couldn't follow. The girl bent lower, and appeared to be straightening the collar of his corduroy jacket, and then stood back to appraise her work. The boy was motionless.

"There," she said, patting the top of his head, "you've earned that," and as the train slowed at the next platform, they turned on their heels, laughing. Looking very pleased with themselves, they sauntered off arm in arm.

The boy looked paralyzed, his face flaming red with shame, only his eyes shifting down to take in the white feather that the girl had pinned to his lapel.

My God, Wells thought.

The boy glanced up, catching Wells's gaze, then snatched the feather off and in his hurry to leave the car, dropped his copy of *Ivanhoe.*

Wells picked it up, expecting him to come back for it, but he did not. The disgrace was too great—he had been given the mark of cowardice, the white feather that young women, many of them suffragettes, had taken to bestowing on men of fighting age who were not in uniform. That boy would never forget this episode; he would never forget the girls' laughter, or seeing the man with the Gladstone bag between his feet looking back at him. What he would never know was there was no disapprobation, but only sympathy, in that man's expression. And he would never again take pleasure in reading *Ivanhoe.*

It was drizzling when Wells emerged from the underground station, and as soon as he got to his flat, he poured himself a healthy shot of whiskey and pulled on his old cardigan sweater. No telling when he'd have another night like this. With his feet before the fire, and rain now pelting the windowpanes, he was settling in with the *Evening News*—the paper Machen wrote for—when the door knocker banged. Several times.

Who could that be? Wells wondered. Almost no one knew that he would even be in London that night. The only people who knew were Jane, Winston, and, come to think of it . . . Rebecca.

CHAPTER TEN

"I look a mess, I know," Rebecca said, standing at the door with a broken umbrella in hand, "and I hope I'm not disturbing you." Her wet hair was plastered to her head. She had so hoped to make a better impression, but there was nothing she could do about it now.

"Not at all," he said. "Come in, come in."

"Are you sure it's all right?" she said, peering over his shoulder to see if Jane might be there, too.

"I'm the only one home."

That was a relief, she thought. Leaving the twisted wreckage of her umbrella at the portico, she entered, shaking the rain from her thick brown mane, and when she turned, he was studying her in, if she were to be honest, a most gratifying way. Perhaps the dishevelment wasn't such a bad thing, after all.

"When I realized that tomorrow was the day you were scheduled to depart"—she wanted it to seem as if it had simply been a passing thought, and not a date with which she had been consumed ever since he had mentioned it in a note days before—"I couldn't bear to not say goodbye."

"I do expect to return, you know," he said, hanging her wet coat on a hook by the door, and ushering her toward the parlor, where the fire crackled in the grate. "But it's lovely to see you." He left the room briefly, and came back to her with a towel in one hand and a glass of whiskey in the other. "First dry, then drink."

She scrubbed her hair, then exchanged the towel for the glass. In the old sweater and scuffed shearling slippers, he looked more endearing than ever. Her eyes roamed the bookshelves, most of them still empty, lining the walls.

"These need filling," she said.

"Yes, they do—I haven't yet decided how to split up my library, between Easton Glebe and here. Inevitably, whatever book I need when I'm here turns out to be in the country, and vice versa."

"You'll have to buy duplicates from now on."

"Not the worst idea."

For the next half hour or so, they made idle chitchat about books and writing routines—he mentioned that he had read with pleasure her piece about militancy among the suffragettes, which she'd sold to the *Clarion*, and she complimented him on a speech he'd given on socialism at the Guildhall.

"You were there?" he said. "You should have come up afterward."

"I tried to," she said, "but you were surrounded by acolytes, and before I could catch your attention, George Bernard Shaw had hustled you out a side door."

"Oh, yes," Wells said with a laugh. "Shaw can't bear to see anyone else being celebrated. But it's hard to imagine that I might have missed you."

Rebecca did not miss the flirtatious note. They could easily have gone on talking in the same vein—about authors and editors and current events—but all the while she was as aware of the subtle, but rising, tension in the room as she was of the rain and wind at the windows. A man of Wells's sensitivity, and with his reputation, could not have missed it, either. A beautiful young woman appears on your doorstep, unannounced, on a blustery night, when you are to leave for the Front in the morning? What reason could there be, other than the most obvious, if yet unspoken, one?

But how to get there? Rebecca had imagined the scene many times—boldly proclaiming herself, initiating the affair, falling onto a divan in a tangle of limbs—but now that she was actually here, in the flat, the fire dwindling in the grate, she found her courage failing her. Would Wells take up the gauntlet?

A church bell tolled in the distance, and on the last bong, she asked if he had already packed his kit for the journey. "If you haven't, I'd be glad to help. I'm quite clever at things like that." Anything to prolong the visit.

He appeared to be mulling it over. "Jane usually does it for me—"

Did he have to mention his wife?

"—but it is indeed a skill I lack. Leave it to me to forget the essentials, and pack only the superfluous."

"Then let me help," she said, clapping her hands together and bounding up from her chair. "Before he vanished into the ether, I used to help my father with his bags. It's one of the few happy memories I have of him."

"You're sure about this?"

"Quite! Where's the bag?"

It was, as she was fairly confident it would be, in the master bedroom—a battered but capacious brown suitcase, with colorful stickers from ports of call all over the world. Despite his less than rousing oratorical skills—those who were standing in the back, as Rebecca had been, at the Guildhall, could barely hear his reedy voice—Wells was a much sought-after speaker from Moscow to New York.

"I was planning to get to this in the morning," he said, opening the case atop the hand-quilted bedspread, which, Rebecca wondered, might have come from Jane's own hand. She tried to put that out of her mind.

"The trick is," she said, "to start at the top and move down to the bottom, then pack everything in the reverse order. So, what have you got for your head?"

"An army officer's cap, which I shall be wearing."

"What else?"

"What else do I need?"

"Something warm."

He obligingly went to the dresser and removed a flannel sleeping cap.

Rebecca smiled and said, "You mustn't let the others see you in this. Now, shirts."

He handed her a fresh shirt, an undershirt, and a black necktie—"Will there be many formal dinners?" she asked, and he shrugged. And so it went, from sweater, to belt, to trousers, to socks, all of the items stacked beside the suitcase. The intimacy of the process—standing close beside each other, handling his clothing, next to the neatly made four-poster bed—wasn't lost on either one of them, and Rebecca could all but feel the heat rising off of Wells. But could he sense her own desire? She had written about love, and lovemaking, in a frank and forthright manner, in essays and stories, but for all of her candor, she was in fact a virgin, as untutored in all of it as a child would be. She'd lyrically praised D. H. Lawrence's work, and assumed the pose of someone more versed in sensuality than she actually was, when, in truth, the whole business remained murky and undefined. Even so, the back of her neck felt as if a warm wind were caressing the exposed skin.

Once the stacks were complete, Rebecca went about putting them into the suitcase, the bulkier items on the bottom, carefully tucking everything in, smoothing out the wrinkles, but when Wells reached out to add another pair of socks—"I've read that trench foot is one of the most uncomfortable calamities to befall the troops"—their hands grazed each other, and Rebecca felt it as if it were an electric shock.

The breath caught in her throat, and she turned her head to Wells. His eyes—that pale blue-gray—were staring into hers, and his expression was one of . . . expectancy? Indecision?

Would she be the one to bridge the gap—those few inches that felt like miles—between the two of them?

Wells opened his lips, as if to speak, but Rebecca didn't dare to wait. *What if it was something about his wife?* she thought. *What if it was a demurral? What if it was anything to destroy the moment?* She closed her eyes, and kissed him.

He neither resisted, nor complied, and in confusion she persisted, pressing her lips against his—though even at that, she was far less experienced than she let on. She felt the slight bristle of his brown mustache—she had never kissed a mustache before—and smelled the faint scent of bay rum from his shaved cheeks. Then, his arms, slipping around her waist, clutched her body to his, bending her like a willow . . . a willow that begged to be bent . . .

She fell back on the bed, the suitcase gaping beside her head, and he lay on top of her, returning her kiss with more passion than she had ever known in her life. Her hands went up to the nubby shoulders of his sweater, coursing across his back and shoulders, then up to the back of his head to hold it even more firmly, more ardently, in place. She wanted the embrace to go on forever, but she also wanted it to lead on . . . tonight she wanted to leave this room, this house, a changed woman, an adult woman, in every sense of that word. She wanted this night to be the Rubicon she had finally crossed, wrapped in the arms of the most eminent lover in the world . . .

And that was when she felt it, like a cold wave, dashing her in the face. Wells had broken off the kiss; he had leaned back—looking intently down at her—and with a tormented sigh, disengaged. He stepped back from the bed, leaving her panting, feeling more naked than she'd have felt with her clothes completely stripped away.

"What?" she breathed. "What is it?"

He shook his head, and looked away. "I can't."

"I want you to," she said.

"And so do I," he murmured, straightening his clothes. "But I cannot do this to you."

"But I give my consent."

"You're a virgin, aren't you?"

"What's that got to do with it?"

"I'm a married man."

"I'm told that hasn't stopped you before."

"And I'm twice your age."

"Nor has that."

The passionate encounter was quickly yielding to debate.

"I see you're aware of my scandalous past."

"All of London is." She rose up onto her elbows, then brushed her damp hair from her eyes.

"It simply wouldn't be right," he said, jamming his clenched hands into the pockets of his sweater.

"A fine time," she said, "to discover your scruples."

He didn't issue a riposte.

But the moment, Rebecca realized, was utterly gone. Her lips still buzzed, her breasts, untouched, ached, but she saw no way to rekindle the blaze.

"Thank you for your help with the bag," Wells said quietly. "I think we'd best return to the study." He left the bedroom, and Rebecca, wondering whether she felt more ravaged or rejected, sat up and straightened her clothing.

What had just happened here? How had it gone so wrong? A student of the dramatic arts, she had played out this scene in her head a hundred times, but this was one denouement she had never foreseen. She could hear Wells stirring the embers in the fireplace with a poker, and she wondered how she would face him. What attitude should she take? What expression should she wear on her face?

The rain was slashing against the windows, the bedside lamp cast a ruddy glow. How long she sat on the bed, she didn't know, but eventually Wells put his head back into the room, and said, "Are you all right, Rebecca?"

Was she? "Yes, fine," she said, putting a few stray hairs back into place. "I'll be right out."

"Take as long as you wish."

Alone again, she glanced at the open suitcase, and on a sudden whim, bent her head to kiss the shirtfront on top. Then, she closed the bag. Standing up, she smoothed her skirt and as if entering an entirely different scene, returned to the front room, her face composed, her shoulders squared, betraying none of the turmoil still raging within.

CHAPTER ELEVEN

Sergeant Stubb lived up to his name, Wells thought. Even in the vast railway station, where lines of young soldiers were being marched onto the trains, their kits and rifles clanking, Sergeant Stubb stood out—an anvil of a man, his head settled onto his shoulders with no intervention from a neck, his bandied legs spread apart. His face, as Wells got closer, was etched with scars and scratches that had never healed.

After introducing themselves—the sergeant's voice, Cockney-accented, was low and raspy—Stubb led the way to an officers' carriage, and all but pushing aside anyone in his way, ushered Wells on board, commandeering a window seat for them both. The senior officers observed them with curiosity, wondering, no doubt, at the middle-aged man in a crisp khaki uniform, closely escorted by nothing less than a bodyguard. Wells had felt conspicuous enough already, emerging from his place on St. James's Court; now, among these true soldiers, he felt positively fraudulent.

And exhausted. He had slept poorly. Every time he had rolled over onto his right shoulder, he had been awakened by the soreness from the inoculation. And his dreams had been troubled, as well—not that that should have been a surprise. After Rebecca had left, he had been tormented by the scene that they had enacted. But he couldn't decide whether he was troubled by how far it had gone, or that it had not gone further. He had never been one to turn down such an offer, and from such a beautiful and talented young woman, to boot. But maybe that was it—he held her in such high regard that he could not proceed without wondering just how deeply he would become involved. Unlike some of his other passades, this one—if embarked upon—threatened to become something of great importance in his life. Rebecca West would not be a passing fancy; she would assume a leading role in his life—he could feel it in his bones—and was he ready for that?

Stubb had folded his hands across his belly, pulled the brim of his cap down over his eyes, and dropped into what appeared to be an enviable sleep. Wells looked out the window as the whistle blew, steam escaping from the billowing stacks of the engine, and the train crept out of the station. There was a half-hearted cheer from some of the men in the other railcars. Wells settled down into his seat.

How many times had he taken just such a journey, leaving London for a lucrative lecture engagement, or a vacation on the Continent, with nothing but pleasure in the offing? Never, in all that time, had he imagined himself on a troop train, embarking for the most dangerous destination in the world. And despite all the assurances that he had given Jane and Rebecca about his own safety—"They're not about to ask me to take out a sniper's nest," he'd said to his wife, "I'm there to bolster morale, not get shot and further depress the national spirit"—he wasn't quite so confident as he made out. Accidents happened and bullets went astray; bombs did not discriminate, and the enemy was not aware that beneath this uniform lay a noncombatant.

For the next hour or two, he meditated, even dozed, but knew that they were approaching the coastline when the terrain became flatter, more desolate. Towns and fields gave way to swaying reeds and tidal wetlands. A flock of white herons, inured to the racket, paid almost no attention as the train rumbled past; and when it was time to disembark, into a vast shed riddled with dozens of tracks, Wells and Sergeant Stubb were herded from the train onto a gangway and then, almost before he was aware of it, to an upper deck of the transport ship that would take them across the Channel. Great cranes were hoisting wagons and supplies on board, while fearful braying mules were being prodded into the hold. It was all admirably efficient, Wells thought, and made a note of it in one of the two-dozen notebooks, and dozen pens, he had packed for the assignment.

While the loading was done, Stubb went below to secure their berths for the night, and Wells lit a pipe at the starboard railing. A younger man—though weren't they all?—was smoking a cigarette a few feet off, glancing at Wells out of the corner of his eye. He wore the red badge of a medical orderly on his sleeve.

"First time over?" he asked, in a somber tone.

"Is it so obvious?" Wells replied.

"Uniform looks like it's just out of the store window."

Wells chuckled, and the orderly said, "Third time for me."

His face betrayed it; by Wells's estimation, he couldn't be more than twenty-three or four, but his skin had an ashen hue. His eyes, too, had a haunted look in them.

"That must be hard," Wells said, "leaving home each time."

The soldier shrugged. "When you're at the Front, you miss your family. When you're with your family, you miss your friends in the trenches." He took a drag on the cigarette, then blew out a cloud of smoke. "We don't belong anywhere. We're all of us unrooted."

Wells made a mental note to remember that.

"Except, 'a course, for the ones who're planted there forever." He was looking off now, talking to himself as much as to Wells. "The ones who're blown to bits, or buried in the ground," he said, tamping some ash over the side, "or worse yet, burrowing under it."

"Under the ground?"

"Oh, yes, they're the ones you got to watch out for. Sneaky devils. Only come out at night. Like bats."

Was this man quite well? he wondered. Should he be going back into combat?

"They don't just want your rations," he said, turning his head toward Wells.

"They don't?"

"Oh, no. They want your soul, they do. And they get it."

What was most alarming was the fact that he spoke as if he were completely rational.

"So you be careful out there, sir," he said, flinging his cigarette butt, still glowing, over the side. "Dead is better than them." And then, laying one finger to the side of his nose, he winked and went below.

Wells's pipe had gone out entirely, and he struck a match to it as the ropes were undone and the boat began to slide away from the wharf. What a strange, and disturbing, colloquy that had just been. And he had never even gotten the man's name.

Juddering and creaking, the ship left the safety of the harbor, brackish water sloshing lazily against its hull. But if anyone had imagined crowds of well-wishers waving handkerchiefs and blowing kisses to the valiant warriors, he would have been sorely disappointed. The sky was a brooding gray, and the only cries were from the flock of gulls flapping around the smokestacks.

A new mood—one of solemn contemplation—seemed to descend like a pall upon all aboard. The soldiers still on deck fell silent, all of them wrapped in their own thoughts, staring out to sea. Suddenly they were leaving England in earnest, and to more than one of them it must have occurred—would they ever be coming back?

CHAPTER TWELVE

Where was her husband right now? Jane wondered. Still in transit, she knew—but at an officers' mess, regaling the others with his marvelous stories? Or on board a ship, staring out to sea? All day long her mind had been returning to such questions, though she told herself that the only way to get through this ordeal would be to try to put it out of her thoughts, and go about her own business running the rectory. There was nothing she could do to affect any of it, so it was equally pointless to fret about it.

While Mrs. Willoughby was set to polishing the silver and changing all the linens, Jane spent the day making a typescript out of the stack of pages Wells had left for her. Only she could decipher his handwriting with any great precision. It was a novel about the home front, another of what she considered his "domestic" novels—treating everything from the zeppelin bombings to relations between the sexes—and a far departure from the earlier books, the flights of scientific fancy, that had made his name. Working so closely on the book made her feel that much closer to him, and made her miss him all the more.

She missed her two sons, away at school, too; the house seemed so empty and barren. When H. G. was in residence, there were weekend guests, and games of croquet or tennis in the yard, and the dining room was filled with lively discussions, even arguments; H. G. liked nothing more than a high-spirited debate. When Mrs. Willoughby pedaled her bicycle back to the village that evening, Jane felt the solitude and quiet even more keenly.

In bed that night, she read a few chapters of the new Joseph Conrad novel that the author had been kind enough to send—she marveled again at how skillfully this Pole had mastered the English language, with all its nuances—before turning out the light. But the weather had turned blustery. The old house wheezed and groaned, the curtains rustled in the draft from every window. Still, among the many sounds she was accustomed to, there was one that was more unusual—a loud and intermittent banging from the yard. She rolled over in bed, trying to ignore it, but when it was joined by the persistent hoot of the barn owl, she knew something was amiss, and rolled out of her warm bed and went to the window.

Sure enough, the barn doors had become unlatched and were swinging back and forth in the cold night wind. Should she wait until morning and deal with it then—though would she be able to sleep?—or bite the bullet and go outside now? The owl hooted again, as if an alarm, and that made up her mind for her.

With her overcoat thrown over her nightdress, and her bare feet stuck into a pair of Wellingtons, she went out the back door, but not without glancing at the ash can to see if its lid had been disturbed. Tonight it looked untouched, though that was no guarantee it had not been pillaged. Holding an electric torch, she picked her way across the yard, where the bucket was swiveling above the well, and slipped inside the barn.

Training the light on the owl, who flew away into the rafters to hide, she turned the beam down toward the empty cow stall, where she saw something, at ground level, darting behind a bale of old straw, and knocking over an old milking bucket as it did.

Something bigger than a rodent. Much.

Whatever it was, it bumped up against the side of the stall, before scuttling for the shadows.

Her immediate impulse was to run, but something in her resisted it, and instead she directed the light in its direction. The intruder slunk along the wall, and only when it was cornered by the beam, and she could see a pair of startled eyes—human eyes—did she say, "Who are you?"

There was no answer, but she suddenly saw the glint of a knife blade, and now she knew she'd made a terrible mistake, and spun around to run.

She was at the doors when she felt an arm sling around her neck and she was dragged back into the barn, the whole weight of her assailant pulling her down. She threw an elbow back to catch him in the ribs, and she heard an *oof*, so she did it again. He lost his breath entirely, but not his grip, and she fell backward on top of him. She still had hold of the torch, and once she had managed to roll enough to one side, she used it to smack him in the head. He waved the knife at her, but half-heartedly, as if he could barely raise his arm from the dirt, and now she could see that it was a young boy—only sixteen or seventeen?—with sunken cheeks and blond stubble. Wearing a torn-up leather jacket, with a patch on its sleeve.

A German patch.

She struggled to her feet, teetering above him, holding the torch out as if it were a sword.

But he was past fighting. One boot was undone, the laces trailing. His eyes were glassy, his breath ragged. Clearly, it had taken all his strength to make this one attack.

Jane's own chest was heaving with the exertion, and for several seconds, they simply remained where they were, speechless. Haltingly, she asked, "What are you doing here?" though she guessed the answer even as she uttered the words. He must have escaped the zeppelin crash.

He must have been hiding all this time in the barn. He must have been surviving on the scraps from the ash can.

He mumbled something in reply, but even if she'd spoken German, she would have had trouble hearing it. It was less an answer than an exhalation, and when it was done, his eyes shuttered closed, his jaw dropped, and his head flopped unconscious to one side. Had he died? She watched for signs of breathing—they were faint, but apparent—and wondered what on earth to do next. If only H. G. had been there . . . This airman was not more than a few years older than her own boys. Gradually, the adrenaline in her veins subsided. The light from the electric torch, damaged in the fight, sputtered and went out. The boy moaned in his sleep, and the hand still clutching the jackknife relaxed its grip.

When it fell from his fingers, she snatched it up. Would he have used it on her, she wondered? Her thoughts were all in a jumble. What she knew she should do was call the police immediately, and then let them turn him in to the military authorities. That was what one did in wartime. To do anything other than that was to court disaster—and charges of everything from harboring a fugitive to aiding the enemy.

So why was she hesitating? What was it in the sight of this injured, helpless boy that gave her pause, any pause at all? And what was compelling her, even now, to unbutton her own coat and drape it over him?

CHAPTER THIRTEEN

By dawn, the ship was off Le Havre, and by eight thirty, Wells found himself, swaddled in his newly issued greatcoat, following Sergeant Stubb through the chaotic harbor scene. Hieronymus Bosch could not have done it justice—twisting avenues lined by bales of barbed wire the height of houses, teetering mountains of crates and barrels, whinnying horses and skittish mules, a thousand shouting voices, little French boys begging for a cigarette or a bit of the breakfast the swarms of soldiers had just been issued: tins of bully beef, along with a biscuit as hard and thick as a fist.

Stubb might just as well have been walking in Green Park, so unperturbed was he by the commotion and discord. Sucking on a Victory lozenge—a hard, medicinal tablet, containing ether and chloroform among its several ingredients, whose slogan, aptly enough, was "It's got a kick like a mule!"—he led his ward to a waiting train. The carriages for the troops were marked *"Hommes 40, Chevaux (en long) 8"* in white paint, and the men, who had hardly enjoyed terra firma for more than a few minutes, were herded into them like the cattle, Wells reflected, they were. At the officers' carriage, in front, a porter was serving up cups of hot tea, and Stubb was once again able, after showing ministry papers to the lance corporal in charge, to commandeer a window seat for Wells.

"I trust that the sergeant has been taking good care of you," the corporal said, after Stubb had excused himself to travel, by choice, with the infantry recruits.

"Yes, quite," Wells replied, "though getting a word out of him is an ordeal."

"Yes, well, it's a miracle he can talk at all."

"Why is that?"

"The mustard gas," the corporal said, as if surprised Wells did not know. "Didn't they tell you he's won an MC for exemplary gallantry?"

"No, no one said a word, least of all Stubb."

"I served with him in the front line. After the Germans had laid down a gas attack, the wind changed, and blew it back into their own damned trenches. Served 'em right. Stubb went over the top to retrieve some of our own who'd been blinded, or couldn't breathe even with their respirators, and carried three of them to safety. By the time he went back for a fourth, the wind had changed again, and he was caught in it; it clings to the ground, you know, in patches like some damned weed, but he still managed to drag a man back by his collar, before succumbing himself."

"And here I thought he'd just had a sore throat."

"The vocal cords," the corporal said, tapping his own throat. "Once burned, they seldom come back."

Wells felt chastened, for not having discovered this story himself. He had been so caught up in his own impressions and thoughts, his note-taking and observations, that he had missed the most moving story of all, one that was right under his nose. He put it down to the slight disorientation he'd felt, the effects perhaps from the inoculation, but resolved to do better, to wake up, which was made no easier by the constant rocking motions of the train. On and on it went, stopping and starting, its shrill whistle preceded each time by the tootling of a little horn that sounded to Wells like some child's instrument. Several times Wells was engaged in brief conversations with other officers, most of whom struck him, as Colonel Bryce would have put it, as "capital fellows"; others impressed him as boors, buffoons, or worse. It was just the mix one would have expected from the officers' corps, composed, as it was, of the aristocrats and public-school boys. But the racket from the train made talking to any of them difficult, and the increasingly stuffy air inside the car seemed to induce a mild drowsiness and inertia.

Wells rested his head against the rattling windowpane, watching as the fields and forests rolled by. French farm women, in loose black skirts, lifted a hand; their children sometimes ran alongside the train, waving wildly. At dusk, the train stopped at an overwhelmed country junction, and everyone was ordered off for a night in the rest area—where thousands of belled tents, like the Indian teepees he'd once seen in the American West, were set up in orderly and endless rows, and a YMCA hut did a brisk business in hot tea and tobacco—before another early departure, on yet another train, the next day. Wells guessed that the soldiers, too, were confused by that same combination of expectation, even exhilaration, and mounting dread that was afflicting him. One minute you could not wait to arrive, finally, at the Front, the next you were relieved to hear, via the grapevine that functioned as well as any telegraph through the train cars, that the battlefield was still hours away.

The first signs that they were approaching their terminus were the occasional abandoned farmhouse, with a neglected yard and caved-in roof, or splintered barn with animals wandering loose. A dead horse lay in a ditch, its body bloated. A row of poplars, every other one of them felled, ran along one side of the tracks. There were no children waving, or hay wagons lumbering down the country roads. And if you listened carefully, above the rumble of the train, the shriek of its whistle, there was a low and steady thunder in the distance. A thunder that grew louder as the train progressed into Belgium. Even the officers in the car quieted down, puffing on their pipes, or hurriedly scrawling some last few words in a letter to their wife or the girl back home.

Wells made a few notes of his own, and when the train began to slow, he looked ahead and saw what looked at first, in the fading afternoon light, like a quaint country village. It was only when they got closer to the covered station that he could see the town was a ruin—all the chimneys down, the windows broken, the rooflines sagging or missing altogether. Arc lamps, casting a paler and weaker glow than the ones at Southampton, were already on above the platform, and when the train ground to a stop, there was a momentary jolt when everything seemed to stop—all motion, all noise—before being suddenly engulfed, as if by a tidal wave, in a flurry of barking orders and escaping steam, doors being thrown open, kit bags hauled from overhead racks, horses' hooves clattering down ramps, a blaring loudspeaker spouting unintelligible gibberish.

Wells felt his very head might explode, but as he stepped down from the train, the ever-reliable Sergeant Stubb was waiting, luggage all accounted for, and ready to escort him to a waiting car. He was deposited in the back seat between a fat major with a walrus mustache and his rail-thin adjutant; Stubb sat in front beside the driver, and as they pulled away from the station yard, past the troops being mustered into marching order, a British plane—one of the de Havilland biplanes used for scouting—swooped low overhead, tipping its wings in salute to the new arrivals.

"Won't be long now," the major said, clapping Wells on the knee, "before we're back in the thick of it, eh." He said it as if they were riding to hounds.

"It appears that way."

The car jounced along what might once have been a main street, pausing only for a mangy dog to drag itself out of the way, before leaving the relative illumination of the town for a gloomy track leading into a dark and stunted wood.

CHAPTER FOURTEEN

It had been a struggle to get him up to the attic, but with Dr. Gruber's help, Jane had managed it.

How she had managed all the rest was a mystery even to her, a day later.

She had driven to the village herself to fetch the doctor, banging on his door to wake the dead. But his puzzlement continued all the way back to her house.

"But what *is* the problem?" he'd said, his medical bag in his lap, his gray hair a wild entanglement. "Whatever it is, it's best dealt with here in my surgery."

"This problem can't be."

"You look fine. And although you're driving a bit recklessly, your motor skills seem unimpeded."

"It's not me."

"But H. G. is away, isn't he?"

"Yes. He's over there," she said, using the common shorthand. "Reporting."

"That's no place to be just now."

"So I told him," she said, trying to concentrate on the road. She seldom drove the car—her husband always said she was a menace to local wildlife when she did—and the night only made it worse. The headlights punched two neat holes in the dark, for ten or twelve feet, but that was all.

"Then who? Mrs. Willoughby is no doubt fast asleep in her own home right now. As I was."

"You'll see when we get there," Jane said, afraid to reveal too much too soon. She was asking the doctor to do something that, for all she knew, was unethical, or even illegal. Helping an enemy combatant? She still wondered, for that matter, why she was fetching medical help instead of simply alerting the local constabulary.

When she led him out toward the barn, the doctor said, "Why didn't you call on the veterinarian? I'm not equipped to—"

But Jane held a finger to her lips, opened the doors, and directing the beam from her electric torch, saw only a patch of disturbed earth where the boy had lain.

Dr. Gruber looked at her as if he were now wondering about her own sanity.

"He was right here."

"Who?"

A track in the dirt led off toward the cow stall. Jane followed it, and at the back, huddled under her warm overcoat, was a shivering figure, eyes closed, and a gnawed bone (was it from last night's pork chops?) lying by his side.

"Who is he?" Dr. Gruber said softly, before fully taking in the leather trousers, the unlaced boot, the scruffy blond beard. "Is he . . . from the zeppelin?"

Jane nodded.

The doctor knelt down by the boy and put a hand on his shoulder to rouse him. Even with only the smattering of German that Jane had— her children had had a German music teacher and tutor for years—she could tell that he had introduced himself as a physician, and told the boy he had nothing to fear. How strange that she had, until now, not even thought about the fact that the doctor's surname was German and that he might speak the language . . . and this in a time when all things German were banned and even dachshunds were being stoned on the street. War threw all common sense out the window.

The boy, hearing his language, turned his head and muttered something. Perhaps he thought he was home again. He clutched the doctor's hand, and when he was asked if he could stand up, tried to do so, pushing himself up against the back wall; the overcoat fell away, revealing the rest of his air uniform, and now, for the first time, he seemed to take in Jane, and in so doing remembered his precarious situation. But instead of threatening her again, he mumbled what sounded for all the world like an apology.

Jane said that it was all right, and with the boy suspended between them, she and the doctor helped him out of the stall. His left leg was dragging, and appeared to have been broken. Maybe it was his ankle, explaining the unlaced boot.

By the time they got to the back door of the house, he had fainted away altogether, and they had to carry him inside. Knowing that Mrs. Willoughby would be coming back again the next morning, Jane took the precaution of having the boy taken all the way up to the attic, where there was a small, unused servant's room under the eaves. She pulled back the coverlet, letting loose a cloud of dust, and they laid him gently on the bed.

"I'll need some water, hot as you can get it," the doctor said, "some clean towels, and perhaps a spot of brandy would not be amiss."

Waiting by the stove for the water to boil, she thought, *What have I done? What am I doing?* She knew only that she had responded in the way most natural to who she was. She saw suffering, and tried to ameliorate it. When she went back up the stairs with the provisions, the boy's clothes were thrown on the floor, and he was undressed but for a pair of ragged undershorts. His chest and arms were scrawny, his ribs showing, and the doctor was tending to an ankle, raised on a pillow, that was as purple and swollen as an eggplant.

Together, Jane and the doctor sponged the dirt and grime off his body—he reeked of sweat, dried blood, and engine oil—and in the process he gradually came back to consciousness. When Dr. Gruber asked his name, he said, "Kurt . . . Kederer."

"Where are you from?" the doctor asked in German, and Jane heard Stuttgart.

"Ah," Gruber said, nodding as he continued to examine the boy's wounds. "Where the zeppelins are made."

At the sound of the word "zeppelins," the boy's eyes shifted nervously to Jane, holding a stack of towels at the foot of the bed. She knew what he was thinking, but her own thoughts were more of a muddle than anyone could ever imagine. This was an enemy soldier, one of the army that might even now be shooting at H. G. This was someone sworn to the defeat of England and working to achieve that aim by dropping bombs on innocent civilians. A baby-killer, as Slattery, the livery driver, had put it before plunging the pitchfork into the rear gunner. So how could she be attending to him now, how could she be seeing not a fierce and fire-breathing Hun, but a broken boy just a few years older than her own, a boy whose beard hadn't even fully grown in yet? There was a dissonance in her head, as if she were hearing two voices yammering at her at the same time.

"Let's try that brandy now," Gruber said, and it was Jane who held the glass to Kurt's parched and blackened lips. He sipped it gingerly, eyes downcast as if in shame, and muttered, *"Vielen Dank"* in a hoarse voice.

"Willkommen," she replied, and at this, his eyes—blue as a summer sky—lifted.

Dr. Gruber pressed the bone just above the ankle, and the boy yelped, a drop of brandy dribbling down his chin.

"If we don't set this, and soon," he said, "the bone will knit improperly and he'll never be able to walk without a terrible limp."

"What do we need?"

"My surgery. To do it right, we'll need to do it there."

Jane's mind reeled at the thought. Finding an opportunity the next day to get the boy down from the attic, and unbeknownst to Mrs. Willoughby, who knew the workings of the house even better than Jane did, would be hard enough; but transporting him into town, unobserved, would be a challenge of an altogether higher order.

Dr. Gruber stroked his gray beard, and gave her a long and level glance. "Right now we could turn him over to the authorities and wash our hands of the whole matter."

"Probably get a commendation for it," Jane said, wryly. "But what would happen to him?"

"He'd be just another prisoner of war—eventually, they might even get 'round to operating on that leg—unless . . ."

"Unless what?"

"Unless, because of the unusual circumstances, he was charged with espionage."

"Espionage?"

"He didn't surrender himself. He's been hiding in the English countryside since the crash, and he could be accused of everything from acting as a clandestine radio operator to an industrial saboteur."

"Saboteur? He's been starving in the barn."

"I know," Gruber said, nodding, "but military tribunals are not overly concerned with the finer points. Especially when the man in the dock is a zeppelin bomber."

Oh, how she wished, at times like these, for H. G.'s wisdom and sage advice. What would he do? Would his natural sympathies and keen curiosity be aroused, or would he cut to the quick and be done with it? Something told her that in this case, it would be the latter—his native patriotism would trump all other concerns.

Kurt, who had to know that the debate was about him, looked beseechingly at the doctor—the German doctor—and speaking in a rush that Jane's acquaintance with the language was too rudimentary to follow, tried to make his case. But for what? Further concealment? Escape? Medical help? In his eyes, she could see naked fear, his hand clutching the doctor's like a lifeline.

Gruber tried to calm him, even digging into his black bag to give him two sedative tablets, which were washed down with a swish of the brandy.

Turning to Jane, the doctor said, "Are you all right with his sleeping up here tonight? He should be unconscious shortly."

Was she?

"Can you lock this room?"

"Yes," she said, "and the door to the attic stairs."

"And your own room, I presume?"

"Of course."

"Then maybe we should let it lie until tomorrow. We both have a great deal of thinking to do."

"Yes, I should say we do. I'm sorry to have brought you into any of this, Dr. Gruber."

He shrugged. "The war spares no one," he said, snapping his medical bag closed. "Two weeks ago, my nephew was killed in action."

"Oh, I am so sorry. I heard nothing of that."

"You wouldn't have. He was fighting for the other side."

CHAPTER FIFTEEN

"Best get used to keeping your head down, sir," Sergeant Stubb reminded him, going so far as to press a hand down atop Wells's newly acquired and uncomfortable helmet as they entered the trenches. "The snipers never let up."

If Wells had imagined a system of deep, straight furrows in the ground, well enforced and plainly laid out, he was immediately disabused of that notion. Though Stubb seemed to know his way about, to Wells it was a veritable maze, with what amounted to three tiers of trenches, eight or ten feet deep, with duckboards underfoot and parapets piled high with sagging sandbags. All the way at the rear, backed by the artillery, were the reserve trenches, then came the support trenches, and finally, there was the front-line barricade; all three were interconnected by communications avenues cut at roughly right angles. The trenches themselves zigzagged every fifty yards or so, designed that way, Wells surmised, so that if an enemy shell landed in one, the explosion and its accompanying shrapnel would be relatively contained; only the dozens of soldiers unlucky enough to be in that particular quarter would be exposed to the full force of the blast. Here and there, short side extensions were cut into the perpetually soggy earth for the English army's own snipers or, more prosaically, for latrines; whenever Wells passed one of the latter, the stench of human ordure and buckets of lime, thrown in to aid in decomposition and hygiene, was so overpowering that he was tempted to pull on his hooded gas mask.

For the moment, all was quiet, and as he passed the mud-covered soldiers sitting on crates, cleaning their Lee Enfield rifles or trying to catch a few minutes of much-needed rest, he knew that he—an older gent, in a spotless uniform, being individually escorted through the labyrinth—was a subject of much speculation. Wells offered encouraging nods and smiles in return for their frank curiosity, while in his heart grew a mounting sympathy for these men who had to survive under such appalling conditions. They huddled in funk holes—tiny caves cut into the trench walls—or under wet macks, or around camp stoves where they might fill a dented cup with tepid tea. Beneath the uneven duckboards, the soil was slick and vile, except where it was altogether invisible under sloshing, stagnant water. And even now, in the full if pallid light of day, an army of black and brown rats went about their business with impunity, scuttling underfoot, burrowing into the sandbags, squeaking with indignation at the occasional well-aimed kick.

"Now we're getting into the posh part of town," Stubb said, gesturing at a metal sign hanging from an upright shovel that said, "Kensington High St." It wasn't the first such sign Wells had seen along the way—there had been others, for "Hyde Park Gate" and "Portobello Road" and "Charing Cross," similarly and haphazardly mounted at various junctures, in part for wry amusement and in part as helpful reminders as to where you might be. Midway down the trench, he saw an incongruous wooden door, with a carved lion-head knocker and a polished brass handle, imperfectly set into a wall of corrugated panels and old oaken boards. "The officers' dugout," Stubb explained. The placard on this door read, "The Reform," the venerable London club where Wells, coincidentally enough, had dined often with Winston Churchill. A good omen. "This is where you'll be billeted."

Banging the knocker, Stubb pushed the door open with his shoulder, then stood to one side to let Wells enter first. After several seconds to let his eyes adjust to the scene, he saw a cramped warren of dimly lit rooms—if they could be so dignified—with low ceilings reinforced by rusted girders, and a few sticks of furniture cluttered with candles and lanterns, plates and bottles, books and maps.

A tall, rangy man peering into a microscope, of all things, looked up, hooked his spectacles over his ears, and said, "Hullo, you must be our honored guest." Rising and coming forward with his hand extended, he said, "Captain Lillyfield—Gerald—Sixth Battalion, Northumberland Fusiliers. At your service."

"Wells. H. G. War Office propagandist."

"It's only because we were alerted to your arrival a day or two ago that we were able to make the place look so inviting," he said, waving his arm to take in the dim and forbidding cavern. "You can't imagine what it looked like before."

Wells laughed, as another man emerged from what must have been the galley, wiping his hands on a filthy apron, and introduced himself as Corporal Norridge, or "Forage, as they like to tell me after each meal."

"Lord knows where he finds all the provisions," Lillyfield said. "He can do wonders with field rations and the occasional fowl freed from a local farmhouse."

"Where do you want me to drop this?" Stubb interjected, indicating Wells's suitcase and gear.

"Oh, right back there." Lillyfield pointed to a canvas cloth hanging open in front of a dark alcove carved from the earth itself. Though he'd expected no more, Wells's heart sank nonetheless at the sight of the gloomy cubbyhole where he would be residing.

"In fact," the captain said to Stubb, "you are welcome to the other bunk, too."

"Not be putting anyone out, would I?"

"No," Lillyfield said, solemnly. "We've had a couple of vacancies since . . . yesterday morning's push."

So they would be moving into dead men's quarters, Wells thought. But then, what weren't dead men's quarters on the Front? There wasn't an inch of soil that hadn't been drenched in blood.

"Well, I'll leave you two to it," Lillyfield said. "I've got some work to do yet."

Wells could see a glass slide, with a smudge of something dark in its center, under the microscope.

"Dinner's at seven, right, Norridge?"

"Or whenever the soufflé rises," the corporal replied.

Wells and Stubb pulled the curtain all the way back on the alcove, revealing two hard pallets wedged sideways into the dirt wall, with a single flat pillow and a striped wool blanket on each.

"Your choice," Stubb said, his voice suddenly so strained it was almost gone.

"As you're more agile, I'll take the lower."

Stubb grunted, and slung his own pack off his back and onto the upper bunk, before hoisting himself up, too.

Wells opened his suitcase, took out the few necessary items he would need that night—his toothbrush, the sleeping cap that Rebecca had made fun of, a fresh pair of woolen socks (his feet always got cold)—and then closed it again and pushed it under the bunk.

Though the table was covered with maps, official army bulletins, and the distinctive green envelopes used for letters home, Lillyfield had cleared a space beside the lantern for his makeshift laboratory. A tray of slides and several chemical vials were arrayed around the microscope, the sight of which took Wells, who had made quite a study of biology and chemistry, back to his school days at the Normal School of Science, to which he'd been admitted, in view of his family's poverty, on scholarship.

"What's your profession?" Wells asked. "Are you a doctor?"

"Associate professor of natural history," Lillyfield said, jotting down a note with one hand while adjusting the lens with the other. "Take a look at this tick." He leaned back on the hind legs of the spindly chair, so that Wells could observe.

What he saw was enough to put him off anything Norridge might rustle up from the galley. A tick—the fattest he'd ever seen—was split open, its eight legs splayed wide, its beak-like mouth gaping open.

"I swear," Lillyfield said, "the war has given nature license to create newer and bigger forms of arachnid life and, as you've no doubt seen on your way to our little haven, vermin galore. They positively thrive on human catastrophe."

It was just the sort of idea that Wells might have employed in one of his earlier science fiction novels, and Lillyfield must have thought so, too.

"It reminds me of your *Food of the Gods*, where the chickens grew as big as a house. I remember reading that book when I was a lad and should have been swotting for my finals at Harrow instead."

Wells removed his eye from the microscope and took a good look at the captain. Under the gaunt and grimy skin, the uncombed hair and wire spectacles, he could see that he was indeed no more than twenty-eight or nine—a lad *still*, in his book.

But one who was in charge of the lives of countless other lads, some as young as nineteen, the requisite age to serve at the Front—and many more, even younger, who had lied about their age to enlist. The recruiters, Wells was aware, were known to turn a willfully blind eye to the deception.

When dinner was served—atop a makeshift table fashioned from old ration crates—Wells found himself pleasantly surprised by the fare. Given the conditions under which the corporal-cum-chef labored, in a veritable cave, over a sputtering gas flame perilously close to ammunitions boxes, beneath a strange agglomeration of tins perched on rickety shelves, it was a miracle he could produce anything edible at all. Mopping up some of the hot Irish stew with a hunk from a crisp baguette, Wells asked if he'd been a cook in civilian life.

"Fish and chips shop. Best in Newcastle." His shaved head still gleamed with sweat from the galley. "My mum always said I could make a dead cat taste savory."

"Is that what's in this?" Lillyfield joshed.

"Ask me no questions, I'll tell ye no lies."

Stubb, Wells noted, chewed his food carefully and long, and swallowed with difficulty, following each bite with a slug of cold water from the earthenware jar. He said nothing, as what voice he could still muster had probably been used up for the day. Wells wondered if he ever used it to complain, but judging from his stoic demeanor, guessed not.

Just as they were enjoying the tinned apricots Norridge had rustled up for dessert, an unwelcome guest appeared in the doorway. Or so, at least, Wells would have thought.

An albino rat, with a missing tail and bent whiskers, sitting up on his hind legs like a dog.

"Alphonse," the captain said, "you're late," before tossing him a leftover crust of bread. The rat lunged for it.

"I do wish you wouldn't encourage this," Norridge said. "He burrowed through a whole box of oatmeal the other day."

"Alphonse is our mascot," Lillyfield explained.

"*Your* mascot," Norridge grumbled.

"He's survived two direct hits, and an unfortunate incident when the enemy actually managed to penetrate the front line. He brings good luck."

"He brings disease," Norridge said, gathering up the empty plates. "And one of these days when you're not around, I'm going to settle his hash."

Wells watched in astonishment as the rat finished his supper, licking his twisted whiskers, and scooted back under the door.

"Shall we join him," Lillyfield suggested, "for a postprandial stroll?"

Outside, it was a moonlit night, and both he and Wells took pipes from their pockets and lit up. The captain walked up and down several of the interconnecting trenches, bucking up the soldiers. Wells got the impression that Lillyfield was a popular officer among the men. And when they came to a breach in the parapet, the captain stood on a firing step and put his eye to a periscope raised just an inch or two above the uppermost sandbag. After swiveling the scope this way and that, he offered it to Wells.

"No man's land by moonlight. A dispiriting sight if ever there was one . . . especially after an unsuccessful push."

Wells tamped out his pipe, took his place on the step, and after a moment or two, got his focus. It wasn't easy to see much—just a couple hundred yards of scarred and uneven terrain, punctuated by leaning posts and shell holes and tangles of barbed wire. In more than one spot, he discerned what, to his dismay, could only be the bodies of dead English infantrymen draped over the wire like dirty laundry hanging on a line. Others were thrown all over the ground, willy-nilly.

"You can't retrieve the bodies?" Wells said, still taking in the awful scene.

"Not unless Jerry wants to call a truce to do the same for theirs."

Wells knew that even if he tried to conjure this bleak landscape for the readers back home, the War Office would never let it go through. Like the letters in the green field envelopes, it would be read first by a censor and then either redacted, or destroyed. He was here to create moral uplift and patriotic spirit, not a blunt account of the horrors of war.

But just before he relinquished his hold on the periscope, something caught his eye. Something moving.

"My God," he said, "I think one of ours is alive out there."

"What do you see?"

"It's hard to say. It's all black. Creeping on the ground."

"Coming our way?"

Wells watched. "No. It's not." It barely looked human at all. It slithered among the fallen bodies like a crocodile. For a moment, its head rose, as if sniffing the air, then went down again, squirming in the muck and mire.

"Here, let me see," the captain said, brushing Wells aside.

Wells stood to one side, a shiver descending his spine. He'd been sent to the Front in search of angels, and instead found this—whatever it was.

"Bloody hell," Lillyfield muttered, then moved to the closest soldier, huddling in a funk hole, and demanded his rifle. Positioning himself on the firing step, he took careful aim, then shot.

There was a muffled cry.

The bolt sprang back, and Lillyfield shot again.

"But what if it's one of ours?" Wells remonstrated.

"Might have been . . . once," the captain replied, firing off another round. "Now it's just another bloody damn ghoul."

Ghoul?

Lillyfield put the rifle down, and quickly peered through the periscope again. "Can't tell if I got the bastard or not."

Wells waited.

"But at least it's not moving anymore. Could just be lying low."

"What was it you called him again?"

"It's not a 'him.' It's an 'it.' Better off dead than a disgrace." Wells was suddenly reminded of the strange warning from the orderly on the transport ship.

Lillyfield returned the rifle to the soldier, with the admonition, "Mum's the word." The soldier, his face caked with mud, nodded. Turning to Wells, the captain said, "Shame you had to witness that."

Witness what, exactly? Wells wondered.

"But what would you say to a spot of cognac?" the captain said, brushing the grime from his hands. "It's going to be a big day tomorrow."

CHAPTER SIXTEEN

Jane drove the car even more cautiously than ever, making sure not to arouse any attention from anyone who might see it going by—though at this time of night, on a country road, there was little chance of anyone being about—and avoiding any pothole or rut that might give a jolt to Kurt, lying flat and under a blanket in the back seat. Although they could barely make themselves understood—her German was only a few words, his English was the same—he seemed to trust her. She had helped him down from the attic and into the back seat of the car, and apart from a searching glance, he had not pressed for more of an explanation, or expressed any reluctance. She suspected that he knew where he was going.

Dr. Gruber's house was on the edge of the town, and his surgery was accessible by a side door, under a porte cochere. He had left the gate light on, as he had promised, and when she pulled in, the door was already waiting open. He came out immediately, and after a quick look about, opened the rear door of the car and helped Jane to get the hobbling Kurt inside. It was only when she closed the door after them that Jane noticed something curious: the brass plaque on his door that used to say, "Dr. Rudolf Gruber, General Physician," had been replaced by a shinier new one, which read, "Dr. Richard Grover,

General Physician." She didn't have to wonder why, but she did wonder when it had happened.

"In here," the doctor said, leading the way to his office, though Jane had been there enough times before, usually dragging one of her boys who had fallen off a swing or collided with a badminton racket. The front room was the consulting parlor, with its desk and book-cases filled with worn-out medical texts; she noticed two conspicuous blank spaces on the wall, before recalling that his medical degrees had once hung there. One, she recalled now, had been from a university in Munich. More evidence gone. The back room was where he performed his examinations and procedures.

The operating table was ready, and Jane steadied Kurt as he eased his way up onto it. He'd had a full bath earlier in the day, and his ruined uniform had been traded for some old clothes of H. G.'s. He looked no different than half the boys she would see on the rugby field in town. Time and time again, she had to remind herself of who he really was, and castigate herself for what she was doing. There could be—there *would* be—consequences to pay, but there was simply something about the situation that aroused her indignation. The war was an insane and costly blunder, committed by foolish and shortsighted old men, on both sides of the Channel, who were prepared to sacrifice thousands—*hundreds* of thousands—of young lives to achieve some obscure geopolitical gain that even they could barely explain. And now, she had a chance, however tiny in the great scheme of things, to defy them, to say, *No, I won't participate, I won't do what's considered right and proper, because it isn't right and proper. I won't be a cog in the immense and destructive war machine. I won't.*

"Jane, may I ask you to go in the kitchen, and bring back the pot of hot water warming on top of the stove? I'm afraid you will have to serve as my assistant tonight."

"Of course," she said, knowing full well that she would be called upon to act as nurse. Normally, the doctor's wife filled that role, but she was conveniently out of town that night, visiting her sister in Berwick Hill. That at least was a stroke of luck, as the operating room would have been unavailable if she'd been about. Mrs. Gruber—Grover—was not only the head of the town war bond drive, but also the head of the local watch committee.

By the time Jane had brought the water back, Dr. Grover, in a clean white smock now, had had Kurt remove his shirt and trousers, and was explaining what he was about to do. Sitting up, in just his underwear, Kurt worriedly asked a question or two, and the doctor reassured him, even placing a hand on his painfully thin shoulder, before laying him flat on the table. As the anesthesia was being prepared, Kurt turned toward Jane, and said several things that she had to struggle to comprehend.

Dr. Grover translated. "He says, he hopes that if you have a son in the war, that he finds someone like you in his own country."

If only he knew, she thought, that she had a husband, not a son, on the front line at that very moment.

The doctor wiped an antiseptic swab across Kurt's arm, then filled two syringes from an upright metal table at his elbow. Holding the first one up to the light, he said to Jane, "Morphine, 1.6 milligrams." That was no surprise, though the second—"scopolamine," he said—was. "It's a drying agent," he said. "Dries up the saliva and ensures better breathing."

Next he lifted a wire frame mask, its shape reminiscent of a fencing mask, and fitted two slips of gauze into its lower portion. "I will want you to hold this gently but firmly to his face," he said, and Jane complied. Kurt's eyes, which until now had been filled with nothing but anxiety, were already showing the effects of the injections. His expression was dreamy, and when the doctor administered several drops of ether to the gauze and instructed him to count from one to ten, he had gotten no further than eight before his eyes closed and his chin fell to his chest.

"I want you to continue to monitor his respiration," Grover said, "and tell me if anything seems to change—especially if the anesthesia is wearing off. If that happens, douse the gauze with just one or two—no more—drops of the ether."

Then he turned to the left ankle, propped up on a wooden block covered with a white cloth; it was purple and blue, and bent at an unnatural angle, and to Jane's horror, she saw Dr. Grover remove from a lower shelf of the metal table a small hammer and a vise the size of a heavy bookend. He placed its sides against the lower shin and carefully assessed the situation, looking it over from every vantage point, the way one might a valuable old vase. After squeezing the limb at several points, he went to work with a scalpel and the hammer, breaking and resetting the bone.

Jane had to avert her eyes, though the sounds were unavoidable. Although Kurt twitched once or twice, he betrayed no sign of becoming conscious. She kept her eyes riveted to his face, even as her thoughts wandered to a time when her son Gip had fractured an arm, and then to the night she had discovered Kurt in the barn, and from there, as they so often did, to H. G. Where was he right now? Was he in danger?

Curiously, and not happily, the next intruder in her thoughts was that girl who had come to the rectory, the young writer, who was so clearly infatuated with her husband. Lord knows there had been enough others before her, and over time Jane had learned not to dwell upon them. Like omnibuses, they came and went. His so-called passades. But to Jane they were never quite so benign. Oh, she always pretended to be a good sport about them, but this last one, this Rebecca West, troubled her. Apart from her beauty, there was real substance to this girl. She might prove to be someone capable of captivating H. G. in ways that the others had not.

Perhaps it was because she was caught up in these thoughts, and overly weary from the night before (she had not been able to sleep, not with the German boy in the attic), that Dr. Grover was alerted to the threat before she was.

"Did you hear that?" he said.

"What?" But now she did, the sound of tires crunching on the gravel of the front driveway.

Then, voices, a woman's—"Thanks again for waiting for my train"—followed by a man's—"Say hello to the doc for me."

"My God," Grover muttered, "my wife's come home!"

"I wonder whose car that is around the side," Maude said. "Hope there was no emergency."

"Need any help with that bag?"

"No, I'm fine. Good night, Mr. Slattery."

"Good night."

Jane glanced at the boy's ankle, straightened now and stitched, but not yet in a cast or splint. She could hear the front door of the house opening. Keys being dropped on a center hall table.

"I'm home, dear."

The doctor hurried to bind the site of the surgery. "I can make the cast tomorrow, at your house."

The door to the front parlor of his office opened, and the voice called out his name—the new one. "Richard?"

By the time Mrs. Grover peeked into the examining room, all she could have seen was her husband finishing up a surgery, with, of all people, Jane acting as his assistant.

"Mrs. Wells?" she said in astonishment.

"Maude," he said, "I didn't expect you until Sunday."

"My sister caught cold, and I didn't want to wait around to catch it."

"We have a bit of an emergency on our hands," he explained. "Can you give us a few minutes?"

"Can I help?" After all, her tone implied, she was his usual nurse.

"No, we're almost done."

Jane nodded politely, flushed and uncertain of what to say, but before Maude withdrew, she felt Kurt stir on the table. She had taken her eye off the ball. She reached for the ether bottle, but Kurt's eyes had flickered open for an instant. Under his breath, he was still counting. *"Nein,"* he said, then more loudly, *"nein."*

"What did he say?" Maude asked.

"Nine," her husband replied. "He went under at eight. Now, please, Maude."

Reluctantly, she closed the door, and the doctor mumbled to Jane, "Not another drop of that."

She put the ether away.

"In about ten minutes, he'll be fully conscious. We will hustle him out to your car, and if my wife interferes in any way, I am going to tell her he is a nephew of yours, who had a motoring accident."

Jane nodded. Why, she thought, had she ever entered into this subterfuge? And now, inevitably, she had implicated the doctor.

She could hear the sound of footsteps upstairs—the master bedroom must be above the surgery—and when the coast seemed clear, and Kurt was ambulatory again, she and the doctor were able to deposit him in the back seat of her car.

"I'm so sorry to have dragged you into this," Jane said.

"Just go," Grover said, pressing a bottle of analgesics into her hand. "Keep his leg slightly elevated, and give him two of those every few hours."

As Jane got behind the steering wheel, she happened to glance up at the window, where she saw Maude Grover standing in full view, between the parted curtains. No wonder she had been appointed the local watch commander. Jane drove back onto the road, wondering all the while if the groggy boy in the back seat might not prove to be her undoing.

CHAPTER SEVENTEEN

"The barrage goes off at five fifteen sharp," Captain Lillyfield said in a low voice, so as not to disturb the sleeping Corporal Norridge or Sergeant Stubb.

"So early?" Wells said.

"Got to catch Fritz unawares," Lillyfield said, attempting to pour a bit more of the cognac into Wells's glass.

Wells put a hand over its rim. "I've had plenty, thanks."

"We pound their positions until seven, then go over the top to mop up whatever's left standing."

He made it sound as easy as a row on the Cam. But from what Wells knew of the stalemate on the Western Front, things never went as smoothly as planned.

Holding his pocket watch close to the flickering candle flame, Lillyfield said, "Almost midnight. Perhaps we should turn in."

"Yes, but not before you tell me more about these so-called ghouls."

Lillyfield had been scrupulously ducking the subject, over and over, and even now heaved a sigh of resignation.

"Who exactly are they?" Wells persisted.

"This goes no further?"

"I can't promise that, until I know what you're about to tell me."

"Who are they? They're deserters. Cowards. Of all stripes—French, Germans, Canadians, Belgians, even some of our own. They live with the rats and the other vermin in all the underground tunnels and abandoned trenches under no man's land. Like the dead men they are, they only come out of their graves at night."

"To what purpose?"

"To scavenge the bodies of the brave men who died that day. Ration tins, tobacco, canteens—whatever they can get their filthy claws on." He threw down the last of the brandy in his own glass. "Some even say," he added, "that they're cannibals."

"Cannibals?" Wells said, his own credulity being stretched to the limits.

Lillyfield shrugged. "I'd put nothing past them."

"How long has this been going on?"

"Months now. But don't even consider writing anything about this. The War Office wouldn't want any word of it to become public knowledge. It's all too ghastly, and the fact that any of our own boys might be among these scoundrels . . ."

For Wells, it was as if someone had confirmed the existence of the Morlocks, the savage creatures from his grim vision of the future of mankind in *The Time Machine*. A race of man-eating monsters, living in darkness, and skulking beneath the blood-soaked battlefields to prey upon the dying and the dead. It beggared even his imagination.

When he did say good night and slip into his cold, damp bunk, he felt as if he were entering their world, and his sleep was accordingly fitful. His dreams were so troubling—skeletal fingers reaching up from the earth, hollow-eyed soldiers mumbling incomprehensibly, hordes of white rats swarming up from a sewer grate—that he didn't regret being shaken awake in what seemed like only a short time later. He'd thought it was a hand disturbing his sleep, but when he opened his bleary eyes, he discovered that it was something far greater. The earth itself was shaking, dirt drifting down from between the beams, everything from the plates in the galley to the pallet he was lying on palpitating.

And the noise—the noise was overwhelming.

The scream of missiles—of all calibers, all sorts—blasting the air above. Heavy artillery, howitzers, mortars. All unleashed on the German lines.

He fished his own watch from the pocket of his greatcoat, in which he'd slept, and saw that the barrage had indeed begun right on time. The shocking roar of the guns had awakened everyone by now, and he could see Lillyfield lighting another lantern as he slumped into a chair at the table and turned a map to see it right-side up. Norridge emerged from the galley, with a pot of tea in one hand and a jiggling cup and saucer in the other, setting them down beside the open map. When he glanced Wells's way and saw that he was awake behind the half-parted curtain—how could he not be?—he said, "Breakfast's served early today."

Wells grunted. "Just some hot scones, coddled eggs, and kippers for me," he said, and Norridge chuckled. "Oh, and clotted cream for my coffee, of course."

"Coming right up, guv'nor."

Even Stubb, a veteran of many an artillery barrage, had swung his legs over the side of his bunk and was loudly stretching. The walls around them shook with the angry growl of cannons, the shriek of shells, and in the distance, the muffled roar of bombs hitting the German trenches. How could anyone, or anything, survive such an onslaught? he wondered. He had read about such warfare from the comfort of his own easy chair at the rectory, and even attended dinners where officers, returned from the Front, tried to describe it. But nothing could have prepared him for the sheer insanity of it, the absolute and ceaseless pulverization, the inescapable din, the seismic disruption of everything from the ground beneath his feet—quivering like jelly—to his own senses, unable to process the magnitude of the destruction being wrought all around.

And given what he'd been told over the cognac, the barrage had another hour or more to go. Over one dinner at the Reform, Churchill had shared with him stories of barrages that had lasted for days on end. *"When they come back from the Front, there are men with bleeding ears and bulging eyes, their nerves utterly shattered. They jump at the closing of a door—when they can hear at all—and awake every night screaming and wet with sweat. It's proving difficult to know how to treat them, or if they will ever actually recover at all."*

Wells could understand it now, in a visceral way that he had not been able to do before. But again, was this—a barrage and its brutal aftermath—anything the War Office would want him to be conveying? More and more, he saw his assignment in contradictory terms. As a patriotic correspondent, he could file stories about the courageous chaps manning the trenches, putting their lives on the line every minute of every day, and put his heart into it, but if he were to tell the whole truth—the albino rat Alphonse and his million fellows, the mud up to your ankles, the ticks and fleas and lice that infested every bed and article of clothing, not to mention the ghastly creatures that wormed their way above ground to batten on the bodies of the slain and the wounded—if he tried to tell all that, Colonel Bryce would recall him to the Ministry of Military Information posthaste. He'd be lucky not to be tried for treason.

Sitting on a crate at the table, he borrowed two of the field postcards from Lillyfield.

"You sure you don't want the green envelopes? Much more room to write."

"That's precisely why I wanted these," Wells said, the table shuddering under his pen. "I just want to dash off a couple of lines, and then go up to see what's what."

Lillyfield grunted, cradling his chin in his palm, as he studied a smudged map of the German lines one more time.

The first postcard he quickly addressed to Jane at home, assuring her that he was doing fine and having a grand adventure. The truth could wait until he got home.

The second card required more deliberation. Addressing it to Rebecca West, care of the *Freewoman* magazine, he took care to say nothing compromising, all the while trying to convey some sense of the longing he felt for her. It surprised even him. He had had a hundred passades, but this young woman, with whom he had shared nothing more so far than a passionate kiss and embrace, haunted his thoughts in a way that he found as exciting as he did alarming.

"Give 'em to Norridge when you're done," the captain muttered. "He'll put 'em in the post." One of the few things that worked with remarkable efficiency at the Front was the mail—a card could be posted and be back in England in no time, and a reply back in a couple of days. The soldiers relied upon it to keep up their morale.

Wells finished up, gulped down a cup of hot tea, then went into the galley to give the cards to Norridge. The man was hunched over a camp stove, his pasty face gleaming with sweat, his hands flying about as he reached for ingredients and pots and pans. How old could he be? Wells wondered. No more than thirty, surely, but in the ruddy glow of the cramped kitchen, he looked like a wizened devil.

"Your breakfast's coming right up," he said, without glancing at Wells.

"Take your time. I'm going up top to have a look around first."

"Won't be much to see."

"But what do I do with these?" Wells said, holding out the cards.

"Stick 'em in the post pouch hanging above my bunk."

On his way to the dugout stairs, Wells buttoned his coat all the way up, and fixed the strap of his helmet under his chin. It didn't do to think too much about the last man who had worn this helmet.

It was still dark enough out that the sky shimmered from the glare of the explosions. The clouds, hovering over no man's land, were briefly illuminated in a fuzzy blaze of white or green or crimson. From a perch on the firing step—surely no sniper could be out plying his trade in the midst of this bombardment—he looked across the tortured landscape, more shell holes than level ground, and saw what might have passed for a breathtaking spectacle under other circumstances. The German line was a strange fountain of erupting lights, bursts of color from the different shells exploding atop it, geysers of black dirt shooting up into the air, commingled with wood and metal and, no doubt, the atomized bodies of the defenders. It reminded him of a fireworks display over the Crystal Palace, from when he was a boy.

The sight was so transfixing, the night air so refreshing compared to the stultifying atmosphere in the dugout, that he remained there, lost in thought, until the dawn broke, and he became aware of the soldiers, roused by their officers to take up their positions, beginning to fix their bayonets and ready themselves for battle. A pair of them, one holding a bucket and the other a ladle, went up and down the line, dispensing a spoonful of rum to each soldier in place. Wells passed on his own—better it should go to one of the lads about to go over the top—and was soon joined by Corporal Norridge. For a moment, he didn't recognize him in the daylight, without his apron on or in the glow from the galley stove.

"There's toast and jam waiting for you down below, Mr. Wells," he said, "and a bit of bacon, whenever you want it," and Wells suddenly felt himself ashamed. Here he was—a middle-aged spectator, a famous author sent to record the derring-do of anonymous men who at any moment might sacrifice themselves for their country—being informed that his breakfast was waiting. How disgraceful. He lost any appetite he might have had.

"Thank you," he said. "And good luck to you, Mr. Norridge."

"The name's Eddie. You can call me that."

"Eddie. And I'm H. G."

"If anything happens to me, do be sure to spell my name right."

Wells did not know what to say. Captain Lillyfield approached, his wire-rim spectacles firmly affixed, his own helmet at a jaunty angle, slapping an encouraging hand on the shoulders of the anxious Tommies, dispensing a bit of advice over the din of the bombardment—"Much as you might want to stop to help a mate, keep on going forward at all costs"—before stopping to talk to Wells.

"Once the barrage ends, in exactly two minutes, the charge will begin. Stay put, and Sergeant Stubb will escort you about a mile down the line."

"Down the line?"

"Yes. We've a surprise for you."

Wells did not like the sound of that.

"It's something that you *can* write about, but only after it's gone off."

"Gone off?"

"You'll see soon enough. Stubb will explain. No time now."

Scaling ladders were being propped against the trench walls. Wells could feel, and see on their faces, the nervousness of the waiting soldiers. Some prayed, eyes closed, some chewed on tobacco, some even tried to make a joke to amuse anyone close enough to hear them over the roar of the cannons. The tension was electric.

Consulting a stopwatch, Captain Lillyfield shouted, "One minute!" and then, in the batting of an eye, "Thirty seconds!" and then "Zero!" As if at his command, the bombardment eerily stopped, only the echo of the artillery still reverberating in the still morning air. "Over we go!" He sounded a shrill blast on a metal whistle, and there was a mad scramble up the ladders. Wells was nearly bowled over by the boys struggling to get up and over the sandbags, and seconds later by the boys falling back into the trench. He assumed that they had simply lost their footing or been jostled off their feet in the melee.

But then he heard a methodical rat-a-tat, an unceasing enfilade of the English line.

How could this be?

There were screams and cries, and pops in the sandbags as machine gun bullets tore into them like hornets.

How could the German machine gun nests have survived the night? How could anything?

His back against the rear wall of the trench, he saw one man fall with his arms spread wide as wings, and another slide back down into the trench with his rifle still clutched in his hand. Another flew backward, landing flat on top of Wells. The two of them lay in a heap on the duckboards, their limbs entangled, and as Wells struggled to get out from under—could the man be saved?—he turned him over.

The face was at once perfectly recognizable—he'd been talking to him only minutes ago—but in an odd way unfamiliar. Where the right eye had been, there was now only a scorched black hole, as if someone had bored an awl into it. Everything else was unscathed.

Wells shook him, as if that might do any good, saying, "Norridge, Norridge," before remembering that they were now on a first-name basis. "Eddie," he said, over and again, to the one vacant and unblinking eye. "Eddie."

CHAPTER EIGHTEEN

There was a neat splotch of blood on the lapel of his greatcoat, precisely where you might wear a medal. But Wells realized that it must have come from the back of Corporal Norridge's skull—from the hole where the bullet had exited.

He had held the man's head there, unwilling to let it simply fall back against the muddy duckboards, or be trampled underfoot by the wave of soldiers who had been moved up from the support trenches to continue the assault on the German lines. Sergeant Stubb had eventually found him there, and bending low to be heard over the cacophony of shelling and gunfire, said, "Got to let go now, sir. Got to let go." He had pried Wells's hands away, allowing the corporal's head to fall back, its one remaining eye staring up at the smoke-filled sky. "We've got to be on our way."

Wells staggered to his feet again, and Stubb, taking him firmly by the elbow, began to move him down the line, dodging the hundreds of soldiers clambering over the reredos, or back rampart, of the trench, before scaling the ladders to an almost certain doom in no man's land. They passed signposts for "Oxford Circus" and "Piccadilly" and "the Strand," while zigging and zagging through the maze, stepping over the bodies that had already fallen back, over the army of rats already swarming on top of them, through ankle-deep puddles stained red with blood and piles of split and sundered sandbags. Eventually, Wells stopped looking at the dead faces—it was too exhausting to register the various expressions of everything from surprise to exhilaration, pain to dismay. Some had been slain in their first burst of exuberance, others in agony and dread. All, no matter how disfigured or seemingly unscathed, lay preternaturally still as everything around them, from the squeaking vermin to their living comrades, swirled and eddied in a maelstrom of confusion and fear.

"Almost there," Stubb shouted, as they rounded a corner marked "Euston Square Station," and waved him on.

Where? Wells wondered—even when Stubb stopped at the end of a communications trench, bolstered better than most with brick and metal sheathing. What looked like the entryway to an officers' dugout was wide open, and to his surprise, he saw a pair of parallel metal tracks, close together, running out from under it, and a battered wheelbarrow propped against the wall. A soldier was, incongruously enough, fiddling with a fire hose and a bellows.

"Welcome to the London Underground," Stubb said, leaning close to his ear. "In you go!"

Ducking his head, and holding his helmet firmly in place, Wells went inside, and was no more than a few yards into a cavern lit only by hanging lanterns dangling from sagging beams, when the din of battle began to die down. It all became a muffled roar, like the sound of the ocean in a conch shell. The floor of this anteroom was littered with empty sandbags, spades, candle stubs, and socks crusted with mud. "Captain Lillyfield thought the best time for you to see this was while the action was going on up top," Stubb said, his husky voice taking on a sepulchral tone. "Fritz will have his hands full right now."

Despite his surprise at finding himself there, Wells was not unaware of the mining activity undertaken by the British forces. The Germans had pioneered the practice of burrowing tunnels all the way under enemy lines, packing them with explosives, and then detonating them—the previous December, not fifty miles from Calais, they had set off ten mines beneath an unsuspecting brigade—but, as Churchill had confided in him on a walk through Whitehall, "we've recruited the best lads from the coal pits in Manchester and Newcastle and they can dig all the way to Berlin if need be." Indeed, two of them, so begrimed that they looked to Wells like chimney sweeps, emerged from the tunnel, pushing a barrow full of dirt and clay along the tracks. They touched the brim of their caps, but went on about their business as if they were merely excavating a sewer main under Camden Town.

"How far does this one go?"

"Far enough. There's a pillbox on a hill—we call it the Beehive—and it's damn near impregnable. Can't take it out from the front, so the idea is to take it out from below."

Very sensible, Wells thought, though the amount of labor and planning must have been immense. "Can we go in?"

"My orders are to let you see whatever you want, with two provisions."

"Which are?"

"To get you back alive."

"Admirable."

"And to remind you, this can't be written about until you get the go-ahead from HQ. We've got to blow up the Beehive first."

"Of course. Any idea when that will be?"

Stubb glanced over at one of the sappers who was just pulling on another pair of filthy socks *over* his boots. "When'ja think, McCarthy?"

McCarthy, a short man with a drooping mustache, shrugged. "A week? Maybe less? Depends."

"On what?" Stubb said.

"On whether Jerry hears us stomping about and blows us all to smithereens first."

Now Wells understood the precaution of wearing socks over the boots. Putting on a pair himself, he followed Stubb and McCarthy—the latter showing no curiosity whatsoever about who he was—out of the cavern and into the tunnel proper. The ground—sandy topsoil at first, yielding then to firmer clay—sloped lower and lower, to a depth of at least twenty or thirty feet, and the passageway became narrower, before leveling off. Wells was stooped over, and had to move slowly, his hands grazing both walls at once. It was a claustrophobic space, poorly lit by guttering candles in makeshift stands, with a thick hose, carrying fresh air to the working end of the tunnel, strapped to brackets in the wall. It was all, by necessity, a hasty job, but Wells was impressed by the sturdy work, the timber frames meeting each other in butt joints without tongues and grooves. Progress was slow, and at any point he knew he could turn around, but he did not want to show any less bravery than the men he was accompanying, and besides, the story would gain from it. He was reminded of the network of eighteenth-century tunnels that had lain beneath the country house, Uppark, where his mother had once worked as a housekeeper; they had fascinated him as a boy, and he had made use of them later on in his art when he created the subterranean labyrinth inhabited by his Morlocks. These wet clay walls, spurting mud through any chink in the wood, could well have been his monsters' lair.

The farther they went, the thinner the air became and the dimmer the glow from the candles. Even a match, struck to light one of them that had gone out, burned a ruby red without actually catching flame. Wells was having trouble getting his breath, and when he started to say something to Stubb, the sergeant whirled around with his finger to his lips. Just ahead, Wells could see two sappers, crouched and absolutely still, at the face of the tunnel, and McCarthy pressing a geophone against the wall, looking for all the world like Dr. Gruber back home with his stethoscope.

Wells, too, remained stock-still, the ceiling so low that he was virtually bent double. Stubb jabbed a finger toward the wall and mouthed, "Boche."

If he listened very intently, he could swear he heard, only a foot or two away, the sound of a tool scraping at the clay. The Germans were digging in the opposite direction, either to intercept the British tunnel or to plant their own mines under the enemy's trenches. No one moved, or said a word. Wells clapped a hand over his mouth to stifle a cough. The digging continued.

McCarthy motioned for them all to retreat up the tunnel, including the two sappers who had been excavating at the face, but the passageway was too narrow for them to do anything but back away, single file. McCarthy removed an electric torch from under his belt and shone its beam down the corridor to help light their way.

But now it sounded as if a pickax were being used—a chopping noise, and to Wells's horror, a hunk of clay fell from the wall, followed by another, and another, until a hole suddenly appeared. A muffled voice blurted something—unintelligible, but unmistakably German—then abruptly stopped.

McCarthy waved at Stubb to extinguish the candle flickering in the holder against the wall, but not before Wells saw a hand, in a fingerless muddy glove, snake its way between two of the bracing planks and grope about. As abruptly as it had appeared, it was yanked back, and McCarthy started to urgently shove them all back up the tunnel. Stubb grabbed Wells by the sleeve, dragging him, but his boot got caught beneath one of the iron rails and he dropped to his knees. Stubb hauled him up, and by the faint light of the candle hanging a few yards farther down the tunnel, Wells glimpsed something that looked like a truncheon emerging from the hole; at one end, a grenade was attached.

McCarthy made a lunge for it, shoving it back where it came from, but it was not more than a few seconds later that the blast rocked the ground. For a moment, Wells thought that the tunnel would hold, the timbers swelling and shivering, but then he felt the shock wave as everything around him collapsed at once. The ceiling caved in, crashing down on his helmet, knocking him flat, his mouth in the pitch dark filling with wet clay and his shoulders pinned under a fallen support beam.

He heard some cries, then nothing but a pounding in his ears and the labored struggle of his own lungs to find some oxygen . . . with little success. Each gasp he expected to be his last . . . until one of them was, and utter silence descended on the darkness where he lay.

CHAPTER NINETEEN

Every day, the office of the *Freewoman* magazine received dozens of invitations to concerts, plays, and gallery openings, from artists and promoters all over the city, in the hopes of generating a review or related publicity. Rebecca, like the other writers, was always on the lookout for the ones that might provide a story, or at least a diverting event. The plays in the West End had already been grabbed, as had the seated dinners, but among the few solicitations that remained, she spotted one that immediately piqued her interest.

Arthur Machen, the journalist for the *Evening News* who had written the much talked-about story of the angels of Mons, was giving a talk for the Spiritualists' National Union on Great Russell Street. It seemed that the tale had been reprinted in a new volume of short stories called *The Bowmen and Other Legends of the War*, and the speech was meant to both celebrate its publication and, of course, increase its sales. (She had known authors so desperate to gain some notice for their books that they had resorted to marching up and down the street wearing sandwich boards.) This, however, held some promise—not so much because of the book itself, but because of the way in which Machen's work had also tapped into the greater current of spiritualism, which was experiencing a sudden boom.

"Mind if I report on this one?" Rebecca asked Mrs. Marsden, the editor in chief.

"Which one?" Marsden shot back, her blue pencil flying across someone else's piece, making quick corrections and edits.

"The Machen event."

"We've already sent the book out for a review."

"To whom?"

"Arthur Conan Doyle."

Rebecca let out an inadvertent laugh. "That's like asking Dr. Watson for an impartial review of Sherlock Holmes."

The pencil paused, and Mrs. Marsden looked up over her bifocals. "Fine. Then you can put on your skeptic's hat, since it fits you so well, and go hear what he has to say. But not in more than 750 words; your work is becoming entirely too prolix."

Assignment in hand, Rebecca had virtually skipped out of the dingy offices, and navigated the increasingly difficult streets—with the threat of an aerial bombardment hanging over the city every night, the streetlamps were hooded, if lit at all, and every window had its curtain drawn, admitting only a sliver of light at one edge or another—to the dilapidated headquarters of the Spiritualists' Union. A costermonger's cart, with the leftover vegetables of the day, was parked at the curb, the weary old horse, head down, slurping from a bucket of water.

At the entryway to the union, a boy was handing out flyers to passersby—"Come hear the man who first reported on the angels of Mons!"—though any number of others were flocking inside already. In the vestibule, a table was set up, with a cashbox and a stack of books for sale. Guarding it was a fearsome-looking brute with a mop of thick blond hair and a bored expression.

The assembly room was at the back, and had seats for perhaps a couple hundred spectators. There were pews instead of chairs, and high casement windows along both walls with stained glass depictions of scenes Rebecca did not recognize. They weren't the traditional biblical scenes, but resembled instead the kind of pictures you might see on tarot cards—women in horned helmets sitting on thrones, knights riding haggard white horses, castles crumbling, men hanged upside down. A grim catalog, all in all, and Rebecca had to wonder who would willingly become a congregant of such a place.

"If time permitted, I would be only too pleased to explain the pictures to you," a man said, blocking her passage down the central aisle. Although under six feet tall, he gave the impression of looming over her from a much greater height than that, and she was transfixed first by his face—pockmarked and fleshy, with incisors that she could swear had been filed to a point—and then by his garb. He was dressed like some Scottish laird in a story by Robert Louis Stevenson, from the tartan thrown over his shoulder to the hilt of the dirk sticking up from his heavy woolen sock. "The Earl of Boleskine," he introduced himself.

"Cicily Fairfield." Sometimes, when reporting, it was best not to use her pen name.

"I've never seen you here before," he said, in what she suspected was an exaggerated Scottish burr, "and I would surely remember someone so young and beautiful."

"This is my first visit."

"I hope it won't be your last."

Several people were anxiously trying to get around them to claim seats, and Rebecca stepped aside to let them pass. Some of them bowed their heads to the man in the kilt.

"Are you interested in spiritualism, or simply in Mr. Machen's book?"

"I'll know once I've heard him speak," Rebecca replied. The earl was overly fond of his aftershave, she noted. And where, she wondered, was this putative earldom of his?

"Fair enough. But if I may give you one piece of advice, sit toward the middle tonight."

"What? Why?"

"Acoustics," he said, before turning to a wiry, ferret-like man, wearing tiny round spectacles, who was tugging at his sleeve.

"Yes, what is it this time, Anton?"

Anton murmured something about the time.

Excusing himself, the earl moved off to take a seat in the front row, just below the raised stage. There, at the podium, a solitary figure somewhere in his late fifties and dressed in a funereal black frock coat, was clutching a sheaf of papers; he looked like a nervous undertaker, and she took him to be Machen himself.

She was not proven wrong. With the notable exception of H. G. Wells, who, despite his thin voice, reveled in public discourse, most authors were solitary creatures, unused to presenting themselves to their readers. They were like moles suddenly exposed to the sunlight. The lights in the room had been dimmed, and black muslin curtains had now been drawn across the stained glass windows. Machen looked out across the crowd—and to Rebecca's surprise, all the seats on both sides of her in the pew were filled—and gripping the podium like a man on a storm-tossed sea, he started to speak in a quavering voice.

"I'm gratified, and somewhat overwhelmed, that you have all come out to hear me," he began. "Going abroad, and at night, is a hazardous undertaking at this unfortunate epoch in time."

From his lilting accent, he was Welsh, Rebecca surmised. For all she knew, the whole United Kingdom might be represented tonight. She made a note of it, in shorthand, on the pad she held discreetly in her lap.

"I am here, of course, to introduce my new book, a collection of stories containing one of my most recent and celebrated tales."

"Speak up, man!" someone shouted from the rear. "Can't hear you!"

"Oh, I do apologize," he said, and the Scottish laird stepped up onto the stage, moving the podium forward and, with an arm around Machen's shoulders, offering him some hushed and overdue advice on the art of public speaking.

Holding his head higher and speaking up, Machen launched into some of the most self-effacing, even apologetic, opening remarks Rebecca had ever heard an author unwisely utter. When he wasn't asking forgiveness for the brevity of the famous tale, he was denigrating it as "an indifferent piece of work," a story that had nevertheless "had such odd and unforeseen consequences and adventures that the tale of them may possess some interest." She almost had to laugh at the man's utter lack of salesmanship. No wonder most authors were as poor as church mice.

"It began on a hot Sunday morning between meat and mass," he said, when he had first heard of the ignominious English retreat from Mons. "I seemed to see a furnace of death and agony and terror seven times heated, and in the midst of the burning was the British army—in the midst of the flame, consumed by it and yet aureoled in it, scattered like ashes and yet triumphant, martyred and forever glorious."

In the space of a few seconds, and to Rebecca's surprise, he had utterly transformed, going from a mouse of a man to an apocalyptic prophet. She didn't want to miss recording a single word of his sudden eloquence.

"So I saw our men with a shining about them," he rolled on, "and so I took these thoughts with me to church and, I'm sorry to say, was making up a story in my head while the deacon was singing the Gospel."

But the more he explained away the tale as one that he had made up out of whole cloth, the more Rebecca could sense a growing resistance in the audience. Looking around, she saw young women already in widow's black, and older couples, misty-eyed and holding hands, perhaps the parents of soldiers now lost to the battlefields of the Western Front. They had come in search of assurance, and like so much of the country, moral uplift. They wanted to hear that God *was* on their side, and that their lost loved ones—defended in Belgium by a heavenly host led by none other than St. George himself—were now enjoying their just rewards in paradise. Machen was offering cold comfort indeed.

"All ages and nations have cherished the thought that spiritual hosts may come to the help of earthly arms, that gods and heroes and saints have descended from their high immortal places to fight for their worshippers and clients. And having written my story, having groaned and growled over it and printed it, I certainly never thought to hear another word of it."

That, as everyone in England knew, was not the end, but only the beginning, of the saga. One journal after another had picked up the story, pamphlets were printed, sermons given from pulpits in every parish church, citing Machen's account as fact, and insisting he provide even more detail. What British regiment was involved? How were the angelic bowmen deployed? Specifically, what commands did St. George give? Several times someone in the crowd threw out a question, or issued a challenge, one elderly pensioner claiming that his own grandson had sworn to having witnessed the apparitions himself. "With his own eyes, he's seen 'em, and he's nowt one to tell a lie!"

It was only when Rebecca thought things could not get much worse that Machen, finally, made another, and rather abrupt, about-face. While sticking to his original story, he observed that some persons "judging by the tone of these remarks of mine, may gather the impression that I am a profound disbeliever in the possibility of any intervention of the superphysical order in the affairs of the physical order. They will be mistaken if they make this inference."

In other words, he *did* believe in the supernatural and the occult, Rebecca jotted down. Machen was not an easy man to categorize.

"They will be mistaken if they suppose that I think miracles in Judaea credible but miracles in France or Flanders incredible. I hold no such absurdities."

He was expatiating on that notion, certainly more in keeping with the spiritualism angle and venue of the night, when from the distance Rebecca could hear an eerily familiar wail. So could the others in the assembly room. Only Machen, intent on his remarks, seemed oblivious.

The wail was picked up by sirens closer to the hall, starting low and then rising in volume, before again descending. Rebecca knew, without being able to look out the curtained windows, that the keening would be accompanied even now by white, anti-aircraft beams frantically probing the sky, in search of the approaching zeppelins.

People looked to each other, quickly consulting what to do. Some grabbed their hats, buttoned up their coats, and bustled up the aisle, no doubt heading for the shelter of the nearest underground station. Others might be making for their own homes; Rebecca's mother always insisted that the safest place for them was under the front stairwell. But home was far from here, and she did not relish the idea of descending into the crowded and fetid tube tunnel. Some of the audience, possibly thinking along the same lines and putting their faith in the stout timbers of the hall, hunkered down in their pews, or crouched down onto the floor.

The Earl of Boleskine had stepped up to commandeer the podium, and announced that anyone wishing to take shelter there was welcome to do so. "The beams in this ceiling have withstood the test of time, my friends, and if we were to summon up the force of psychic will that resides within us all, we could bolster them even more." The sirens were screaming now, the noise echoing around the vaulted chamber. Under it, Rebecca could hear the *ack-ack-ack* of the anti-aircraft guns and even more menacingly, a low and sustained roar, like the growl of some dinosaur; it was a sound she had heard before, the thrumming of the massive engines in the zeppelin—the baby-killer—soaring high above the city. It was just a matter of time—seconds—before she would hear its bombs exploding on the streets and houses of London.

"Focus your thoughts," the earl was imploring them over the cacophony, "and send your spirit energy to ward off the danger! Together, in the name of the powers whose temple this is, we can make of these bricks and timbers an impervious sanctuary!"

Rebecca sent no spirit energy to hold up the roof, but she did slink to the floor, where a gray-haired couple were already holding each other tight, and on the other side a bearded young man, eyes closed, was clutching a rosary and reciting a prayer. She could still see, just above the back of the pew, the earl holding the stage, head and arms upraised, his ferret-like friend crouching at his feet and the blond brute from the vestibule, clutching the cashbox under one arm, sticking close to his side. The earl was shouting something indecipherable—it sounded as if he were calling upon strange and ancient gods—before there was a cataclysmic explosion that shook the whole building. The pew rocked in place as a wave rattled through the slate floor, and the curtains billowed out on both sides of the hall. The stained glass windows shattered into a million gleaming shards that sprayed the room like shrapnel; people closest to them screamed as the dagger-like fragments tore through their clothing, or into their exposed skin. One green glass piece, pointed as an icicle, pierced a pew across the aisle, and stayed there, vibrating. But Rebecca wasn't hurt, nor were the others who had been seated, as she was, in the middle of the assembly hall.

Only when the attack was over, and the zeppelin had moved on, and the all-clear was sounded by Boy Scouts blowing bugles from the back of taxi cabs, did Rebecca dare to lift herself up. Brushing the dust and debris from her coat and hair, she was glad that she had paid attention to the earl's advice about the acoustics. But was that really why he had advised her to sit where she had? She had the momentary, and unsettling, impression that he had known a bomb was going to rock the hall—an impression that she just as quickly dismissed as impossible.

The earl was attending to several of the shaken parishioners, or so she thought of them, at the front of the hall, but before she followed some of the others, wounded or not, out to the vestibule, she saw his gaze settle upon her. So did his little accomplice's. It looked as if they were even exchanging a word or two about her. But perhaps it was just conceit on her part. Her mother told her that she had always thought, even as a little girl, that she was the center of everyone's attention, even when she wasn't.

Outside, she saw a crowd milling around, some still nervously glancing up at the sky, others peering into the huge black crater smoldering in the middle of the street. At its bottom she could see the wreck of the vegetable wagon that had been parked outside, along with the mangled remains of the poor old horse that had drawn it.

CHAPTER TWENTY

Wells was awake long before he let on. He lay on the straw-stuffed pallet, listening to the voices around him. One was speaking German, another was answering in English. Accompanied by the wheezing of an accordion, someone sang a few lines from a popular French song, in French, and when he finished, to the clapping of hands and a "Bravo!" the place fell silent again.

Where was he? Wells wondered. What had happened? The last thing he remembered was being crushed under a pile of timbers and a ton of dirt and clay. If he had died, this could hardly be heaven where he found himself now. It was much like the officers' dugout where he had billeted with Captain Lillyfield and his crew, but felt, if that were possible, even more subterranean. Deeper, and more clandestine. The ceiling was lower, the space more cramped, the air thinner. The light, from an assortment of candles and lanterns, flickered more feebly, and the walls of clay were punctured by low portals, more like bolt-holes than doors of any kind.

Turning his head on the pillow—a coarse sack that reeked of old potatoes—he saw three men going about mundane tasks—mending a jacket, reading a magazine, fiddling with an accordion. They all wore different uniforms, some of them in tatters, others relatively intact, as if the garments had been acquired more recently. But what struck him most was the pallor on the men's faces; they were white as ghosts, except where their sunken cheeks betrayed a hint of sickly green. How long, he thought with horror, had these men been at the Front? They looked as if they had never seen the light of day.

The one in a gray German uniform was the first to notice Wells was awake.

"Guten Morgen." He was thin—they all were—and about thirty or thirty-five years old. Old enough to be an officer, which, judging from the stripes on his sleeve and the one epaulet still clinging to his shoulder, he'd been. *"Sprechen Sie Deutsch?"*

"Now why would he *sprechen* that?" the one in the uniform of a Tommy said. Taking over from his perch on a rations crate, he said to Wells, "You with the Northumberland Fusiliers?"

Wells was still too disoriented to answer.

"'Cause I am." He plucked at his sleeve to display his badge, a circlet of St. George and the dragon, inscribed with the words *"Quo Fata Vocant."* Or, "Whither the Fates carry me."

"Where am I?" Wells asked. "How did I get here?"

The Tommy lifted his chin toward the German, who was sitting at a table made of a wooden plank suspended between two ammunition boxes. "Fritz there found you, dragged you out by your heels."

The one who had been singing in French was lying on a heap of old coats with an accordion in his lap. *"Moi aussi. C'est moi qui vous ai permis de respirer."*

He was the one who'd gotten Wells breathing again; Wells could speak French well enough to understand that much. A bandage, encrusted with dried blood, was wrapped around one of the Frenchman's hands.

Teetering from one side to another, Wells sat up. He had the oppressive sense of being a deep-sea diver, so far down it would be nearly impossible to reach the surface ever again.

"What about the others?"

"What others?" the Tommy asked.

He thought first of Sergeant Stubb. And McCarthy. And the two sappers who had been working at the face of the tunnel. "The British soldiers I was with."

The Tommy shrugged. "They mighta got out, can't say for sure. We found four dead Jerries," he said, adding, "No offense" to the German soldier, who appeared to take none. "Blown up with their own grenade."

The last time he'd seen Stubb, the sergeant had been trying to drag him to safety. Had that last act of valor cost him his life? Wells would never forgive himself if it had.

"If you're hungry, help yourself," the Tommy said, gesturing at a pile of dirty and dented ration tins. "The French ones are the best, no offense to Whitehall."

Wells couldn't make out the labels from where he sat, but he could tell they were from all different armies. "No . . . thank you," he said. "Maybe later."

"Suit yourself. So who are you, anyway?"

"The name's Wells. Bertie," he added, rather than using the initials he was best known by. "And you?"

"I'm called Tommy, 'cause that's what I am. A Tommy." Pointing at the German, he said, "And he's Fritz, naturally. And the Frenchie here is called Nappy, after Napoleon, of course."

"That makes things easy."

"That, and because once you're down here, you're a dead man, anyway. Not much point in names anymore."

Down here. Dead men, anyway.

The German officer—Fritz—brought him a chipped porcelain cup, with some murky brown tea swimming in it. "It is not, I do not think, of the best," he said, in his halting English, "but it is hot."

Wells took the cup gratefully—there were baggy dark circles under the man's eyes, and his mustache had turned a premature gray—and drank. The tea was sweet with sugar. But his mind was succumbing to the inevitable realization.

"Good, yes?" Fritz asked, hovering like a headwaiter, and Wells nodded without looking up from the cup.

Ghouls. He was in the underground den of the ghouls—the deserters from every army. The cowards who had abandoned their fellows-in-arms to save their own lives. The men Lillyfield declared would have been better off dead than so disgraced.

"You do not look such as a miner," Fritz observed.

"I'm not." The living dead . . . and he was among them.

"Ah, you are then an engineer?"

"No, not that either."

Nappy had gone back to fiddling with his accordion, but awkwardly because of the bandage around one hand. Was he the one who had been hit by Lillyfield's potshot the night before? Tommy returned to leafing through a ragged magazine.

"May I sit?" Fritz said, as if asking to draw up a chair at his club.

"Of course." What else could he say to the man who had apparently saved his life?

Fritz pulled up a packing box and perched on it. "In what capability, then?"

"Capacity?"

"Yes," Fritz said, "that is the word. Excuse my English."

"Nothing to excuse. I've almost no German." Realizing that he still hadn't answered the question, he said, "As an observer."

Fritz looked puzzled.

"A reporter. Correspondent. On the war effort."

The German nodded. "And what is it that you have reported?"

What is the man? it occurred to Wells. *A spy?*

"Nothing much so far, I'm afraid."

"Is anyone winning?"

Much as he might have liked to say otherwise, Wells replied with honesty. "At the moment, no one. It's a stalemate."

Fritz dolefully shook his head. The answer did not seem to surprise him. "And do you, may I ask, live in London?"

"Some of the time."

Fritz was up to something, that much was clear. There was a knowing, and eager, glint in his otherwise weary blue eyes. To turn the conversation, Wells asked him his real name.

"Friedrich," the man said, as if with relief at recovering it. "Friedrich Von Baden. Major in the Imperial German Army." He extended a hand, and Wells found himself shaking it. His skin was so paper dry, Wells felt as if he were shaking hands with a mummy. But the German did not relax his grip for several seconds. He was studying Wells.

"I know who it is you really are," he finally confided in a low tone.

"Because I've just told you." The man had been a major, Wells was thinking, and was now consigned to this veritable grave? How did *that* happen?

"No. It is because I have seen also your picture in my books."

"Your books?"

"*Ja*, in *The Time Machine*. And *The Invisible Man*. And in the one that is my favored, *The War Between the Worlds*."

Wells was aware that his books had been translated into German, printed there in fancy leather sets with his portrait on the title page. Judging from his royalty statements, they sold quite successfully. He saw no point in denying it, and when he didn't, Friedrich grinned and clapped his hands together in delight.

Nappy and Tommy glanced over, curious, then went back to their respective tasks. The accordion wheezed.

His voice even softer now and leaning close, Friedrich said, "Now I know. You have been sent here on a purpose."

"Yes. To report. As I've said."

"No," he replied, dropping his head and shaking it. "You have been sent to *me*."

"To you?"

"*Ja*. And on a more great purpose than that."

"Really?" The man was mad, apparently, but who would not be under these circumstances?

"More great than you even know."

Wells wondered what was coming next. "And that momentous purpose would be?"

Raising his head again, and looking Wells squarely in the eye, he said, "To save your country."

CHAPTER
TWENTY-ONE

The moment Jane saw the car marked Easton Livery Service turning up the drive, with Maude Grover in the back seat, she muttered an unladylike epithet under her breath. This was absolutely the last thing she needed. She had so hoped that the woman had put the incident in the surgery out of her mind, but that would have been asking too much. Maude was, after all, the head of the local watch, a job that she took to entail nosing into every single thing that happened in Easton Glebe.

By the time Jane got downstairs to answer the door, Maude was busy affixing a white nurse's cap to her thinning brown hair. Oh, this was too much.

"Good afternoon, Jane! I was making my rounds today, and thought I'd just stop in to see how your nephew was doing."

"Oh, that is so kind of you. But your husband has the situation well in hand."

"Does he? Sometimes I worry about the poor man—too much on his plate these days. Too much on everyone's plate," she added, with a false laugh.

"Yes, there's no getting around the war," Jane said, standing fast with one hand still on the door. The burly Mr. Slattery had lumbered out of the car and was leaning against the hood, lighting a cigar.

"But could you spare me a few minutes? I have some things to discuss."

"It's not a good time, actually, as I was just—"

"I'll be here and gone in no time," she said, and before Jane could physically interpose herself, Maude had snaked past. Mr. Slattery tipped his cheroot and blew a cloud of smoke in the air to signal that he would be fine waiting in the driveway.

Maude had already gone into the front sitting room, where she was admiring—or pretending to admire—a new set of Wells's novels, translated, that had just arrived the day before.

"Good gracious," she said, "I can't even make out what language these must be in."

"It's Norwegian," Jane said, coolly. "H. G. is quite popular in the Scandinavian countries."

"Is he? I expect his work is popular most everywhere by now."

Jane waited for her to come to the point, while Maude, she suspected, was waiting to be asked if she'd like a cup of tea. Well, she wasn't going to get one.

"Is the great man at home?"

"No, he is out of town for the time being." She saw no reason to advertise his perilous mission; people would read about it soon enough when his dispatches appeared in the papers.

"That's a pity. I'm sure he'd have been supportive of what I'm about to suggest."

At that, Jane did prick up her ears.

"It's about my sister," Maude said, quite unexpectedly. "Seems she's taken a turn for the worse, and I'll be having to run back and forth between here and Berwick Hill for the next few weeks . . . provided she recovers at all."

"I'm sorry to hear it."

"We were never very close—she's five years older—but blood's blood, as they say."

Jane had her first intimation of where all this was going.

"Which leaves an extremely important role in the village unoccupied in my absence. I mean, of course, commander of the local watch."

The words fell on Jane like an anvil. To come at a time when she was harboring an enemy fugitive in her attic, unbeknownst to her own husband . . . Thinking fast, she said, "Surely, Mr. Slattery would be honored to accept the post."

"Mr. Slattery is in his cups by eight every night."

Jane was well aware of it. H. G. had regaled her with stories of Slattery, weary after a day of shooting hares and grouse, slipping off his bar stool at the Four Crowns pub.

"No, I was wondering if *you* might be willing to fill in as deputy commander on those occasions when I'm away? No one is more respected in Easton Glebe and I think having Mrs. Wells herself would be considered quite a feather in our cap."

"While I'm flattered by the offer," Jane fumbled, "I'm afraid I have my hands full, as it is."

"With what?" Maude said, rather sharply. "Your husband's away, your children are off at school—I should think you would welcome the opportunity to be of service."

"I am of service, as you call it. I manage all of H. G.'s business affairs. Right now, I'm transcribing and typing the pages he left of his new novel."

"I meant to the country."

Jane's neck prickled. "We all do our duty, as we see fit."

"Yes, well, of course we do," Maude said, securing the nurse's cap to her hair again. "I'm not asking you to give an answer right now. Why don't you sleep on it? Will you do that much for me?"

Jane nodded assent.

"Good. Then all I'll need to do is look in on the patient, and be on my way. Mr. Slattery will be wanting us to finish our rounds."

"Look in on? What do you mean?"

"See if he's doing all right."

"He's doing quite well, thank you."

"The doctor will want to know that, from my own professional observation."

"Surely he didn't send you."

"He didn't need to. Even if I were not the watch commander, it would be my responsibility."

Jane was flummoxed, and Maude seemed to sense her momentary advantage. "Your nephew, you say? How old is the lad? From the glimpse I caught of him, he was of an age to volunteer."

Ignoring the implication, Jane said, "He's sleeping, the best thing for him, and I do not want him disturbed."

Maude paused, and then, in a lower key, said, "He's not a conchie, is he?" A conscientious objector. "Because you can tell me if he is."

"No," Jane said, snatching at the only thing she could think of. "He's considered reserve personnel, and doing home service."

"Oh, that's quite impressive, especially for someone so young. May I ask in what area?"

"That, I am not at liberty to divulge." In for a penny . . .

Maude nodded, though Jane could not tell if she had actually made the sale or not. Maude looked as if she were still mulling it over, and if for no other reason than to get her off the track, Jane said, "I won't need to sleep on it, after all. You're right, Maude. I accept your offer."

"To be deputy watch commander?"

"Yes."

"Ah, then, all's right with the world and God's in his heaven."

"I'm not sure I'd go that far."

Reaching into the pocket of her cloth coat, Maude removed a creased pamphlet and said, "The duties are all outlined here." She laid it on the mantelpiece, next to the Norwegian books. "If you have any other questions, you have only to ask."

"Yes, thanks, I will," Jane said, all the while shepherding her toward the door. "And thank you for stopping in."

Outside, Mr. Slattery was just stubbing out the end of his cigar on the gravel.

"And I do hope your sister is well again soon," Jane said, wearing the closest facsimile to a smile that she could muster.

Maude fluttered a wave over her shoulder before getting into the back seat, and Jane remained at her post until she was quite sure that the car had gone. Once she had closed the door, she put her forehead against the heavy oak frame and breathed a sigh of relief. *Deputy watch commander,* she thought. H. G. would have a laugh at that.

CHAPTER
TWENTY-TWO

So deep underground, time passed unnoticed, or not at all. Wells could consult his pocket watch—the crystal had cracked, but miraculously the hands still turned—without knowing if it was noon or midnight. Everything seemed to proceed in a murky, jaundiced light, as thin as the fetid air. When he'd asked how they managed to get any oxygen down so far at all, Tommy had pointed out a ventilation shaft, with a hanging leather flap. "Got a bellows system up top, and when it's safe and there's no gas about, we use the blower. The flap's for when it's not."

"Is it safe now?" Wells asked, and Tommy shook his head.

"Bombardment going on. Put your head up above ground and you'll get it handed to you in a basket."

"Who's doing the bombing?"

"Does it matter?"

"How long will it last?" He could hardly hope to wait out the war here, drinking from brackish canteens and eating from salvaged ration tins.

"Long as it takes to kill every living thing."

Tommy had been right about one thing, though—the French tins *were* better. Easily spotted by their white *Chevalier-Appert* labels, he had just finished a *cassoulet pur porc* and *haricots blancs à la tomate*. Hardly the Ritz, but perfectly edible.

Most of his time underground, Wells had spent working on his dispatches, wondering if they would ever see the light of day, much less print. Gradually, he had become aware of the extent of his surroundings. Nappy had crawled through what he had imagined to be merely a funk hole but was in fact another very narrow tunnel, before returning with, oddly enough, a ragged teddy bear. He had swapped a surplus German gas mask for it, with someone no doubt inhabiting a subterranean cavern similar to this one. Pressing his ear to the clay walls, Wells could occasionally hear voices, subdued, and movements, muffled. It was an entire world of moles, burrowed into the earth, and communicating through air shafts and drilled holes and tortuous, abandoned passageways. A world of ghouls—men who, as Tommy had explained on Wells's arrival there, had no need of proper names as they were "dead men, anyway."

It had taken Wells some time to fully appreciate the truth of that sentiment. Deserters from their various armies, they all faced the same fate—summary execution, if discovered and captured. Already reported as missing in combat and presumed dead, their names included on some newspaper roster in Munich or Marseille or Bristol, their families notified, their earthly possessions dispersed, they could never return to their former lives, any more than they could hope to escape the battle zone, which stretched for miles in every direction.

This war, Wells noted in his journal, was different from any other in so many ways—not only in its unfathomable casualties and barbaric weaponry, but also in its sheer geographical scope. A soldier at the Battle of Agincourt could, if weary or wounded or simply faint of heart, have traipsed into some neighboring forest, or over some empty green hill, and have laid himself down beneath a towering oak. A soldier in Wellington's army at Waterloo could have at least caught a breath by lying flat among the dead, without being pulverized from above by unceasing shellfire, or smothered in a creeping ground fog of mustard gas. For soldiers in this war, however, there was no recourse. You either obeyed your orders to go over the top and into a withering fusillade of machine gun fire, from which you would be lucky to escape with only a serious maiming, or you could cut and run—but where? The lines stretched through entire countries, and went just as deep in every direction, and if you weren't brought down by an enemy sniper, you were caught by your own comrades and court-martialed for your cowardice.

"Three platoons," Tommy confided to Wells, his identity disc carefully tucked away under his collar. "Three platoons and every time I was the last one left. By the fourth, I was a bad luck charm and lucky not to get shot, accidental-like, by one of our own. I spent two nights lying in a foxhole in no man's land, with a dozen rotting corpses—half ours, half theirs—before I found, at the bottom of the sinkhole, the way down here."

"How long ago?"

"What month is it now?"

"February."

"Three months, then."

Wells made note of the story, and of others. Gradually, word had spread through the underground network of his presence there, and like penitents coming to confession, men who could no longer seek expiation above ground came to him to unburden themselves. Their stories were all unique, and all the same. One Belgian soldier was blind from a chlorine attack, a Frenchman had refused a command to stand up and walk directly into the enemy line of fire, a Canadian volunteer had enlisted with two boyhood friends who had been blown to pieces in front of his eyes and when ordered to somehow reassemble their bodies for burial, had punched the officer in the face. A capital offense.

Wells did his best to record the stories, to pass no judgment, to offer no cheap absolution—who was he to offer anything but an ear?—but he could no longer think of these wretched creatures as ghouls. Not even as deserters and shirkers. In the face of unthinkable evil, they had made an unthinkable choice. Asked to commit themselves to a ritual death, for a few yards of mud, they had rebelled. Were they madmen, or were they, quite to the contrary, the sanest of them all?

He knew where Major Friedrich Von Baden stood on the issue, though his story, as it turned out, was even more complex than the others. After his declaration that Wells had been heaven-sent to save England, Friedrich had retired to his makeshift bunk and dug out a notebook of his own. He had been reluctant to share it except when everyone else was asleep, absent, or paying no attention. And at first, Wells thought the man might have become delusional. He claimed to be the scion of an ancient Prussian family "of the royal blood, descended from Frederick Barbarossa," and that as a result he had been privy to councils in the kaiser's chambers in the Charlottenburg Palace in Lietzenburg. "Only two years ago, I was one of the honored guests at the marriage of his daughter, Victoria Louise. There I met both the czar and your own Prince of Wales."

Exaggerated as his claim might be, Wells knew it could conceivably have happened—the royal families of Europe and Russia were all intimately intertwined, the bloodlines of Saxe-Coburg-Gotha coursing through the veins of monarchs who, instead of acting as loving cousins, were presently pursuing paths of mutual annihilation.

Among his many accomplishments were saber duels—he bore the requisite scar on one cheek—steeplechases, and Alpine mountaineering. But in his youth, he had declined a career in the military—the standard occupation for Prussian nobility—to study medicine at the renowned Guy's Hospital in the borough of Southwark. "And that is the reason I was—what is the word?"

"Recruited?"

"Yes, that is it. Recruited for the job, the very secret job in London. I could speak English, and I knew my way in the city. A year or two before this war was declared, I was called back to Germany. To be trained."

"In what?"

"Extermination."

And there the story first began to take on a shape that chilled Wells to the bone, especially because he could see, as Friedrich continued, its genesis in his own published works—works that Friedrich had enjoyed in his youth, that thousands of German readers had read in translation. Books that explored fantastical scientific ideas, carried to their extremes, and tales of future warfare waged with unconventional weapons.

"You are familiar with the Royal Prussian Academy of Sciences?" Friedrich asked.

"Yes. I have—or, had—several friends there."

"Ah, and you are much respected there. Not just for your stories, but for your articles about the topics of biology. They have helped to formulate many ideas, ideas that I fear are now to be used in this war. But did you perhaps ever know Dr. Koch?"

Though Wells had never actually met the man, who had died several years before, he knew him by reputation—Robert Koch had been the world's most eminent bacteriologist, winner of the Nobel Prize for his work on tuberculosis, and after whom the Koch Institute of Infectious Diseases had been named. It was Koch who had revolutionized microbiology by inventing methods for creating and harvesting pathogenic bacteria, free from other organisms, in pure culture. "Koch's postulates," as they had come to be known, laid out the conditions that had to be met before any particular bacterium could be accepted as the cause of a specific disease. Wells had relied upon his findings in the creation of one of his own best-known scientific fiction stories, "The Stolen Bacillus."

"I know of his work," Wells replied, "but no, I never had the opportunity to meet him."

"Dr. Friedrich Loeffler, then? Dr. Koch's most able lieutenant, and successor, at the research institute?"

Wells racked his brain. He had attended several symposiums in Germany over the years, but Loeffler . . . Loeffler . . . it was only vaguely familiar. "Something to do with horses?"

"*Ja, ja,* that is the man. He was the man who discovered the virus of the hoof-and-mouth disease. He worked also on the deadly diseases of anthrax and glanders. His experiments, they were so dangerous that the institute said he could not do them in Berlin. What if it escaped the laboratories? He was sent to Reims."

"Reims? France?"

"No, the small island of that name. In the Baltic. There, we had thousands of horses, all in neat and separate stalls—all very modern, very efficient—and we used them to make antitoxins. The experiments were not easy, and they took much time. But after we injected the horses with dead tetanus virus, for example, and then drew their blood, we were able to inoculate every German soldier against the disease."

But where was all this going? Wells wondered. All he could say so far was that it did not bode well . . .

"I was among his assistants. And when Dr. Koch died, and Loeffler was called to Berlin to be in his place, I went with him."

Even this far down in the earth, Wells felt a tremor in the dirt under his feet. Had a bomb landed just above? Or had an underground mine, packed with explosives, ignited? He saw Tommy look up from his magazine, watching the roof for a possible collapse, and when it didn't come, go back to reading the tattered pages. Nappy was asleep, his head resting on the teddy bear like a pillow.

"But how is it that this information about a tetanus vaccination will help me to save my country?"

"Because the high command changed the work. Now they were not trying to save lives. They were using the research to find ways to kill—horses, mules, donkeys, cattle, all pack animals—by the millions."

Wells was stunned, and Friedrich could see it.

"Your armies need these animals to drag artillery, *ja*? To deliver supplies? To be cavalry? To be food? Without them, an army cannot fight."

"True enough."

"When I knew that this was now the mission—no, I said."

"You said no?"

"I am a German nobleman, and I am a doctor. I am not a barbarian. I do not kill horses, I do not kill civilians."

"Thousands of them die here every day," Wells scoffed.

"Never by my hand," he said, shaking his head.

Wells waited. The story so far had been intriguing, to say the least.

"Take this," he said, pressing the ragged notebook on him. It looked as if it might fall apart at any second. "I will not be party to crimes."

Wells accepted it.

And then, removing a sealed letter from his pocket, he handed that over, too. "I do not want harm to come to this person."

Wells saw that it was addressed to a Miss Emma Chasubel, Head Nurse, Communicable Diseases Ward, at Guy's Hospital in London. "Please to deliver it for me."

"What's in it?"

Here, Friedrich hesitated. "There are . . . certain sentiments."

"Ah, a love letter."

"I was not able to say goodbye in a proper manner."

So, now he was to act the part of the go-between in a war-torn romance?

"But it is more than a billet-doux. Miss Chasubel had a patient—this was just before the outbreak of the war—and he was delirious. His name I cannot remember—he lived in England, but was of German ancestry—and so she asked me to translate some of his ravings. He seemed to go back to German in his fever talk and in scraps of paper he wrote on."

"What were these ravings about?"

"Horses. Churches. Saints. London."

"A plot?"

"I do not know for certainty. But I think yes."

"Was it connected, do you think, to anything in Dr. Loeffler's lab?"

Friedrich shrugged. "Many others worked under him, and I did not recognize the name of this man. But once they knew of my resistance, I was . . . disposed."

"Dismissed?"

"Yes—that is it—and sent to the Front. To be rid of. I believe that the generals had orders—quite plain—to make sure I did not come back alive. That is why I had to take refuge," he said, surveying the dank underground pit, "here."

There was suddenly another explosion, but this one was not from above—this one was smaller, but more concentrated, and seemed to emanate from their own underground level. It shook Nappy awake, and caused Tommy to drop the magazine flat. Even Friedrich shot to his feet, his eyes wide.

There were cries from the tunnels, as a green mist started to descend from the ventilation shaft like a jungle snake. Nappy leapt for the leather flaps to close it off, but his one good hand was fumbling and the flap wouldn't fasten tight. Tommy snatched up a gas mask—the English variety, a canvas hood with thick mica goggles—and yanked it down over his head.

"Catch!" his muffled voice shouted, as he tossed another one to Wells. Friedrich had scrambled for his own mask—the German model, with elastic straps—from under his bunk.

Wells had just gotten his on when he heard a muted blast from behind and, turning, saw, through the blurred lenses, a new and gaping hole in the wall. Scrambling through it was a gangly British officer—good God, was that Lillyfield under the mask?—with an electric torch shining in one hand and a gun blazing in the other!

CHAPTER
TWENTY-THREE

The first shot from Captain Lillyfield's pistol caught Nappy in the gut, sending him reeling back onto the pile of coats. The second shot exploded the teddy bear he had clutched to his chest.

Through the filtered mouthpiece of his hood, Wells was shouting for the firing to stop. But by now a pair of British sappers, also hooded and blasting away with their bolt-action rifles, had clambered into the chamber. Wells ducked behind the table as a bullet slammed into a lantern behind him, ricocheting and sending sparks and shards of isinglass flying into the pale green air.

Tommy was the next to go, holding up his hands and wildly plucking at his sleeve to show the Northumberland badge of St. George, but it made no difference. One of the soldiers trained his barrel on him and fired a shot that punched a hole in the hood, and he collapsed like a marionette whose strings had been cut.

Friedrich had immediately dropped to the floor, and through the mist and shadows scurried out, on all fours, through the main tunnel. Wells would have tried the same, but he was suddenly tackled around the knees as if in a rugby scrum, and driven hard to the ground. The breath was knocked out of him, and trying to draw in another—heavily laced with the glycerin and sodium thiosulphate that coated the helmet as a protection against chlorine—was painful in itself. The chemicals scorched his throat. He struggled to say who he was, but the man bearing down on him, covering him with his own body and gripping him by the shoulders, suddenly became familiar. It was Sergeant Stubb! Wells stopped fighting, and lay still, trying simply to regulate his breath. Lillyfield and the sappers had followed Friedrich, and seconds later Wells heard a cry of "No, I am a friend, friend to English!" before a burst of shots broke out.

Only a pair of candles lit the room, but by their feeble glow Wells could dimly discern the search party returning. Stubb rolled off him, and shouted to the others, "It's Wells! Wells!" and then hauled him, wobbling, to his feet.

The captain clapped Stubb on the shoulder, then directed the two sappers to finish their job. Wells saw them wedge delayed charges into the walls. A cloud of green gas swirled in the tunnel behind them, and then they were all stumbling back out the hole they had blown in the dugout. Only a few yards on, they connected to the passageway Wells had first been taken down. He recognized it from the remains of its timbers and wheelbarrow tracks . . . and from the bodies of McCarthy and two of the men who had been with him on that initial voyage. They lay like rugs splayed under his feet, though their limbs were stiff and strangely contorted. This, it crossed Wells's mind, was the only grave they would ever know.

With Stubb urging him on, and both of his arms outstretched like a tightrope walker's, Wells staggered down the tunnel, repeatedly banging his head on the roof, and trying desperately to see more than a foot or two ahead. Through the grimy thick goggles, everything was murky and shadowed, like looking up from under a dirty pond, and the hood made hearing almost as hard. The journey seemed endless, under the stifling hood, and by the time they emerged into the British trenches again—Wells could have kissed the sign that said Euston Square Station—Wells was ripping at the top of his mask and gasping for fresh air.

Stubb and the others snatched theirs off, too, but held them tight until they had ascertained that there was no hint of gas in the air. The sun was shining bright—what a blessing!—and Wells, closing his eyes, put his face up to it, just to feel the unaccustomed warmth.

"Good God, old man! You're alive!" Lillyfield exulted.

Stubb, crouching down, quietly unwrapped another Victory lozenge, and offered one up to Wells, who declined. They were almost as bad as the chemicals in the hood.

"I've received such a blistering communiqué from Colonel Bryce in London, it's a miracle I wasn't taken out and put before a firing squad."

"For what?" Wells managed to get out.

"For what?" Lillyfield exclaimed, incredulously. "For losing H. G. Wells, that's what! For being entrusted with a national treasure and getting it buried under a ton of mud. We were dispatched just to retrieve your mortal remains, at any cost. And what've we done instead? Rescued you, the living specimen himself, and from a bunch of damn ghouls at that!"

"Those 'damn ghouls,' as you call them, saved my life."

"What?"

"They saved my life. After the German grenade went off, it was the Tommy who pulled me out of the tunnel."

The two sappers, leaning with their rifles against the wall, were immediately dismissed by the captain. Plainly, this was nothing he wanted them to hear.

"And the Frenchman, I'm told, was the one that got me breathing again," Wells went on. "He was the first one you shot."

Lillyfield was silent.

"The German—his name was Friedrich—I gather you caught up to him, too."

"We did."

Wells debated saying something about the trove of information that the German officer had been imparting, but thought better of it. Either what he'd been told was utter balderdash, the ravings of a deranged deserter—in which case it was all best kept to himself—or it was of such great significance that it would need to be guarded at the highest levels of security. That was a call for Colonel Bryce to make. The notebook was still safely nestled inside his jacket, but it would need to be translated and its contents carefully studied.

As for the letter to Miss Chasubel at Guy's Hospital, that was different. In gratitude to one of the men who had helped to save his life—one of the despised, and now slaughtered, ghouls—he would deliver that himself.

CHAPTER TWENTY-FOUR

"The Earl of Boleskine?" Mrs. Marsden said, looking up from the pages Rebecca had turned in for editing. "Seriously? You saw him there? You talked to him?"

"Yes. Why?" It was just a bit of color that Rebecca had decided to add to her piece about the Machen lecture, especially as the evening had been so truncated by the zeppelin raid. "Is it important? I can easily take that part out, if you prefer."

Slipping her glasses back up the slope of her nose, Marsden said, "Why would you take out your brief encounter with the wickedest man in the world?"

"Pardon?"

"The Beast 666."

"Who?"

"The Great Satan himself. Does none of this ring a bell?"

"I'm afraid it does not."

"Aleister Crowley."

Ah, at last—that name did. Although unaware of the other monikers, she did know him by his proper name, if "proper" was a word that could ever be attached to a man of such vile reputation. A notorious libertine and self-proclaimed magus, author of pornographic (and thus largely suppressed) poetry and prose, Crowley cut a scurrilous figure on the London, and even international, scene, and Rebecca kicked herself for not recognizing who he was.

"But the Scottish accent? The clothes?"

"Crowley has more getups than a circus clown," Marsden said. "More impostures, more poses. He bought an estate in Scotland, not far from Loch Ness, called Boleskine House, and went there with his followers—he always has some, usually depraved young women and lost young men—to practice his arcane rites and rituals."

"Are you talking about the Golden Dawn?" Rebecca asked. The secretive spiritual order had its own reputation for occult mumbo jumbo, though it included W. B. Yeats, among others, as members.

"Not exactly. That whole world is an especially fissiparous one"— Marsden sniffed—"with allegiances changing daily. It's all hocus-pocus and nonsense, of course, but Crowley manages to keep his name before the public."

"A charlatan, then."

"I didn't say quite that. For all the foolishness, he is a serious man, and in some ways I suspect a dangerous one. I would not want to cross him."

Her last words stirred something in Rebecca, something with which she was all too familiar. A challenge. What was it about this self-styled Scottish nobleman that inspired such trepidation, even in people as hardheaded and down-to-earth as Dora Marsden?

"Perhaps I should write something more about him," Rebecca mused aloud. "Interview him even?"

"Not by my authority," Marsden replied. "I would never send a Christian into the lion's den."

"Who says I'm a Christian?"

"I'm saying he's the lion."

After responding to Marsden's edits on the Machen piece, and making the necessary changes, Rebecca used the office files to find out something more about Aleister Crowley. Apparently, the magazine had reviewed a performance of Oscar Wilde's *Salome* that Crowley had orchestrated—"salacious as it is inane, overblown as it is underwhelming" was the verdict—and in the editorial notes she found a number of interesting details: Born into a wealthy brewer's family, who were members of a strict religious sect called the Plymouth Brethren, he had rebelled against their teachings, dropped out of Cambridge just short of earning his degree, and traveled the world as a mountaineer. All of this before he became the master magician, or Scottish earl, he fancied himself today. Most importantly, she found, jotted into the file, his address in London: 67 Chancery Lane.

She could be there in under an hour.

It was late afternoon when she left the office, and the sky was a sulky gray. By the time she arrived at the townhouse Crowley occupied, it was nearly dark, which made the tall narrow house, painted black from roof to cellar, even more ominous. All the curtains were drawn, and the iron railing separating the stairs from the sidewalk was prominently spiked. For a moment, she wondered if she should even knock on the door, but then she thought, *I've come all this way—why falter now?* All the way there, she had been formulating her questions—What did he think of Arthur Machen's abbreviated speech? Did he accept that the story of the Mons angels was a fiction? What exactly had he been declaiming from the lectern, in some indecipherable tongue, while the zeppelin was thundering overhead and dropping its bombs? And beyond all that . . . how had he known to tell her to sit in the middle of the hall? She didn't fully accept that it was all a matter of acoustics. It was as if he had anticipated the explosion somehow.

Mounting the front steps, she saw a curtain to one side of the door part an inch, emitting a sliver of light, before closing again. And when she banged the knocker—shaped like the head of the Medusa, with a swirl of snakes for hair—she heard a rustling in the vestibule. The door gave a theatrical creak when it opened, and standing there, in a diaphanous gown and holding a candle in one hand, was a young woman with bright scarlet lips and a fall of long black hair over one shoulder. Rebecca's first thought was of the *belle dame sans merci.*

"You were expected," she said, languidly waving her inside.

"I'm afraid I was not," Rebecca said. "And this is terribly rude of me, simply to appear without—"

"You were expected," the woman repeated, closing the door with a decided thump. Behind her rose a steep staircase with a curving banister.

"My name is—"

"Rebecca West," she heard from the landing, as a man in a long ivory-white caftan came into view. It was unmistakably the earl, but he had shed his Highland garb for the look of a Bedouin chieftain. Mrs. Marsden had been right about his bountiful wardrobe.

"Machen enlightened me," he went on. "He is a toiler in the same fields as you. Says your stuff is often cutting. Cutting, I like." The Scottish brogue was gone; now he sounded like any other Cambridge toff.

He had stopped where he was, looking down into the gloomy foyer and, Rebecca surmised, making sure this image was indelibly imprinted on her mind. It was as if he were posing for a portrait.

"Circe," he said, "where are your manners? Take the girl's coat."

Circe? Rebecca thought.

Resting the candle on the bottom stair, the girl held out her pale white arms and allowed Rebecca to drape her coat and scarf over them.

"Come upstairs," Crowley said, "where I can get a better look at you."

The idea of being inspected was not a particularly welcome one, but Rebecca followed him up, and then down a narrow hallway, lit by red-shaded sconces, with closed doors on either side. Behind them, she had the sense of other people going about their own business. Behind one, she heard a raised voice, as if in argument, behind another something that sounded suspiciously like the rhythmic hit of a headboard against the wall.

At the end of the hall, Crowley turned into a surprisingly roomy chamber—the house was somehow wider than it appeared from the street—dominated by a massive fireplace, with a roaring fire. But the heat in the room could not be attributed only to that—two radiators hissed before the curtained windows. It was like a hothouse. And leaning with one hand on the mantelpiece was the ferret-like man she had seen at the speech; with his other hand he was feeding the last of some papers into the fire. Gray ashes were flying up the flue. He turned as she entered, looking none too pleased.

"I believe you've met," Crowley said. "Rebecca West, Dr. Anton Graf."

From behind his little steel-rimmed spectacles, Graf shot an admonitory glance at Crowley, saying nothing.

Rebecca nodded, but kept her distance, taking a chair Crowley beckoned her to. It was a Georgian piece, with a stiff back, tapestry seat, and elaborately carved armrests that were finished in demonic faces. Crowley sat opposite her, in what might have passed for an oaken throne; its back was covered by a silk crimson cloth with a pentagram emblazoned on it.

"I hope I'm not intruding," Rebecca said, "but—"

"You wouldn't be here if you hadn't hoped to intrude," Crowley interrupted, setting her back on her heels. But it wasn't said with asperity so much as amusement. He was trying to keep her off-balance, just as the girl, Circe, had done, by implying that she had been expected.

"It's just that I had not known who you were when we met the other night."

"Ah, but I knew you," he said. "I knew you by your essence."

Apparently, he never let up.

"You are no Cicily Fairfield," he said, crinkling his formidable nose. "A name fit for some garden posy. You've got fire and brimstone in you, like that name you purloined from Ibsen."

He paused, while Circe, who had wafted into the room on bare feet, placed a goblet—silver, chased—of red wine on the small table to her left. At least Rebecca hoped it was red wine—in this house, one had to wonder. The girl drifted out again, as if blown by an errant breeze.

"But you're here because you want to know what I thought of Arthur Machen's oration."

"Yes, among other things."

"Arthur is a dear friend, so I say this with all the malice that only a friend can muster, but he's behaving like a perfect ass."

"Why do you say that?"

"Why? Why, the man has written a sensation, the equivalent of a shilling shocker, and he can't get out of his own way. Why does he deny the story? Why doesn't he give the public what it wants—when what it wants is *to believe*. Every time he opens his mouth he does himself a disservice—and me, too."

"You?"

"I've devoted my life to opening the eyes of the ignorant masses, to lifting their heads out of the trough, to revealing the mysteries of this world, and the next, and here comes old Arthur, like a dray horse fit only for the knacker's yard, braying about his perfidy."

"But he is just being honest."

"Try the wine," Crowley urged, "it's come all the way from Provence. Not much of it getting here anymore."

Hesitantly, Rebecca sipped from the goblet. It was, thank God, nothing more than an exceedingly smooth claret, and blessedly cool. Lifting her eyes, she only now noticed the words etched in stone above the mantel where Dr. Graf still stood: "Do What Thou Wilt."

"Honesty is one of the simplest and yet most inane of the so-called virtues," Crowley said. "Machen should give it up."

At this, Graf, polishing his glasses with a white handkerchief, snorted in agreement.

"Show me an honest man, and I'll show you a man lying in the gutter, stripped of everything but the rags on his back—a fool destined from birth for just such an ignominious end."

"The words above your mantelpiece . . ." she said.

Craning his neck as if he needed to be reminded what they were, he replied, "They are the Whole of the Law."

"What law?"

"The law of Thelema. The philosophy I have created, and preach to my many disciples, thousands of them, the world over."

One could not accuse him of hiding his light under a bushel. To Rebecca, the words seemed nothing more than a permission to indulge one's basest appetites.

There was a muffled scream from down the hallway. Rebecca was startled, but Crowley didn't so much as turn a hair.

Then there was a thump, and another, quickly stifled, from the same quarter.

"Shouldn't Dr. Graf check to see if someone is in need of medical attention?" Rebecca said, and Crowley laughed.

"Unless that was a pig being stuck, he'd be of precious little use."

Rebecca was confused.

"Dr. Graf comes to us from the Military Veterinary Academy in Berlin," he explained, and Dr. Graf, plainly vexed, stepped in to commandeer the conversation.

"I am marooned here," he declared, "by international circumstance. Nothing more. A temporary problem. But if I may be frank, I am still unclear on what has brought *you* to this house."

What *had* brought her? Other than her innate curiosity—her mother used to remark that curiosity killed the cat, and that if she wasn't careful, it would get her, too—there was the sense that a story of some kind, a story that she could uncover and then make known to the world, was lurking here. It was all just a matter of rooting it out.

"Beautiful young women, and gifted ones at that, need no excuse to visit my house," Crowley interjected on her behalf.

"Let her answer," Graf insisted.

"Who cares what has delivered her to my door? I'm more interested in what she has to say about the wine."

"It's very . . . refreshing," Rebecca said.

"Because the room is so hot?"

"Perhaps."

"I dress, as you can see, accordingly." He plucked at the front of his caftan, but in such a way, and in such a spot, as to suggest he wore nothing underneath.

"Have you come as an acolyte?" Graf said, persisting.

"No."

"Then as a journalist?"

"Yes."

Graf shot a warning glance at Crowley, lounging on his throne. "Do you think this is wise?" he asked him.

"As our late friend Oscar once said, the only thing worse than being talked about is not being talked about."

"Your friend, not mine," the doctor shot back, before turning toward the door, where steps were approaching. Not the barefoot steps of the maiden, but the slapping of damp leather shoes.

"Have you seen this?" Machen said, entering in a long shabby overcoat, with a rolled-up newspaper brandished in his hand. His attention was entirely fixed on Crowley.

"What is it?"

"The *Times*, your letter to the editor. The one in which you dispute my own account—my own account, mind you—of the bowmen story."

"I'm doing you a favor, as I have just explained to my guest," Crowley said, gesturing at Rebecca, who sat quietly with goblet in hand.

Machen, still in a lather, only now registered her presence, and it brought him to a full stop.

"Miss West?"

"Yes. I was at your lecture the other night, before the zeppelin so rudely interrupted."

"And I once heard you declaim in Hyde Park, on suffrage. You were fiery and impressive."

"Ah, but I didn't have a finale like yours."

"One that I'd have been happy to do without," he said, his lank gray hair plastered to his forehead by the heat in the room. He glanced at the surly Dr. Graf, then at Crowley, and then back to Rebecca. His gaze, she noted, fell on her goblet of wine for a second. It was as if he were assessing a complex chessboard, and making up his mind what move to make.

Tossing the newspaper into Crowley's lap, he said, "I'll thank you to stay out of it from now on. You and the whole OTO, for that matter."

What, Rebecca wondered, *is that?*

"I'm afraid you have no sway over me, or, for that matter, the *Ordo Templi Orientis.*"

"Yes, yes, I know," Machen retorted. "Go ahead and do what thou wilt. No one's stopping you. Just leave this bowmen business to me."

"You're not forgetting the rites, are you?"

"Not at all. I shall, as always, be there."

"And do your part?"

"And do my part." Then, turning to Rebecca, he said, "Will you allow me the honor of escorting you out?"

"Who said she was leaving?" Crowley demanded.

"I do, Aleister," he replied, in a freighted tone that Rebecca could not have missed.

"I don't see why."

"You don't?" Machen replied. "Surely you don't want me to elucidate."

The atmosphere had grown charged, and Rebecca, taking the hint, placed the goblet on the table and rose from her seat. The heat in the room was so great she felt a tiny bit unsteady on her feet at first, and Machen came quickly to take her elbow. Without a glance back, he all but hauled her toward the door, and as they made their way down the long corridor, Rebecca heard wicked laughter from one of the rooms, followed by the crack of a whip, the rattle of a chain. A woman groaned.

"Shouldn't we help?" she said, just as the door was flung open and she saw, standing bare-chested with a whip in one hand and his suspenders hanging low, the same blond brute who'd been minding the cashbox at the lecture.

"Heinrich," Machen said, acknowledging him, before quickly correcting it to "Henry," all the while tightening his grip on Rebecca's arm and drawing her on. Machen's clothing, she noted, was matted with cat hair.

"Who is he?" she said, dragging her feet and still wanting to intervene.

"Heinrich Schell—Graf's cudgel. He's no one you would ever want to tangle with."

"But the woman in there—"

"She is no doubt there of her own accord, hard as that might be to believe."

Glancing back, she saw the suspendered man still watching, with a flat malevolent gaze.

"However strange they might seem," Machen cautioned, as he hustled her down the stairs, where Circe awaited them with Rebecca's coat already draped across her arm, "in this house it is wise to leave things be."

CHAPTER
TWENTY-FIVE

"No, I do this," Kurt said, sitting up in the bed, his leg still propped on a pillow. He put the bowl of pea soup, generously laden with ham, in his lap, and took the spoon and napkin Jane held out. He looked so proud of himself.

Perched on the chair by his bedside, she went back to studying the tattered English–German dictionary that Dr. Grover had given to her. Trained in medical schools both in England and on the Continent, he said that he'd never attended a lecture without it, "though, even then, it was notably faulty about any word or invention from the previous thirty years." Its publication date was 1864.

But it helped. For the past few days, as she and Kurt had passed it back and forth, pointing to words and expressions to make themselves understood, they had come to know and, though she recognized what a leap this was, trust each other. Simple things were easy (food, water, an extra blanket, an opened window) to communicate about, but the more important questions—what was to happen next? where was Kurt to go? how long could he remain a fugitive in this cramped attic?— were considerably harder to address or explain, especially as Jane could never come up with what she thought was quite the right answer. She had debated the issue not with Kurt, but with Dr. Grover, all the while aware of the fact that she had only so much time to come to a conclusion; by the time Wells came back from the Front, it would all need to have been sorted out.

Since his departure, she had had only one field card from him—a rudimentary missive printed by the military that was routinely read and redacted for any mention of an exact place, or army unit, or plan. She knew he would have his hands full, taking copious notes for his newspaper dispatches, but she waited for the postal delivery every day in the hopes of receiving something more substantial.

"This . . . it was . . . *gut*," Kurt said, placing the empty bowl and spoon on the bedside table. His color was restored, Jane thought, and unless she was mistaken, he had already put on a pound or two. Dr. Grover had been by to check on the ankle cast—he'd whipped up the plaster in the kitchen—and seemed satisfied with the boy's progress. The worst part of it for Kurt, she now surmised, was the confinement; he was young—seventeen, he told her, though he had lied about his age to be accepted into the air corps—and he was eager to get outside and into the winter sunshine. But she was still afraid to let him out into the yard or the barn, even when she had given Mrs. Willoughby the day off. In fact, she had told her to come much less frequently, on the excuse that with Wells gone, the house did not need so much attention. Mrs. Willoughby was not happy about her reduced hours.

Waving one hand to indicate the whole house, Kurt said, "Empty?"

Jane nodded. Here it was again.

"Out?" he said, gesturing at the window.

"*Nein*," she said. "Too . . ." Quickly, she looked up the word for danger. "*Gefahr*. You never know when someone might come around."

Often they both slipped into full sentences in their own languages, confident that context and tone would carry the day—which it generally did.

But he cast his blue eyes despondently toward the window again—a bank of fluffy white clouds was off in the distance—and she felt the way she had when her sons Gip or Frank had begged to have a pony ride, or to skip their lessons for just one afternoon.

"At Germany," he said, "I was out. Worked in . . ."

"Fields?"

"*Ja*. Farm. *Kühe und Hühner.*"

Cows and chickens.

"With your brothers? *Brüder?* You've said that you had several brothers."

"*Ja.* I was the—" He pinched his fingers together to indicate that he was the smallest or youngest.

"Are they still at home," she asked, "or in the war, too? Fighting?" Though so far voluntary, the mobilization in Britain had been so extensive, she imagined that it must be the same in Germany. Every man—or boy, who could pass for one—wanted to be a part of the action, wanted to suit up in a uniform and strut around the town square to be given admiring smiles from the girls. The worst fate that could befall you was to have one of those pretty young damsels present you with the white feather of cowardice. Again, she thanked God that her two boys were young enough to be spared.

"*Ja,* all in war. Albert," he said, shaking his head. He made the motion of a plane flying, then crashing.

"I'm sorry." But what was she saying? That she regretted the loss of a pilot whose job it was to kill her own people?

"Caspar," he added, shaking his head again. This time, he made the gesture of a gun being pointed, a trigger being pulled. A tear glimmered in his eye.

So that was two—and by now, his family would have been informed that they had lost a third child to the war—their youngest. She could not imagine what it would be like if she ever lost one, not to say both, of her own sons.

In their halting way, they talked for another hour until it was time for one more of Kurt's analgesic tablets, which always made him drowsy. Before she left the room, he pointed out the window at the waning sun and said, "*Nacht?*"

"Soon, yes."

"No," he said, drowsily. "Out. *Nacht.*"

He was asking if he could go out after dark. "Let me think about it," she said, tapping her temple to indicate that she was mulling it over.

"*Danke,*" he said.

"*Schlaf gut,*" she replied, before descending the narrow staircase and then locking the door at the bottom, not to keep him in, but, despite the fact that they were alone in the house at present, to guard against any unwarranted intrusion from an unanticipated visitor.

At her desk, she sat down to write another letter to H. G. Unlike mail to most personnel at the Front, hers had to be rerouted through Colonel Bryce's office at the Ministry of Military Information. No one was to know that Wells had been posted to the battlefield. But all the while she wrote, telling him about being appointed the deputy watch commander, or the arrival of the Norwegian editions, she felt like a fraud. She was deceiving him. She wasn't telling him her deepest, darkest secret, the one that was sleeping upstairs under the rafters, the one that posed a genuine dilemma. Her pen often paused, but if she had even *considered* divulging what she had done, the thought of her letter being opened for censorship purposes made it quite impossible. No, this would be a question that only she and Dr. Grover could solve.

Accustomed as she was to H. G.'s absences—on lecture tours, to conventions and meetings on the Continent, to his extended stays in the London flat—this one was *sui generis*. This one, unlike all the others, involved the real threat of death. Oh, she knew that the army would take every precaution to protect him and get him back safe and sound, but at the battlefront there was only so much that could be done. The enemy was not about to observe any special rules of conduct because the other side had sent an eminent figure into the fray.

After another hour or two of typing up handwritten pages for H. G.'s next book—she never failed to marvel at the variety and volume of his output, from love stories to scientific treatises—she prepared a light supper for herself, and brought up a tray to Kurt. He was still groggy when she came in, but quickly roused himself—his appetite had returned in no time—propping himself up against the headboard and accepting the plate of mutton and mint jelly with relish. His nap had apparently refreshed him—his eyes were bright and clear—and he had no sooner finished than he glanced again at the window. The moon was full, and he looked at it as longingly as a wolf who wanted to sit back on his haunches and howl.

"Out? *Ja?*" he said. *"Nacht!"*

Jane scrunched up her face, to indicate that she still thought it was a bad idea, but he put his hands together, as if in prayer, and looked at her so imploringly she could hardly stand it.

"Ich will den Himmel sehen."

Taking the dictionary, he pointed out the German word for "sky"— *Himmel*—as if it were the name of his beloved, and for a farm boy raised in the countryside, and then made an engineer on a zeppelin, it made sense that the sky, and the open air, would be so important to him.

She glanced at the clock on the table. It was after eight. What were the chances that anyone would be out and about the rectory at this hour? Next to none. What harm could it really do?

Plainly, he could see her wavering, and a big toothy grin broke out on his face. His teeth, she noted, were solid and white, much better than most British boys' of his age. It must be the result of all the fresh milk and eggs and cheese he ate, growing up on a farm.

"We go?" he said, drawing the blanket off his legs. "Out?"

"Ja," she conceded. "Yes." She held up one hand. "But wait." She went to the old dresser and removed the pants and tunic she'd found

him in; she had laundered them, but they were mostly rags. Still, she knew that if Kurt was ever found out, or turned over to the authorities, it would be essential that he be wearing a uniform and not civilian clothes. Civilian clothes spelled spy, and certain execution.

Teetering in his underwear by the side of the bed, one ankle still in the cast, he let her help him into the clothes, and then, leaning on one of H. G.'s old walking sticks, hobbled to the door. Getting down the stairs was a perilous journey, made no easier by his eager haste, and then down the main flight again, and through the downstairs rooms. Kurt looked around in wonder. He had registered so little of this on his previous trips, sedated or barely conscious at all. Now he had plainly become aware of the rich Oriental carpets, the mahogany bookshelves gleaming with leather-bound sets, the fine furniture, and the oil paintings, in gilded frames, hanging on the walls. Jane guessed that he had seldom, if ever, been in such a fine house.

At the back door, she gave him one of H. G.'s old overcoats to put on—no point in saving him from amputation only to have him succumb to pneumonia—and after donning her own, stepped out first for a reconnoiter. A pair of rabbits froze on the lawn, then hopped away into the brush. An owl hooted in a tree overhead. But as was to be expected, there was no sign of a human being anywhere.

Kurt was still just inside, but champing at the bit to get out. She waved him on, and putting the cane out in front of him, he left the cover of the house, his head already tilted up toward the sky. It was a clear and cold night, and the stars were twinkling. He came only a few yards, before stopping beside a tree, and using its trunk to keep balanced, looking all around—at the vegetable bins, the empty tennis court, the barn where he had hidden himself after the crash. Jane wondered what he was thinking. This alien place, this house in the middle of nowhere, had become his refuge, his sanctuary, his only real experience of England—home of his sworn enemies. And apart from Dr. Grover, she was his only human connection, not to mention his savior. How did it feel, she wondered, to be so marooned, in such an unlikely and dangerous place?

But looking at him now, she knew he was thinking of none of that. He was entirely in the moment.

"*Schön,*" he said—beautiful—closing his eyes for a moment and taking a deep breath of the night air. He inhaled it as if it were the finest perfume. Then he opened his eyes again and walked a few steps from the tree, into the open yard, and gazed straight up, studying the stars. Pointing at a particularly bright asterism of seven stars, he said, "*GroBer Bär.*" It was, she knew, the Great Bear constellation; H. G. had often taken the boys out in the yard at night to point out to them the various heavenly bodies and configurations, but left it to her to tell them the myths behind each one. This one she remembered well.

Jupiter, king of the gods, had lusted after a young woman, a nymph of Diana, named Callisto, and Juno, the god's wife, in a fit of jealousy turned her into a bear. But not before a boy, Arcas, was born. Years later, on a hunting expedition, Arcas was about to kill the bear—his own mother—when Jupiter intervened to stop such a terrible crime from occurring; he transformed the son into a bear, too, and put them both into the sky, the boy as Ursa Minor. If only she, Jane, had those same powers—if she did, then that young Rebecca West would not be any worry now. She would already be a handful of stars in the night sky.

As for relating the tale to Kurt, it would be far too much to narrate in her faulty German. Besides, he might have heard the story in his own tongue, perhaps from his parents, standing by their own barn in the German countryside.

In the baggy overcoat, he had ambled over toward the vegetable plots and was poking about in the barren earth with the end of the walking stick, perhaps recalling the nights he had dug around for any petrified root to gnaw on, when something put Jane on alert. It was the sound of an automobile engine, coming up the country lane. She turned quickly, just in time to see its headlamps searching for the end of the rectory drive.

"Kurt! Hide!"

He turned around, and seeing the car's lights already sweeping toward the house, lurched off toward the darkness of the barn.

Who could this be? Jane shielded her eyes from the glare of the headlamps, and it was only when they dimmed, and a car door opened, that she could make out Mr. Slattery, stepping out, with something in his hand. As he came closer, she could see that it was an envelope, the kind telegrams arrived in.

For a terrible moment, she was paralyzed with fear. H. G.

"Evening, Mrs. Wells."

"Good evening, Mr. Slattery. You're working late."

"This came in late," he said, "straight, I'm told, from the War Office. The orders were to get it to you quick as it could be done."

She took the envelope, but hesitated to open it.

"You want me to wait, in case there's a reply?"

She was about to say no, then thought better of it. Whatever news the envelope contained, it was better to open it straightaway and deal with it. "Let me get some light," she said, walking closer to the open back door.

"That your nephew?" Slattery said, following a few feet behind.

"What? Who?"

"Maude Grover said your nephew was staying with you. Had some kind of accident."

"What about it?" she said, slipping a fingernail under the flap to unseal the envelope.

"Thought I saw someone out here in the yard with you."

"No, there was no one." Why oh why had she given in to Kurt's pleas?

"You sure? Not over by the barn?"

"Quite sure," she said, at last able to focus on the unfolded telegram. Its opening words were enough to quell her fears and slow her heartbeat.

ALL WELL DEAR BUT NO THANKS TO JERRY STOP MUCH TO TELL YOU STOP RETURN TO LONDON ON WEDNESDAY FOR DEBRIEFINGS STOP THEN HOME BY WEEKEND STOP LOVE TO YOU H. G.

My God, she thought, dropping the hand holding the telegram; it was still shaking. A telegram, delivered at night, with orders from the War Office, was a terrifying thing. Thousands of other families, with loved ones at the Front, would attest to that same fact. But where was Slattery? She lifted her gaze only to see him ambling toward the barn.

"Mr. Slattery?" she called out, suppressing any note of alarm. "Where are you going?"

"Could have sworn I saw somebody," he said, his eyes scanning the hard earth for footprints.

"There was no one, I assure you."

"Well, with Mr. Wells away, and your boys off at school, I wouldn't want any trouble to happen out here at the rectory."

"That's very kind of you. But why don't you come inside for a minute? You can have a glass of brandy while I compose a reply to this telegram."

The brandy, as she thought, proved a sufficient lure to turn him around, and once he was inside, she glanced back at the barn—the door was ajar, but otherwise nothing looked amiss—and led Mr. Slattery to the front parlor, chattering all the while about the news of the day. While he enjoyed a generous shot of H. G.'s best brandy, she composed a warm but innocuous message to her husband, and then escorted her guest out the front door, waiting, waving gratefully, until he had backed all the way down the drive and turned the livery car toward town. Only when his taillights had faded into the night, did she take a full breath and then, go back out to the yard to find Kurt and give him the all-clear.

She would not run a risk like this again, but what, she wondered, was the alternative? To keep him imprisoned in the attic—and somehow unnoticed by her husband—until the end of the war, whenever that might be? That, too, was impossible. Only in a world as consumed with hatred and violence as this one could an impulsive act of compassion have led to such a quandary.

"Kurt?" she said, slipping into the barn. "It's all right to come out now."

His cane was lying by the floor of the ladder to the loft.

"It's only me."

His head poked over the edge of the loft. *"Ist es sicher?"*

"Yes, it is safe now." She was surprised that he had been able to get up there with the bad leg. "It is safe," she repeated, but with far less conviction than she might have wished.

CHAPTER
TWENTY-SIX

"When are you going to be done with that blowtorch?" Graf asked, impatiently. "I have important things to do in here today."

"You told me to make this," Heinrich Schell replied, still tending to his work, "so I make it." The flame was white hot, and with goggles on his eyes and his huge hands stuffed into a pair of asbestos-lined gloves, Schell was welding together two tin panels stripped from an empty Guinness barrel. He had seen, and repaired, any number of these barrels in his time running the Prussian Guard, a public house on the so-called Charlottenstrasse of London. Now he was molding a cylinder eighteen inches long, closed to a point at one end and capped at the other.

It was shaped like a miniature zeppelin, Graf reflected, but if all went well, it would be even more devastating. Much as he hated having anyone else in his laboratory, there was no way around it. He simply couldn't do everything, metallurgy for instance, himself. And so he had handed over to Schell the instructions, sent by secret courier from the Colonial Office, for the construction of the canister. When completed, it would be hidden away in the battered viola case under his bed.

Rather than distract him again, Graf took a few minutes to comb over the diagrams once more, for the fuse, the burster, the filling port.

Such a device, commonly employed for the dissemination of poison gas on the battlefield, had never been used for the purposes he had in mind, but he was certain that his scheme would prove as workable as it was elegant. He, Dr. Anton Graf, would win the war without employing a single cannon, plane, or submarine. But how odd, he thought, that his sole accomplice should be this stolid dullard, with whom he had not much more in common than nationality and a deep-seated antagonism toward all things English. It was odd that they even knew each other.

The previous September, very soon after the outbreak of the war, Graf had been in the Prussian Guard one night, celebrating the cultivation of a particularly promising culture, when another boatload of Belgian refugees had come to London with their tales of German atrocities, tales Graf immediately discounted as pure propaganda. But as usual, the British mob had been riled up, and headed for the German district of town to square accounts. It was a surprisingly warm and summery evening, all going well, until a crowd, including many of the pub's regular customers, suddenly converged on the place with bricks and bats and a thirst not for beer, but for blood. Graf saw them through the front window, which was shattered a moment later by a barrel thrown right through the glass. It caromed off one table and thumped onto Graf's, who ducked in the nick of time. The door was banged open, and the mob surged through, overturning chairs, smashing mirrors and anything else in sight. Fire quickly followed when a burning torch was tossed onto the alcohol spilling from the broken bottles behind the bar.

Schell, taken by surprise, tried to fight at first, but even a man of his size and fury could do only so much against the seething mass of frenzied Britons. Graf saw him hurl three or four men out of his way with Herculean strength, sending one of them all the way back through the smashed window, and crowning another with a heavy beer mug. It was only when Schell's barking dog, Munchen, a schnauzer named after the town where Schell had been born, was lifted up by a man in the mob and hurled directly into the flames now rising to the rafters that he seemed to lose his senses altogether, digging a meat cleaver out from under a counter and slashing through the mob willy-nilly. In the distance, Graf, cowering behind a coatrack, had heard the shrill sound of police whistles, the rumble of fire wagons, and had somehow managed—shouting orders at him in German—to stop him from fighting anymore and run out the back door of the pub before it was too late.

Dazed and bloodied, Schell had tried one more time to rescue his dog from the fire, but the animal had already been consumed by the flames, and as if he were leading a lost blind child, Graf dragged Schell into the deserted alleyway, then through the labyrinth of streets and all the way back to his own safe haven in Aleister Crowley's townhouse. There, Schell had hunkered down ever since, nursing his thirst for revenge and becoming a devoted worshipper at the altar of all things perverse and occult. At the latter, he had proven to be a quick study.

"There," Schell said, extinguishing the blowtorch and lifting the goggles from his eyes. "It is done."

"Try the cap. See if it fits."

"It will fit," he replied, lifting the three-pronged cap and screwing it to the open end of the cylinder. "*Ja?*"

"*Das ist gute Arbeit.*"

"Now are you going to tell me what it's for?"

"In good time, in good time." Graf was reluctant to share his plans with anyone, particularly someone as prone to drink, and inclined to rage, as Heinrich Schell. Even Graf's distant overseers, in the Schutztruppe branch of the Colonial Office at Wilhelmstrasse 62 in Berlin, didn't know precisely what he was up to. Better that way.

"The Master keeps asking me when he will see some gold," Schell said. "He says that he is tired of experiments. He is tired of excuses. He needs gold."

Graf carefully removed his spectacles and cleaned the lenses with a handkerchief before answering. "You may inform *your master*"— pronouncing the last two words in such a way as to imply that while

Schell might regard Crowley as his master, Graf did not—"that the work will be done when it is done. In the meantime you may show him this," he said, producing a burgundy velvet pouch from his vest pocket.

Schell opened the drawstring and peered at the golden dust and nuggets jumbled inside. "You made this?"

Graf hooked the sidepieces behind his ears and blinked at Schell through his polished lenses. "What, do you think the Bank of England gave it to me?"

"How much of this can you make?" Schell asked.

"It all depends on how long I am left alone to do my work." In fact, it all depended on how many more times the Colonial Office was willing to smuggle him similar pouches. As far as they knew, Graf was just dunning them for his laboratory expenses. If they had known it was to convince a character like Aleister Crowley that alchemy was being successfully performed in his cellar, they'd have laughed themselves out of their chairs. It was a joke he would share with them one day when the war was over and won. But for the moment, all he wanted was his lab back.

"Now, take that pouch and leave me be."

Schell pocketed the sack, tossed the goggles and gloves onto the worktable, and trudged up the steps. Once Graf heard the door at the top of the staircase close, he pulled the viola case out from under his bunk and opened it. Lifting the empty cylinder, still warm, he laid it inside the green felt interior.

Soon, he thought, it would be traveling like an arrow straight at the breast of the British empire.

CHAPTER
TWENTY-SEVEN

When the train from Southampton finally arrived at Waterloo Station, it was late on a drizzly afternoon. Wells, with the ever-dependable Sergeant Stubb by his side, waited in the carriage until the wounded had been helped off. Soldiers with missing limbs, bandaged heads, gauze masks to conceal the hideous damage from gas, shot, and shell, limped into the arms of waiting nurses, or were loaded onto stretchers and carried down the platform. As Wells watched through the grimy window, one of them, half-blind, stumbled into a stanchion post, another fell to his knees and retched onto the tracks. They moved like phantoms in the gray station light, and when Wells finally followed the grim parade outside, he saw a long row of Red Cross ambulances, supplemented by private cars and even horse-drawn bread vans, courtesy of Lyons bakeries, lined up to receive them. From here, they would be transported to several of the nearest hospitals including Charing Cross, London in Whitechapel, and on the South Bank, Guy's—where he would soon be making a sad mission of his own.

"I'll be quite all right now," Wells said to Stubb, taking back his suitcase, now much the worse for wear.

"Quite sure?" Stubb said, rasping around the Victory lozenge. The brief re-exposure to the gas underground had exacerbated his problem. "My orders are to see you all the way home, you being a national treasure and all that." A smile flitted at his lips.

"This national treasure can find its way to St. James's Court, unassisted," Wells said, extending his hand and clasping Stubb's. "I shall see you again, Sergeant."

"Right you are."

"And thank you." So inadequate to the weight of all that he owed him, but he knew that Stubb would understand its full import.

And then the sergeant was gone, and it was up to Wells to walk several streets away, in the rain, before he was able to commandeer a cab just dropping off a gaggle of young people, erupting in laughter, outside a popular hotel.

"The whole bottle of Dom? All by herself?" a girl crowed.

"Yes," a young man replied, "and without a glass!"

The others cheered, and fell into the door being held open by a bellman.

When Wells climbed into the back seat and the cabbie saw his uniform and suitcase, he harrumphed and said, "Glad to be rid of that lot. Were you over there?"

Wells confirmed it.

"Welcome back to Blighty."

"Good to be back."

"Me, I was over in Africa, I was, fightin' the Boers. But lor', that was fifteen—no, sixteen—years ago now."

For the remainder of the ride, Wells was happy to let him expatiate on his service in South Africa, but when the cab pulled up before his building, and Wells looked up at the darkened window, the drapes standing open but no one waiting between them, he was touched by a familiar melancholy.

Opening the door to his flat, it was hardly a hero's welcome he received. A curtain stirred in the draft, and the smell of stuffy, dusty air assailed his nostrils. But it was blessedly quiet, and private, and serene. He leaned against the back of the door, and simply took in the unreality of it. This was the first moment that he felt he had well and truly escaped from the Front—and by the skin of his teeth.

He knew the sensation was one to be savored because he also knew it would pass, swiftly and inexorably; that was both the blessing and the curse of human nature. The horrors would fade, but with them the appreciation of the beauty of the commonest things in ordinary life— the comfortable chairs, the clean tea towels, the soft carpet underfoot. If only one could forget the former hardships, while preserving the latter sense of joy; that would be a trick worth mastering.

As he went about his business, turning on the lights and drawing the curtains closed, banging on the radiators to get them going again, he found himself at loose ends in the flat. After shaving and bathing (ah, the miracle of hot water!) and putting on his civilian clothes—an old tweed suit and waistcoat—he took the notebook and letter that Friedrich Von Baden had given him, and sat down in one of the wing-back chairs that flanked the fireplace.

The letter, still sealed, was addressed in English, but the notebook was written in German. Colonel Bryce, to whom he would hand it over the next day, would want it translated immediately. Wells wondered what it would reveal. Would it indeed contain the seeds of some terrible scheme to further the kaiser's war effort, or would it be the ravings of a man consigned to a life among the living dead, a man, like all the others down there, with no country to return to?

The notebook page that Wells was looking at—where several chemical formulas were entered—suddenly swam before his eyes, and he pressed two fingers to the skin just above the bridge of his nose and squeezed, hard. Ever since that night in the underground, when the gas had leaked into the chamber, he had been prone to these sudden but brief attacks of neuralgia. His eyes would become momentarily unfocused, sounds around him muffled, his temples throbbing. Sometimes the air was tinged with a murky, unpleasant scent. And then, in a minute or two, the feeling would pass, leaving him drained but all right again. He would have to ask Bryce for a referral to a London physician who might be familiar with such symptoms. He could hardly be the first to have experienced them.

He was just preparing a plate of some stale biscuits and a tin of sardines—all that he could find in the cupboard—when he heard the shrill whistle of an air-raid warden outside. Hurrying to the front windows, he glanced outside—night had fallen—and yanked the curtains tight. As he returned to the kitchen, there was a peremptory knock on his door. Had he failed to secure them properly?

"I come," he said, as he made his way to the foyer. He didn't bother to peer through the peephole, but opened the door and then stood, surprised, as Rebecca said, "I hope you won't think I'm making a habit of this."

"How did you even know I was home?"

"Your curtains were drawn. They've been open ever since you left."

"You've been checking?"

"I could deny it, but what would be the point?"

Neither had moved an inch.

"Aren't you going to ask me in?"

Wells moved to one side, and once the door was shut, felt her arms wrap around his neck, and her lips pressed to his cheek. He was caught so off guard that he did not respond, his arms hanging limply at his sides.

"I must say," she murmured, "I had hoped for more of a greeting than that. I was so worried about you that I've barely been able to sleep."

"You should not have been."

"Yes, I should have," she said, holding him at arm's length and studying his face. "You've been through something terrible—I can see that."

He was not about to challenge it.

Nor did he challenge her when she tossed her coat over the back of the sofa, or when she kissed him again—this time with even greater ardor—or when she took him by the hand and led him, not unwillingly, toward his own bedroom. What had gotten into the girl? It was as if she had thoroughly rehashed their last encounter here, perhaps all the time he was away, and was determined now to rewrite the script, to make it play out the way she had originally intended. He already knew she was a girl of bold convictions, and this appeared to be evidence of it yet again.

But what of his own convictions? Even as he lay back on the bed, atop the quilt that Jane had made, he recalled balking, the last time, at anything further. But he did not have that kind of resistance in him now. He had seen so much death, he needed this reaffirmation of life.

This was nothing new to him; for years, young women had been irresistibly attracted to the nectar of his renown. But for every one of them that he had seduced, there was another who had done the seducing. Even so, in Rebecca he sensed something very special, something that would render this much more than a mere dalliance. His desire for her was as great as any he had ever known—at the Front, it had only grown—and when her face hovered above his for just a moment, and he gazed into the dark liquid pools of her eyes, he was overcome with passion, the kind he had felt as a young man still making his way, and his name, in the world.

He rolled her over, and she let out a sigh—recognition that the battle had been won, the tide had turned, *he* now wanted *her*—and his fingers tore at the buttons of her blouse. She laughed with pleasure, and clawed at him playfully, like a big cat.

"Oh, so you're a panther now, are you?" he said.

"I could be, if you wanted me to," she said, nipping up at his neck.

"I do."

"But only on one condition." Her perfect teeth shone white in the darkness. "You must be my jaguar."

"Then that's what we'll be," he said, slipping his hands up under her skirt, nimbly unfastening the tops of her stockings, and dragging them down—his fingernails, ragged from the trenches, deliberately scratching her skin as they went. "Jaguar and panther."

Could it be that he had hit upon his ideal counterpart, a girl who relished the playful aspect of sex as much as he did?

Once he had undressed her, he leaned back on his haunches and, as was his wont, simply surveyed the beauty of her body—the full breasts, sloping gently to each side, the heaving rib cage, the darker triangle between her legs. Most girls—nearly all, truth be told—folded their legs, or demurely covered themselves with one hand when they saw him looking there. But not Rebecca. She stared up into his eyes, eager to see his reaction, to see the quickening of his passion, which fed her own.

"Panther," he breathed, stripping off his own clothes, then bending his head, and his bared teeth, to her breast.

"Jaguar," she whispered, her hand snaking down, catching him from below with a firm grasp. Her fingers were supple and cool and, for a newcomer, surprisingly adept.

Their embrace was fierce, and her face, at the moment of consummation, was revealed in a flash of light from a searchlight beam that penetrated a slit in the bedroom curtains. She cried out and he gripped her tight, holding on until, minutes later—both of them spent—they lay together in the dark, limbs still entwined, letting their normal breathing return.

"Are you all right?" Wells asked, tracing a finger tenderly along her upturned jaw.

"Better than that."

"No regrets, then?"

"Should I have?" she replied, pressing a quick kiss to his lips.

Disentangling herself, she got up and crossed the hall into the bathroom, even then displaying a confidence he did not often see. She didn't scurry off with head down, or wrap her naked body in a sheet, but moved unhurriedly. He heard her turn the faucets on the tub, heard the rush of the water in the pipes. When she closed the door, he stared up at the ceiling, asking himself what he had just done.

The searchlight beam sliced between the curtains again.

He had launched another of his passades—that much was undeniable. But this time it was with someone who, until that evening, had been a virgin, and with whom, he knew in his bones already, he would experience passion, and a welter of other emotions, utterly foreign to married men of his years. His life would be simpler without such escapades, but it would be immeasurably less interesting, too. Decades of fidelity, to one woman, in one bed, in one redundant embrace, was a fate he could not fathom. The very springs of his creativity would dry up without the occasional foray into new and forbidden territory. It was his way of priming the pump, stoking the engine. Eros was his inspiration, and without it he felt he would be utterly enervated.

When Rebecca slipped back under the sheets, they kissed again, and when he excused himself, he went to the sink and ran some warm water onto a hand cloth. He scrubbed the sticky patches of his skin— the water gave off a rusty odor—before turning on the cold water tap, bending his head to the basin and splashing his face.

Instantly, he regretted it.

The neuralgia, or whatever the hell it was, burst like a grenade in that spot between his eyes, and he again squeezed the skin firmly, with two fingers, to try to squelch the pain. He fumbled for a towel and wiped the water from his eyes, but his vision remained blurry. He swung open the medicine chest mirror, retrieved the aspirin bottle, and swallowed several pills with a handful of water. It was only when he swung the mirror closed again that he was so startled he dropped the bottle and stared into the glass as if he'd seen a ghost.

Or had he?

He whipped around, but the bathroom door was closed and he was quite alone.

He looked back at the mirror. It was empty, apart from his own reflection.

But the image was indelibly imprinted on his mind.

Just behind his shoulder he had caught a glimpse—as evanescent as it was shocking—of Corporal Norridge—and not as he was in life. The bullet hole that had been drilled like an awl straight through his right eye was as black and bloody as Wells, who had cradled the dying man against his overcoat, remembered it. Norridge's remaining eye was open, and his lips were, too—he was saying something, but so softly Wells had not been sure of what it was.

Yanking his robe from the hook, he pulled it on, and threw open the bathroom door, dreading what he might see, but the hallway held only shadows. He went into the bedroom, where Rebecca was lying under the blanket, her back against the headboard, and looked around the room, before leaving again.

"H. G.?" she said.

He poked his head into his study—nothing and no one there—and then turned on the light in the front parlor. His eyes took a few seconds to adjust, but again the room was just as he had left it.

"What's wrong?" Rebecca said.

Turning, he saw her standing in the archway, the quilt gathered around her.

"You look as if you'd seen a ghost."

When he didn't answer, she said, "Did you?"

He pressed two fingers to his forehead—he felt as if all the energy had just been drained from his body—and she came to him, opening the quilt and wrapping it around the two of them.

"Come back to bed."

"But I could have sworn . . ."

"Could have sworn what?"

How could he answer? That he'd seen a soldier—Eddie, he remembered now, was the man's first name, Corporal Eddie Norridge—but as he was just after he'd been killed by machine gun fire?

"Bed," she said, shuffling them both back toward the hallway. "You need rest," adding, as encouragement, "Jaguar."

He offered her a weak smile, though his mind still reeled, and his nostrils twitched with a faint scent of the trenches.

"Panther," he replied.

They slipped back into the bed, and though Rebecca swiftly fell asleep, her head nestled on his chest, Wells lay awake, staring at the ceiling and trying to determine what the dead soldier had said. It wasn't at all clear, but had he been mumbling something about a saint?

CHAPTER
TWENTY-EIGHT

In the cellar of Crowley's townhouse, where he had set up his laboratory, Dr. Anton Graf heard the sirens announcing another zeppelin incursion and wondered for a moment if he should postpone his mission that night. On the one hand, he had no more desire than the English did to be blown to bits by an incendiary bomb, but on the other, the attack might provide extra cover. Most people would be rushing into the tube stations for shelter, or cowering under a kitchen table in their homes. They wouldn't be out in the open, on the streets, much less carrying a dangerous cargo in their leather satchel, as he would be.

He finished up what he had been doing—very carefully wrapping the glass vials, with their murky yellow and green contents, in swaths of cotton before fixing them into their slots in the velvet-lined sample case; the brass box had been given to him by Dr. Loeffler himself, in recognition of his work for the Imperial Colonial Office. He had just snapped it closed when he heard footsteps on the stairs and turned to see that strange, barefoot girl—the latest of Crowley's many disciples—with a shawl wrapped around her shoulders.

"Haven't I told you never to come down here, Sally?"

"Circe. The Master said that was my new name."

Crowley redubbed them all, the gullible lost souls he inducted into his sect. "Why Circe?" he could not resist asking.

"Because he said that I was so beautiful he acted like a swine around me." She shrugged, indicating that the classical allusion had been squandered on her.

How *did* he find them all? Graf had often wondered. Or did they somehow find him?

"There's an air raid," she implored. "It's safer down here."

"Look around you," he said, waving a hand at the many beakers and flasks, the incubators and burners and bellows, the petri dishes and chemical bottles, cluttering the work tables. "Do these look safe to you?"

She seemed uncertain on that score. "You're just making gold, aren't you?"

Sometimes it was all he could do to contain his temper, even with Crowley himself. Yes, the story was that he was performing great feats of alchemy down here—turning lead into gold, discovering the philosopher's stone, the universal alkahest—and he had to keep up that subterfuge, for his own good. But, *Gott in Himmel*, there were times, like this one, when he longed to dispatch them all, so he could get on with his work in peace. With great deliberation, he slipped the brass box into his satchel.

"Go and hide somewhere else," he said.

"Where are you going to go?"

"Out."

The sirens screamed more loudly.

He pulled on his hat and overcoat, scarf and gloves, and with the satchel in one hand, and the other hand pushing Circe up the stairs ahead of him, he emerged from the cellar. Despite the fact that he was Crowley's guest here—and a secret guest at that, harbored in plain violation of the Alien Restrictions Act—he would have to put a strong lock on this door. Crowley forbade locks in his house, as they were an impediment to his goal of unfettered freedom and access, but now that his endeavor had reached its critical late stages, he simply could not risk exposure, intrusion, or meddling of any kind.

Outside, the streets were nearly deserted, with just a few stragglers making for whatever protection they thought best, when, in fact, Graf knew it was all just the luck of the draw. Even if the zeppelins had wanted to drop a bomb on a specific target, they could seldom manage it. Winds and weather made precision too impractical for the gas-filled dirigibles. But they achieved, nonetheless, their major aim—which was to instill fear and uncertainty in the civilian population. Looking up at the sky, scissored by white search beams, Graf saw, a couple of miles to the east, the dull black silhouette of two of the behemoths and the glow of a fire below them. Fine, he thought, if the airships stayed over there, they would not impede his journey toward the Horse Guards Parade.

After securing his box in the wicker basket of the bicycle that he kept below the street stairs, he climbed on and set off. A trip like this would be hard enough on a night when the streetlamps were lit and the shop windows blazing, but in the dark it was especially difficult. He had made the journey many times before, so he knew which stretches of pavement were straighter and smoother, but several times he almost missed a street corner where he was meant to turn. Twice air-raid wardens shouted at him, warning him to seek shelter, but he simply tucked his face into his scarf, waved one hand, and pedaled harder.

As he approached the edges of St. James's Park, bordering the parade grounds, he could smell the wet trees . . . and the horses. Thousands had been shipped here from all over the countryside, and plenty more all the way from America, to be checked by veterinarians and then transported to the battlefields of France. Without horses, an army could not function, and at the opening of the war, the British army had only twenty-six thousand on hand—a fraction of the number that would be needed. The British Remount Services had put out the call, and requisitions officers had scoured every farm and hamlet in the kingdom. There were so many horses assembled here now that there wasn't room to stable them all, so the surplus was corralled on the parade grounds itself and others in a sequestered section of the park. The sirens and smell of distant smoke in the air would be sure to make the animals, nervous and scared to begin with, even more jittery than usual. But Graf was good at calming them; in Reims, he'd become famous for it.

He had visited the parade grounds enough times before the war had broken out that he knew his way around, and he counted on the over-saturation of animals, compounded by the chaos of the zeppelin attack, to afford him additional protection tonight. Stashing his bicycle in a clump of bushes, he slung his leather satchel over one shoulder, like a quiver, and crept toward what he knew was a low and rusty old gate at the eastern end of the grounds. Even here, he spotted a sentry marching back and forth, his rifle over his shoulder. But he had only to wait until the soldier had reached the far end of his circuit before scurrying out, and then scrambling over the old gate.

Entering the vast stables, in which the horses of the Life Guards were normally kept, would prove to be more difficult, but he was counting on old Silas to be minding the feedlots, and he was right. Before the war, Graf had occasionally acted as a consultant to the British veterinary corps, but had taken the precaution, even then, of giving the old man only a false name—Dr. Eulenspiegel, after the famed German trickster—rather than his own. Even then, he had foreseen this day might come.

When Silas looked up to see him, and Graf greeted him with a smile and a hearty hello, Silas gave him a gap-toothed smile in return and said, "What brings you out in an air raid, Doctor?"

"That's why I've been sent," he said, "to see to the horses' agitation."

"Good luck to you with that," Silas said. "They been skittish all day, like they knew what was coming. Barely et a bite."

"But you have filled the troughs and bins for the night?"

Silas nodded. "See for yourself."

Dr. Graf passed by the huge storerooms, where bales of hay were stacked to the ceiling and barrels of bran and oats, each one the size of an automobile, were lined up as far as the eye could see. Another pair of sentries was patrolling the lots. But it was too risky to do his work in here, anyway, and besides, it was the horses and mules outside, the ones most likely to be shipped soon, that were his quarry.

He walked slowly, so as to call no attention to himself, down the wide, dirt-floored concourse, through the areas where the incoming livestock had been processed. The smell of seared flesh was in the air here, from the red-hot branding irons, with the broad arrow of the British army, which had been pressed into the animals' flanks—it took half a dozen men to hold down each one—then he went on past the hogging stalls, where manes were trimmed and tails squared in the military fashion. Graf, an expert on equine care, knew that they routinely cut away too much of the horses' natural coat, especially given the rigorous conditions the creatures would encounter at the battlefront. The horses could freeze, catch pneumonia . . . or, as no one knew better than he did, suffer even worse fates than that.

There was another guard at the archway leading to the parade grounds, but since Graf was already coming from inside the stables, he was able to saunter right under his nose unchallenged, with a salute and his leather veterinary bag now clutched in one hand. Stepping out into the open parade grounds, he saw that it had been partitioned off into at least a dozen vast corrals, separated by hastily constructed barriers of wood and wire. In some there were horses, in others mules, and in some a mix of the two. At one of these, he saw what were unmistakably Missouri mules, animals that might well have come all this way from the Guyton and Harrington Mule Company, centered in a little American town called Lathrop; G&H had been supplying animals to the British army since the Boer War years before. These American-bred mules were especially prized for wartime duty as they were strong and sturdy, and a good deal more easily managed than draft horses.

He continued along the outside fencing, to make sure he was as far from the stables as possible, before finding what he needed—a convenient tree stump that would serve as a table. Looking all around, he opened his satchel, removed the brass case, then replaced his leather gloves with a pair made out of thick, reinforced rubber; these, he pulled halfway up to his elbows, under his coat sleeves. Wearing them would make his work a bit more difficult—he would lose a fine sense of touch—but not wearing them could cost him his life. Unlatching the case and folding its lid all the way back, he surveyed the pair of syringes secured on top, and then the quartet of vials, two marked "A" and two marked "G."

The "A" stood for anthrax, the "G" for glanders.

Where to start? All the horses and mules were shifting nervously in their pens, alarmed by the vagrant smoke in the air from the zeppelin raid, but they were crowded in so close it would not be hard to get at them. As delicately as he could, Graf lifted out the two syringes, each one about two inches long, and slipped off the cork stoppers protecting the steel needles. Opening two of the vials, he dipped the needles into the bile-colored broth—cultured in his own lab—and, laying one of them on the stump, approached the wooden perimeter fence with the other held tightly between two fingers.

"Come to me," he said to the nearest animal, a chestnut-colored shire horse with shaggy white hooves. Its great dark eyes were fearful, but he crooned to it and held out his hand as if it held a lump of sugar. The horse bowed its head several times, and paced in place, before growing curious enough to extend its nose over the water trough that rested against the boards of the pen.

"That's it," Graf said, "*das ist gut.*"

As he stroked and petted its head, gaining its trust, he took aim and then plunged the needle into its neck. The horse whinnied in pain and reared back, kicking out and hitting another horse crammed in behind it. When that horse swiveled around to get out of the way, Graf jabbed it, too, in its flank.

Now the whole pen was in motion, ramming and butting each other, aware of some immediate danger, crying and braying and snorting in alarm. Graf recharged the syringes and when a pair of mules—sorrel males—came within reach, he stuck one in the haunch and another, a strong plow animal, in its shoulder. That one twisted its neck back at the injection and snapped at his hand, nearly taking off his fingers, but Graf cursed it and reloaded again, methodically moving from corral to corral, luring animals close and then jabbing at them, wherever he could reach, with the dripping steel needles. Infecting every creature he could reach with the two deadly contagions.

He had almost run out of the bacteria when a guard, alerted by the whinnying and kicking of the injured beasts, appeared a couple dozen yards away. Graf just had time to dump the rest of the germs into the water and feed troughs before the sentry spotted him and shouted, "You there! Stop!"

Graf snapped his case shut, threw it into the satchel, and scrambled for the shadows.

"I said, hold!"

But Graf ran toward the shelter of the trees in St. James's Park. A shot rang out and a branch snapped over his head. Glancing back, he collided with the end of a wooden bench, and tumbled over it, onto the hard ground. The open satchel flew out of his hand and the brass box clanged against a tree trunk. A shrill alarm whistle sounded, and on all fours Graf scuttled after the bag. He had it in hand when another shot splintered the bark of the tree where his empty case lay, glinting in the moonlight no more than a yard or two away. He darted out to retrieve it, but this time the shot spurted the dirt up around his feet, and he had no choice but to race in the other direction. He put as many trees as he could between himself and his pursuer, and by the time he reached the spot where his bicycle lay hidden, he heard no more shots, or any indication of close pursuit. His lungs were ragged, but he got on the bike, and with legs aching from the collision with the bench, pedaled away.

By the time he left the park grounds, the all-clear alerts were sounding—constables ringing hand bells, Boy Scouts on bicycles blowing their bugles—and civilians were starting to emerge from the shelters and tube stations. He was finally able to steer the bike into an alleyway and stop, his heart hammering in his chest. With one hand, still in its rubber glove, supporting himself against the redbrick wall, he vomited copiously from the sheer exertion of it all.

A warden in his round helmet called out, "You all right, mate?" and Graf nodded wearily.

"It's all over now," the warden added. "Looks like we'll live to fight another day."

Graf nodded once more, to signal agreement, and the warden moved on. He spat out the sour taste of the vomit, then peeled off the gloves and let them drop onto the cracked pavement without any further contact.

Yes, he thought, you English might live to fight another day, but in the end, the time would come—thanks to brilliant and inventive men like himself—when the kaiser would ride in glory through the gates of Buckingham Palace itself. Dr. Anton Graf, he felt confident, would be not far behind in his retinue.

CHAPTER TWENTY-NINE

It was the strangest of sensations, and Wells had heard about it from several soldiers, after they had returned to the Front from a leave back home. One had said, "They treat me as if I've just been gone on a bender." Another had said, "Even though I don't want to talk about what I've seen here, it doesn't matter—they don't want to hear about it, anyway." More than one had complained to him that they'd returned home to find their sweetheart had already taken up with someone else. "I told her, I'm not dead yet, love—couldn't you have waited? It won't be long." A heartbroken young corpsman had shown Wells the engagement ring he had taken back, and wore now on a chain around his neck, along with his identity disc. "Let Fritz finish what she started."

Standing on the street outside the War Office, Wells had that same sense of unreality, of disorientation. Only a short time before—the sort that could be calculated in hours—he had been mired in mud and blood, riddled with lice and overrun by rats, deafened by artillery bombardments and sniffing the air for deadly gas, even buried alive in an underground trench of lost men . . . and now? Now he had to remind himself to step back from the curb as a crowded bus went clanging by. Now he was surrounded by civilians with bowler hats on their heads and newspapers under their arms. Cars and taxi cabs honked their horns, church bells rang the hour, shopkeepers hawked their wares from open doorways—it was an unusually temperate day—and shoeblacks tried to talk him into a polish. How could this world—of bustling and benign activity—coexist with the world of death and destruction that he had just departed? Such a negligible distance separated them, but they might just as well have been in different island universes, millions of miles apart.

Remembering as best he could the vertiginous route up to the Ministry of Military Information, he climbed one flight of stairs after another, passing dozens of young men and women in uniform, hurrying about with important folders tucked under their arms, and found the door to Colonel Bryce's office standing open.

"Come in, Wells, come in," Bryce said. "Just airing the place out a bit." The windows behind the desk were raised, too.

Wells gratefully took a seat, plopping his briefcase in his lap. He hadn't had much sleep the night before, what with Rebecca's visit, the air raid, and then the awful hallucination in the bathroom mirror. This climb up the stairs had almost finished him.

"Can't tell you how shocked and dismayed we were at the initial news of your disappearance on the battlefront," Bryce said.

"No more than I, of that I can assure you."

"And how relieved we were to get the news of your rescue from Captain Lillyfield."

Wells could see, even though it was upside down, that a copy of his first dispatch was lying on the desk. There were red pencil markings on it, something any writer could spot at a hundred paces.

"But you are well now? Everything's all right?"

"Yes, fine, thanks." No point in bringing up nightmares now. "Sergeant Stubb was an exemplary chaperone."

"Yes, we thought he might be."

"In fact, I'd like to take him to dinner at my club. Least I can do."

"It'll have to wait, I'm afraid."

"For what?"

"Sergeant Stubb has been returned to his unit."

"What? Surely the man earned a furlough at least."

"It was at his own request."

Wells had heard of that phenomenon, too—soldiers who felt disoriented away from the lines, or were convinced that they were letting down their comrades.

"We've run your first article through all the necessary channels," Bryce said, now slipping the edited pages across the desk, "and only some minor redactions were required."

Wells took the papers and quickly glanced over them.

"It's just what we were looking for," Bryce said, "giving a boost to our troops, while reminding the folks back home of the great sacrifice these men are making."

Wells took no issue with the edits eliminating what might have been considered military information, but wherever he saw that the officious pen of some bureaucrat had tried to alter a word or passage for some putatively artistic purpose, he took out his own pen and crossed it out, writing "stet" in the margin. Who were these people to think that they knew more about writing than he did? The gall.

When he handed it back, Bryce did him the courtesy of not checking his corrections, but simply stamped it with the seal of his office and, presumably, put it aside for dissemination to the press. Normally, of course, Wells, or his literary agent, would be responsible for that, but this was not a normal assignment. He was working for the ministry, not himself.

"And I have something else for you," Wells volunteered, reaching into his briefcase and taking out the journal that Friedrich Von Baden had given him. "It's in German, and I don't read German."

Bryce looked it over, noting the dirt and stains and, inside, the cramped handwriting. "What is it?"

"A ghoul's last testament," Wells said, and when Bryce gave him a quizzical look, added, "It was given to me by the German deserter who saved my life." And then, as Bryce listened with mounting astonishment, he elaborated on the strange concatenation of events that had landed him in the ghouls' den, deep below no man's land . . . talking to a German scientist whose research had involved equine stock. It became increasingly clear to Wells that Captain Lillyfield had relayed a much sanitized, or should he say "redacted," account of what had occurred to him.

"And you say that this Von Baden was a nobleman?" Bryce said, still studying the document.

"So he said." Wells found it typical that Bryce's first question would be about the man's social standing. An ordinary conscript turning deserter would not have surprised him nearly as much.

"And a medical man, to boot?"

"Yes, with a specialized background in zoonotic bacteriology."

"We'll have to get this translated, immediately. Should take no more than a day."

But Wells could see that some other part of his narrative had piqued Bryce's interest.

"This business about horses," Bryce said, placing the journal on his desk, his fingers drumming on its soiled cover.

"Yes?"

"You say that he told you he'd been involved in experiments with them?"

"In Berlin, and on that island in the Baltic."

Bryce sat back in his chair, his eyes toward the ceiling as he plainly pondered what next to say.

"What I'm about to tell you is still top secret. You may share it with no one. Is that understood?"

"Understood." Wells was irritated by the superfluous admonitions.

"Last night, there was an incident, at the Horse Guards Parade."

"What sort of incident?"

As Wells was told the details, he sat up in the chair. An intruder had penetrated the corrals, and then been chased into St. James's Park, where the feedlot overseer had later found a brass box, with test tubes in it. The box, which bore an inscription from the Colonial Office of Germany, had been sent on to the chemical weapons department for further analysis. In Wells's way of thinking, the incident bore all the hallmarks of what the Prussian doctor had told him about the planned sabotage of the Allies' equine stock.

"May I be kept apprised of this investigation?" Wells said.

"Under normal circumstances, and given your civilian status," Bryce hedged, "that would never be done."

"Damn my civilian status! I've just put the proof of a German plot to win the war by some awful and ingenious means right on the desk in front of you."

"I recognize that fact," Bryce said, to mollify him, "and depending on what we learn from this journal, we may need to enlist your help again. If Winston, who inducted you into all this in the first place, is willing to back me up, I see no impediment to further disclosures."

Then it was a done deal. Churchill was not only Wells's friend, but his most tireless promoter. Not to mention one of the Admiralty's most valued leaders.

For now, Wells was eager to get on with the next part of his mission, the part that he was keeping secret even from Colonel Bryce. The part he felt he owed to Friedrich Von Baden, who had proven himself not to be a ghoul—some coward lurking in Stygian gloom to scavenge the dead—but that very rare thing, a man with a moral compass . . . in a world that seemed to have lost its own.

CHAPTER THIRTY

"Oh, you're home!" Lettie said, poking her head into Rebecca's bedroom, then calling out to her younger sister, Winnie, to come quick.

Rebecca had hoped to sneak into the house and out again without anyone noticing. "Shh," she admonished Lettie, "I don't want to have to deal with Mother."

"She's out at the market," her sister said, perching on the edge of Rebecca's bed—conspicuously unused from the night before.

"But did she notice that I didn't come home last night?"

"What do you think?" Lettie replied. "She notices if an antimacassar is askew."

"You're not going to be out again tonight, are you?" Winnie said, breathless from running up the stairs. "Mother will pitch a fit."

"Let her," Rebecca said, hastily cramming a fresh blouse and skirt, and assorted other items, into the satchel on the bed. She didn't know where she would be spending that night, or the next—right back there, or at Wells's flat—but she wanted to be prepared for any eventuality.

"You were with him, weren't you?" Lettie said, and Winnie put in, "That's what Mother believes."

"She would not be mistaken," Rebecca said, tossing her hairbrush into the bag.

Both of her sisters blushed at once, and put their hands to their mouths. They were older than she was, but almost as unsophisticated as she had been . . . until the night before.

"My God," Lettie said, "does that mean that you have become—"

"His mistress?" Winnie said, completing the thought.

It was a question Rebecca had wrestled with all that day, ever since awakening in the flat in St. James's Court. Opening her eyes, she had been momentarily confused—where was her bureau? the familiar bedposts? why did she have no nightgown on?—and then Wells had rolled over to face her, and mumbled, "Morning . . . Panther."

She had done it. She had stepped into the lion's den—or jaguar's, to be more precise—and lived to tell the tale.

"Good morning," she'd replied, as if this were the most matter-of-fact way to awaken.

His hand had slid under the sheet and onto her hip, drawing her closer. He kissed her on the tip of her nose, as you would a kitten, and looked deep into her eyes.

"Did you sleep well?"

"The sleep," she said, "of the unjust."

He smiled. "But are you happy?"

She frowned, thinking it over. Happiness wasn't exactly what she felt, and she was not one to put the wrong word to something. "Triumphant."

"What," he said, rearing back, "have you conquered me?"

"That was the easy part. I conquered myself. My own fears. I did what I wanted to, despite any social brickbats that might come flying my way."

"None have to," he replied, soberly, "if we exercise discretion."

"Discretion has never been your long suit, H. G."

He mulled that over. "Neither has it been yours."

"Correct. It appears we're doomed."

"In which case," he said, slipping his arm around her and pulling her so close that her breasts rubbed against his chest, "we might as well make the most of it!"

He pressed his lips to hers, his bristly mustache scratching her cheek, and she felt a rush of blood pounding through all her veins, and her hips, almost as if they had a will of their own, grinding against his groin. It was somehow even more powerful than it had been the night before; then, she had been consumed with the novelty, the surprise, even the shock of a carnal embrace, and to some small extent had remained an observer, as writers are wont to do. But this time there was none of that. This time, she entered into the moment fully and physically.

"What was . . . *it* . . . like?" Winnie asked, and there was no question what she was referring to.

"Is it as transcendent as the romantic novels would have us believe?" Lettie said.

Rebecca did not know what to say. She hardly wanted to serve as some corrupting influence on her sisters—both of whom were pursuing careers of their own, and could by no means be considered delicate hothouse flowers—but she also didn't want to hew to the conventional lines and downplay the enormity of the experience. Men, it was generally accepted, were consumed with desire and a commensurate enjoyment of sex, but women were assumed to be not much more than willing vessels, able to enhance their partners' pleasure and, if sufficiently free and modern, capable of experiencing some pale simulacrum of those same sensations that the men felt. Younger writers like D. H. Lawrence were challenging that assumption (and finding their work dismissed because of it), but even H. G., in his recent novels of domestic mores, had given it a go. It was still with some embarrassment that she remembered the review in which she had described him as an old maid whose books were clotted with a sex obsession like cold white sauce. In bed, he was anything but temperate or old-fashioned, and though she had no one to compare him to, he was as energetic—and creative!—as any lover she could imagine.

"Well?" Lettie pressed. "Have you been transformed?"

"Yes," she said, "I've become a jungle cat," and her sisters laughed, not realizing that what they'd just heard was a confession and not a jest.

The sound of the front door opening put a stop to the conversation, and their mother's voice called up the stairs, "Come and help me with these packages!"

"Right down," Winnie called, then whispered, "Shall we cover for you?"

"No, best to face the music," Rebecca replied, and with her satchel in hand, she followed her sisters down the stairs. Mrs. Fairfield was still in the foyer, with several bags from the grocer. When she saw Rebecca, standing halfway down the flight, her eyes touched on the satchel, then went back to Rebecca's defiant face.

"I don't need to ask where you've been, do I?"

"Probably not."

"Or where you are going?"

Rebecca didn't answer. Why prolong this?

"If you think you can lead this life, and use this house only when you find it a convenient refuge, you are mistaken. This is my house, and I make the rules."

"Fair enough," Rebecca replied. "I'll take a flat in the city."

"His flat?"

"My own."

"With what, may I ask?"

"I work, and I've put some money by." In truth, she hadn't put much money by, and the practical implications of what she was doing were just sinking in. Still, she couldn't back down now.

"Once a woman has gone down that path—"

Rebecca interrupted her to say, "What path is that?"

"You know perfectly well what path I mean, and once a woman has chosen to go down it, it can be very difficult to return."

Rebecca saw no point in continuing the back-and-forth. Elbowing her way past her silent sisters, she went to the door and threw it open in the kind of theatrical gesture she had been taught, and usually failed to carry off, at the Royal Academy. This time, she muffed it by banging the bulging bag against the doorframe, which put her off-balance. She stumbled to the front steps before recovering. When she heard the door slam shut behind her—over her sisters' protests—she found herself wondering what in fact she had just done. Wells had invited her to spend the night with him again, and she had come back simply to pack some overnight supplies. She'd anticipated a possible skirmish with her mother, but not an all-out war—much less one that she had apparently lost.

Without intending to, she had lived up to her adopted stage name, the reckless character from the Ibsen play. That character would never look back, and so she didn't, either. Marching off down the street, she held her head high, despite the misgivings in her heart.

CHAPTER
THIRTY-ONE

Wells had always had a soft spot for Guy's Hospital, as it had been the place where John Keats, a hundred years before, had completed his medical training with a dressership, or appointment as a surgeon's assistant. Of course, what the young poet had experienced here, holding down writhing patients as doctors amputated limbs without the benefit of anesthesia, or in the dissecting rooms, where students played games poking maggots out of their hiding places in the corpses salvaged from the city prisons, had been enough to turn him away from the profession entirely—to the lasting benefit of literature. But Keats embodied, like Wells, a great curiosity about the physical world at the same time that he evinced an overwhelming literary compulsion. He wanted desperately to understand the basic underpinnings of life as much as he wanted to find a way to transcend them and celebrate, in lyrical and enduring words, the higher things. Wells sometimes wondered if his own work would hold up for so long and so well.

The entranceway was much as it had been since 1721, when Thomas Guy had founded the hospital with a fortune he made in the South Sea Bubble. Passing between the two stone columns that flanked the iron gates, Wells entered the wide forecourt, with Boland House on his left and the chapel on the right. He knew his way about a bit, and soon found his way to the Communicable Diseases Ward, where he stopped a young medical student, his face still spotty, and asked where he might find a Miss Emma Chasubel.

"That's her, over there," he said, pointing to a bosomy woman shaking a thermometer at the foot of a patient's bed. Her dark hair was piled under a nurse's cap so crisp and white and majestic it resembled a nun's wimple. This ward, unlike many others, featured better ventilation than usual—the long windows had been kept slightly open, despite the cold drizzle starting outside—and the beds were not only more separated, but featured netting or screens between each one and its neighbors. When she had finished with the patient, she went to a sink and table in the center of the room, washed her hands, and dried them on a fresh towel. Only then did she notice Wells standing in his overcoat, letter in hand.

"Were you waiting for me, sir?" she asked, and when Wells acknowledged that he had been, she came to him, not accepting his extended hand, but nodding politely. When he introduced himself, she appeared taken aback. "Are you sure it's me you were looking for, Mr. Wells, and not one of the physicians?"

"Not unless it's their name on this envelope," he said. "Is there someplace we can talk?"

"Of course," she said, ushering him into a private alcove just off the ward, where there were two hard-backed chairs and a little round table with a single green bud in a vase. Someone had left a book on one of the seats. Wells guessed that this was where the night nurses sat to keep watch over the patients in their charge.

He put the book on the table—it turned out to be *Sons and Lovers*, by that upstart D. H. Lawrence—and sat down opposite Miss Chasubel, who still seemed flustered at being in the company of such a well-known person. To make her more comfortable, he joked that he would have to send some of his own books over to complement their library.

"Oh, we would be so honored. The patients would love it!" She was a strong woman, he could see that, with a wide-open face and kind eyes as big as saucers.

Which made his task only that much harder. After a few more moments of pleasantries, Wells placed the letter squarely on the table and said, "I have brought this for you all the way from the Front."

"You have?" She picked it up, saw that it was indeed addressed to her, and from the expression on her face, immediately recognized the handwriting. At first she appeared thrilled—but then, fearing what the letter might contain, troubled.

Lowering her voice, though there was no one near enough to hear her, she said, "Is it from Friedrich, then?"

"Yes."

"Is he all right?"

Wells dropped his gaze, let a pause fall, and said, "I so regret having to tell you this, but no. He is not. A short time ago, he was killed in action."

She sat as still as a stone.

"But only after saving my life."

"He saved *your* life?" she murmured.

"It would be difficult to explain, but before he died, his one wish was that I find you and give you this letter."

The letter remained unopened. "Though I hesitate to impinge on your privacy," Wells continued, "I think it's best if you read it now, because I will need to talk to you afterward. I can step away if you like."

She shook her head to indicate he could stay where he was, and with trembling fingers, she unsealed the envelope and took out two or three small pages, pale blue and closely written. Wells did not want to study her as she read, so he picked up the Lawrence book and pretended to peruse the opening pages. But after a minute or so he detected that same strange scent that he had come to associate with his attacks. It was the harbinger of the pain that now blossomed between his eyes, like a match that had just been struck. His fingers squeezed the bridge of his nose, and when he lifted his eyes from the book, his vision was blurred.

The ward, gloomy to begin with, had become even darker from the rainstorm outside. A patient moaned in his bed, another coughed like a dog barking. And at the end of the ward, behind a thin muslin netting, Wells saw a man sit up on the bed. He moved stiffly, poor chap, but then, after consolidating that gain, he drew the curtain to one side and stood up. Why he wasn't wearing pajamas, or a hospital gown, was strange enough, but the fact that he was wearing a uniform—a military uniform—came as an even greater surprise.

Wells debated whether or not he should call the man to Miss Chasubel's attention, but she was so intent upon the letter, tears rolling down her cheeks as she turned the pages, that he thought it better to wait and see what happened next. It wasn't as if the fellow was about to run off—his legs were wobbly, and he could barely navigate his passage between the two rows of iron bedsteads that lined the room. But as he grew closer, Wells became even more astonished and perplexed.

The uniform was gray. Prussian gray.

He could wait no longer. "I'm sorry to interrupt you, Nurse Chasubel, but one of your patients has—"

The breath caught in his throat as the man staggered closer still. He doubted that Miss Chasubel had heard a word he'd just said.

The face of the man was as deadly a green as that of any soldier felled by gas in the fields. But this man, Wells knew, had not died in the fields; he had died in the filthy, labyrinthine tunnels beneath no man's land. And no doubt he lay there still, unwanted and unmourned by anyone other than the woman now grieving, her breast heaving mightily, in the chair at this very table.

A hallucination, Wells thought, that's all it was. Like the dead soldier in the mirror at his flat.

The man was now looming right behind the nurse's chair, and as she dropped the hand holding the tear-stained pages to her lap, he laid a consoling hand upon the shoulder strap of her white smock.

Although she did not openly acknowledge the touch in any way— how could she, this was nothing but a ghost, and one that only he could see!—she did, for whatever reason, raise a hand of her own to the exact spot, as if unawares, and hold it there in silent communion. Von Baden's eyes, filled with grief and inexpressible longing, rested on his beloved, before lifting to take in Wells, flattened against the back of his own chair.

"*Danke schön*," he said, though again, only Wells seemed to be aware that he had spoken at all.

Miss Chasubel had fished a crumpled handkerchief from the pocket of her smock and was using it to dab her tears. "I know he was German," she said, "but he was a good man."

Wells nodded in agreement.

"A good man," she repeated, reading again whatever fond farewell appeared at the bottom of the last page. "We did love each other," she said, as if challenging him, or anyone, to deny it.

"And that is why," Wells said, as much for her benefit as that of the silent, sad apparition behind her, "he sent me here."

Von Baden nodded, then bent to kiss the top of her nurse's cap.

To Wells, it seemed a pity, and a puzzle, that she could not behold him, too—though if that would have been a solace to her, he could not know.

CHAPTER
THIRTY-TWO

Graf hurled his wet umbrella into the foyer, yanked off his coat, and stormed back down the stairs to his laboratory.

"You could watch where you throw that," Circe complained, pushing the door shut against the wind and pulling off her own damp coat. "Other people live here, too."

Oh, how Graf wished he could remedy that! He was only really happy when he was surrounded by his petri dishes and bacterial cultures, his flasks and beakers and vials. Today, however, he had had to make an exception. He had not only had to leave the confines of Crowley's townhouse, but take this brainless girl along with him for camouflage. Ever since his narrow escape from the Horse Guards Parade, he'd been haunted by the thought of his brass sample case, left behind among the trees. Had it been found, and worse yet, been turned over to the authorities? It did not bear his name, but the engraving did indicate that it was from the Colonial Office of Germany. He had needed to go back and see if it could possibly be retrieved, and a man strolling in the park with a pretty young woman would be far less noticeable, he thought, than a single man rooting through the brush.

When they'd set out, the weather had been clear, but by the time they crossed Birdcage Walk and entered into the spacious grounds of St. James's Park, it was already becoming overcast. Casually twirling his furled umbrella, with Circe hanging on his arm, he had led her onto the Blue Bridge that spanned the ornamental lake, and waited there, looking around, just to make sure that no one was following him. He suspected everyone. From this central vantage point, he could see Buckingham Palace to the west and to the east the tower of Big Ben and the perimeter of the parade grounds. Several people on the bridge were feeding the ducks and the famous pelicans, whose progenitors had been a gift from the Russian ambassador in 1664.

Sometimes, at times just like this, he had to remind himself that these people were the enemy, that his mission was to help defeat them and bring their nation to its knees. He had made a fine start so far by disrupting their supply of horses and pack animals, and was already concocting a fresh batch of deadly bacteria to administer on an even wider scale. But killing these dumb creatures was only a rough experiment for the grander scheme that he had hatched—a scheme that would devastate the human populace. Once that was done, and the plague and its terror had been fully unleashed upon this proud capital, he'd have done his part—*more* than his part—for the fatherland. He would one day be hailed as a hero to his country, his name enshrined not only as an equal to the great scientist Robert Koch, but also to the kaiser and Generals Ludendorff and Von Hindenburg. Schoolchildren would all learn his name, and in Berlin's Tiergarten—a more beautiful park than this one could ever be—among the statues of Goethe and Lessing and Queen Louise, there would be a monument to him. In idle hours, he had sketched out ideas for what it might look like.

"It's getting cold just standing here," Circe had complained. She was wearing a scarlet coat that he had wished she hadn't—it was too conspicuous—but there was no dissuading her. "Can't we keep moving?"

He escorted her off the bridge, her arm crooked in his. Despite the chill, she was enjoying this. He could tell. As much as he dreaded leaving the house on Chancery Lane, she relished it. But then, he didn't spend his time there as a sex slave to a British pervert.

In 1912, Crowley had joined the *Ordo Templi Orientis*, a mystical order founded by the German occultist Theodor Reuss, and risen quickly through their ranks. In a ceremony in Berlin, he had dubbed himself "Baphomet" and been declared "the Supreme Rex and Sovereign Grand Master General of Ireland, Iona, and all the Britons," head of the British branch of the OTO. But what really attracted him to the order, Graf knew, was its emphasis on "sex magick," the notion that by harnessing sexual energy—the orgasm, specifically—one could transcend the ordinary world and bring whatever one visualized to reality. Crowley had even broken new ground by working various perverted acts into the ritual initiations of those members of the group who had been elevated to the Eleventh Degree.

As a scientist, Graf had to laugh at such errant nonsense, but as the German intelligence services knew, such a man—who remained anathema to their British counterparts—could be useful, especially as his natural sympathies lay in their own direction, anyway.

When Graf had come back to London, he had first found lodgings in the old German quarter of the city, but when those had proven unfeasible, and he had had to look for a place to set up shop anew, Crowley's place had immediately sprung to mind. There was no one in the city who was at once so gullible and so compromised, so open to the most extravagant claims (like alchemy), and so eager to do anything to increase his own notoriety. Graf pretended to be an acolyte—Crowley was never hard to convince of that—and had readily been accepted into the fold. But when he had moved some of Crowley's rudimentary torture equipment out of the cellar to make room for his laboratory, Crowley had complained.

"My dungeon is dear to me," he'd said, "and necessary for certain rituals of initiation."

"But think of the dungeons you can construct once I have refined my alchemical experiments, turning mere dross into gold," Graf had countered. "You will be as rich as Croesus, and you'll be able to build an underground kingdom worthy of Pluto and Persephone."

The very thought of that—untold riches and an unlimited supply of maidens to ravish, like the lord of the underworld himself—was enough to overcome Crowley's objections. The iron chains and leather straps had been relocated to an attic space, and Graf had moved not only his lab equipment but himself into the subterranean chambers. In an alcove, close to the furnace, he had set up a bedstead and rudimentary privy of his own. This way he could watch over his lethal cultures, brewing in their flasks and dishes, like a hen watching over her eggs, by night and day.

"Oh listen, there's music!" Circe said, drawing him on in the direction of the St. James's Park bandstand. By the time they got there, a small crowd had gathered to hear half a dozen Scotsmen in full ceremonial garb, playing their bagpipes and marching back and forth across the shallow stage.

Surveying the audience, Graf remembered coming here on St. George's Day, a year earlier, to hear an orchestral concert to celebrate the Britons' patron saint; it had begun to rain, as it threatened to do even now, and he had gone home, shivering and weak, to the top-floor flat he had inhabited at that time, a dismal suite of rooms that no one else had wanted, due to the unsavory reputation of the penny arcade just below it. In the morning, he had been so sick, running a high fever, that, much as he had wanted to avoid it, he had had no choice but to check himself into Guy's Hospital under his assumed name of Eulenspiegel. He knew two things: Guy's had a ward that specialized in communicable diseases, and what he was suffering from was an accidental exposure to one of his own research elements.

For the next week, he had been in and out of delirium, always fearful of what he might have said while unaware, but well attended by the doctors and nursing staff. It was a pity that they, like the rest of the city's population, would now have to suffer so at his hands. But that was war, which had been fermenting, like his bacteria, for some time before the recent outbreak. Graf prided himself at being among the first to see it coming.

After a few minutes, he got restless—he hadn't come to the park to listen to the screeching of bagpipes—and he dragged Circe off toward the parade grounds. The closer they got, the stronger was the aroma of the horses, still crowded into their makeshift pens and awaiting transport. But Graf was trying to calibrate the exact spot where he had run from the sentries, where the bullet had scathed the tree, where the brass box had fallen. He remembered falling over the bench, but there were several located close to the pathway.

When he diverted Circe off the pavement and onto the grass, she said, "Where are we going? My boots are going to get all muddy."

He didn't answer—he was focused too closely on his surroundings. Did he recognize anything? Was he in the right location? And most important of all, was there anyone else lurking about, some soldier or Scotland Yard plainclothesman hoping to catch the perpetrator returning to the scene of the crime? After a few minutes, with Circe complaining the whole time, he spotted the tree stump where he had laid his paraphernalia, and from that was able to judge roughly where he might have reentered the park grounds in his flight.

"Look at all the horses," Circe said in amazement, surveying the maze of pens and corrals.

Graf glanced across the wide dirt road, too, wondering how many of them might have already begun to manifest symptoms, and spread the contagion.

"Why are there so many? Ooh, I wish I had an apple or a lump of sugar to give them."

That was a good idea, Graf thought. In the future, he should find a way to stabilize the germs and simply infuse lumps of sugar with lethal doses.

An armed sentry was posted twenty yards down the fence, and lest they be spotted, Graf pulled Circe back into the shelter of the park.

Turning, he passed a bench—was it the one he had tripped over?—and began scouring the tree trunks for a splintered patch. He must have studied dozens before he suddenly noted a fresh white scar on an old oak. That must be it! His eyes jumped to the ground, praying that he might see a glimmer of the case in the underbrush, but he caught a glimpse instead of a man in a long coat, a bowler hat pulled low on his forehead, casually lighting a cigarette. Instantly, his nerves were on alert, and as he had planned in advance, he pulled Circe into a tight embrace and pressed her up against the damaged tree.

"What do you think you're—"

But he shut her up by pressing his lips against hers, slipping a hand between the buttons of her scarlet coat and fondling a breast.

Pushing him off, she said, "You could at least ask."

"I'm asking," he said, renewing his effort, and to his own surprise, she offered no further resistance. Crowley knew how to pick them.

He pretended absorption until he heard the man cough, and approach holding an open badge in his hand.

"What are you two doing there?"

Circe pulled back and laughed. "Guess it should be pretty plain, constable." She wasn't cowed in the least.

"Yes, it is," he said, sternly, "and I'm not a constable."

"Then what's that?" Circe countered, nodding at the badge.

"It's what tells you two to move along. This is a public park, and no place for shameless display."

Graf had lowered his head, as if mortified, and slipped his hands into the pockets of his coat. At the bottom of the right-hand one, he felt the hole through which he had lost countless coins and once a souvenir cigarette lighter.

"Come along now, love," he mumbled to Circe, and then to the officer—whose badge bore an army emblem of some kind—"Quite right, you are. We'll be on our way." A drop of rain fell on his spectacles, and then another.

"You do that," the man said, "and behave properly from now on."

"Yes, of course."

But Circe, defiant to the end, threw a haughty glance at the officer. Graf was afraid she was about to make the situation worse. He slipped his arm through hers, and firmly drew her back toward the pathway. Under his breath he muttered, "Keep your mouth shut."

"Why should I? All my life blokes have been trying to tell me what to do. The Master says to ignore them, and to do what thou wilt."

Good Christ, she had swallowed that Whole of the Law business—hook, line, and sinker.

People on the gravel pathway were unfurling their umbrellas, turning up the collars of their coats, and moving briskly for the park exits. Graf, frustrated in his mission, pulled Circe, now moaning about the mud on the boots that had been clean just that morning, toward the street, in hopes of finding a cab.

"Aren't you at least going to take me out for tea and sandwiches?" Circe said. "Any gent, who'd taken the liberties you just did, wouldn't think twice about that."

"I'm not a gent."

"I can see that now."

They had spoken barely a word in the horse-drawn cab ride back to Chancery Lane. Circe had flapped the tails of her coat, hoping to shake off the rain—"The Master gave me this coat, and I won't have it ruined"—while Graf had fretted over the fate of his brass case and how it might affect the success of his grand plan; he had dubbed it "Operation Ottershaw," after the observatory from which the Martian invasion was first spotted in that novel by H. G. Wells. In the story, the humans had seen the cataclysm coming—the gaseous plumes and blaze of light on the alien planet's surface as their hostile rockets were launched—but they had not understood it until it was too late.

By the time the people of Earth had grasped the scope and scale of the danger, the enemy, like Graf, had landed on their very shores and the war of the worlds had begun. What better metaphor, and in Britain's own canon, could he have found?

CHAPTER
THIRTY-THREE

"Mr. Wells!" the doctor's wife exclaimed upon opening her front door. "To what do we owe the honor?"

Her eyes flicked to the suitcase in his hand, puzzled.

"I thought I'd like a brief consultation with your husband, if he's at home."

"Of course he's home—these are his office hours. Come in."

Wells came in, dropping his bag in the vestibule. He was glad to be relieved of its weight.

"You've been away," Maude observed. "In London?"

"Yes, and elsewhere," Wells replied. "Jane wrote to tell me she'd been appointed your deputy."

"Yes, that's true."

The doctor, hearing the commotion, came out of his office, shook Wells's hand vigorously, and escorted him to the inner sanctum. Maude, Wells could guess, was terribly frustrated by the closed door.

Almost as soon as they were alone, the doctor mentioned his recent name change, "for reasons I need hardly explain."

Wells had seen it happen all over the country. Theirs was a time, he reflected, when identities had become muddled, friendships strained, alliances shattered. There was a great sorting out going on in the world.

"But you've not been about for a while," Grover said. "You were in the very teeth of it, weren't you?"

"How would you know that?"

"Jane might have mentioned something."

Odd, he thought, that she would have confided in the doctor. "I've written some dispatches," he admitted, "the first of which should appear in tomorrow's papers."

"I'm pleased to see that you appear to have escaped unscathed."

At that, Wells hesitated. "Not entirely true. It's why I've come straight here, instead of home. I don't want Jane to know."

"Know what?"

How to start? All the way up on the train, he'd wondered how much he could, or should, share, without violating the warnings from Colonel Bryce: *Do not breathe a word about your time in the under-ground den of ghouls. It would be very detrimental to both the military and the national morale.* "Let me just say, I witnessed horrors I could not have imagined."

"For someone of your imaginative powers that is a surprising statement."

"And yet it still does not do justice to the reality."

Dr. Grover sat silently, waiting for the patient to continue.

"Some of those horrors seem to have followed me home."

"How so?"

He described the vision of Corporal Norridge in the bathroom mirror, and then the even more prolonged visitation of a ghost—his German nationality skirted altogether—in the ward at Guy's Hospital. "The apparition even seemed to hold my gaze, as firmly as you are holding it now."

"These soldiers you see—they are all dead?"

Wells nodded.

"And when you perceive them, do you experience other physical symptoms?"

"Yes, I do," and he went on to retail the pain between his eyes, the blurred vision, the olfactory disturbances. "I would like you to examine my eyes, my ears, and anything else you deem appropriate, and then prescribe for me something to calm my nerves—these episodes must be nervous in origin—and help me sleep. I can't go to bed without starting awake, often several times, in the dead of night."

Dr. Grover asked him to remove his coat and shirt, then listened to his heart and lungs, tested his vision and auditory capacities, even his reflexes—earning a quick kick in response—before going to his cabinet, where he withdrew a green glass bottle labeled "Veronal." Shaking a handful of cachets, small white capsules, into a paper packet, he said, "These should help, but no more than one at a time. And for heaven's sake, don't wash them down with liquor."

"What are they? Chloral hydrate?"

"No, they're a barbital. A dozen grains' strength. German synthesis—you can't get them anymore." The doctor paused. "They will address the sleeplessness, and some of the physical manifestations, but as you know, perturbations of the mind are beyond the ken of us country physicians. Much less the ones as old as I am."

Wells tucked the packet into his shirt pocket.

"Jane will be very glad to have you back," the doctor volunteered, before adding, in a curious tone, "She does know you are coming, right?"

"Yes, of course—I sent her a telegram."

Grover nodded, stroking his chin. "Good. Then I'm sure she will have everything well in hand by the time you arrive."

"She always does," Wells replied, putting on his coat and hat.

On the drive over, sitting in the back seat of Slattery's livery car, Wells wondered just what it was that Grover thought Jane had to have so well in hand before he got home. On the front seat of the car, between the gearshift and a shotgun, a pair of dead grouse lay.

"Good hunting on these grounds," Slattery observed, "especially out by the wreckage of the zeppelin."

Though Wells would never be able to forget the sight of Slattery plunging the pitchfork into the German gunner, he now had a veritable catalog of other atrocities in which to include it.

Clambering out of the back seat with his suitcase, he was embraced by Jane, who held him tight all the way to the front door of the house, which stood open.

After all the hardships he had endured, it was good to be home, better than he could ever have imagined. The fire in the hearth, the gleaming andirons, the rich Oriental rugs on the floor, the crystal decanters on the bar cart. His loyal and adoring wife. Long ago, he had learned the trick of compartmentalizing his love life, accepting his passades for what they were, while acknowledging that his marriage was the bedrock on which the whole edifice of his life rested.

So why was this Rebecca never far from his thoughts? It wasn't customary.

Jane had prepared a lovely dinner, and they ate by candlelight, enjoying some of his best port afterward. Too much, given the fragile state of his constitution just now. And whether it was his own distraction that was affecting Jane, or there was something on her own mind that wanted airing, he couldn't say, but the conversation between them, which had always flowed as smoothly as a mountain stream, repeatedly stopped and started. She listed the foreign editions that had arrived in his absence—the war had proved a boon to his sales, especially his more apocalyptic titles such as *The Time Machine* and *The War of the Worlds*—discussed the preparation of the pages he had left to be typed, and chuckled at her appointment as deputy of the local watch. But all the while, he felt like there was something being left unsaid, something skimming along beneath the surface like a great gray shark.

Once or twice, he felt she was on the verge of divulging whatever it might be, but each time she retreated. In the candlelight, he noticed more than a few strands of her hair had gone silver.

He had his own reticence to deal with, too. Jane had of course inquired, several times, about his exploits at the Front, but it was not something he wanted to revisit. "Whatever I can share, I will share in the newspapers," he said, and, intuiting his discomfort, she dropped the subject. It was only when the grandfather clock on the landing struck ten, and he felt his entire body sagging with exhaustion, that he swallowed the last of his port and suggested they go upstairs to retire for the night. At her bedroom door, at the opposite end of the hall from his own, he kissed her tenderly, and she folded herself into his arms.

"You cannot imagine how hard these nights have been," she said, her voice muffled against his shirt. "I've been so worried."

"Worry no more. All's well that ends well."

She turned her face up to his, begging another kiss, which he bestowed. But she wanted more than a kiss, and that he could not give. Not just then. Between his fatigue and the nagging thoughts of Rebecca, he wanted only solitude, and slumber. The packet of Veronal pills crinkled in his pocket against Jane's cheek. "Good night, my dear. Thank you for keeping the home fires burning."

He turned down the hall, embarrassed by how trite his words had been, and waiting to hear Jane's door close behind her, but it didn't—not until he had gone into his own bedroom—where he could barely make it to the pitcher on the bureau; there, he poured himself a glass of cold water and swallowed one of the pills. Tonight he meant to sleep soundly, in the safety and security of his own bed, untroubled by those sporadic bouts of wakefulness, not to mention the nightmares or visitations. Pulling his shirttails loose, he fell sideways onto the bed, feeling distinctly remorseful. For all his talk of free love, all his advanced and modern thinking, he was not immune to sorrow at the hurt he knew his views inflicted on others—most notably his wife, a woman he cherished and respected in every way, but to whom he could no more remain exclusively bound than he could stick to a lifelong diet of bread and water. He just wasn't made like other men. (Or was he?)

Before he could even take off the rest of his clothes, he fell into a stupor, a half-conscious state in which he could scarcely move a muscle. His legs hung over the side of the bed, his arms spread wide. How long he lay like that he couldn't know, but to be in his own bed, safe and secure, on a night when the wind howled at the windows, was a blessing in itself. His dreams were tangled, all in a swirl, bringing together everything from an ashen Von Baden to the nubile Rebecca, and he was somehow asleep and aware at the same time, watching the pictures pass through his mind in an endless cavalcade.

At some point he became aware of an ache in his back, no doubt the result of his posture on the bed, and sat up, his head swimming. The room was dark, but it no longer seemed like his bedroom—it was just another dugout, another funk hole. And there was a noise upstairs, under the dormers. His thoughts were thick as mud and muddled as a stew. But the sound came again—a creak and a thump—and he wasn't sure if it was rats in the attic, or sappers working at a tunnel. Regardless, he needed to investigate, that much he knew, and stumbling to his feet—why was the ground tilted so under his feet?—he rummaged around in the bottom of his suitcase and retrieved the Webley revolver that the colonel had issued, and allowed him to keep.

The wind battered the windows, and the curtains stirred, but he fumbled for the door handle and went out into the hall. The grandfather clock ticked on the landing, and he wondered if it wasn't the ticking of a bomb. He padded in his stocking feet toward the door to the attic, and opened it; to his surprise, there was a faint glow coming from the top. The third floor was not electrified. As stealthily as his dizziness would allow him, he crept up the stairs, the light growing brighter as he went. Close to the top, he paused and poked his head just above the level of the floor.

An oil lamp was burning, a bed had been made up, and a pair of his own pajamas came into view. *What was this?*

He rose up another step, his finger on the trigger of the gun, and now he saw the intruder—a young man with blond hair, limping about in his stocking feet. Wells felt a sudden surge of outrage. Waving the revolver, he tried to charge into the room. But he tripped on the top step, the gun going off and the bullet shattering a mirror above the dresser.

"*Herr* Wells!" the man shouted, backing away with his palms raised.

But Wells knew the enemy when he saw—and *heard*—it. *Herr* Wells, indeed!

"Who are you?" Wells bellowed, trying to level the gun. "What are you doing here?"

"*Ich bin Kurt!* I am Kurt!"

None of this made any sense.

"Lie down!" Wells ordered, unable to think of what else he could do. "On the floor!"

But the man—boy?—approached him instead, saying something, then reaching for the gun that was wavering in Wells's hand. Wells didn't want to shoot him in cold blood, but he was not about to surrender his weapon, either. "Stop where you are!" he shouted, backing up and colliding with the open drawer of an old dresser. The room was dark and starting to spin, and as Wells went down, the gun went off again, the bullet demolishing the window.

The boy was on him in an instant, wrestling for the gun, and very nearly had it when Wells heard Jane crying, "Stop it! Both of you! H. G., stop it!" and in her nightgown prying the boy away. "Stop it!"

The boy relaxed his hold, and fell back, grimacing and clutching one ankle. Wells could hardly breathe, and rolled to one side, his chest heaving. Jane crouched down beside him, saying, "Are you all right?" over and over again, and stroking his arm.

Wells, coughing, nodded his head.

Jane stayed where she was, calming him and gently removing the pistol from his grip, while the boy scooted on his bottom toward the bed.

The wind whistled through the splintered window frame and broken glass.

Wells was so confused, he wasn't sure what to make of any of this. What had just happened? Where was he? He closed his eyes, spent, and the last thing he remembered was Jane's hand rubbing his arm and her voice as she repeated, "Tomorrow I'll explain everything, H. G., tomorrow, I promise, I'll explain . . ."

CHAPTER
THIRTY-FOUR

Waking up, alone, in Wells's flat, Rebecca felt utterly disoriented.

After her dramatic exit from her family's house, she had wondered where to go. She had put a bit of money aside, but for a single woman seeking inexpensive but furnished accommodations in overcrowded London, not to mention on an immediate basis, it would not be easy. Wells had taken pity on her, and said that as he was traveling up to Easton Glebe for a few days, she was welcome to stay in his flat until he returned. Rebecca had jumped at the offer.

The morning papers were left at the door, and she was thrilled to see a dispatch—billed as the first in a series—from H. G. on the front page of the *Times*. It carried an account of his journey from the city to the battlefield, and what he had observed, accompanied by one stolid sergeant, in transit—the crowded trains, the night crossing to Le Havre, the camaraderie of the troops, the moments of deep and silent introspection that every soldier underwent, wondering when, and if, he would ever return to England. It stopped short at his arrival at the trenches and his first grim view of the legendary no man's land. "Who could doubt that the hearts of St. George or his angels would not be inspired to action by such a desolate sight?" It was a neat trick, she observed, to end in such a way, neither endorsing the story that Arthur Machen had himself disavowed, nor dismissing it out of hand.

It was only when she'd finished the piece, and resolved to dash off a few lines of congratulation to Wells, that she noticed another story, less prominently displayed, but billed as an exclusive and arresting nonetheless. Apparently, there had been an incident at the Horse Guards Parade, in which a saboteur had attempted to enter the pens and do harm to the animals. Anyone with information about the possible perpetrator was advised to contact the newspaper, which would then facilitate communication with the proper authorities.

The first thing that popped into her mind was her visit to the Crowley townhouse, and the strange veterinarian—who'd studied in Germany yet—leaning up against the blazing hearth. Could there be a connection? From what she already knew of that bunch, it was not something she would put past them. But before she went to any other publication, her reportorial instincts kicked in. If there was something to this, then she should be the one to uncover it and even perhaps trumpet it to the world in the pages of the *Freewoman* magazine.

She had just thrown on her clothes, resolved to go to the Horse Guards Parade and see what she could find out for herself, when there was a knock on the door that brought her up short. She was not exactly keen on being discovered there. Quietly peering through the peephole, she saw, turned to one side, a man in a black coat, long gray hair over the back of his collar and a newspaper tucked under his arm. When he turned around to knock again, she saw that it was, of all people, Arthur Machen.

Opening the door, she could see the confusion on his face, and she quickly explained that her friend Mr. Wells was allowing her to stay in his flat while he was out of town. Whether Machen bought the entire story was uncertain, but he recovered neatly and brandishing the paper said that he had been in the neighborhood and dropped by to congratulate Wells on the piece.

"A capital job, as always. His writing has an enviable vigor to it."

Rebecca did not disagree. There was no one better than Wells at capturing a scene with just a few strokes, and moving the narrative forward. "I was just going out," she explained, retrieving her coat and gloves.

"Where to?"

She hesitated. "Did you read the item about the sabotage at the Horse Guards Parade?"

"I did. The Germans are behaving like bloody swine. It's one thing to kill a man—that's war—but to deliberately endanger or injure animals is beyond the pale."

It was a common sentiment among Britons, unless the animal happened to be a dachshund or German shepherd. "I'm going to go there and see what I can find out for myself."

"They'll never let you get near."

"I have my press card."

He scoffed. "And I have mine. But let me accompany you. A man stands a much better chance than you do."

She couldn't disagree with that, either. Despite her publication credits, she was often dismissed out of hand; it was just the sort of discrimination that the *Freewoman* magazine was dedicated to ending.

It was a cold, clear day outside, and apart from the bomb craters in the streets here and there, or the demolished storefronts, London looked itself, the Houses of Parliament standing tall along the Thames, Big Ben proclaiming the hour, the noble dome of St. Paul's Cathedral, the highest point in the city, gleaming in the wan winter sunlight. But as Machen and Rebecca disembarked from their cab, they could not help but note the cordon of policemen standing every thirty paces, arms folded behind their backs, truncheons at the ready, all along the fence erected around the perimeter of the vast parade grounds. The earthy aroma of the horses and mules, coupled with the sound of their neighing and snorting, filled the air.

"Let me take the lead," Machen said, and as much as she resented it, Rebecca held back.

Stepping forward, he said, "Good morning, officer," to the police captain guarding the main gate, and engaged in some kind of male banter that Rebecca could not quite hear. She saw Machen proffer his press credential, and even heard the words "golden bowmen" and "Agincourt" fall from his lips. The captain seemed duly impressed, and instructed the two constables behind him to open the main gates. It was then that Machen turned and gestured for Rebecca to join him. "My secretary," he explained, and with her head down—chiefly so that they wouldn't see the annoyance on her face—she followed close behind him, as the gates swung closed again.

There was a narrow aisle down the center of the grounds, like the nave in a church, with perpendicular paths cutting right and left between the various pens and fences. Rebecca had never seen, indeed could never have imagined, so many horses in one place, their long heads hanging over the railings, their tails switching and twitching, their big dark eyes watching them warily as they passed. Dozens of boys, fifteen or sixteen years old, were pouring buckets of water or bags of oats into long wooden troughs; others were mucking out the grounds, filling wheelbarrows with clumps of wet manure and straw. Rebecca hadn't gone more than ten paces before her shoes were caked with mud and worse.

"This was once the tournament grounds for Henry the Eighth," Machen, a renowned student of history, said over his shoulder. "The jousts were held here."

But Rebecca was in no mood to cast her mind back in time. She was determined to focus entirely on this moment, on the sights and sounds and sensations that struck her. Where, exactly, had the saboteur struck? And what had been his plan? The *Times* had been deliberately opaque on those scores, and on one other—had he succeeded in whatever nefarious scheme he had hatched? Who, she wondered, could she interview?

As they approached the stable entrances, part of the extensive stretch of venerable structures that encompassed the northern end of the grounds, the Old Admiralty and Citadel, she saw that the constables had given way to soldiers, with set faces and rifles slung over their shoulders. Although she was following close on Machen's heels, she still drew puzzled, and even hostile, glares from the guards, and once inside the cavernous interior, which echoed with the jangle of bridles, the squeaking of leather saddles, and the cries of hostlers and members of the Household Cavalry in their distinctive red tunics, she wasn't sure which way to turn.

"The Duke of Wellington's office was upstairs," Machen said. "In fact, his original desk is still in use by the head of the guard."

Rebecca had the sense that Machen would have liked to act as her docent and give her a historical tour of the premises.

"The duke kept living quarters there, too. Shall we go and see if there's anyone upstairs who might be able to shed some light on the incident the other night?"

While she wasn't averse to questioning figures of authority, Rebecca had already learned, from bitter experience, that most of the time they stonewalled, confiding nothing and in some cases turning the tables to ruthlessly interrogate anyone with the temerity to ask a question of them—especially when that someone was an attractive young woman. She had been rudely escorted out the door of several government premises and private clubs.

"Why don't you go and see if you can find anyone who can enlighten us further," she suggested, "while I poke around on my own a bit?"

"Let me just see who's about. I used to know one or two of the cavalry officers."

Machen, in his old-fashioned black frock coat, went up a winding stair, and Rebecca wandered through several of the connecting rooms, some filled with tack and others with horse stalls, where each occupant held its head out over the gate, hoping to snag an apple or a rub of the muzzle. Rounding a corner, she heard a cough from an adjoining corridor, and saw an endless row of massive feed barrels, stacked to the vaulted ceiling. The cough came again, and this time she traced it to an old man, bent over a rusty pail. Before she could say a word, he started coughing so violently she thought he might not be able to catch his breath again.

"Are you all right?" she asked, coming closer, and his bald head, though still down, nodded vigorously. He spat into the bucket.

"Can I get you some water?"

He held up a canteen, still without looking at her, and when he did lift his eyes—rheumy and bloodshot—he registered only a dull comprehension.

Rebecca introduced herself, claiming to be attached to the War Office as a civilian volunteer, but the subterfuge was hardly necessary. He was beyond caring. When she asked him who he was, he gestured at the hundreds of barrels surrounding them, and said, "Provisions master. Silas Drummond."

Normally, she might have shaken his hand, but she was not only wary of coming too close, but also saw now that his right hand was red and swollen.

"Were you here the other night, when the intruder got in?"

He nodded.

"Can you tell me what happened?"

He shook his head no. "Didn't see anything, not at first."

She waited, which was one of the first things she had learned about reporting. Let people fill the silences.

"Everything usual." He coughed again, and wiped his mouth with the back of his filthy sleeve. This man had no business being up and about, she thought; he should be in a ward somewhere, being properly tended to. "Saw the doc come by, to check on the horses."

"Was that routine?"

He thought about that for a second, then said, "No. But the zeppelin attack had them riled."

The attack had destroyed an empty school and several warehouses a mile or so away. Only three dead, this time. "Which doctor was it?" Perhaps she could track him down and secure an interview.

"They asked me that already. The one with the long name. Oil something. Never could catch it."

"So you didn't actually see anyone else in the parade grounds?"

"No. I only went out when I heard the shots." Then, proudly, "But I was the one that found the box."

"Box?"

"The brass box." He paused, as if possibly it had occurred to him that if she were part of the investigation, she would know that already.

"Yes, of course," Rebecca said. "The one that you turned over. Thank you for that. It's been very helpful."

"Hope so," he said, shaking his right hand. "It was dark and when I opened it up, I pricked myself on one of them damn needles."

Needles?

"Ah, so there you are," Machen called out, walking toward her with an officer in tow. "Major McGuire tells me there's little that he is able to add to the account in the paper."

At the sight of the major, Silas levered himself up onto his feet, and tried to straighten his clothes.

"Any inquiries must be addressed through the War Office," McGuire was admonishing Rebecca. "To be blunt, you have no business here."

This was the kind of reception Rebecca was used to.

"If Mr. Machen were not here to vouch for you," he continued, "I daresay you would be under arrest."

Before she could say a word in her own defense, Silas, plainly unable to remain erect, suddenly stumbled backward, then forward, his eyes rolling up into his head. Arms outstretched, he fell flat, dust flying up into the air.

"Good God!" McGuire exclaimed.

Machen started to come to his aid, but Rebecca grabbed him by the elbow and said, "He might be contagious."

"What?"

With what, she had no idea. But this, she imagined, was how plague victims must have looked just before the end. "Don't touch that hand," she said, indicating where a pustule had burst, leaving a purple splotch.

The major shrank back so fast, he banged up against a post. "What's wrong with the man?"

Silas let out a low groan, and Rebecca had to resist her own urge to lift him up and tend to him.

"You'll need to call for an ambulance," she said.

"I'll contact Guy's Hospital," McGuire said, "and get them to send one right away." He hurried off as fast as he could.

Machen stood, wringing his hands, and in his black coat looked like an undertaker simply waiting for the opportunity to perform his sad but necessary functions.

But Rebecca was already turning over in her mind the questions Silas's remarks had raised—who, for one, was the mysterious Dr. Oil? And what could have been in that needle?

CHAPTER
THIRTY-FIVE

"Are you sure?" Wells asked again, and Jane assured him, again, that no one else knew about Kurt. "Only Dr. Grover and I know."

"But what about Maude? The watch commander of all things?"

"The doctor knows that telling his wife would be disastrous, especially as he has already been complicit by caring for Kurt and setting his broken ankle. He would never divulge anything."

Wells was slumped in his chair, holding his head up with both hands. Jane refilled his cup with hot tea.

"Can I get you some more toast? Another egg?"

Wells grunted no. He just needed to think this through, and his head wasn't helping any. The night before he'd made the mistake of mixing the barbital with port wine, and after the scuffle in the attic—it was a miracle that no one had been seriously injured or killed—he'd fallen into a slumber that had lasted into early afternoon. When he did finally awaken, he'd prayed that it was all a nightmare—that there wasn't really a German soldier living in his attic—but now, after three cups of tea and a very late breakfast, he knew that it was real.

"Where did you say he is right now?"

"I told him he could go outside."

"Is that wise?"

"He can't stand being cooped up. He's just a boy."

"A German boy, may I remind you, who was dropping bombs on English boys, and girls, and anyone else unlucky enough to be under the zeppelin's path."

"I'm well aware of that."

"Sometimes I wonder."

"I told him to stick close to the house and barn."

Wells was still having trouble assessing the situation. He was no sooner back from the Front, where the Huns had very nearly buried him alive, than he'd found one of them lurking under his own roof. Jane had explained to him, slowly and carefully, just how she had discovered him, wounded and starving, in the barn, and how, at that critical juncture, she had made the decision to help him rather than immediately turning him over to the authorities. It had been, in his estimation, a terrible decision, but he did recognize that, once done, there was no going back. With every hour, every day, that she had harbored him, her own complicity had grown more egregious, and the boy's situation, too, more dire. When he'd landed in his parachute, he'd been an enemy combatant. When he'd traded his uniform for civilian clothes, and lived in hiding among the people of Easton Glebe, he'd become, in the eyes of any military tribunal, guilty of espionage. Several spies, who had already been unmasked, had been executed by firing squad in the Tower of London.

And now he, Wells, was also a party to the crime, unless he called the police, or the army—he wondered which it should be—and turned him over forthwith. His head pounded with the internal turmoil.

"Didn't you think this through at all?" he said, unable, and unwilling, to keep the frustration and disappointment from his voice. "Didn't you foresee any of this?"

"You stumbling onto him in the attic, armed with a revolver? No."

"Not that. Looking down the road, what did you imagine would happen? Were you planning to hide him until the war was over, and then discreetly ship him back home? Because I have seen this war up close, and despite my own, and others', early forecasts, it is not going to be a brief affair. I would not be surprised if the trenches being dug today were still inhabited a year, or even two years, from now."

Jane's jaw was set, her arms folded across her bosom, and he knew that he was doing no good by browbeating her now. What was done was done. But somewhere in the back of his mind, a small thought was brewing, one that he could not express. Had she acted in this way as a sort of muted protest? Was she angry about his passades—and Rebecca West in particular? Was this her convoluted way, perhaps unclear even to her, of demonstrating her own agency and volition? Of acting independently, dangerously, as he did in his own life—in everything from his romantic adventures to his mission to the Front—though within her more limited scope? A problem like Kurt didn't normally fall from the sky—except of course in this case, where it had.

If only he could focus, with a clear mind, on what to do next.

"It's doing no good for us to engage in recriminations," Jane said, with some asperity of her own. "The only thing to do now is to figure out how to go forward."

Aye, and there's the rub, Wells thought.

"Kurt poses no threat to us, or to any of our neighbors. Of that I am firmly convinced."

"I'm glad one of us is."

"It's just a question of knowing what to do with him for the time being. Where to put him where he'll remain safe, and we'll no longer be in the position of harboring a fugitive."

"But what if he tells someone that you helped him, and hid him?"

"He knows not to do that."

Wells snorted. While everything Jane had just told him was reassuring, he could not judge its veracity. Wouldn't an enemy soldier do his level best to make just such an impression, when his very life and freedom depended upon it?

"He can't hide in our attic forever, that's for certain," Wells remarked, still thinking.

"I agree. And I doubt we could find a way to smuggle him out of the country."

"Which would only allow him to reenlist and come back to bomb us again. That hardly seems an ideal solution. We need him neutralized. Placed somewhere he'll be as inconspicuous, and harmless, as a young German in England can possibly be just now."

Ironically, as Wells knew well, London had long provided a safe and welcome home for tens of thousands of native Germans. In the East End, they had congregated around Whitechapel, and in the West End in Soho and St. Pancras north of Oxford Street. Charlotte Street, west of Tottenham Court Road, was so famed for its row of German restaurants and clubs that it was commonly referred to as Charlottenstrasse; he had occasionally enjoyed a bratwurst in one of the beer gardens. There were a dozen German churches in London, a couple of German language newspapers, a German gymnasium at King's Cross, a German hospital at Dalston. In many neighborhoods, there was a good chance that the neighborhood baker and butcher were German, and before the war, well liked. Wells had seen it all change virtually overnight. With the outbreak of the war, German establishments became targets for wanton vandalism and destruction. Thousands of Germans were rounded up and repatriated, and thousands more, many of whom had married English citizens and started families, were herded into internment facilities in empty exhibition halls, such as the Olympia and the Alexandra. Wells himself had seen the vans going by, packed with sorrowful Londoners who had lost their homes, their occupations, their livelihoods, on their way to an uncertain future in a crowded and euphemistically titled "camp."

It was then that it hit him. If he could find a way to sneak Kurt into one of these holding grounds, where he would fit right in with his countrymen and yet be *hors de combat*, as it were, Wells would have neatly solved this difficult equation. While getting *out* of a place like the Olympia, past the sentries and barbed wire and locked gates, was well-nigh impossible, getting *in*—something which no one wanted to do—was almost certain to be easier. All that Kurt would need was identity papers of some kind—forged—and perhaps an order of internment, ideally signed by some government official sufficiently high up the chain of command to sidetrack any deeper inquiry. But to whom could Wells turn for such a monumental and risky favor?

It was almost as if Jane had seen the wheels turning in his mind. "What are you thinking of?" she said, just as Churchill came to his mind.

"A solution," he said, still running through the obstacles and impediments that would have to be surmounted. Winston, for one, would surely want to exact a price for such a concession; in return for his sponsorship, he would want to interrogate Kurt on everything from the zeppelin's internal engineering—the only examples that the British had been able to study were burnt and demolished—to the logistics, such as where it had been launched from. If Wells could assure him of Kurt's cooperation, he felt confident that Winston, an eminently practical man, would agree to the transaction.

But would *Kurt* cooperate?

"You say the boy is out back?"

"Yes. But why? What's this solution?"

"Let me get the lay of the land first," he said, rising too quickly—he had to brace himself against the table for a moment—"and then we'll see."

Once dressed, and bundled into his overcoat, Wells stepped out the back door and into the cold gray afternoon. The ground, hard as concrete, was dotted with patches of ice that crackled under his boots.

Looking around, he saw no sign of Kurt. He saw no sign of anyone. Thinking he might have gone into the barn, Wells pushed the doors open wide and surveyed the interior. Aside from the flitting of some birds in the rafters, there was nothing. Hadn't Jane warned him not to wander off?

Looking out across the barren fields and meadows behind the house, he still saw no one, and on a hunch, he walked around the side of the house and out to the front lawn. He wouldn't be foolhardy enough to return to the scene of the crash, would he?

As Wells crossed the road, and entered the empty cornfields, he remembered the night of the accident—the exuberance of the crowd at the fall of the dreaded "baby-killer," the roaring fire, the smell of burning oil and human flesh . . . the rear gunner crawling from the wreckage. Impaled by Slattery's pitchfork. In the field, the steel framework of the fuselage, scorched and bent, still lay where it had crashed, like the bones of a beached whale. And standing in its twisted carcass, Wells saw the German boy. Had he lost his wits altogether?

Wells was within twenty yards before the boy even noticed him, and then, as he turned to run, Wells shouted, "It's only me, you bloody fool!"

When he got closer, Wells said, "But what if it hadn't been? What are you doing here?" He had to remind himself that the boy spoke only a few words of English, though he seemed to have had no trouble understanding the import of Wells's words.

Gesturing at the wreckage, Kurt said, "Friends. *Freunde*."

"Dead friends," Wells corrected him. "*Tod*. Gone. And you will be, too, if you're spotted out here."

The boy looked at him blankly.

"We're trying to help you, you damn fool, though I'm not entirely sure why."

"*Es tut mir leid,*" Kurt said, bowing his head, and Wells grasped that it was an apology for the fight the night before.

Wells whisked a hand in the air to indicate that it was all forgiven. "I've got something important to discuss with you," he said, knowing full well that only the tenor of his voice could carry any meaning.

But before he could cajole him back to the house, where Jane and the bilingual dictionary could help to make his case, a shotgun blast echoed across the field. From the same copse of trees that had sheltered Kurt on his parachute landing, a flock of birds flew out in all directions, wings beating in terror.

Wells grabbed the boy by the sleeve and dragged him away from the zeppelin's skeleton.

A second blast reverberated in the air, and Wells shoved Kurt toward the house. "Run!"

He turned to see if they were being pursued, but couldn't spot anyone. The hunter must have been shooting from the other side of the grove of trees. Wells ran, close on the heels of the hobbled young soldier. Jane had heard the shots, too, and was standing at the open door. She shooed Kurt into the house and up to the attic, and as soon as Wells, winded and holding a hand to his chest, stumbled through the door, too, she slammed it shut and peering between the curtains in the front windows, kept watch for the next minute or two.

"What do you see?" Wells said, slumped into an armchair.

"Nothing so far. Maybe it was just a hunter."

"Looks like it."

"But you don't think he saw you two?"

Wells couldn't be sure. But he did know that there was no time to lose in explaining his scheme to Kurt, and as long as he was in agreement, getting him out of the rectory and into the sanctuary of the Olympia internment camp as fast as humanly possible.

Next time they might not be so lucky.

CHAPTER
THIRTY-SIX

"That's the damnedest story I've ever heard," Churchill said, once Wells had finished. "Jane, harboring a wounded Hun in your own attic?"

This, even though Wells had done his level best to make it seem less extraordinary than it was.

"And all while you were at the Front," Churchill added, "wielding your mighty pen as a war correspondent." It was one of the many things that had bonded Wells and Churchill—in his youth Winston had served as a reporter in the Second Boer War, and despite his immense governmental duties, had been an inveterate writer ever since.

"But good Lord, you haven't left your wife alone in the house with him?" he asked now, incredulous.

"She's quite safe," Wells replied. "If he was going to commit any mischief, he'd have done so by now."

"Mischief? I call dropping bombs from a zeppelin something more than mischief. We need to get this Kurt fellow into custody and interrogate him as soon as possible."

"And in return you'll give him what I've asked—a safe berth in one of the internment camps?"

Churchill grunted his approval. The man was as good as his word, or in this instance his grunt, and it was why Wells had known to take this scheme across the street from the War Office—and away from Colonel Bryce, to whom he had just delivered the text of another dispatch. He had gone straight to the Admiralty House, where his friend reigned as First Sea Lord. Lacking its own entrance from Whitehall, and entered through a sheltered courtyard, the Admiralty was a less imposing building than the War Office—just three stories of yellow brick, but with ornate neoclassical interiors and a rear facade that looked out directly onto the grounds of the Horse Guards Parade.

"Cigar?" he said, lifting the lid from the humidor on his desk, and after Wells declined, took one out and rising from his chair, stood by the window to light it. "As it happens, you can do me a favor in return," he said, between puffs.

"Name it."

"You've read about the incident down there," he said, gesturing with the lighted cigar at the herds of horses and mules crammed into the pens outside.

"A small item in the *Times*."

"It's not a small matter, though. We are trying our best to contain the story, though we clearly have failed in that regard." He turned back toward Wells and summarized what was known so far, before adding that a brass case had been retrieved, a case engraved with the imprimatur of the Colonial Office. "The *Imperial* Colonial Office," he added, to make clear that it was of German origin.

"Colonel Bryce mentioned this. He said there were test tubes in the box?"

"It's a field kit, equipped with syringes and vials of an unknown liquid. They're over at the biochemical labs right now."

"What have they found out? Are we looking at some bacterial or viral agent?"

"Too soon to know. But the man who found the box has been taken to the hospital. He's at death's door, from what I've been told. Before he crosses that threshold, I'd like you to go over there, take a look at him, and see what if anything you can ascertain."

Although he could guess the answer before asking, Wells said, "What hospital?"

"Guy's. The Communicable Diseases wing."

Of course. It was the natural choice. He felt as if the ghost of Von Baden was summoning him back, and perhaps because of that he felt a sudden twinge between his eyes, which, fortunately, subsided as quickly as it had come. "I'll go straight over."

"Take this," Churchill said, handing him a letter stamped and signed with the Admiralty's seal, and carrying Wells's name as the bearer. So Churchill had known in advance, as soon as this appointment had been made, that Wells would take the bait; he was a shrewd judge of men. "Use one of our cabs. There's always one waiting under the arch."

All in all, Wells thought, as he crossed the courtyard and hailed the cab, it had been a fair trade. Now he just had to convince Kurt, when he got back to the rectory the next day, to cooperate.

The street in front of Guy's had been newly sown with sawdust to cut down on the noise of passing traffic, and a wide banner read, "Quiet, please, for our War Wounded." The shell-shocked, Wells knew, were the most affected by any clamor. Several other men, missing limbs, were bundled in blankets and arranged in a row of wheelchairs by the main gates, smoking or simply turning up their faces toward the weak late-day sun. One of them was holding a cigarette to the lips of another, left with no arms and only one leg. The horror and waste of it all, Wells thought.

Climbing the stairs to the top floor, he heard a familiar voice before rounding the last landing.

"It's my grandfather," the voice pleaded. "I really must be allowed to talk to his doctor."

"I'm afraid that's impermissible," another voice, also familiar, replied. It was then that he saw it was Rebecca who was posing as the grief-stricken granddaughter, and the head nurse Emma Chasubel who was blocking her passage into the ward. Emma caught his eye, and attempting to dispense with Rebecca, said, "Nothing can be done about it. Your grandfather is under strict quarantine."

"I suspected he would be," Wells said, and when Rebecca turned, she at least had the decency to blush at being caught in her subterfuge. "But I can answer for this young lady."

Emma skirted Rebecca, and came to Wells, whose hands she took warmly.

"I wasn't sure if you would ever want to see the likes of me again," he said, "given the awful news I brought you last time."

"Oh, no, it was a blessing, really. Terrible to hear, of course, but it's always better to know. I keep his letter with me all the time," she confided, patting a pocket in her white smock. "Sometimes, it seems as if I can even feel him with me."

No surprise there, Wells thought.

"But what brings you here today?" she asked.

He flourished the note from the Admiralty, and said, "I do need to see the patient from the parade grounds, and speak to the physician in charge of his care."

He saw the light go on in Rebecca's eyes at hearing this.

"The patient is under the most restricted observation," Emma said. "You will need to wear a gown and face mask."

"That's fine, and please do provide the same to this young lady. I will take full responsibility for her."

"Are you sure? The doctor was quite explicit about the quarantine."

"I understand, but she may be helpful to me."

As Emma went to a closet across the hall, Wells murmured, "What on earth are you doing here?"

"I could ask you the same thing."

"I'm here on orders from Winston Churchill."

"What's the Admiralty got to do with this?"

"What's the *Freewoman* magazine got to do with it?"

"I think these will fit you both," Emma said, handing them two white hospital gowns and a pair of face masks.

Rebecca's gown trailed all the way down to her ankles.

"It's this way," she said, leading them into the long ward where Wells had been before. In a couple of the beds, he recognized the occupants; in others, there was a new, but equally sickly, patient. The windows were propped open to let in fresh, if chilly, air. As they walked all the way down the ward, his eyes flicked to the bed, surrounded by the muslin curtain, from which he had seen the apparition—hallucination?—of the German officer arise. The bed was now tenanted by a wheezing British soldier with a white bandage across his eyes—blinded, perhaps by gas?—and skin of an ashen hue. He could not be long for this world.

At the end, Emma guided them into a short corridor behind an iron gate hung with a sign that read, "Authorized Staff Only—Danger of Lethal Contagion." The walls were whitewashed and the cells, which numbered no more than half a dozen, were separate, each one with a steel door that had a glass window, crosshatched with wire, for viewing. One door stood ajar and inside the dimly lit room Wells saw a tall, thin doctor, wrapped in a gown with its collar raised and all but his glasses concealed behind a mask, like the ones Wells and Rebecca and Emma were all wearing, with a white cap covering his hair and rubber gloves on his hands. My God, Wells thought, he looked as if he were in the same sort of disguise that his own invisible man, in the novel of the same name, wore. Maybe Oscar Wilde had had a point about life imitating art.

In the bed, his head thrown back, mouth gaping open to reveal the bare stubs of a few brown teeth, lay the frail but still breathing body of Silas Drummond. One of his hands was loosely tied to the iron bedstead, as he gently rocked himself to and fro, mumbling what sounded like some children's nursery rhyme. His skin was peppered with welts and boils, some of which were leaking noxious fluids into the linen dressings, and his face was as inflated as a balloon. His nose was red, while his eyes, leaking tears, skittered about, from the blank walls of the cell to the group of visitors now assembled outside. It was as if the man were deliquescing before their very eyes.

When the doctor stepped out—lowering his mask and introducing himself as simply "Phipps, chief of pathology"—Wells proffered his letter. After the doctor had taken a moment to review it, Wells asked him, "Will Drummond survive?"

Shaking his head, the doctor said, "Lucky to have made it this long."

Wells could not imagine the man's condition to be considered lucky under any circumstances.

"But what is it that ails him?" Rebecca queried. "He looks like he's being ravaged from within."

"And you are?" Phipps said.

Before she could perpetuate her ruse, Wells leapt in by saying she was there under his authority—he could feel her bristle without even looking at her—and asked what Phipps could tell him of the case.

"I'm aware of your background in science, Mr. Wells—and let me say that it's an honor to meet you—so I believe you'll understand when I say that this appears to be a zoonotic disease, most commonly seen in solipeds, consistent with percutaneous infection."

A transmissible equine disease, in other words, introduced through a skin prick or open skin lesion.

"The symptoms—excessive lacrimation, photophobia, copious nasal discharge—indicate a unilateral axillary lymphadenopathy."

Even Wells needed a second to sort through all that. Did the man always talk like this? But it would account for the swollen face, raw nose, and encrusted tears.

"What about pulmonary involvement?" Wells asked, as that would be the most dangerous route to widespread contagion. Was the patient simply dangerous to touch, or could his very breath be deadly to anyone in close proximity?

"Mr. Drummond does present pleuritic chest pain, high fever, and mucoplurent sputum, all of which would point to a disseminated infection."

"But the lungs?" Wells pressed. Could the man ever speak in plain English?

"We'll need to do the autopsy to see which organs have been most colonized by the bacterium, but I would hazard a guess—a highly confident guess—that we will see abscesses in the spleen, the liver, and yes, the lungs. I haven't seen anything like it since just before the war. A veterinarian was admitted, sick with a much less virulent variant."

"Do you remember his name?" Rebecca burst in.

The doctor, taken aback by her sudden interruption, said, "As a matter of fact, I do. It was an unusual name, a German name. Eulenspiegel."

For some reason Wells could not imagine, Rebecca clapped her hands together as if with satisfaction. What was so marvelous about that discovery?

"Would you have his address?" she asked. "Or any other information about him?"

"Do we?" Phipps asked his head nurse.

"I'll have to check his records, but I would assume so."

"Then I would like to see what you have," Wells said, trusting that Rebecca had asked for some important reason.

Emma, indicating the cell, cautioned, "Doctor, I think something is happening."

As all three turned, Silas raised a quivering arm from the bed, and, like the ancient mariner, pointed a finger at them. He opened his mouth to speak, but all that emerged was a bubble of blood.

"I haven't seen him move like that," Phipps said, raising his mask over his mouth and nose again. "I wonder what's stirred him up."

A moment later, Silas was on his feet, the loose bandage with which he had been tied to the bed trailing onto the floor like a mummy's rag. By the time they realized he was lurching for the door, it was too late, and he had flung it open, staggered through, and lunged at Rebecca. She fell back, with Silas's bony fingers clinging to the bottom of her white gown. He was still trying to speak, even as his knees buckled and he slid to the floor. Wells grabbed him by the collar of his blue hospital shirt and tried to yank him away, but the old man's grip was tight.

"Let go, damn you," Wells barked, "let go of her!"

Emma threw an arm around Rebecca's waist to steady her and keep her from being dragged down, and when Silas did lose his hold, he swiveled his head, raising his bloodshot eyes so imploringly Wells wondered what it was he wanted.

Then it became crystal clear.

Seeing his route unimpeded, Silas mustered a last reserve of strength and scrambled on all fours to the exit.

"My God," Phipps shouted, "stop him!"

But he was already through the door and making straight for the open ward. Gibbering like a baboon, he staggered into the center aisle, colliding with a terrified young nurse, then reeling away toward the bank of casement windows. Wells saw him pause, and, as if inspiration had struck, run between two of the beds to get at one of the more open windows. He pushed it wider, and though Wells would not have guessed it possible, squeezed himself into its gaping frame. He hesitated for just a second, looking down at the courtyard several stories below, and then, his scrawny arms flung wide, launched himself like an eagle taking flight.

Wells was close enough to hear the splat when he landed, and when he craned his head out the window, to see the broken body, exploded like a ripe plum, on the cobblestones. A couple of patients, who had been smoking in the courtyard, were looking on in shock. The blanket draped across one of their laps was spattered with gore; the other was slack-jawed, a pipe dangling from his lower lip.

"Don't touch him!" Wells shouted down. "Get out of there!"

When he turned around, he saw Rebecca—pale and stricken—with the bloody paw prints soiling her gown. Coming to her, he said, "Hold your breath and close your eyes and put your arms out straight." As deftly as he could, he removed the gown, wadded it into a ball, and keeping his own face averted, shoved it into a receptacle for soiled linen, making sure that the lid was clamped down tight. Doctor Phipps, shouting instructions to Emma to keep all the patients in their beds until further notice, charged out of the ward.

For Wells, who had seen so much death of late, this was just another horror, but what was it like, he wondered, for someone as young and sheltered as Rebecca? He wrapped her in his arms, expecting her to cling to him for comfort, but he was wrong. Her back was stiff with resolve, and when he drew back, she said, "I think I know who Dr. Oil is."

Puzzled, Wells said, "Who? What's this about a Dr. Oil?"

"The German prankster of legend and lore. *Eul*enspiegel," she said, emphasizing the proper pronunciation of the first syllable. *Oil*. "I believe I've met the man, at Crowley's house, who has disguised his identity that way."

Now he was more confused than ever.

"We have to stop him, H. G."

"From doing what?"

"That I don't know yet."

"Then why are you so sure it must be stopped?"

The dread in her voice was as real as the crumpled body lying in the courtyard below. "Because, if I'm right, it will be terrible." Nodding toward the open window, she said, "That is only its harbinger."

CHAPTER
THIRTY-SEVEN

Before rushing to catch the evening train back to Easton Glebe, Wells warned Rebecca to hold off. But she did not want to hear that.

"I'll be back in a day," he told her. "I'll go and see Winston and we can pursue this lead to the mysterious Dr. Eulenspiegel then."

"But what's so pressing at the rectory?" Rebecca asked. "What could possibly be more urgent than this?" Finding Dr. Anton Graf—whose pseudonym struck her as just the kind of wicked joke he might make—took precedence over anything.

"It's a personal matter, nothing I can explain just now."

"Then it's to do with Jane?" she said, trying hard to keep any note of jealousy out of her voice.

"In a way," he said, uncharacteristically evasive.

He kissed her on the cheek, jumped into a cab and Rebecca, surprised and more than a little vexed, turned on her heel and marched right back into Guy's Hospital. She found Nurse Chasubel enforcing a strict beds-only policy on the ward, as Dr. Phipps had ordered, and it was only by waiting an hour at a table where a copy of the controversial *Sons and Lovers* sat—with three separate bookmarks sticking up from its pages—that she prevailed upon the nurse to look in the file cabinets and dig out the records of the veterinarian who had checked himself in.

"I'm afraid there isn't much," Emma said, handing her a thin folder with just a few pages in it. "He was delirious when he arrived, so the intake form is largely blank, and he left without any notice or word to anyone on the staff, between shifts."

Rebecca scanned the documents quickly, noting that the address given was a flat on Tottenham Street in the old German quarter, not Crowley's townhouse, and there was no place of employment. Nor were there any relatives listed. On the medical charts, she read a précis of the conditions she already knew about, some of which she had just witnessed in the old man who had leapt to his death. Dreadful as it had been, she understood exactly why he'd done it. Who else, suffering as he most plainly was, would not have done the same? She was actually relieved for his sake that the ordeal was over. She did not necessarily believe in any afterlife, but in this instance, all that mattered was putting an end to the present one. Making a few of her own notes, Rebecca thanked the nurse and returned the folder.

Sliding it back into the drawer, Emma said, "And how is it that you know Mr. Wells? I wasn't sure."

"Family connections. But how is it that you knew him?"

The nurse blushed, and with downcast eyes, said, "He had met someone, at the Front, that I cared for. He acted as a courier and brought me a letter from him."

"That was kind," Rebecca said, reminding herself that there was so much about her lover that she still didn't know. "And will you be seeing the letter writer again soon?"

Emma shook her head tightly. Rebecca did not have to guess at what that meant. "I'm so sorry."

Emma drew a lace handkerchief from the pocket of her smock and, turning away, dabbed at her eyes. "But I do sometimes wonder . . ." she murmured.

"Wonder what?"

"Whether he is truly gone." She shook her head as if to dismiss such embarrassing thoughts. "I'm sure you would think me silly—I would have thought so myself, until recently—but as I told Mr. Wells, sometimes I can feel a presence." She sniffed, and thrust the bunched handkerchief back into her pocket. "I don't know why I'm telling you any of this, especially when you have just lost your grandfather and in such a terrible way."

For a moment, Rebecca was stumped, before remembering the lie she'd told about Silas. Vaguely ashamed, she placed a consoling hand on the nurse's shoulder and said, "It's a dark time just now, for all of us." And that was no lie at all. "The whole world is shared with ghosts." A telling look crossed Emma's face, and Rebecca put it down to the fact that it must be a common sentiment these days, what with the endless scroll of the war dead in the papers, the black armbands of civilians in the streets, the church services and tolling bells for the missing and deceased.

By the time she emerged again onto St. Thomas Street, dusk was falling and Rebecca saw that the maimed soldiers she had passed on her way in had nearly all been rounded up for the night. The last of them was being wheeled in through the gates, a kerchief drawn across the lower half of his face. Rebecca offered him a sympathetic smile, just as a vagrant breeze lifted the bottom of the cloth, revealing . . . nothing. Below his nose, his face had been entirely shorn away.

The soldier followed her with a forlorn gaze. Rebecca let her feet guide her down the street, past the banner pleading for quiet, around the corner and into the hurly-burly of the evening traffic. She was grateful for the ordinary noise and commotion; there was something reassuring about bumping into the other people on the sidewalk, even when one of them accidentally knocked the notepad from her hand and she had to turn abruptly and bend down to pick it up. A man in a shabby herringbone overcoat and a hat with a slouched-down brim was ogling a fancy silk smoking jacket in a store window across the street—who had the money, or the desire, for such luxuries today? Not she.

Armed with nothing more than her notes, she set off for 92 Tottenham Court Road. As she approached the tall, rickety building in the middle of the block, she heard the muffled crack of gunshots from the second story, and saw the last glimmerings of a lighted marquee— "Fairyland Shooting Gallery"—just before an air warden supervised its extinguishing.

"You'll want to be getting home for the night, Miss," the warden said. "Clear sky tonight, and Fritz will be wanting to take advantage of it."

Fairyland, she thought, of all places. Had Graf really lived above this penny arcade and shooting range, the place that had become infamous a few years back, when the Indian nationalist Madan Lal Dinghra had practiced his marksmanship here before going on to assassinate Sir William Curzon Wyllie? And as if that weren't enough, the arcade had achieved further notoriety when two suffragettes had reputedly used the facility to train for an attempt on the life of Prime Minister Herbert Asquith. It was at once a shock, and strangely fitting, that Graf had holed up here. Along with the coin-in-the-slot machines, billboards advertised "Expert Advice in Firearms." She checked her notes again, but this was indeed the address the putative Dr. Eulenspiegel had given.

Men's voices carried into the open arcade, along with the scent of cheap cigars and cordite, but when she went into the lobby proper, all motion and talk seemed to cease.

"Help you, Miss?" a man growled. "The perfumery is down the corner."

There were several snickers among the men loitering there, and behind a counter she saw the proprietor in a striped vest, the stub of a dead cigar wedged in the corner of his mouth. "Yes, you might be able to help," she said, withdrawing her pad and flipping to a blank page.

"You ain't one of them damn suffragettes, are you? Your lot ain't welcome here no more. The country's got bigger fish to fry."

Not surprising, Rebecca thought, that he felt that way; most of the nation did.

"There's a war on," he said, for further emphasis, "case you haven't noticed."

Although the issue of voting rights for women was one of many that had had to be put aside in view of the present crisis, Rebecca accepted the practical argument. "I've nothing to do with that. I'm here on behalf of the War Office."

She applauded herself for the ease with which she now conjured up one identity or another. Grieving granddaughter, War Office employee—what next?

"Oh no, you don't," the owner said, rummaging around beneath the counter, "you won't be writing me any fines. I've got a license for the guns and ammunition used here."

From the floor above, Rebecca heard a round of shots and a man cursing his aim.

"None of it's fit for present combat use," the owner went on, as Rebecca, falling into the role, pretended to inspect the certificate he slapped on the counter. The line for proprietor was signed "Henry Morton."

"This all looks in order," she said, making a note of his name on her pad. "But I'm chiefly here to check on the whereabouts of a tenant."

"You think anybody'd live above this racket?" one of the eavesdropping bystanders cracked. "He'd have to be balmy."

But Morton screwed up his face, and told him to butt out of it. Leaning over the counter to lower his voice, he said to Rebecca, "You referrin' to that rum bastard used to live up top?"

"That depends. What was his name?"

"You tell me. Had a different one every week. Did his best to cover up the German accent, but I can smell 'em from a mile away."

"When did he move out?"

"Why? What's he done?"

"That, I am not at liberty to say."

"He left oh, maybe seven, eight months ago. Middle of the night, no word. But lucky he had, 'cause I'd have thrown him out after that first zeppelin attack. Yes, I would 'ave. Him and his cages."

"Cages?"

"Had animals, he did, in cages, all over the place. Rabbits, rats, even a cat or two. They're up there even now."

"May I see them?"

"The animals? Oh, they're dead and gone."

"No, the cages."

Little as she relished the idea of ascending into the uppermost recesses of Fairyland, and in such dubious company, she still wanted to find that one indisputable piece of evidence that would confirm it was Anton Graf—alias Eulenspiegel—who had resided here. That it was Anton Graf who had perpetrated the attacks at the Horse Guards Parade. As soon as Wells returned from his own mysterious mission to Easton Glebe, she wanted to have an indisputable case so well in hand that together they could go straight to the authorities . . . and on her own she could go straight to press in the *Freewoman*.

"Nothin' much to see up there," Morton grumbled, lifting the board to come out from behind the counter, "but if you insist. Sully, watch the till," he said to the bystander who had interrupted earlier.

"You take as long as you need," Sully said, in a suggestive tone.

What was she getting into? Rebecca wondered.

Morton went to a side staircase, where a sign with a bright red arrow pointed the way to the "Shooting Gallery—Must Be Sixteen Years of Age or Older." Below it, a second smaller, hand-lettered sign read, "No Ladies or Dogs Allowed." As they rose, the racket got louder, and at the top Rebecca saw that the long and narrow room, its walls and ceiling lined with thick cork, had been divided into three lanes, with a bull's-eye at the end of each one, and a box, painted in yellow, at the other end; three shooters stood in separate boxes, two with revolvers and one with a rifle. All of them turned to frown at her.

"He used to shoot once in a while," Morton said, gnawing on the butt of the cigar.

"Was he any good?" For all she knew, it was a piece of information that might prove vital.

"Given the glasses he wore," Morton said with a shrug, "yes." Then, he motioned with his electric torch for her to follow him up the next and even narrower flight of stairs, at the top of which he put his shoulder against a warped wooden door that screeched as he shoved it open.

"Grease for hinges ain't easy to come by these days," he said. "Nor's gas or the electric. I shut 'em all off."

Once inside, he went to the window and pulled back the blackout curtains. Pale moonlight spilled into the room, as the electric torch beam picked out a jumbled stack of empty cages against the back wall. Sloppily made, of wire and wood, they were falling apart at the hinges, and Rebecca had to wonder why Morton had bothered to keep them at all. In the air, there was a faint, but noxious, chemical scent that made her sneeze.

"Haven't you thought of airing the place out?" she said, going to the window herself and yanking it up. She stood there, to take a couple of breaths of fresh air, and only then noticed down below, across the street from the arcade, a man lurking in a doorway, with his hat brim pulled down to conceal most of his face. He was smoking a cigarette and stamping his feet to keep them warm.

"Nobody'd want it, anyway," Morton replied. "Every once in a while, a bullet comes up through the floor."

"You're joking."

"It's spent by the time it gets through. No danger, really."

As if she didn't already have reason enough to hurry, Rebecca now had another, and borrowing the light from Morton she inspected the ramshackle cages, not even sure what she might be looking for. But apart from a few patches of fur or feathers, there was nothing to see.

"Had a couple of pigeons, he did, but I tossed 'em out the window. Dropped like they was stones, not birds."

No doubt because Graf had subjected them to some horrible experiment, Rebecca surmised.

Beside the cages, there was a fruit crate with broken slats, and in it she saw a jumble of other loose items—a rubber glove, some cracked flasks, a few papers. Crouching down, and holding her handkerchief over her fingertips, she gingerly sorted through them; the yellowed papers at the bottom included everything from theater stubs to train schedules, a pamphlet on theosophy to a souvenir postcard of St. Paul's Cathedral. But nothing that would identify, much less definitively incriminate, Anton Graf.

Attempting to light his cigar, Morton said, "Told you there wasn't nothing to look at." The flame wouldn't catch, and he tossed the dead match to the floor. But instead of using another, he drew a fancy gold lighter from his vest pocket.

The glint of it caught Rebecca's eye, and Morton said, "This was the only thing left that was worth anything. Found it on the staircase."

"So it was his?"

"He left owing me two pounds."

She asked to see it, and turning it over in her hands she saw, to her surprise and delight, that it was engraved. On one side, it bore the patent mark of Hahway, a well-known Bavarian manufacturer, and on the other the initials "AJG," with an even more pointed inscription— *Reichskolonialamt*. The German Colonial Office.

"I'll need to requisition this," she said.

"The hell you will."

She dug into her purse and just managed to come up with two pounds, which she stuffed into his breast pocket.

"The War Office thanks you for your service," she said, clamping her bag closed with the prize inside, and absconding before an errant bullet could pop up through the floor and graze her ankle.

CHAPTER THIRTY-EIGHT

Wells had never been so frustrated at his inability to make himself readily understood. In English, he was a master of every idiom and means of expression, but without much German in his arsenal, it was difficult to convey his plan to Kurt, much less to persuade him of its wisdom.

Jane, with Dr. Grover's old bilingual dictionary on the table in front of her, offered constant translations, and Wells could see that it was better to let her carry the ball. Kurt trusted her in a way he would never trust Wells. Right now, she was explaining to him, yet again, how comfortable his life would be at an internment camp in London.

But that did not seem to be the sticking point.

Kurt, his eyes lowered to the teacup and a half-eaten scone on the plate, mumbled something about his country, his duty to it, his unwillingness to betray his comrades. Wells and Jane had been over this territory several times already and even without knowing all the words, Wells had been able to gather the gist of what the young man was going on about. If, God forbid, one of his own sons had ever been faced with a predicament like this, he would hope that the boy would behave in much the same fashion.

"But your presence here is now known to the government," Jane said, slowly, before piecing together the same thought in rudimentary German and reiterating it. "You have no choice now. This is the only way to keep you safe."

By saying everything twice, in each language, she was able to keep both Wells and Kurt apprised of the discussion.

Glowering at Wells, whom he plainly regarded as having betrayed him, Kurt slapped the tabletop hard enough to make the crockery jump, shoved his chair back, and stood up. "*Nein, nein, nein,* I can't"—stopping to search for the English words—"do this thing." He lapsed back into a torrent of German that even Jane appeared to have trouble keeping up with. She exchanged an exasperated look with her husband.

"Tell him he'll be arrested and tried as a spy if he doesn't," Wells said.

"I've told him."

"Tell him that you'll be arrested."

Jane hesitated.

"Tell him that you'll be shot, too."

"That goes too far," she mumbled.

"Does it? If it weren't for my friendship with Winston, what do you think would happen to you? If it weren't for my fame, not to put too fine a point on it, what kind of treatment do you think you would receive for having harbored and nursed back to health a German airman?"

Kurt was observing them closely, like a child watching his parents bicker.

"Oh, and let's not fail to mention that Dr. Grover, with whom he shares a kinship with the fatherland, will also be arrested for aiding and abetting the enemy," Wells continued. "Does he want to bring doom down upon every single person who has helped him here? Does his loyalty to the kaiser supersede his loyalty to the people who have actually saved his life?"

Carefully, Jane went about assembling the sentiments in German and expressing them to Kurt, who limped back and forth in the kitchen. Wells could see the torment on his young face. The worst thing a boy like this should have had to be worrying about at this age was whether or not the farm girl he fancied had fancied him back, but instead here he was, wrestling with questions of life and death—his own, and others'.

"You, they would not shoot," Kurt finally stammered, fixing on Jane.

"They most certainly would," Wells corrected him. "And they will."

"Then I can run."

"Where? All the way to Germany?" Wells said, throwing up his hands to emphasize the utter futility. Gesturing at Kurt's damaged leg, he added, "And you wouldn't get far, anyway."

"I don't know what else to say," Jane sighed. "H. G., how else can we convince him that cooperation is his only salvation? He's as stubborn as a mule."

"The Teutonic temperament at its worst." Wells rubbed his chin contemplatively. He'd known that the task wouldn't be easy, but given that there was no other reasonable course of action, he had not expected it to be this hard, either. Surely, the boy would see the light. All he had to do was provide Churchill with a few details about the operation of the zeppelins, all under the strictest secrecy, and he could be safely ensconced for the duration of the war among his displaced countrymen in the heart of London. By all rights, he should have jumped at the chance.

"No one need ever know that he talked to our War Office," Wells said. "Does he fully grasp that?"

"I'll try, one more time," Jane replied, but before she could start in, there was the sound of an approaching automobile—or several.

"You weren't expecting anyone, were you?" Wells asked Jane, and she shook her head.

"Kurt—run to the barn," she said, hurrying to the back door and throwing it open. "Hide there!" No translation was needed. Jane grabbed an old overcoat from the rack and tossed it over his shoulders as he hobbled out into the yard, where a light dusting of snow lay on the ground. Fortunately, it was a dark night, with a thick cloud cover. Slamming the door behind him, she turned to Wells and said, "Go to the front and see who it is!"

But he was already on his way. Headlamps swept the parlor windows as he peered outside. Leading the procession was Slattery's livery car, but close behind there was a black police van and a camouflaged military vehicle. As soon as they had pulled up in front of the house, doors were flung open and the occupants leapt out. Slattery, flanked by two constables, raced to the door, banging the knocker hard, while four or five soldiers fanned out around the house. It had to have been Churchill, Wells thought, who had authorized the raid; there was no other explanation. Had he not trusted Wells to get the job done?

"Coming!" Wells shouted as he went to the vestibule. "Don't knock the door down!"

"We've a warrant to search the premises," one of the policemen said, brandishing the paper, as Slattery nodded his head vigorously.

"I knew it all along," he declared. "There was somebody out where the zeppelin went down. I saw him!"

The policemen brushed right past Wells, one of them barging up the stairs. Jane stood immobile as the other, gun drawn, poked around the ground floor.

Slattery had an odd look on his face, as if he wasn't quite sure what to make of this. Were Wells and his wife collaborators? Were they involved in some nefarious scheme that he was not permitted to fully comprehend? Whatever was actually going through his mind, Wells could see that his blood was up—he lived for the hunt, and the hunt was on.

"What are you looking for?" Wells said, as benignly as he could.

"Not what—a who." His shotgun was strapped behind one shoulder. "I been tellin' your wife there was somebody lurkin' about, and I bet it's one of them Germans from the crash."

Wells did not reply, but Slattery was already done with talking. With the fox in the fields, he wanted to run with the hounds. He stepped away from the door, and lifted his chin, as if sniffing the air, before disappearing into the night.

From above, Wells could hear the thump of the constable's feet. Jane shot him a worried look.

"What should we do?" she whispered.

Wells wasn't sure, either. They could just give Kurt up—tell the officers where he was hiding—but that would only confirm that they had been complicit all along. What, he wondered, had the constables been told? How much did they already know?

The one thing he did need to do was make sure that he was there for the arrest, or surrender, if they found him. He might need to act as the boy's shield.

"You stay here," he said, "I'm going to see what's happening out back."

Jane nodded, as the policeman came back down the stairs.

"Why is there an extra bedroom made up?"

"My husband and I sleep in separate bedrooms."

"I mean the one up top, in the attic."

Wells left her to make up some story—he heard her saying something about the children—as he walked back through the dining room, as nonchalantly as possible, glancing out a window, where a soldier was nosing around in the bushes. Once in the kitchen, he parted the curtains by the stove and saw a figure outside—Slattery—with his shotgun in his hands, and his head down, studying the ground.

Footprints, in the snow. *Damn.*

Slattery's head came up. Looking toward the barn, he set off at a trot.

Wells couldn't wait any longer; he would have to get to Kurt and orchestrate his being taken into custody. He just wished that Winston had not forced his hand like this.

Wells stepped outside, and called to Slattery to slow down. "Don't do anything rash!"

But Slattery didn't lose a beat, and by now two of the soldiers had begun to converge on the barn, too.

Wells picked up his own pace, but slipped on the snowy ground and went sprawling. He clambered to his feet, and called out, "Wait!"

One of the soldiers threw open the barn doors. Slattery was the first one through.

"Wait for me!" Wells cried out. He only hoped that Kurt was hidden well enough that he could get there in time to negotiate the boy's surrender himself. "Wait!"

And then a shotgun blast split the frosty air.

No, Wells thought, *it can't be.*

Another shot rang out.

Slipping and sliding, he reached the barn. A gray owl was fluttering wildly around the roof beams, before swooping out into the night.

Slattery still held the rifle butt to his shoulder. A wisp of blue smoke coiled around the barrel.

Hanging upside down on the ladder leading to the loft, his legs still entangled in the rungs, was the body of Kurt. His head and arms, in the oversized coat, hung down limply.

"What did you do?" Wells shouted. "What did you do?"

Slattery, looking triumphant, lowered the shotgun. "Killed a baby-killer, that's what I done."

The constables and soldiers crowded in.

"He was comin' for me," Slattery declared, to justify the shooting, "so I let him have it."

Coming for you? From the ladder? Wells thought. *No. He was surrendering.*

"We'll take it from here," the policeman who had carried the warrant said. "And not a word of this, from any of you, to anyone around town. Understood?"

The other members of the search party signaled their assent.

"Good. That's on strict orders from the First Lord of the Admiralty."

As two of the soldiers went to the ladder to free the body, Wells joined them. It felt wrong to leave the boy so friendless, manhandled by strangers.

From the barn door, he heard a muffled cry. He looked up to see Jane, hand to her mouth, frozen there. As the soldiers carried the corpse out, one holding it by the feet and the other under the arms, Wells followed, his hand resting on the boy's broken ankle.

Jane was shivering, as if from the cold, but he knew better. Without a word to Slattery or any of the search party, Wells escorted her back to the house and quickly closed the door. He did not want their private shock and grief to further betray the truth.

CHAPTER
THIRTY-NINE

Rebecca had eaten crow, and she did not like the taste of it. The feathers were still stuck in her teeth.

She had not thought it wise to spend another night at Wells's flat—not so long as he was up at the rectory attending to some private business that involved Jane. What if he unexpectedly came back to London with her? She hadn't heard a peep out of him since his departure, and as she had not actually followed through on her oath to find a flat of her own, she had had no recourse but to retreat to her family home. Her sisters had been unabashedly delighted to see her, but her mother had been unable to resist gloating.

"I'm not even going to ask you to explain where you've slept on your nights away, Cicily, because I see no point in listening to a lie."

Cicily. Not Rebecca. Her mother would never call her by her own chosen name.

"I can only assume that the notorious Mr. Wells has had his way with you, and like the others who have come before you, you have now been discarded. I hope you are quite proud of yourself."

From her favorite perch on the piano bench, Mrs. Fairfield leveled a damning gaze, one that Lettie and Winnie, squashed together on the loveseat, tried to divert by calling attention to themselves.

"Did I tell you that I've been given a promotion, Mother," Lettie said, "and a pay raise, too?"

"Oh, and I passed my certification course," Winnie said, "with the highest score of anyone."

But Mrs. Fairfield was not so easily distracted. "So what have you got to say for yourself? Don't tell me that the cat's got your tongue."

Oh, how Rebecca longed to say something cutting, but a defiant gesture now would only land her back out on the cold and lonely street, from which she had just come. Sometimes silence was the better part of valor, so she stayed mum.

"You may stay here, but only if you acquit yourself in a proper manner. I won't have you setting an improper example for your sisters."

"Mother," Lettie said, "we're older than she is."

"And thoroughly corrupted already," Winnie added, with a wink at Rebecca.

"This isn't a subject for amusement," their mother said, rising from the bench. "One day you will understand that. You have no idea how hard it has been, since your father abandoned us, to keep our heads above water. I've done the best I could, but it has never been easy."

"And I do understand that," Rebecca said, in a rare concession, one that seemed to take her sisters by surprise. "I am forever grateful for the sacrifices you have made." Mrs. Fairfield appeared confused by the admission.

But Rebecca did mean it. Much as she resented her mother's control, she *did* recognize what a difficult row she had had to hoe. It was all part of the reason Rebecca fought so hard for women's suffrage, and women's rights overall. The war had forced such issues onto the back burner, but it wouldn't last forever, and once it was over, she planned to pick up exactly where she had left off. In the meantime, she could see that even the war had moved the cause of women's rights forward; with so many young men enlisting to fight, jobs that had once been off-limits were now being filled by young women—everything from bus conductors to munitions factory workers. Women were being given a taste of greater economic freedom and, as Rebecca had just written in a piece for the *Freewoman* magazine, it was a taste that they would not readily relinquish at the war's end.

With relative tranquility restored to the house, Rebecca was able to enjoy a civilized dinner—her mother's culinary skills, though hardly refined, were demonstrably better than her own—and once Mrs. Fairfield had retired to her boudoir for the night, Rebecca tossed her reporter's pad into her handbag, and threw on her coat and hat.

"You're not going out again at this hour?" Winnie said, lounging on Rebecca's bed.

"And not just after going to all the trouble of forging a peace agreement," Lettie put in, from the window seat. "Everything was going so well!"

"I'll be back later, but right now there's something I need to do."

"It can't wait till morning?" Winnie complained. "We could all play cribbage together."

"No, in spite of the overwhelming appeal of playing cribbage at home with my two older sisters, I am going to go out."

"You needn't be so sarcastic," Lettie said.

"That's right," Winnie concurred, in a playful tone. "We could form a knitting circle, if you prefer."

Rebecca slung her handbag over one shoulder and waved one hand backward as she crept past her mother's room, down the stairs, and out the front door. All day long, she had awaited some word—at the office, at Wells's flat, or even at the Fairfield home—to let her know when H. G. was returning to London, and when they could go to the War Office, or the Admiralty, with what they had found out. She was eager to show him the incriminating gold lighter, which she carried in her purse, even as she recognized that it was just one more way in which she sought to gain his approval. Whether it was a compliment on one of her published pieces, or a laugh at one of her clever remarks, she was in his thrall and wanted above all to impress, as well as enrapture, the great H. G. Wells. Some feminist, she scoffed at herself.

It was another cold and bitter night, and she set off at a brisk pace, composing her thoughts as she went. Her first impulse had been to break into the Crowley house and find out if Anton Graf actually lived there; if he did, she meant to discover his secret laboratory and thereby close the case, definitively. But the more she mulled it over, the more she felt the task of penetrating the house, unnoticed and unaided, seemed beyond her talents. That was when she hit on the notion of Arthur Machen once again; Machen was a regular presence there, and if anyone could contrive to take her under his wing and in through the doors of Crowley's temple to indulgence and depravity, it was he.

When she arrived at his address in Notting Hill Gate, she took a deep breath before entering the dilapidated building, and climbing to the top of the stairs. As Wells had once told her, she smelled the place long before she reached it. Cats and incense. When she knocked, she heard a clawing at the door in response, and had to knock again before she heard a gruff and surprised, "Who's there?"

But as soon as she announced herself, the door was instantly flung wide, and a face out of some nightmare greeted her—a stony gray mask with carved curls of hair and eyes buried deep in hollow sockets. Behind the unmoving mouth, she glimpsed a hint of lips and heard a muffled, "And have you come to join in the rites of Eleusis?"

"The rites of what?" The disguise reminded her of the comedy and tragedy masks that hung above the entryway to the acting academy where she had once been enrolled, but the sight of Machen wearing one was unnerving, to say the least.

"Eleusis, where the ancient Greeks explored the great mysteries of the afterlife."

His words remained indistinct, and Rebecca was not about to keep talking to a man in such a strange getup. "Take it off, please. I can barely understand you."

Lifting the mask back over the top of his head, Machen breathed a sigh of relief. "It's really quite stifling under that." A few stray gray hairs sprouted in all directions. "But please, do come in," he said, nudging a black cat away from the open door with his foot.

The smell of cedarwood and sour milk was overwhelming, and every surface was cluttered with books or bric-a-brac of one sort or another. The long room, with its musty curtains and battered antique furniture, felt like a tomb that had not been aired out for centuries.

"Although I am delighted that you have sought me out, and eager to hear why," Machen said, "I'm afraid I am late for an appointment."

"In that?" Rebecca said, glancing at the papier-mâché mask he held in his hand.

"Given the occasion, it is de rigueur."

"A costume party?"

"Oh, much more than that. Twice a year, we observe the Eleusinian Mysteries at Crowley's townhouse. I will be making some preparatory remarks."

Rebecca could hardly believe her luck. "So that's where you're going now?"

"Yes."

"Then take me with you."

Machen appeared dubious. "It's not—how shall I put this—a safe event for the uninitiated."

"Then you shall initiate me on the way over."

"Why? After what might have happened to you the last time you were there, why would you want to run that risk again?"

"I will explain in the cab, if you will explain these mysteries to me."

"If I do take you, you mustn't go astray there, or wander off on your own."

"I won't," Rebecca said, knowing full well that that was exactly her intention.

"And whatever you witness, you must not publish. Too many reputations are at stake."

Her curiosity grew with every word. "I won't." Another promise she would probably not keep.

Machen still looked unsure if he could trust her, but after she offered him her most beseeching look, he relented, and said, "You'll need to look less conspicuous. Wait right here."

Leaving her under the watchful eye of the black cat, now perched atop a dusty bookcase, he disappeared into a back room and when he came back out, carried a white robe with a golden belt, a wreath of silken flowers, and a pair of delicate Greek sandals. "Put these on."

"To be *less* conspicuous?"

"We haven't time to debate. Do as I say."

"Where did you come by such things?"

"I haven't always been a wretched old bachelor," he replied. "But hurry, or we'll be late."

As he stood by the window with his back turned, she took off her coat.

"As you no doubt know," he declaimed to the cat and the curtains, "the ancient Greeks explained the changing seasons through the myth of Demeter, the goddess of nature and the harvest, and her beautiful daughter, Persephone, the maiden who signified springtime."

The robe she was able to pull on over her dress, though it snagged in her hair.

"When the lustful god Hades first spotted Persephone, he decided he had to have her as his queen. He abducted her, and dragged her down to the underworld. Her mother looked everywhere for her, wandering the whole earth in search of her lost child. But in her despair, Demeter neglected her responsibilities. She left the crops to wither and die, the trees to become bare, the fields fallow and sere. Famine descended upon all mankind."

The robe was so long that Rebecca had to hike it up and cinch it with the golden belt below her breasts. "Go on," she said, though the outlines of the myth were familiar to her.

"It was only when Zeus, the king of all the gods, intervened, that his younger brother Hades was finally forced to relinquish his unwilling bride, who had, quite wisely, refused all food and drink from his hand. In her joy at the reunion, Demeter, who had tarried in the town of Eleusis, allowed the earth to thrive again."

The sandals would leave her feet cold, but they were otherwise comfortable.

"Hades, however, had been clever. After agreeing to return her to her mother, but just before she had set foot above ground again, he had persuaded Persephone to eat four pomegranate seeds. Because she had done so, she was obligated to return for four months of every year to the underworld—a time when her mother grieves again."

The wreath settled upon her brow like a tiara.

"That's why we have winter," Machen said, almost as if he believed the story himself. "The rites we observe tonight are both a celebration of life and an acknowledgment of death, a recognition that it is all one journey, with its own attendant joys and miseries all along the way. Are you done dressing?"

"Yes," she replied, feeling ridiculous in the outfit.

He turned around, with one more item in hand, and said, "Put this on when we get there, and never remove it until we are gone."

It was a gray mask, made of clay. She slipped it into the pocket of her coat, which she threw on over the rest of the getup.

Outside, they had to walk several blocks in search of a cab, and in the sandals, her feet were indeed freezing. In this downtrodden part of the city, cabs were not as plentiful as in more affluent districts, and she felt that the two of them—an elderly man in an old-fashioned coat, and a young woman with a wreath in her hair—stood out to some of the more menacing characters they passed on the street. Once or twice, she even turned to see what looked suspiciously like a man in a slouched-down hat ducking into a doorway, before they were finally able to hail a taxi.

On the drive, she asked why she had to wear this costume while he got away with only a mask.

"The rules, you will find, are quite different for women and men, though great latitude is afforded either way. You will see things you cannot expect."

"What I hope to see is conclusive evidence that Dr. Anton Graf is the same veterinarian whom Silas Drummond saw visiting the Horse Guards Parade."

"Ah, yes—the mysterious Dr. Oil."

She nodded, taking care not to disturb the wreath.

"And that poor man Drummond," Machen said. "Do you happen to know what happened to him once he was transported to Guy's? I meant to inquire."

"He died there. I witnessed it."

"You witnessed it?" He sounded impressed. "You *are* an enterprising young thing, aren't you?"

Rebecca wasn't sure how to take that remark.

But looking out the window of the cab, Machen said, contemplatively, "So he has embarked on the next step of the universal journey. He was at death's door when we saw him—I can't say that I'm surprised he's passed through it."

The cab drove slowly through the darkened streets.

"But surely you don't mean to go snooping around the house in the midst of all the revelry?" Machen said. "If experience is any guide, many people will be there."

"So this should come in handy," Rebecca said, slipping on the clay mask.

"As should this," Machen replied, putting on his own as the cab came to a stop before the tall black townhouse. All the windows were covered, the porch lights extinguished. It looked absolutely untenanted, and Rebecca wondered if Machen had not gotten the night wrong.

That illusion was dispelled the moment they knocked and the door was swiftly opened by a hulking man in a black butler's jacket straining at the seams. It took Rebecca a second to place him, but then she remembered his square jaw and sullen brow from the lobby of the assembly hall on the night she first heard Machen lecture.

"Heinrich," Machen said, with a nod, and after looking them over, the giant moved to one side to let them pass.

"Leave your things in the parlor," he growled, and there she did see a host of overcoats and hats and scarves, scattered across the divans and center table. But what puzzled her was the number of other garments, ranging from waistcoats to skirts, pants to pantaloons, neatly folded or carelessly flung about the room.

"I did warn you," Machen said, as he draped their coats on the back of a chair. "The motto of the house prevails."

The motto, Rebecca remembered from the chiseled words in the salon upstairs, was simple: *"Do What Thou Wilt."*

The main staircase was lighted by a series of torches, in wrought-iron stands, and as Rebecca and Machen rose up the stairs, she could hear the strangest mixture of sounds—laughter, weeping, cries of jubilation, moans, exultations, whoops—all of them inextricably mingled, growing louder, some coming from open rooms, others from behind closed doors. And music, too—what sounded like a Gypsy band, violins screeching, tambourine banging, wooden flute trilling. As she rounded the landing, a girl with nothing on but black stockings and a white-lace bridal veil raced past her, with a fat, bare-chested man in hot pursuit. Rebecca could hardly believe her eyes, though Machen seemed oddly unfazed.

What had she gotten into? She made sure her mask was tightly affixed to her face, and her wreath secured.

The long hallway, which she had gone down once before, was also torchlit, with sheaves of wheat strewn about the floor.

"Emblematic of the harvest," Machen explained.

On either side, doors were thrown open to reveal tableaux of people—all ages, all shapes and sizes, all wearing masks or disguises of some kind, but little else—cavorting on beds, on carpets, on strange leather and metal contraptions that would not have looked out of place in a stable or a torture chamber. There was the snap of whips, the clanking of iron, the swish of silk, and the rustling of crinoline. Also, the unmistakable slap of flesh against flesh. The air reeked of perfume and patchouli, burning tar from the torches, and spilt liquor. It was, in the truest sense, a bacchanal, a wild and obscene spectacle of lust and unfettered license. Was this what humanity resorted to, Rebecca thought, when the central precept of Thelema—Crowley's manufactured faith—was observed?

At the end of the hallway, the main salon was more brightly lit, by a crystal chandelier with pink shades that cast a fiery glow around the tapestried walls and the words engraved above the roaring fireplace. If the house was hell, then this was the devil's own chamber.

And the devil was at home—seated on his throne in a purple gown, a golden goblet in one hand, a scepter in the other. Unlike so many of his guests, he wore no mask. His bald head glistened with sweat; his features were twisted into a gleeful sneer. Eyes glittering, he waved the scepter like a baton, to conduct the Gypsy players ranged against the back wall, who wore red vests, black trousers, and white blindfolds over their eyes. What was the point of acting as conductor, Rebecca wondered, if the orchestra couldn't see you? A raven-haired girl, in a loose skirt and ropes of beads, whirled like a dervish, shaking a tambourine and banging it against her swiveling hip. Perhaps thirty or forty spectators lounged about the room, on sofas and cushions, or simply propped against the walls, drinking from earthenware jugs and pewter mugs.

But even in the midst of this maelstrom, Rebecca felt Crowley's attention shift from the dancing girl to the one who had just entered the chamber, in her wreath and robe, sandals and stony mask. It was as if he had simply sensed her presence—and she did not welcome his notice.

"He has a nose for you," Machen said. "Bad luck, that."

Rising from his throne, thus revealing its backing embroidered with the crimson pentagram, Crowley clapped his hands together several times, and shouted at the band in what sounded like their native tongue. The girl, exhausted, dropped to her knees, and the musicians lowered their instruments.

"The time has come," he declared, "to assemble for the rites of Eleusis."

The other guests stopped whatever they were doing as word traveled throughout the house, and others drifted in, silent and respectful now, from the neighboring rooms. But she saw no sign of Dr. Anton Graf among them.

"The mysteries will be revealed," Crowley announced, arms spread wide in the billowing sleeves, and his incisors filed to a point like fangs. "The veil between the world above and the world below shall be forever rent. Let us celebrate the wedding of Hades and Persephone!"

Looking around, from beneath her own mask, at the half-naked crowd of wastrels and wantons, their skin damp or flaccid, their eyes wet with tears of delight or satiated desire, she thought she had never seen such a ghoulish gathering. Had it not been for her mission, she'd have ripped the white gown away from her limbs, tossed away the wreath, and even in the sandals run for her life.

But she had not come this far only to fail now.

CHAPTER FORTY

"I'm telling you, it's her."

"Put some clothes on," Graf said, huddled over his workbench. "I can't talk to you like that." He would have to remember to secure the lock at the top of the stairs, regardless of what Crowley declared to be the house rules.

Circe leaned closer, her bare breasts hovering above the tallest beaker by only an inch. "The girl with the dark hair, the one who left last week with that old man, the writer. Machen. And he's here, too."

Machen he could understand. The old man was a believer in much of the claptrap Crowley dished out to his followers; he was even supposed to play some part in the evening's festivities. But the girl—Rebecca West—that was a surprise. He didn't think she'd have the nerve to come into this house again, not after the close call she had had the last time. If Machen hadn't shown up when he did and personally escorted her out, she might well have fallen under Crowley's spell. Most young women did.

"She's up to no good," Circe said, hands planted on the table. "You should do something about it, before she spoils the party."

Party. That was hardly what Graf would have called it. Crowley liked to bill it as an exploration of ancient Greek rituals, but that was just a cover story, as far as Graf was concerned. The Eleusinian Mysteries, meant to reveal the secrets of the soul and immortality, were just one more excuse for an orgy, fueled by mystical pronouncements and jugs of wine that Graf had helped to doctor with hallucinogenic chemicals first pioneered in the German labs at Reims. (As Crowley's houseguest, he felt obliged to help out in whatever small ways he could.)

But Anton prided himself on two things—his bacteriological genius, and his intuition. It was the latter that had kept him alive and out of prison. And his intuition was telling him now, in no uncertain terms, that the girl—a magazine writer, no less—was here for a malignant purpose. She was nosing around, and he could not have that, not now, not when he was so close to fulfilling his plan. The prudent thing would be to deal with her, to find out what she knew—and what she was planning to do with that information—tonight.

"I'll come upstairs in a few minutes," he said. "Keep an eye on her."

"What are you going to do?"

"That is not your concern."

When she turned, the fringes of the long leather skirt she wore flapping round her otherwise bare body, Graf quickly attended to the items on his workbench. First, he made sure the metal canister he had been inspecting was stowed away in the viola case, and under the bed. Then, he closed and latched the lid on the makeshift tin box in which he now kept his vials and syringes; it could not hold a candle to the brass box he had lost in St. James's Park, but it was the best Heinrich Schell had been able to fashion on such short notice. From the glass cabinet against one wall, he took out a small brown bottle of a powerful horse sedative, and very carefully loaded yet another syringe with it. One poke with this, and the inquisitive Miss West would be rendered immobile. Best of all, in the frenzied scene upstairs, once everyone was affected by the adulterated wine, her paralysis would pass unnoticed, and Graf would be able to take his time with his interrogation, in private.

But if he hoped to blend in with the crowd here to celebrate the mysteries, he would need a disguise. Fortunately, he had the laboratory goggles, large enough to fit over his spectacles, and the mask he wore over his mouth and nose whenever working with possible inhalants. Festive it was not, but utilitarian; he would be able to get right next to his victim without her recognizing him until it was too late.

Anticipating a somewhat hasty return to his underground warren, he left the door again unlocked, but warned Schell, still guarding the front entrance, to see that no one entered in his absence.

"Who would want to go to that filthy place?" Schell replied, tugging at the ill-fitting jacket that had visibly split under one arm.

"Just be sure they don't."

As he ascended to the upper floor, he heard not the sound of the Gypsy violins, but the sonorous drone of Machen's voice, holding forth on ancient Greece and its pantheon of gods. That he could hold an audience rapt with such dull twaddle was, to Graf's mind, the greatest mystery of all. But this was why Germany would win the war; while the English could be taken in by such nonsense, the Germans could not. The Germans revered science over superstition, fact over fancy. And when they got drunk it was with strong beer, not weak wine.

The jugs were already being passed around, and Crowley, his purple robe billowing open to reveal an exaggerated silver codpiece beneath his ample belly, was blessing each person as he or she imbibed. The women he kissed full on the mouth, nibbling with his incisors at the lips of the most beautiful, and the men he kissed on the forehead—unless they happened to be particularly young and striking. If they were, they received the same benediction as the women.

Quickly scanning the room where some of the people who had drunk first were already experiencing the mind-altering effects of the drug—slumping to the floor, or swaying unsteadily in place—he spotted Circe, standing beside a woman in a gray mask and long white robe, cinched with a golden belt. Unlike many of those around her, this woman was still attending to the speaker. Machen, dressed as always like an undertaker, had removed any mask he might have worn, the better to read some incantation from the notes he held in one hand, as he stood on the dais, before Crowley's empty throne. He'd better finish soon, Graf thought, or his audience might, like the maenads of yore, rend him limb from limb in an intoxicated ecstasy.

Weaving his way through the crowd, Graf approached Rebecca from behind, the needle primed and protruding from his sleeve, his thumb on the plunger, ready to strike. Circe saw him coming and sidled even closer, to lend whatever aid might be needed. Her eyes shot down to the glistening needle tip, and she nodded her understanding. She slipped an arm through Rebecca's, who cocked her head, puzzled, just as Graf came within range.

But something must have alerted Rebecca to the danger, because she turned suddenly, her eyes surprised even under the mask. He thrust the syringe at her, hoping to hit an arm, but her sudden movement threw off his aim. The needle struck her bodice instead, glancing off something hard and brittle underneath the robe. Circe tried to intervene, holding her fast as he thrust again, but this time the needle, dripping with the drug, jabbed into Circe's wrist.

Circe dropped her grip and staggered back in shock, her knees instantly wobbling. Rebecca leapt away, crashing into a couple sharing one of the jugs. The jug shattered on the floor, the wine splashing up.

Rebecca backpedaled into a corner, hitting the wall, and then, assessing the situation, made a mad dash for the archway leading to the hall.

Machen, absorbed in his incantations, droned on, oblivious to the drama unfolding in the back shadows of the vast chamber.

Graf, whipping off the goggles and face mask, swiveled to catch Rebecca, but she was too nimble and quick, slipping past him.

"Help me!" Circe whimpered, collapsing in a puddle to the floor.

But Graf gave her no thought. Rebecca was already halfway out, and he raced after her, tripping over a woman writhing on the floor, then scrambling back to his feet as Rebecca entirely disappeared from the salon.

He hurtled into the hall and saw the flash of her white robe in the torchlight, heading for the stairs. The dress was so long, she had to hold it up with one hand as she ran. A wreath flew from her hair. Grabbing the banister with the other hand, she rounded the staircase and scuttled down, two or three steps at a time. Before she reached the bottom, a sandal spun off one foot, she stumbled, and slid to the floor of the foyer. She ripped the mask away, gasping, and in her eyes he saw naked fear.

Was there anything more delicious, he thought, than the terror of cornered prey?

CHAPTER
FORTY-ONE

As it was the last train to London that night, Wells found it sparsely occupied. He had the entire compartment to himself, and leaving his coat and hat on the rack, he made his way to the dining car, where one elderly gent was snoozing with his head against the blackout shade and another was largely obscured behind an open newspaper page. Ordering a whiskey and soda—"and make it a double"—from the barman, Wells turned, saw the newspaper page come down and heard, "I thought that sounded like you."

It was Dr. Grover, looking particularly haggard and worn.

Wells joined him at his small table, littered with empty glasses, lime rinds, and an ashtray filled with burnt matches and cigarette butts.

"What takes you into the city at this hour?" Wells asked.

The doctor sipped from a glass still containing a finger or two of gin, and said, "I need to see my solicitor, first thing in the morning."

Wells did not need to ask him what about. It had to be Kurt.

"When they saw the boy's cast, and knew that his ankle had been set, the authorities came calling earlier today."

"What did you tell them?" Wells knew that Jane's decision to rescue Kurt had directly embroiled Grover, too.

"I took cover behind my Hippocratic oath. But it failed to make much of an impression."

Wells felt a great responsibility for the trouble the man was now in. He looked sick with worry.

"And Maude, of course, is ready to have my head. The watch commander, of all things, and this happening right under her nose."

Wells drank from his glass, welcoming the bite of the whiskey, and said, "The domestic problem, I cannot help you with. My apologies."

"No need to. I made my own decisions."

"But as to the larger issue—the legal predicament—there, I believe I can."

Grover lifted his downcast gaze.

"I'm to see my friend Winston soon. Let me assess the situation, and see what can be done to contain the damage."

A spark of hope ignited in Grover's eyes. "Do you think you can?"

Wells recognized that he had asked a great deal of his friend Winston already—exoneration for Jane, a safe berth in an internment camp for Kurt—and that asking for yet another favor might be pushing him to the limit. But on the other hand, Churchill had not trusted him enough to let him peacefully enlist Kurt's cooperation, and look at how that had wound up. In a telegram that morning, Churchill had apologized for the bungled capture the night before, adding "at times like this, sometimes even friendship must yield to the exigencies of war." Winston had always been a man in a hurry, and this was one instance where his haste had backfired, drastically.

"Let's just say, that he will owe me a debt of gratitude after our meeting." Wells planned to share whatever news it was that Rebecca had been so eager to share with him, the identity or whereabouts of a mysterious German agent. "I will barter it wisely, and on your behalf."

Now that the doctor saw some glimmer of good news, he shook out another cigarette from the pack, offered it to Wells, who declined— "strictly a pipe man"—and then searched for a match. Wells offered him his lighter.

Grover inhaled deeply, and sat back in his chair. The train ground to another halt, with screeching brakes. Unlike the regular trains, this last of the day stopped at virtually every station to pick up mail and produce, along with its few passengers. The man dozing at the other end of the car sat up in his chair at the cessation of the rumbling wheels, straightened his shirtfront, and returned to his compartment.

"But tell me," Grover said, "about the problem we discussed in my office. The Veronal, has it helped you to sleep?"

In truth, Wells had not used it since the night he had discovered Kurt in the attic, and almost shot him. Even though he knew he had taken it improperly, on top of several glasses of port, he still did not trust himself under its influence, and continued to sleep poorly, snatching an hour or two at most before awakening, often with a start.

"I am holding it in reserve," Wells said, diplomatically, removing a silver pill case from his vest pocket, and opening it. "An aspirin, however, might not be amiss." He felt that warning twinge between his eyes.

"You have had no more . . . visitations?"

"Not for several days," Wells said, his mind flashing back to his last such encounter, with the dead German officer at Guy's Hospital. "I can only hope that I am free of that sort of disturbance."

"That's good," Grover replied, though Wells could see that he was chiefly preoccupied with the fortunate turn in his own affairs. Only minutes ago the doctor was picturing himself in the docket for aiding and abetting a German spy, and now he had seen redemption. His sense of relief was palpable.

Wells drained his glass, stood up from the table, and said, "I'm going to try to catch a bit of shut-eye. With all these stops, it'll be midnight before we get to London." He offered his hand to Grover, who took it gratefully.

"Thank you again, H. G. You've saved my life."

As the train lurched back into motion, the gas lamps flickering, Wells headed back to his carriage and, he hoped, some brief, and whiskey-assisted, rest.

CHAPTER
FORTY-TWO

Rebecca had hit the marble floor so hard, the breath had been knocked out of her, and the only reason she didn't crack a kneecap was the padding provided by the robe and the dress underneath. The bone buttons had already saved her from the prick of the needle.

But glancing back, she saw Graf, ripping away his goggles and mask, letting them fall, as he slowly descended the stairs, confident that he had her dead to rights.

She struggled to her feet, gasping for air, and was staggering toward the door when she heard him shout, "Heinrich! *Hören Sie auf!* Stop anyone!"

The brute who had answered the door planted himself squarely in front of it, arms across his chest.

The only other way to run was toward the back of the house, and she did, but what she really wanted was a weapon. All she could see was another torch, burning at the top of a cellar door, and she made for it, wrenching it back and forth until it came loose from its stanchion. Graf was approaching, warily, and she waved the unwieldy torch to keep him at bay.

"Stay back!" she warned.

"Or what?" he sneered.

"I'll set fire to the house."

He laughed, and took another step forward. In another few seconds, he would be on top of her, and though she was loath to descend into a cellar, it was the only option she had. There had to be another way out down there; all of these old townhouses had back entries for coal deliveries and such. She yanked the door open, jumped inside, and found a feeble latch up top—a mere hook and ring—that she fastened with fumbling fingers, before turning to hold the torch out to light her way. It was a steep set of stairs, made of old and buckling wood, and at the bottom she glimpsed a chain dangling from a light fixture in the ceiling.

She hurried down the steps, kicking off the one remaining sandal, and jerked the lights on just as she heard Graf rattling the door. That latch wouldn't hold for more than a minute.

Although she saw a bed and dresser and a coatrack crammed against one wall, the room was for all intents and purposes a secret laboratory. Everywhere she looked she saw flasks and vials, test tubes and petri dishes, and a stack of cages—just like the ones she had seen in the flat above the penny arcade—teetering in front of an old iron door that was boarded over with two heavy planks of wood to keep it sealed.

The door above burst open—she could hear the crack as it split apart—and Graf shouted down, tauntingly, "Can't we just have a civilized conversation?"

She ran to the cages, frantically hurling them aside with one hand while clinging to her weapon with the other, to get at the door leading to the coal stairs. Graf's footsteps, deliberately loud and plodding, echoed into the chamber.

"I must ask you to be careful," she heard him warn. "I'm conducting some important experiments down there."

She bet that he was! This was undoubtedly the breeding ground, the central headquarters, for the plague that was afflicting the horses at the parade grounds and that had already killed Silas Drummond. Now that she had seen it, she knew for certain that Graf could not allow her to live to tell the tale.

He was in the room now—she could see his shadow on the coal door as she labored to remove the planks—but instead of coming for her, he had stopped. She threw a quick glance over her shoulder and saw that he had gone to the worktable, where he was removing something from a tin box. He appeared to be in no hurry.

"It's a pity you came this way," he said. "But a human subject is something I have longed for."

He held something up to the light—a spurt of liquid darted from the top of the needle.

The first plank tumbled loose, but the other was stuck harder. She dropped the torch and using both hands struggled to pry the plank loose from its iron slat.

"That's enough now," Graf complained, in the tone one would use to stop a willful child. "No one's going anywhere."

Rebecca gave up on the plank, snatched the torch from the floor, and jabbed it at Graf as he approached with the syringe in hand. He ducked each thrust, carefully guarding the needle.

"You English, such indomitable spirit," he said, "however misguided."

She swung the torch like a club, and he backed off. From the smile on his face, he was enjoying the match.

But he was also moving in such a way as to protect the laboratory behind him. It was the only thing Rebecca thought he might fight to save.

She shoved the blazing torch, sparks and ashes dropping from its end, at his chest, over and over again, each time maneuvering him toward the bed and dresser, and the moment she saw enough of an opening, she rushed toward the worktable, where the tin box and the dozens of beakers were arrayed, banging it with her hip so hard that the glassware spilled to the floor. Graf looked stricken, but when she tried to outflank him, she sliced her bare foot on the broken glass. He lunged with the needle, the game over now, and snarled, "You'll regret that!"

Dodging the syringe, she smacked his arm with the torch. He grabbed for its wooden shaft. For a moment, they fought for control, but his grip was tighter and she let go so suddenly that the torch flew from his hands, too, and skidded under the bed; there, it butted up against what looked like a violin or viola case.

"*Mein Gott!*" he exclaimed, running to the bed and dropping to his knees to bat wildly at the burning torch, trying to push it away from the instrument case. A hem of the sheet caught flame.

Rebecca leapt past him and scrambled up the stairs, past the door that was dangling from its broken hinge. Poking her head out, she saw that the giant, Heinrich, was still standing guard, but an unruly group of masked revelers were clamoring and pushing to leave. Keeping her head down, Rebecca scurried into their midst, throwing her arms lasciviously around a fat man in an extravagant fur coat—who welcomed her embrace—and with her face buried in his collar, she was out on the front steps and into the night air before her bloody footprints on the marble had alerted the sentry that the quarry had just slipped through the trap.

Machen was standing at the curb, peering up and down the street. "Ah, so there you are," he said, taking in her bloody foot and disheveled clothes, and looking quite confused. "They said you had gone."

She clung to him like a sailor clinging to the mast.

"Is everything all right?"

"No, it's not."

"What's happened to you?"

"We must get away," she murmured, slinging her arm through his and dragging him down the street.

"I say," the abandoned fat man shouted, "what's your name? Where can I find you?"

Rebecca waved him off, as a wisp of smoke rose like a cobra from a sidewalk grate. Looking back, she saw a faint orange glow from under the front stoop of the townhouse. "We need to sound the fire alarm at once!"

CHAPTER
FORTY-THREE

On the way back to his train compartment, Wells reflected on the situation in which Jane's impulsive act of humanity had landed them all, and regretted that he had been quite so sharp with her about it. Yes, it had been dangerous, in a myriad of ways, none of which he needed to elaborate on any further—he had already done so, in spades—but he also understood, and respected her for, the difficult choice she had had to make, and under the worst and most exigent circumstances. She had found herself in an untenable spot—torn between wartime duty and her own instinctive decency and compassion—and the latter had won out. That decency was precisely the sort of thing that had made him fall in love with her in the first place, and for him to chastise her for it now was, even in his own estimation, reprehensible. When he got to his flat, he would have to sit down in his library and write her a letter expressing that very sentiment.

Assuming he would find the place untenanted.

He had not heard from Rebecca, nor she from him, during his sojourn in the country. It was safer that way. But was she still residing at St. James's Court, or had she retreated, tail between her legs, to her mother's home? Why, Wells wondered, did he insist on making his own life so complicated? Why could he not rule his heart with the same cool mastery that he ruled his professional life?

The train rumbled onto a siding, no doubt to take on some additional cargo, and Wells plopped onto the seat in his compartment just before losing his balance. Too much whiskey, too little sleep the night before. Fortunately, he had his quarters all to himself. The seat was old and worn, the tufted buttons missing in several spots, the flooring was warped, and the very fact that this train had no electrification confirmed that it had been mothballed and only brought back into service because of the increased wartime demand. The gas lamps, which had replaced the oil lamps of a previous generation, were fueled by Pintsch gas, a compressed fuel derived from distilled naphtha, which cast a brighter glow and could withstand the vibrations of a bumpy railroad journey better than most gases.

Its inventor, Julius Pintsch, was German.

How had it come to this? How had two nations, who had traded together to their mutual benefit, whose populations had mingled freely and in peace, once again come to such a disastrous crossroads? These were among the great questions that Wells hoped to confront in the book he had long been contemplating—*The Outline of History*—a book inspired by Diderot's *Encyclopédie*, but encompassing the entire scope of human history, from the Neanderthals to the present day. It would be a monumental undertaking, and one that did not promise the same easy rewards as his popular novels, but he felt a growing compulsion to do it. Humanity needed a lesson in its common origins, its most significant achievements, and its most unfortunate failings, or else this war—the bloodiest and most barbaric in human history—would one day be superseded by something so monstrous and destructive as to be unimaginable by the standards of the present day. In a story written years before, he had already predicted something he called an atom bomb, a weapon that could be dropped from a high-flying plane and whose power, unleashed by a nuclear reaction, could level whole cities.

There was a clanging of bells, a hiss of releasing steam, and a grinding of wheels as the train rolled back onto the main line and resumed its journey toward London. Wells extinguished the gas lamp, and once the compartment was fully black, fumbled to lift the shade. Once his eyes adjusted, he could make out, through the shivering pane of glass, the signal box, where a railway worker was huddled over a glowing stove, and the empty fields beyond. The sky was clear and strewn with stars.

He leaned back against the headrest, but it was so hard that he took his hat and overcoat down from the rack and put them on. He raised the coat collar to cushion his neck and tilted the hat down to cover his face. He settled into the seat, closing his eyes, letting the steady rumble of the wheels lull him into something akin to sleep—a meditative doze, perhaps, one in which his mind roamed free while remaining, vaguely, aware of his immediate surroundings. It was a familiar state, one in which he often came up with the most original ideas for his novels and stories. It was in just such a state that he had first envisioned such creatures as his hydrocephalous Martian invaders . . . his Selenites on the moon . . . his hulking Morlocks burrowed beneath the earth like worms.

How long he had rested like that, before sensing that something in the compartment had changed, he didn't know. Nor could he tell if it was something he had heard, or smelled, or simply felt, that stirred him back toward greater consciousness. He only knew that his skin had prickled and a distant alarm had begun to ring in his head. The pain between his eyes was sharper, the vagrant odor in his nostrils more pungent. At first, he was reluctant to acknowledge any of it—if ignored, the whole sensation might pass—but then it became too persistent for that. He felt as if his attention was being demanded.

Slipping a hand out of his coat pocket, where it had retreated for the warmth, he tilted the brim of his hat up. He glimpsed a pair of scuffed boots, and khaki pants stuffed into their muddy tops. Lifting his gaze, he saw an equally soiled tunic, with the badge of St. George on the torn sleeve.

He was afraid to look farther.

The air in the cabin was tinged with the scent of the trenches—blood and soil, stale tea and cigarette butts, carnage and cordite.

"You'll have to look sometime," a voice said.

When had this person come in? he wondered. How had he not taken notice when the door must have slid open, when the soldier had stowed his gear, when he had taken his seat directly opposite?

And why was the voice—filled with gravel—so familiar?

He saw two dirty hands, unwrapping a packet of lozenges—Victory brand—and as the lozenge was raised to the man's mouth, Wells's eyes followed it.

"You said we'd meet again," the visitor said, "and now we have."

Sergeant Stubb. His protector and guide, the savior who had pulled him from the wreckage of the ghouls' den. Wells was overwhelmed with relief, even joy—the man had survived, somehow, after all! But at the same time, his fear did not entirely subside. There was something about the sergeant, wreathed in shadow, which was not quite right. He rubbed his eyes and tried to focus better.

"How did you find me?" Wells asked.

"A man as famous as you?" Stubb said, with a sly smile. "Not so hard."

Although that was not an answer, Wells let it go. "But what are you doing here?"

"My job. Guarding you."

"Now? From what?"

Stubb pulled a handkerchief from his pocket—a filthy, wadded-up affair that Wells would never have allowed to touch his own lips—and dabbed his mouth with it. Even in the darkness, Wells could see that it was matted with blood.

"You don't look well," Wells said. "You should be in hospital, not here."

"Too late for that," he said, raising lusterless eyes.

A shudder ran down Wells's spine, the joy vanishing, the fear surging. If he had harbored any doubt that his friend was dead, it was gone now. It was just as if he had encountered Corporal Norridge again, or Von Baden, or any of the ghouls who had been slaughtered in their bunker.

"When did it happen?"

Stubb shrugged, sucking on the lozenge. "Yesterday."

"Where?"

"Between Oxford Circus and Piccadilly," he said, referring to the street signs placed in the trenches.

Wells was not surprised that Stubb had died, with his comrades, at the Front. "How?"

"Big Bertha." Slang for the heaviest German artillery. "A direct hit, buried me alive."

"I'm sorry." My God, how inadequate was that?

"I was long overdue."

The train whistle blew, shrill and discordant, as they passed through a junction.

"You know, you're not the first . . . visitor I've had," Wells said.

"No, not surprised."

"You're not?" He had to suppress his astonishment at conversing with a ghost, but with each exchange he was emboldened. "Why not?"

"You lived among 'em."

"Who?"

"The dead," Stubb whispered, matter-of-factly, in his ravaged voice. "The ghouls—they were good as dead when you met 'em. You breathed the same air, slept in the same grave. You took their confessions, food from their hands, and drink. They've got a claim on you."

Wells had been to Hades, he reflected, and now its denizens had come back to haunt him.

"And now I'm just another one," Stubb said, as if admitting to something hardly worth a mention. "Another name on the casualty roster."

"You lived, and died, a hero," Wells insisted.

For the first time, the sergeant assessed him with a skeptical gaze. "There are no heroes in that bloodbath. The only difference is, some die standing, and some die cringing. Surely you can see that."

He could, though he would always hold the sergeant in a reverential regard. How could he not? The train rattled over a trestle bridge, the cabin shaking.

"What is it like?" Wells finally dared to ask. "The afterlife?"

Stubb seemed to fade from view for a moment. "If you're not careful," he said, in a voice even more sepulchral than before, "you'll know too soon."

"What do you mean?" Wells said, leaning forward. "Can you see into the future?"

"The future, the past . . . it's all a bit like one of those magician's tricks, you know. An illusion."

"But the war . . . how will it end? Will we achieve victory?"

"Victory . . . another word. Hollow. Ask Wellington, entombed like me. Or Lord Nelson."

But there was something urgent in his tone, despite the fading in his volume. "Ask *them*," the apparition repeated.

Something remained unsaid. But before Wells could follow up, the door to the compartment slid open, and light from the corridor spilled in.

"So there you are," Dr. Grover said, holding out his hand. "You left your pillbox in the dining car."

Wells glanced at Grover, wondering why he did not react to the sight of the dead soldier in his tattered uniform, but by the time he glanced back, the sergeant was gone. Evaporated.

"I say, Wells, did you just awaken from a nightmare? I hope you didn't take a Veronal on top of that whiskey and soda."

Wells slumped back in his seat, feeling, he thought, as Coleridge must have done, when his visitor from Porlock interrupted the composition of "Kubla Khan." Grover dropped the pillbox onto his lap, and sat down where the apparition had just been.

"God, these old trains reek, don't they?" the doctor said. "It smells like a pack of wet dogs in here."

Despite the bad air, Wells took a deep breath—the first he had taken in some time—and played over in his mind the counsel he had just received, or, more to the point, *not* received. The sergeant had hinted at Wells's own fate, but never more than that. And he had skirted the query about the outcome of the war with talk of tombs and long-dead heroes.

If only Wells had had another minute, even a few seconds, to pursue matters . . . but Grover, still basking in his friend's promise to intercede on his behalf, was prattling on, mixing effusive praise with heartfelt gratitude. Under the circumstances, it was all Wells could do not to question his own senses, and wonder whether he had not entirely taken leave of them.

CHAPTER
FORTY-FOUR

"Not on your life," Henry Morton declared from behind the penny arcade counter. "I've got half a mind to call the coppers on you, as it is."

Graf had expected just this sort of reception, but he was hard-pressed and hadn't been able to think of any other safe haven on such short notice.

"You still owe me two pounds from the last time!" Morton went on. "And all that junk you left is still upstairs."

Graf laid the viola case on the floor between his feet, then turned to Heinrich Schell, standing behind him like an overburdened donkey, with a bulging satchel in one hand and a wooden crate tucked under an arm, and said, "Give it to me."

Schell carefully put his things down, and fished a velvet pouch from his pocket, which he passed, grudgingly, to Graf.

"Open it," Graf said, and Morton did, his eyes widening at the glint of the golden nuggets and dust inside.

"This real?"

"Have it appraised, if you like."

But Morton looked sufficiently dazzled.

"We just need to stay for a night or two," Graf went on, "and then we will be gone. There will be another pouch for you, just like this one, when we leave."

Morton looked torn between his patriotic duty and the unbridled greed that Graf had been counting on. Graf knew enough not to trust the man, but he did trust in his avarice. Morton would wait until he'd extracted that last golden ounce from his tenants, and then, an instant later, try to turn them in to the authorities.

But long before that, Graf would be gone, his apocalyptic mission complete and all of England reeling.

"You know the way," Morton said. "Door's open."

On the way up the stairs, they were greeted by the racket of gunfire—two men were shooting what resembled muskets at the paper targets backed by the cork wall—and above that, the door standing ajar to the dusty room, where Graf saw his old cages, along with yellowed papers and cards, scattered about the floor, the detritus he had left behind in his haste. The place was a dismal wreck, but he would not need to be there long. He would need only the next day to complete his preparations, and by nightfall he would be ready to strike.

"*Hier ist der Ort?*"

"English, Heinrich, English, from now on. Even in private. And yes, this is the place."

"This is . . . bad."

"Yes, I know that. But we had little alternative."

None, in fact. The fire that had broken out in his cellar laboratory had quickly ignited the ceiling beams and from there raced into the upper floors of the house. Schell had barged down the smoldering stairs in time for Graf to point him at the rear door, where he had pulled the planks loose with his bare hands. Graf had thrown as many of his supplies as he could into the satchel and the wooden crate, and with the viola case cradled in his arms, he and Schell had escaped into a back alleyway.

Crowley, like most of his half-naked guests, had barely managed to flee into the street as flames burst from all the windows and the ceiling caved in. The house was now a smoking ruin, as if it had been hit by a bomb in one of the zeppelin raids.

Graf instructed Schell to sweep up this new refuge—an old broom lay in the corner, atop a pile of rags—and stack the fallen cages against the wall, while he dusted off the top of the table and then opened the satchel. From it, he removed a burner, several flasks and culture dishes, and other implements of his trade, which he arranged in the same places they had been on the counter in his cellar lab. In his line of work, one could never afford to absentmindedly reach for the wrong chemical or specimen. The gas masks, of the German prototype, he left in the bag.

Then, he put the crate on the table, and as gently as if he were handling nitroglycerin, he lifted out the precious vials and tubes that contained the fruits of so many years of intensive labor. The weapons of Operation Ottershaw, as he had dubbed it in one of his more whimsical moods, were finally to be deployed. Too bad that H. G. Wells, the author of that famous tale from which he had drawn his inspiration, would never know. Graf had seen the man once, years before, when he gave a lecture in the Royal Albert Hall. Wells had been talking about certain scientific advancements, and Graf remembered thinking that, despite his reedy voice, his words were worthy of a German speaker. The highest compliment he could bestow. After the speech, Wells had mingled with the crowd, and although he had noticeably paid special attention to the young women, he had shaken Graf's hand when he offered it and expressed his hope that the lecture had been interesting.

"Oh, yes, very interesting indeed," Graf had replied.

"You are, if I'm not mistaken, German?"

"My accent is still so strong as that?" He resolved to work harder to disguise it.

"Your country has much to be proud of when it comes to science," Wells said, citing the geographer Von Humboldt, the physicist Carl

Friedrich Gauss, and, finally, the bacteriologist Robert Koch. When Anton said Koch's work had been an inspiration to him, Wells replied, "Then let nothing daunt you, my friend. There are many great advances just waiting to be made," before the swarm of other well-wishers had interrupted their colloquy. If only exceptional Englishmen like Wells, Graf thought, could be spared the mayhem that was to come.

"I am hungry," Schell said, leaning on the broom.

Graf was, too. They had spent the better part of the night in transit, hiding from constables and air-raid wardens whenever necessary, and hadn't dared to stop for a decent meal. Graf took a few pound notes from his wallet, and said, "Go out and get whatever you can find. Enough to last us until tomorrow night. We won't be going out again until then."

Schell pocketed the money and stomped toward the door.

"And try to make yourself inconspicuous," Graf said, though that was like asking an elephant to disappear in an ant farm.

Schell grunted, slamming the door behind him.

And Graf swiftly went to work.

CHAPTER
FORTY-FIVE

"I think you should see a doctor," Winnie said, tilting Rebecca's foot to one side to better catch the morning sun streaming through the bathroom window. Examining the cut on the sole more closely, she added, "It might need stitches."

"Maybe tomorrow," Rebecca said, her foot propped on the edge of the bathtub, "if it gets worse. For now, just finish dressing it."

"What did you say you cut it on?" Lettie asked, as Winnie swabbed the wound with alcohol, then wrapped a strip of gauze around the foot.

"A broken wine bottle," Rebecca fibbed.

"You weren't having a squabble, were you . . . with Mr. Wells?"

Even though Rebecca knew that her sisters were endlessly curious about her private life, it was as close as they had come that morning to probing into it.

"No, nothing like that." Imagine, she thought, if she told them how it had really happened—fleeing from an orgy in the home of Aleister Crowley, the most reviled man in London. "Did Mother hear me come in last night?"

Her sisters exchanged a look, before Winnie, the middle sister, said, skeptically, "What do you think?"

"Have you ever known her to miss a thing?" Lettie put in.

"No."

Winnie tied off the bandage, and said, "Maybe you shouldn't walk on it too much today."

Good as that advice probably was, Rebecca was not about to follow it. She had all the information she needed now—including the inscribed lighter she'd procured from the arcade owner—to establish who the enemy agent was, and she just had to figure out how to get that news to the proper authorities, so that it could be acted upon before he managed to strike again—in the parade grounds, or God knows where else.

From downstairs, they heard a knock on the front door, and after Lettie craned her head out the window to try to see who it was, she pulled her head back in and said, "All I can see is a cab, idling at the curb."

"Plainly, not the postman," Winnie said.

But who was it, then? Rebecca wondered. Could it be? She had barely formed the thought when she heard, to her horror, her mother's voice, saying, in response to another knock, "Coming."

"Quick," she said, pulling on her shoe, "we have to go down!"

But by the time she had rounded the stairs, it was too late. Her mother had opened the door, and found herself face-to-face with her nemesis, the defiler of her daughter. Rebecca had not heard the initial exchange, but if she was waiting for her mother to slam the door in his face, or give him a thorough tongue-lashing, she was much mistaken. Wells was being politely ushered into the parlor, and she could hear him saying something about the charming garden her mother had planted in front of the cottage.

Her mother, even more surprisingly, was thanking him, an unaccustomed and timorous note in her voice.

Rebecca hurried down to join them, her sisters close behind, and she was delighted to see a spark flare up in Wells's eyes at the very sight of her.

"Ah, here she is now," Mrs. Fairfield said, and it was then that Rebecca understood, from the awestruck look on her mother's face, what was happening. For all of her disapproval of Wells on moral grounds, she was no more impervious to his fame than anyone else. He was arguably the most famous writer in all of England, his books on everyone's shelves, his photograph in the papers, his articles in the daily newspapers and monthly magazines, and she was astonished to find him occupying her own humble parlor.

"And may I introduce her sisters, Letitia and Winifred."

The two young women, blushing and falling all over themselves, nodded, and Winnie had the courage to step forward and shake hands.

After another minute or two of pleasant banter, during which Rebecca had to wonder what had prompted him to come all this way on no notice, and to leave a cab waiting outside, her mother offered to set out some tea and biscuits, but Wells declined, saying, "I'm afraid I've come to fetch your very talented daughter Cicily—"

How clever of him to use her given name in front of her mother.

"—on some pressing business matters."

"Business?" Mrs. Fairfield asked.

"Literary stuff," Wells said. "But on a rather tight deadline. She is one of the most astute readers, and editors, I have come across in many a year. I predict a bright future for her in journalism, if she should choose to pursue it."

Her sisters were dumbstruck, and her mother looked at her again, with—was it?—newfound appreciation in her eyes.

"I'll just get my coat and hat," Rebecca said, going to the hall closet.

Wells was offering up some other kind remarks as he took his leave of each one of them by name—her mother still uncharacteristically tongue-tied and unable to issue even the slightest remonstration—and then ushered Rebecca outside, and into the waiting cab. It was not until the car had turned the corner that he took her in his arms and said,

"I've been looking forward to this for days." He kissed her full on the lips. "And nights."

"Then why didn't I hear anything from you?"

"It was best, I felt, to remain incommunicado until we could see each other and talk in private." His eyes flicked to the driver, and lowering his voice, he said, "I have so much to tell you."

"So do I. But where are we going?"

"Whitehall."

"The Admiralty?"

Wells showed her a telegram that said simply, "COME AT EARLIEST OPPORTUNITY. WINSTON," and though it was unlikely the cabbie would have been able to hear much over the rumble of the engine, they whispered their news to each other. Rebecca went first, telling Wells about her discoveries at the flat above the penny arcade—even opening her purse to display the gold lighter with Graf's initials on it—and her narrow, barefooted escape from the burning Crowley house. His jaw fell open at the bravery and resourcefulness she had displayed. Clutching her hands, he said, "I am in awe of you."

Rebecca basked in his praise.

And then, with some evident trepidation, Wells sketched out for her the situation he had been attending to in Easton Glebe—an enemy flier, hidden in his own home—and Rebecca had to remind herself that she should never again jump to conclusions, or assume that she knew what was going on in someone else's life; while she had been imagining him conducting a passionate reunion with his wife, and tormenting herself with visions of his domestic bliss, he was in fact entangled in subterfuge and confusion.

"And then, to top it all off," he said, lowering his eyes as if unsure of what he was about to say, "I had another visitation."

"Another attack?" she said, sympathetically. "Bad as the last one at the flat?"

"He simply showed up on a train."

"The dead corporal again?" The next morning, he had divulged the details of what she had, at first, regarded as his hallucination.

"No. My old friend and guardian, Sergeant Stubb."

He had spoken of him several times, and with great fondness. But judging from this encounter, Stubb was gone, too, now. The whole world seemed to be loitering in death's anteroom these days, whether from bullets at the Front, or bombs from a zeppelin overhead, or mysterious ailments requiring the strictest quarantine. In yesterday's paper, she had seen the names of two of her old classmates at the Royal Academy, who had joined up in the same unit, and been killed in action the same day.

"And he had a rather urgent message for me," Wells confessed.

"Saying?"

"I'm not sure. It was all so veiled, in talk of Wellington and Nelson."

"And you can't summon him again?" It amazed Rebecca how easily she had fallen into acceptance of what Wells was telling her.

"No more than I could summon a breeze at will."

By the time the cab arrived at the Admiralty building, where the driver gave Wells a wink to congratulate him on such a young and lovely companion, the morning sun had been eclipsed by a thin scrim of clouds.

To reach the offices of the First Sea Lord, Wells and Rebecca had to clear several checkpoints and pass through a number of doors and corridors and stairwells; along the way, Wells noticed that she was favoring her right leg, and asked what was wrong.

"In my escape from the debacle last night, I cut my foot on some broken glass. It's nothing," she said, with greater confidence than she felt. In truth, it was stinging.

He put a hand under her elbow, and as they finally approached Churchill's inner sanctum, they could hear his gruff voice emanating from an open door, issuing an order to "make sure you get word back to me as quickly as possible."

A tall man in a herringbone overcoat, his hat brim pulled down toward his eyes, was just exiting, but Rebecca, startled, grabbed him by the arm and said, "It's you!"

The man looked at her with an even gaze, betraying nothing, but she knew he recognized her. How could he not? He had been trailing her for days.

"What's this all about?" Churchill said from behind his desk.

And Rebecca, who had hoped to make a better and more composed impression, was left to make her claim, to which Churchill barked a laugh.

"Looks like you've been spotted, Donnelly," he joshed, "and by an amateur, no less."

"Sorry, sir."

Wells, to whom she had yet to convey her suspicions on this score, looked baffled, too.

"Donnelly is normally one of our most invisible agents," Churchill said.

"But why was he following me?"

The agent looked to his boss, who nodded for him to go ahead and answer. "I wasn't planning on it, Miss. I was actually dispatched to keep an eye on Mr. Wells—"

"Me?" Wells burst in, glancing at Churchill.

"But when you came into his company," Donnelly said, choosing his words carefully, "and he got on the train to Easton Glebe, I decided to let our agent there pick up the job, while I kept a watch over you."

"You were *protecting* me?"

"If it had come to that."

"We have borrowed Inspector Donnelly from Scotland Yard," Churchill explained, "and he is given a fair amount of discretion in the field."

Rebecca was nonplussed. She'd been apprehensive enough about this meeting, but now, here she was in the thick of it, and perhaps this little imbroglio had proved a blessing in disguise. She wasn't nervous at all, and a smiling Churchill said, "We must let the inspector go on his way now," and Donnelly wasted no time excusing himself.

"Why don't you sit here, Miss West," Churchill said, directing her to one of two spindly chairs facing his desk. Through the broad window she could see the parade grounds, still teeming with horses and mules. Wells sat beside her, his chair creaking, and said, "So your surveillance was strictly precautionary?"

"You're a national treasure, H. G."

"And a risk?"

Winston plainly took his meaning, but remained silent.

"Didn't you trust me to get the job done at home?" Wells persisted.

"We couldn't brook any delay, of any kind. The information he might have provided was too critical." Then, glancing at Rebecca, he said, "But perhaps we should debate this at another time."

"She already knows everything."

Churchill scowled. "Was that wise? Miss West is, among other things, a member of the fourth estate."

"You may rely utterly upon her intelligence and discretion."

It was odd for Rebecca to find herself under discussion.

"Apparently, I shall have to," Churchill said. "But I did wish to express my regrets—both practical and personal—on how it turned out. A bad business, all around."

"Yes, it was that. Jane is still terribly distraught."

"There was so much we could have gleaned from a German aviator. But I shall send her a note. In the meantime, please give her my apologies."

Odder still, to be sitting there while the two men talked about Wells's wife.

"And then, of course, there's that affair at Guy's Hospital," Churchill said. "Another dreadful turn of events." Addressing Rebecca, he said, "I understand that you were present for the poor man's death."

"I was. And I had interviewed him on the parade grounds."

"At the risk of redundancy, may I repeat that what we are discussing here is not for publication?"

Rebecca chafed at the restriction, but acquiesced.

"Yesterday, I received the report from the chaps in the chemical weapons lab"—he touched a document lying on the desk between his humidor and a toy cannon—"so our worst suspicions have been confirmed. The brass box is from the Colonial Office, which has long served as a cover and a conduit for the Imperial war department, and now we know what was in the vials and syringes it contained."

"Anthrax," Rebecca interjected.

Churchill nodded, before adding, "Glanders, too."

"And Miss West, through diligent investigation, has identified the culprit," Wells said.

"You have?" Churchill exclaimed, grabbing a pen and turning over the lab report to write on its back.

"His name is Anton Graf. Dr. Anton Graf."

"A medical man?"

"A veterinarian, German, and a friend of Aleister Crowley."

"We have always doubted Crowley's loyalty to this country," Churchill said, scribbling furiously. "Apart from his occult mumbo jumbo, his past writings have betrayed a very pro-German slant."

"Graf lives in the cellar of his house at 67 Chancery Lane."

Churchill looked up. "Not anymore, I suspect. The morning papers report that a fire burned the place down."

"I know, I was there," Rebecca said, and Churchill regarded her with even greater interest.

"You were there? Miss West, I believe the intelligence services should have enlisted you long ago. Go on."

And so she did, digging the notebook out of her purse to aid her memory and to make sure she was supplying all the correct details, including an account of the celebration of the Eleusinian rites and Arthur Machen's part in it.

"Machen, too, eh?" Churchill said. "His tale of the bowmen at Mons was so helpful to the country and the cause. I hate to see him mixed up in this."

Backtracking, she supplied the address of the penny arcade where Graf had once lived. "This is his lighter, engraved with his initials," she said, handing it across the desk. Churchill examined it, before returning to his interrogation, and when Rebecca had exhausted her cache of information, he jumped on the intercom and summoned an adjutant and a secretary to the office.

"We will need to act on this immediately," he said, and Rebecca and Wells knew enough to recognize that their meeting was being abruptly terminated. Coming around the desk, he took Rebecca's hands in both of his own and looked deep into her eyes. "Although it may be impossible to acknowledge all you have done in a public manner, let me say here, in private, that the nation owes you a debt of gratitude. If there is ever anything you require, you have simply to ask."

"The vote?" she said, and after a moment to register her cheek, Churchill guffawed. Clapping Wells on the shoulder, he said, "These suffragettes, they've got more backbone than many a guardsman. But keep alert, you two! Donnelly is off the case, and you're on your own."

The adjutant and secretary bustled into the room and before she had made it out the door with Wells, the two assistants were already perched on their chairs and taking a brisk series of orders, which began with the words, "We must start a manhunt throughout the city!"

CHAPTER
FORTY-SIX

"Hold it still, for God's sake," Graf growled from under his face mask, and Schell, also masked, clamped his meaty paws down more firmly on the cylinder.

This was the especially tricky part of the process, transferring the fragile tubes that contained the live pathogens, painstakingly cultured and brewed, from their compartments in the packing box and in through the filling port. Any disturbance now could fracture a tube prematurely, and release a cloud of particles, refined and concentrated to a hitherto unheard of level, that would kill Graf, Schell, and anyone else unlucky enough to stumble across their dead bodies, or even breathe the air left permeating the Fairyland arcade. How long the fatal conditions would last, how swiftly the contagion would take to kill its victims, and how easily it might be transmitted from one human host to another, were all questions he would have liked to explore through further experiments; that was the way his gods, men like Koch and Ehrlich, had done it. But fate—in the shape of that awful, interfering termagant Rebecca West—had intervened, and now he had to improvise, and under rather adverse circumstances at that.

Still, the effects of his attack—striking to the very core of the kingdom—would be felt throughout the country. And whatever the immediate death toll—which he hoped would be quite high indeed—the repercussions to the national morale alone would be immense.

"Now the gas?" Schell said, and Graf nodded. He had debated which one would be the best to fill the canister and provide a pressurized, disseminating agent, as it were, for the deadly pathogens. The war had already given birth to several contenders, all of which had their relative virtues—tear gases, chlorine, phosgene, diphosgene, and the ubiquitous mustard gas, which clung stubbornly to the ground like a scurvy weed. That's why he had chosen that last one. When his attack was over, the place would have to be quarantined for days, if not weeks, though in his heart he hoped that no one would ever again dare to set foot inside.

Using a heavy rubber tube connected to the gas cylinder, he pumped the bomb full and then hermetically sealed it. Once that was done, he pulled off the mask, which had made his breathing difficult and obscured even his vision. Schell did the same. By comparison, the stuffy odor of the flat came to him like a summer breeze.

"The detonator? Do you want me to set it?"

"Not yet," Graf replied, "no point in risking an explosion before we get there." The tip contained enough nitroglycerin to guarantee that when the bomb landed, the explosion of the pressurized gas would blanket the area with lethal bacteria, carried on a tide of choking, blinding gas. There would be no escape for anyone in range.

Leaning back from the table, Graf surveyed his handiwork—crude in its way (Schell was no Cellini), but powerful and resourceful, too, all things considered. And it would more than do the job.

"I'm hungry."

No news there. "Eat whatever's left," Graf said. Glancing out the window at the waning afternoon light, he said, "We'll leave in an hour." No reason to expose themselves to the world sooner than they had to. "After Operation Ottershaw is complete, we won't be coming back here."

"Operation what?"

"Nothing you need to know." It would hardly be worth explaining the reference to someone like Heinrich, who might not even know who H. G. Wells was. There were only two people in the world who knew the name of his mission—the other one was Wilhelm Solf, a secretary of state sitting behind a desk in Berlin, and even he was unaware of its full dimensions. That was the way Graf had wanted it.

He had been planning to launch the operation on St. George's Day— while the British were celebrating their patron saint, whom they astonishingly believed could intercede on their behalf on the battlefield—but that was still weeks off and he could no longer delay. God was smiling on him, regardless—today was Ash Wednesday, and he would be sure to find a rich and variegated audience for his performance. Since these worshippers were going to give up something for Lent, anyway, why should it not be their lives?

CHAPTER
FORTY-SEVEN

Once they had left the Admiralty and were out on the street again, Wells felt strangely depleted, like a sponge squeezed dry. He and Rebecca had shared their secrets and discoveries, and now found themselves relegated to the sidelines while Churchill and his emissaries took over the mad search for Dr. Anton Graf. Lost in thought, the two of them walked arm in arm, from Whitehall toward Trafalgar Square, passing people on the street who wore the smudged sign of Ash Wednesday on their foreheads. Wells was far too much the iconoclast for such things, and he guessed that Rebecca shared that sentiment. But if ever there was a time when people needed the consolations of religion, this was it.

Dusk would soon be falling, and the air was cold and raw. Rebecca's limp was worse than before, and when they came to the four recumbent lions guarding the base of Nelson's column—the statue of the great admiral, victor of the Battle of Trafalgar, towering over a hundred feet above them—Wells encouraged Rebecca to sit down for a moment so that he could examine her foot.

Reluctantly, she removed her boot; her hosiery, he was alarmed to see, was sticky with blood.

"Don't look," she said, overwhelmed with embarrassment, but he rolled the fabric away to view the cut on the sole of her foot. In the fading light, it was angry and striated with pink lines connoting an infection of some kind.

"Does the lady need a hand?" a passerby asked, but Wells shook his head.

"What the lady needs is a doctor," he said, quietly, to Rebecca. "And right away." He did not like the look of that foot at all, especially given where and how it had been wounded.

"The lady needs to figure out where Anton Graf is planning to strike," she said with some asperity, ignoring his advice. "I don't think he can afford to wait any longer than he has. His safe haven has burnt to the ground. He knows that I escaped after seeing his laboratory, and that I have undoubtedly reported him to the authorities. No, he will do his worst tonight, I am sure of it, unless we can stop him."

"The horse parade grounds are thoroughly well protected now. He would not dare go back."

"H. G., do you really think he will confine himself to horses? Look what happened to Silas Drummond. Graf has bigger aims."

Wells, without saying so, had been thinking along the very same lines, as, he was sure, Churchill and his staff were doing. In this war, nothing, it seemed, was forbidden, from poison gas to burning oil, and no one was safe, from the soldiers in the forward trenches to the helpless civilians whose towns and cities were destroyed by ever more powerful bombs.

"But how can we anticipate where, in the whole of London, he will choose to attack?" he asked, his eyes falling on the immense lions flanking the pedestal—created, he never failed to recall, by the famed Victorian sculptor Sir Edwin Landseer, now entombed in St. Paul's Cathedral. As was, of course, the admiral, the nation's greatest seaman, standing high atop the Corinthian column.

When Wells, in the train car, had asked about the prospects of victory, he remembered that the specter of Sergeant Stubb had told him to ask Lord Nelson. Or Wellington. Entombed, Stubb observed, as the sergeant himself had been.

But in the crypts of St. Paul's Cathedral.

Which was, itself, the single most potent symbol of Great Britain.

Could that be right? Had Wells just intuited—no, deduced—his enemy's plan of attack? Or had his imagination run away with him, as it so often did? Was he being too clever by half?

Sliding the shoe back onto Rebecca's foot as gently as he could—she winced, nonetheless—and lacing it, he stood up and said, "I am going to put you in a cab to Guy's Hospital. Go and see Nurse Chasubel the moment you get there, she will know what to do, while I chase down a"—he paused, not even knowing what to call it—"a premonition."

"Of what? Where?"

"Of Graf. Launching his assault." The cathedral would be filled with worshippers for the Ash Wednesday evensong. Wells's intuition seemed more likely by the second.

"Then I am going with you."

"You most definitely are not. If I'm right, there is no time to lose, and even less to argue about it."

"Then don't."

"Rebecca, I can't put you at any more risk."

"And how, may I ask, do you plan to stop him on your own? You don't even know what Graf looks like."

To his chagrin, she was, of course, right.

"But I *do* know," she declared, getting to her feet and putting an end to the debate. "If you're so sure of where we're going, H. G., and an attack is imminent, then hadn't we hurry?"

CHAPTER
FORTY-EIGHT

The night sky was clear, and the moon was full—all but inviting an aerial attack. The deadly airships could soar across the Channel and follow the shining silver thread of the Thames all the way to their target. The dome of the cathedral, sitting high atop Ludgate Hill, would gleam like an ivory bull's-eye in the bombardier's sights.

Graf's only fear was that a zeppelin might eclipse or undo his own achievement. All the more reason to work fast.

"I do not like heights," Schell said, sitting beside him in the back seat of the cab.

"Keep your mouth shut," Graf muttered, training a watchful eye on the driver.

"I won't go up. That is all I am saying."

"You will do whatever I tell you to do," Graf snarled under his breath. "Now shut up."

Graf hadn't liked the way the driver had looked at them when they got in and told him their destination. His curiosity wasn't so surprising, since they did make an odd pair—a bespectacled type, cradling a viola case, and a hulking brute with a shock of blond hair, expensively attired in a felt brown hat and a long, fur-collared overcoat. He had stolen them from the pile left by the guests on the night of the Eleusinian rites.

The cab hit a pothole, and Graf instinctively hunched over the viola case, holding it close to his chest.

"Sorry 'bout that," the cabbie said. "Bomb crater."

"Watch out for them. This is a very delicate instrument I'm carrying."

"Not easy, with the blackout and all. You play the violin?"

"Viola. Yes."

"You playing at the cathedral?" he said, turning around. Only now did Graf notice the soot marking his forehead for Ash Wednesday.

"Yes."

"Oh," he said, nodding and visibly relaxing his shoulders. "Then don't you worry. I'll get you there in one piece."

When they arrived, Graf paid the fare and, just to ensure that the man would have only good feelings and no nagging suspicions about his passengers, gave him a generous tip. Stepping out in front of the church, he saw a stream of parishioners already passing under the plane trees, whose spindly branches were bereft of leaves, and climbing the stairs surmounted by the twelve mighty columns. It was an impressive edifice, Graf had to grant, comparable to the cathedrals of Paris or Cologne. Built by Sir Christopher Wren—now entombed there along with this country's other great heroes, Nelson and Wellington—it had reigned over this spot, where four previous churches had stood, since the end of the seventeenth century. Graf had visited it several times already, and even taken a guided tour overseen by the deacon's office, making careful mental notes all along the way. He knew all there was to know about the history and the construction of the church—erected after the Great Fire of 1666, dedicated to the patron saint of London—but more to the point he knew all of its vulnerabilities. He knew the way to the popular Whispering Gallery, a hundred feet above the floor of the nave, and from there the winding staircase that would take him even higher up into the dome if need be. He knew the spot from which he would be able to look straight down onto the very pulpit itself, onto the bowed heads of the worshippers and the upraised faces of the choristers in the choir stalls . . . and strike the hammer blow that would resound forever after.

"You see that?" Schell said, nudging him in the ribs as they passed through the massive doors, standing open. A dozen members of the St. Paul's Watch, in helmets and brown uniforms, were stationed on either side, with buckets of water and hoses, lanterns and sandbags, ready to deploy should a zeppelin score a hit.

"Just follow me," Graf said, skirting a priest dispensing ashes, and turning toward the south aisle leading to the Chapel of St. Michael and St. George, and just past that the Holman Hunt portrait entitled *The Light of the World*; in the picture, Christ knocked at a closed door, inviting any man to open it and let him in. In Graf's view, few, if any, ever did admit him, and those that did received precious little for their trouble. Religion was a swindle; it was only science, in his book, that could be relied upon. Although jostled by the other people, and clutching the viola case close to his chest, Graf controlled himself lest he betray any of his eagerness or anxiety. Those around him were in solemn, but good, spirits, greeting friends and wishing each other well.

"Hope Jerry stays home tonight," said one.

"Well, if your number's up, your number's up," his friend joshed, "and no better place than this to get the news."

These English displayed a remarkable, though disturbing, pluck, Graf reflected.

The crowds moved slowly, many craning their necks simply to marvel anew at the eight exquisite grisaille panels, picked with gold, in the vaulted ceiling, depicting scenes from the life of St. Paul, from his conversion on the road to Damascus to the punishment of the sorcerer

Elymas. Graf could tell that Heinrich, raised Lutheran and respectfully holding his hat in his hands, was cowed by his surroundings.

For that matter, the enormity of what they were about to do weighed heavy even on Graf's shoulders. He was going to wage war as no one else had ever done it, in the center of the enemy's capital, in their most consecrated space, and using science not brute force. Any moral qualms he might have felt, and in truth he felt barely any, could be assuaged by the prediction that H. G. Wells had often propounded—that this would be the war to end all wars.

Seen in that light, he was only advancing the cause—making war a thing of the past—and, in his own way, doing God's work.

CHAPTER
FORTY-NINE

Please God, no, Wells thought, not now.

Rebecca said, "What's wrong?"

Wells pressed his fingers to the bridge of his nose, and squeezed the skin tight. He bent over in his seat, the other passengers on the Underground train taking note, and one of them asking Rebecca if her father needed some help.

"No, we'll be all right," she replied.

But Wells had heard it, and might have been amused if the pain between his eyes was not so sharp.

"What can I do?" she asked.

"Pray," he said. But the symptoms were familiar enough now that he knew what was coming—the smell of the trenches, the visions. He hardly dared sit up and look around.

Leaving Trafalgar Square, they had been unable to flag down a taxi and rather than risk any delay, they'd hurried down into the tube station at Charing Cross. The train was full with people heading home for work, or, as this was Ash Wednesday, to an evensong service at their church. It was only a short trip, less than a couple of miles to the cathedral station, but each time the train jolted or made a stop or swerved on the tracks, he felt another stab of the knife between his eyes. Bad at any time; right now an attack would spell disaster. He would need his wits about him for whatever challenge was to present itself when they got there.

"You can lean on me," Rebecca said, but he was not about to do that—especially as Rebecca herself was hobbled by the injury to her foot. A fine pair, they made, to thwart Anton Graf and his henchman Heinrich Schell, whom Rebecca had intimated would most assuredly be accompanying his boss. When the train screeched to a halt at the St. Paul's station, Wells took a deep breath and got to his feet, swaying slightly, and the other riders made way for them to step out onto the busy platform . . . which is when he was brought up short and stopped in his tracks.

The British soldier—who had never shared his true name with Wells—the ghoul he had simply known as Tommy, was leaning against a rusted column, his face black with dirt, the front of his khaki tunic torn to pieces and splotched with blood. Was this how Captain Lillyfield and the sappers had left him, deep in the secret labyrinth? Other people bustled all around, paying no attention, and when Wells looked to Rebecca, she, too, seemed oblivious.

"Over there, by the column," he said, "what do you see?"

"What do you mean?"

"Do you see someone standing there—a soldier?" He did not add the word "dead."

"No." And then, "But you do?"

Like the ghost of Corporal Norridge, Tommy seemed to be saying something—was it simply "St. Paul's"?—but his words were swallowed by the station noise and his image was obscured by the other travelers in the station.

"Let's go on," Wells said, trying to brush the intrusion aside and leading Rebecca toward the stairs. He cast one look back, and Tommy, though remaining in place, was following his progress with doleful eyes, and nodding encouragement.

When they came up out of the station, Great Paul, the largest bell in England, was ringing in the tower of the church, and worshippers were streaming past the statue of Queen Anne that stood before the west entrance—the grim spot where in 1606 Father Garnet had been taken to be hanged, drawn, and quartered for his role in the Gunpowder Plot. Under the portico lights, which were dim and hooded, members of the fire brigade were perched on the steps, their round helmets tilted back, searching the darkening sky.

"What do we do now?" Rebecca asked. "Did your ghostly visitor offer any clue?"

"No," Wells said, "we're on our own," though the pain between his eyes was lessening. "We simply have to spot them before they spot us." Beyond that, even he was unsure. Assuming his hunch was correct and they were there, what would their plan of attack be? He looked back again, to see if the apparition was anywhere in evidence, but all he saw were parishioners, most of whom had presumably fasted that day, hurrying to attend the services and then get home to a hearty meal. But the mere fact that Tommy had appeared at this particular place, and time, offered him some confirmation that he might be on the right trail, after all.

Just inside the narthex, a priest in his purple and white vestments was ministering to the faithful, reciting, "Remember that you are dust, and to dust you shall return," as he daubed the forehead of each one with ashes made from the burnt fronds from the previous year's Palm Sunday observance. Wells and Rebecca dutifully submitted, but as they moved past him, Wells felt her grip on his arm growing more forceful. It struck him that it was less for his benefit than her own. She was limping badly, and in the light of the candles and lanterns, all of which were ready to be extinguished at a moment's warning, he saw the gleam of perspiration on her brow. He raised the back of his hand to her face, and the skin was warm. Too warm.

"You're not well," he said, and rather than deny it, she declared, "I'm not about to quit now. I'll go to hospital later."

He was torn between love and duty, but he also knew her well enough not to argue the point. He still needed her to identify the culprits; the cathedral was full, and the low hum of the multitude of voices and the shuffling of their feet reverberated off the walls and false-coffered ceiling so high above. There were two ways to go now—to his left, the north aisle of the nave, with its chapel of St. Dunstan and Lord Mayor's Vestry, or the south aisle, with its famed geometrical staircase and, beyond that, the entrance to the crypt where, along with the cathedral's builder Sir Christopher Wren, the Duke of Wellington and Lord Nelson were entombed. He turned in that direction. Would whatever destruction Graf and Schell planned to unleash be hatched in that underground chamber?

Passing the chapel of St. Michael and St. George, he was reminded of the role the latter saint had played in Machen's story, marshaling the ghostly bowmen on the battlefield at Mons, and the importance of that account to English morale. By now the tale had become as integral a part of British mythology as any ancient legend had to the classical Greeks. Several people were kneeling inside the enclave, heads bowed in silent prayer.

He felt Rebecca's fingers clench his arm like an eagle's talons, and when he looked at her to find out why—was she about to faint?—he saw her gazing toward the pulpit and mumbling, "Straight ahead. Look!"

There was a sea of faces and hats, coats and canes, and even a wheelchair or two, with legless soldiers being pushed down the aisle, but he could not tell what she was looking at.

"The big man in the beaver hat."

The crowd parted for a moment, and he glimpsed a thatch of blond hair spilling over a fur collar.

"And the man with the viola case."

Beside him, a smaller man in wire-rim glasses was holding the instrument against his chest rather than by its handle, as a musician would normally do.

Then, as if he had felt their attention, the smaller man turned. His eyes flicked to Rebecca, then back to Wells, with a shock of recognition, and in the next instant he bolted toward the nearest interior door. Schell, taken off guard by his master's flight, looked all around, then barreled after him. In seconds, they were gone.

"Where are they going?" Rebecca said, already trying to give chase and pulling Wells in their direction.

A door slammed after them—the door, Wells knew, that led to only one place. "The crypt. They've gone into the crypt."

CHAPTER FIFTY

If there was one thing that Graf had learned from his many years of study in bacteriology, it was that you had to control for all the variables in any experiment. But this intrusion was not one that he had anticipated; Rebecca's appearance he might have foreseen—she had a knack for getting in his way—but H. G. Wells? That was something he could not have even remotely contemplated.

Nor had he planned to be descending this narrow stone stair, with Schell lumbering after him, into the cathedral's subterranean chambers. All he knew was that he had to get them off his trail, whatever that took. At the bottom, he crashed into a watchman in a metal helmet, and nearly lost hold of the viola case.

"This area's closed," the watchman said sternly, waving a lighted electric torch. "No exceptions. Out you go."

"Heinrich," Graf said, nimbly stepping to one side, as Schell smashed a fist into the man's unsuspecting face. He went down like a plank, but to make sure he was out cold, Schell crouched down, and lifting his head by his collar, punched him again and again, until his head lolled on his neck like a broken stalk.

Looking around, Graf took in the gloomy vault, the feeble glow of the gaslights illuminating plaques mounted on the walls, and the two immense sarcophagi holding the nation's greatest admiral and general. Before concealing himself behind one or the other—Wellington's topped with red granite, Nelson's a black slab—he stopped to listen, and heard the sound of footfalls on the stairs.

Damn, he thought, Wells and that pestilential young woman were going to be an impediment, after all . . . though not one he would have to tolerate for long.

"Get rid of them," he said to Schell. "Do whatever you have to, but be quick and quiet about it."

Schell, wiping his bloody fist on his pants, grabbed the watchman by his feet and dragged him out of sight, his helmet and truncheon, electric torch and loose change, rolling about on the blood-spattered floor, as Graf scurried to hide.

Wells paused a few steps from the bottom, seeing the watchman's things littering the stone slabs. He put out a hand to stop Rebecca, who was following close behind, clinging to the handrail. With no weapon, he knew that in a confrontation he would be no match for his quarry. "Go back up," he urged her, "get help!"

"I'm not leaving you here."

"You must!"

He'd been foolish to go in hot pursuit, but it was too late to turn back now. The truncheon was only a few yards away—he would have to make a grab for it.

Keeping low, as if going over the top and into no man's land, he ducked out of the doorway and swooped down, picking up the truncheon in one hand and the torch in the other, then pivoting in place to search for the Germans. A trail of blood drops led to a dark alcove, its archway strung with cobwebs—cobwebs that were still swaying as if caught in a breeze. Wells trained the light on the enclosure as he approached, announcing out loud that there was no escape, the guards were on their way, and surrender was the only option.

The beam of light shone on a brass plaque depicting "The Lady with the Lamp," Florence Nightingale, before her silhouette was suddenly eclipsed by a blinding rush of motion. His head down like a bull, Schell charged out of the recess, bowling Wells over and sending the torch and iron baton flying. Knocked flat on his back, Wells put up his hands to deflect the flurry of blows raining down on him, but the man had his knees on his abdomen and he could barely breathe. He tried to hit back but he had no purchase or angle, and when he felt the meaty fingers grappling at his throat, he feared he had only seconds left before blacking out.

The face above him—fleshy and broad, topped by a smooth beaver hat—was grinning with unconcealed pleasure.

He struggled to loosen the grip, but the man was simply too strong, and too determined. His lungs bursting, Wells dug his nails into Schell's thick fingers, trying without success to pry even one away, when the beaver hat unexpectedly sprang off his head . . . and the fingers slackened their hold.

Wells gasped for a breath, and saw the face rear back, stunned, a bloody gash now smearing the temple. Before he could make sense of it, there was a blur as the truncheon struck again, and this time Schell slumped to one side. Wells gulped at the air, as the body toppled over.

"H. G., are you all right?" Rebecca said, dropping to her knees, the weapon still in her hand.

He couldn't speak yet, but nodded instead.

"Just try to catch your breath."

"What about . . . Graf?" was all he could get out.

"I don't know," she said, quickly casting a wary look around the morbid environs. "I don't see him anywhere."

"But he's here," Wells wheezed, painfully raising himself on one elbow, and inching away from the prostrate Schell. "He has to be . . . and he's not done yet."

In confirmation, a shot rang out, the blast echoing off the Portland stone of the walls, off the gleaming porphyry and red granite of the mighty caskets lying in state. Rebecca, who had been crouching low, slumped over in a heap.

CHAPTER
FIFTY-ONE

Graf's heart leapt with joy the second after he'd pulled the trigger. Judging from the way the girl fell over, Graf had scored a direct hit— even though it was Wells he had been aiming at. But good enough—his target practice at the arcade had paid off.

By the time he managed to get off a second round, however, Wells had rolled on top of her, and was dragging her toward the alcove where Schell had stashed the dead watchman.

Graf realized he could stay and fight—part of him would have liked to—but the gunfire would only bring down other guards and he could wind up trapped in this cellar. If that happened, his grand scheme would be utterly thwarted and the final death toll would hardly register—even with the celebrated H. G. Wells among them. The great massacre he had planned would have devolved into a minor skirmish, hardly worth a mention in the papers the next day. No, there was only one course open to him—he had to make his way out of the crypt, and up to his planned destination, before it was too late. Already, he could hear the distant echo of the bishop's amplified voice from the pulpit, reciting some biblical passage as part of the service.

Keeping low, the viola case pressed to his chest and one eye on the alcove, he ran past Schell's body—his fallen Goliath, the blond hair matted with blood—then onto the steps. Halfway up, he bumped into another watchman coming down, who said, "Who're you?"

"A musician," he replied, "with the choir."

"What was that noise down here?"

"Oh, that," Graf said, slipping one hand back into the pocket of his overcoat and firing the revolver directly through it and into the man's gut. The watchman crumpled over, groaning, then slid down the steps as Graf climbed the rest of the way up. Just before he emerged into the hall, he composed himself, straightened his collar, and stepped out, holding the viola case by its handle now. Everyone's attention was focused on the pulpit, but a young man in a blue navy uniform, confined to a wheelchair at the end of an aisle, looked at him curiously. Graf smiled and nodded an acknowledgment, before walking with slow deliberation around the south transept and the baptismal font, then ducking into the stairway that led up to the library, the Whispering Gallery, and the massive dome that towered over not only the bulk of the cathedral, but the entire city of London itself.

His destination was only a few hundred feet up, and with no further interruptions, he should be able to reach it in a matter of minutes. At that point, he anticipated nothing but the memorable crescendo to Operation Ottershaw.

CHAPTER
FIFTY-TWO

"Were you hit?" Rebecca whispered in the darkness of the alcove.

"No, were you?"

"No," though the moment she had felt the first bullet whiz within an inch of her cheek, she had dropped to the floor. The second shot had ricocheted off the wall.

"Do you think he's gone?" H. G. murmured.

"I heard footsteps on the stairs, and another shot."

Wells said, "You stay here," and of course she refused. When, she wondered, would he ever take her true measure?

He poked his head out of the archway, then ventured a few feet into the crypt. Rebecca followed, but slowly and unsteadily. The cut on her foot felt as if it were on fire, and her head was hot and feverish. Whatever she had sliced her foot on in Graf's laboratory, it had infected her, just as Wells had suspected. Swinging the truncheon had taken every ounce of strength she had left; now she could barely stay upright.

Wells had stepped over Schell's body, and made his way to the staircase, where she now saw that another body—in the brown uniform of the St. Paul's watchmen—lay crumpled. Wells had turned him over and was feeling for a pulse, in the wrist and then the neck. Looking up at her, he shook his head.

"H. G., you have to go after Graf."

"But what about you?"

"I can manage," she said, with as much false conviction as she could muster. "Just hurry! I'll raise the alarm."

As Wells slipped the standard-issue nightstick loose from the dead man's belt and disappeared up the winding staircase, Rebecca suddenly felt her legs give out under her and she folded to her knees. Her hands tingled from the force of the blows she'd administered, and there were spatters of blood on the sleeve of her overcoat. She'd killed a man. The body was lying only feet away, as motionless as a statue. He was certainly someone who deserved to die, she'd had no choice, and even now felt no regrets. But a man was dead, nonetheless, and she—Cicily Fairfield—had done it. It was a thought that she would have found almost impossible to accept under the best of circumstances. But here, at this moment, in the crypt of St. Paul's, on Ash Wednesday, with a fever smoldering inside her, it was all but incomprehensible. She felt as if her head would burst at the seams.

Unable to remain erect at all, she lay flat, pressing her cheek to the cold, hard stone. The sensation was so blissful, she could not contain a sigh. As if holding a seashell to her ear, she could hear the faraway echo of the great cathedral, like a living thing, its breath rising and falling, all around her. Rising, and falling. In her mind's eye, she envisioned an ancient dragon, slumbering in its cave. "But you must wake," she was urging the dragon. "You must fight!" And it was then that she lost consciousness altogether.

CHAPTER FIFTY-THREE

The winding stone steps were smooth and worn from centuries of use, and Anton Graf had to navigate them more slowly than he'd have liked. He didn't want to risk slipping, or colliding unexpectedly with yet another watchman. He disliked killing on an individual scale—it was entirely too personal. And this was not personal. This was war.

Schell was only its most recent casualty—and that had been to some extent his own fault. The sight of Wells being strangled was so riveting that he'd neglected to keep an eye on the ever-resourceful Rebecca West. When she'd swung that club at Schell's skull, he'd been grudgingly impressed by her initiative . . . until he realized it had left him with little recourse but to take the revolver from his pocket and start shooting. He'd hoped to avoid such a noisy overture to the grand symphony that was to come.

From the pulpit, he could still hear some sort of exhortation to the faithful, the empty, indecipherable words echoing around the immense chamber, lulling the multitude into an artificial sense of security. Well, let it be. Let them rise, with prayers on their lips, toward heaven; he would help them along.

Rounding the second landing, he came to the library door, where he knocked, waited, then knocked again. Turning the handle, he found it unlocked, and slipped inside. The windows were concealed by black-out curtains, with a single gas lamp illuminating the tiered shelves of dark wood, packed with theological tomes. The chimney breast was adorned with a portrait of some bewigged church functionary, and a marble bust of Sir Christopher Wren, the size of a loaf of bread, presided over the main librarian's desk. He locked the door behind him.

This, he thought, was as good a place as any. He turned up the lamp, then, clearing away an open book of psalms, laid the viola case atop the desk, putting it down as gently as if he were consigning a baby to its cradle. Undoing the clasp, he opened the case and gazed at his makeshift bomb. A thing of beauty it was not, with one end blunt and one pointed, and a portion of the Guinness label still adhering to one of its tin panels, but it would more than do the job. It was a pity that, like a bee undone by wielding its stinger, the weapon itself would expire in the cataclysm. He would have to fashion an exact facsimile one day, for the kaiser's private *Wunderkammer*.

"Oh, so you must be the new verger?" he heard, and his head shot up in astonishment. An old man, bent nearly double, emerged from the towering shelves, with a heavy leather volume under his arm.

The new what? Graf kicked himself—how could he have blundered like this? "Yes," he said, buying time, "I'm the new one."

"What was that?" the old man said, cupping a hand behind one ear. "I didn't expect you during services, for goodness' sake."

No wonder he hadn't heard him knocking, Graf thought, as he carefully closed the case again. The man was nearly deaf.

"I decided to come in tonight."

The old man was coming closer, inching forward like a crab, and Graf did not dare to fire the gun again—not here. Looking around, his eye alighted on the bust of Wren.

"I'm Spenser, though I'm sure you know that," he said, plopping the book on the desk and extending a palsied hand. "Head librarian, lo these thirty years."

Graf shook it, but did not give a name.

"What's this?" Spenser said, regarding the viola case. "You are also a musician?"

Graf could not brook any further delay. It was unfortunate, but time was of the essence, and as the old librarian bent to open the viola case, he took hold of the bust of Wren, and brought it down hard on the back of the man's head. Stunned, the old man dropped to his knees, but remained upright. It took another swipe before he toppled over, but even then, to Graf's surprise, his fingers grasped at the cuff of Graf's trousers and held on.

"Let go of that," Graf said, shaking his leg and trying to jerk away, but in so doing his hip jarred the desk, the leather-bound book bumped against an inkstand, and then that, too, fell over, sending a sea of black ink spilling toward the viola case. Graf tried to stanch the flow with his sleeve, his arm inadvertently banging up against a brass desk lamp, which went crashing to the floor. What *else* could go wrong?

"*Gott in Himmel!*" he muttered, ink dripping from his sleeve.

And deaf old Spenser, against all odds, was still hanging on, as if to a lifeline. Graf delivered a swift kick to his head and the wind finally went out of the old fool's sails.

Good God, when would these nuisances stop? Graf thought. There was work to be done.

CHAPTER
FIFTY-FOUR

When Wells had come up into the cathedral again, he'd looked in every direction, but the place was full, and there was no sign of Graf anywhere. The raised pulpit was straight before him, the minister delivering the close of his sermon—"And in this time of war, let us use the season of Lent to reflect upon the many hardships and sacrifices made by those who protect our kingdom from afar"—while Wells surveyed the choir stalls to his right, packed with young boys in black and white, holding their scores. Past them stood the high altar and the elaborate baldachin that sheltered it.

But no, he thought, Graf could not have run there, not in full view of the choir and congregation. Wells turned the other way, back around the south transept, where the baptismal font stood. As he did so, his head swiveling anxiously to catch any sign of Graf, he saw a navy man, in a wheelchair, waving a hand to catch his eye. The man cocked his head and made the motion of someone sawing away at a violin.

"Yes," Wells mouthed, nodding his head vigorously. *That's the man I'm looking for.* The sailor pointed at the arched doorway, with a brass plaque marking it as the staircase to the library. This was also the doorway to the renowned Whispering Gallery, constructed so cleverly that if someone whispered something to the wall at one end, his utterance could be heard perfectly by someone holding an ear against the wall anywhere else along its circumference. Wells charged to the door, threw it open, but saw no one ahead. He started up the winding steps, and at the second landing, had to pause, winded, clutching the banister. A door to his right was marked "Library Archives," and he might have gone right by it, if it weren't for the fact that behind it he heard what sounded like a tussle and a lamp crashing to the floor.

He tried the handle, but the door was locked. He knocked forcefully, and all sound abruptly stopped. A moment later, the small sliver of light that had emanated from the threshold went out.

"Graf, I know you're in there!" Wells said, raising his voice to be heard above the first striking chords from the cathedral's massive pipe organ. "Whatever you were planning, it's over now!"

The organ swelled, the full diapason from its mighty pipes rising up through the walls and floor, and Wells used the cover from the noise to bash the old door handle with his truncheon. Three quick blows and the antique brass fixture crumpled to pieces. Wells shoved the door open with his shoulder, but in the light spilling from the gas lamp on the landing, he saw no one. A lamp and a marble bust lay on the floor beside the main desk. Nothing moved inside the book-lined room.

"I know you're in here," Wells announced. He kept himself low and to one side of the door, to make himself less of a target. "No point in running now." Out of the corner of his eye, he now glimpsed an old man, absolutely still—dead?—sprawled behind the desk, in a pool of blood. Or could it be . . . ink?

Cautiously, he stepped a few paces into the room, trying to stay in the shadows of the towering shelves, which stood in rows as orderly as soldiers on parade. "Game's over," he said.

"Hardly, Mr. Wells."

His ears pricked up. Where precisely had the voice come from?

"Though I had not expected you, of all people, to interfere."

"You know me?" Wells advanced slowly, trying to pinpoint the sound.

"In a war of civilizations, the most technologically developed will prevail."

What was he talking about? Only one of his books came immediately to mind. "Not in *The War of the Worlds*, it didn't," he retorted.

A chuckle, but from where? The man was weaving among the shelves.

"Only because you introduced a *deus ex machina*. Germs."

His adversary's stock in trade, Wells thought.

"I thank you for the inspiration," Graf said, now strangely close. Clutching the club, Wells surveyed the shelves looming all around him—the confessions of St. Augustine, the lives of the early church fathers—trying to peer between the hidebound volumes to see into the next aisle.

"The humblest bacteria—" Graf murmured.

Wells whirled around, the voice sounding now as if it had outflanked him.

"—defeating the alien horde."

As if to taunt him, a single volume slid from an upper shelf, pushed by a finger, and splatted open to the floor behind him. Graf was plainly moving about.

"That was just a story," Wells said.

"No. That was a *manual*."

"For what?" Wells simply wanted to keep him talking, to figure out where he was and perhaps get close enough to grapple with him.

"It is a shame we have to finish now," Graf said, "but I am on a rigorous schedule," and Wells, hearing the click of the revolver a foot or two away, leveled his arms and shoved a couple dozen books into the opposite aisle, ducking down just as the shot ripped through the space where they had been. He caught a glimpse of Graf's narrow face, spectacles glittering, before it flitted away. Wells crawled into the next aisle, and squatted there, perfectly still, heart pounding.

"If that one didn't hit you," Graf called out, his voice growing farther away, "the next one will."

But the next one did not come.

Wells played dead until he heard the footsteps receding, then the door slamming shut, closing off all the light from the hall and leaving him in total darkness. He groped for an upper shelf to raise himself by, and then, praying that he had oriented himself correctly, moved toward the front of the library, feeling his way, elbows out, among the bookcases. He was desperate not to lose any more time in the pursuit . . . especially now that he had a much better—and more horrifying—idea of Graf's plan.

One that his own book had inspired.

CHAPTER
FIFTY-FIVE

At first, the sensation was comforting. Warm. Embracing. Rebecca welcomed it, and although she knew that she had to get up and do something—raise an alarm?—she wanted to linger just as she was, the cool, grainy surface of the stone against her cheek, the languid arm across her shoulders. Her limbs felt as if they had no strength of their own, and her mind was foggy and uncertain.

"Jaguar," she murmured, imagining the arm to belong to her lover.

But there was no reply. Only a hot breath on the back of her neck. Hot and foul.

Something was wrong.

The arm pressed down, and the bulk of a body seemed to be joining it. There was something damp on her skin. Spittle. She squirmed.

"Sie schlagen mich."

Even her rudimentary German could translate that. *You hit me.*

He lay almost entirely on top of her now, a dead weight like an elephant.

She tried to wriggle away, but it was almost impossible to move at all. Even to breathe.

Schell's breath was ragged, too.

She tried to buck him off, but his bulk was too great. How had he survived the strikes to his head?

"*Hure.*"

That, too, she understood. *Whore.*

A surge of adrenaline coursed through her veins, and lifting her head from the floor of the crypt, she tried to focus her eyes. But then a hand, fat fingers spread, pushed it back down again so powerfully she nearly cracked her teeth.

"*Sie schlagen mich.*" Again.

And he was going to settle the score.

The truncheon she had hit him with was lying only a few feet away—she stretched an arm out toward it—but it might just as well have been a mile. He grunted in derision, and she felt a splat of blood and spit fall from his mouth and onto her cheek.

"English bitch."

Bracing herself on her elbows, she rocked her hips, back and forth. He gripped her shoulders to hold her still. From far above, she heard the swell of an organ's pipes. As he bore down, hoping to crush her, she reared up, just enough to throw him off-balance. She did it again, and this time raised her body sufficiently high to topple him. He slipped to one side, groaning. The blows to his head *must* have taken *some* toll! She was able to turn over at last, and see him—his eyes were cloudy, and his thick blond hair was creased and matted to his skull with dried blood. If only she had hit him one more time when she'd had the chance . . .

Her feet scrabbling sideways at the floor, she managed to put a few inches between them, enough to get to her knees, and then to stand, however unsteadily. Her left shoe felt like a red-hot vice around her swollen foot. Picking up the truncheon—it was slick and unwieldy in her hand—she steadied herself. He was bobbing on his knees, shirttails hanging loose, a gas mask, strangely enough, dangling from one pocket of his overcoat. He was twisting his mouth to say something, but he never did get it out. With both hands on the truncheon, Rebecca swung it so hard that his head spun nearly all the way around, blood and teeth flying, before he flopped onto his belly, his chin smacking on the floor. Panting from the exertion, she waited to see if he moved again—she was not going to make the same mistake twice—but he did not. Still, just to be absolutely sure, she rested her good foot on the small of his back and pressed it there.

The hunter, claiming her kill.

CHAPTER
FIFTY-SIX

Graf knew, from a previous trial run, that it was exactly 295 steps from the floor of the cathedral to the commanding heights of the Whispering Gallery, set on a cornice running the circumference of the dome. But he did not remember being so winded from the climb that last time he had tried it. Of course, on that trial run he had not encountered the turmoil in the crypt, or in the library, nor had he been carrying the viola case. When he emerged into the gallery now, it was very different than it had been during the day. The long rectangular windows that surrounded it, each set of four punctuated by a niche containing a piece of classical statuary, admitted only moonlight, which cast an eerie bluish glow all around.

And tonight, unlike before, he was quite alone there.

Far below, but directly beneath him, lay the more brightly lighted expanse of the church, and the reverent worshippers listening to the choristers—thirty young boys, their voices raised in sweet harmony—singing to the booming accompaniment of the mighty church organ. The music echoed around the gallery, reverberating from the curved walls, soaring to the top of the dome overhead, so stirringly that even the painted Gospel figures adorning the spandrels seemed to have come to life. But Graf had already picked out his spot, and doing his best to block out the noise and distraction, he went right to it, gently resting the viola case on the wooden bench that ran the length of the space. *Concentrate,* he told himself, *concentrate.*

Peering down from the iron railing, he could see the pulpit to his left, the endless nave straight ahead, and in the very center of the floor the great circular medallion marking the apex of the dome itself. It was a multicolored mosaic, a round sun emitting spike-like rays, and bordered by a black marble ring advising, in Latin, that anyone seeking Christopher Wren's monument should simply look around them. The medallion could not have made a better target.

Stepping back from the rail, he took from one pocket of his coat a pair of rubber gloves—the thinnest, but most durable, from his lab— and snapped them on. From the other pocket, he removed a gas mask, then unwound its straps and looped it around behind his ears. Since the goggles interfered with his vision, and the lower portion with his breathing, he would only raise it to his face at the last minute—just before arming the bomb and hurling it over the rail.

There was a break in the music, the last chords of the hymn dying down. A few words were being preached from the pulpit, largely inde-cipherable from up here, and of no importance, anyway. With all the deliberation of a surgeon about to embark upon a complicated opera-tion, Graf unlatched the case and lifted its lid. The canister lay cradled in its black velvet berth, with soft rags, made from Schell's old coat, tucked into every corner around it to provide extra cushioning. Schell . . . he had hoped to have him up in the gallery, too, not only as an accomplice, but as a witness to his achievement. Who would vouch for him? There was the secretary of state Wilhelm Solf, back in the Colonial Office in Berlin, but even he didn't know much about the plan. Graf had pur-posely kept him, like everyone else, in the dark.

Still, he could not dwell on that now. The *act* was the thing.

Sitting down beside the case, he lifted the bomb out with both hands, and laid it in his lap. The minister was still prattling on—Graf could occasionally make out a phrase or two about the enormous sacrifices made by the nation, or the resolute character with which Britain was meeting the brutality of the savage Hun—as he carefully loosened the screw on the tip of the canister. Beneath it, the nitroglycerin charge lay. Schell had assured him that he had weighted the bomb in such a way that it would fall headfirst and explode on contact. But from this great height, Graf was certain that however it landed, the detonation would occur, and its lethal contents would burst out on a cloud of poisonous gas. All he needed to do first was give it a shake or two, enough to crack the tubes inside, and mix the deadly brew.

He had anticipated this moment for so long, he was reluctant now to proceed. He would wait until the music died down, and only then, as the organ pipes subsided, as every voice went silent, as the worshippers sat enraptured, would he ignite this long-planned Götterdämmerung.

CHAPTER
FIFTY-SEVEN

How long it took him to fumble his way out of the dark library, Wells could not be sure—but it was too long, that much he knew. He had banged up against several shelves, then circumvented the fallen librarian, before stumbling over the andirons and almost landing in the hearth. Regaining his balance, his hand fell on one of the pokers, which he gratefully gripped harder. At last, he thought, lifting it from the rack, he would have some kind of weapon. Not a gun, as Graf had, but *something*.

Groping for the handle to the door, he eventually found it, and stepped out into the dim gas-lit corridor. The walls echoed with the strains of the pipe organ—Bach's "O Man, Bewail Thy Grievous Sin," if he was not mistaken. But the only sign of Graf was a footprint smudged in black ink . . . heading toward the end of the hall, where a velvet cord had been dropped and a winding staircase led to the upper gallery.

Poker twitching in his hand, Wells went to the stairs and started up, wary of alerting Graf to his pursuit, but eager to close any distance between them. He knew he was on the right track when he saw yet another smear of ink on a step. But he heard nothing and saw nothing of the man himself. What, he wondered, was his plan? And what, more to the point, was in that viola case he had been carrying?

As he rounded the last landing, he saw a brass plaque that read, "The Whispering Gallery: In addition to proper decorum, visitors are reminded to observe all necessary safety precautions." Wells moved even more slowly now, keeping close to the inner wall—the stone thrummed with the music—until he could stick his head out enough to look around the gallery's vast circumference.

In the gloom, it was hard to see anything clearly—a golden aura from the lamps in the nave below had turned the gallery into a flickering magic lantern show—and Wells wondered if he'd somehow lost the man's trail. But how? The stairs had led nowhere but here. Exhausted already, unsure of what he could possibly do next, he leaned his head back against the wall. Having come this far, was he going to fail in his duty now?

"Straight across," he heard, softly, "on the bench," and nearly jumped. The wall was whispering to him, but in an unmistakable voice. Hoarse, gravelly. The voice of Sergeant Stubb.

Whose ghost was nowhere to be seen.

Wells's eyes sprang wide, and looking where he'd been told, he discerned the outline of a lone, dark figure now, sitting on the curved bench that went all the way around the gallery. He held something in his lap, to which, head bent low, he was carefully attending. Resting beside him, barely visible behind the wrought-iron railing, was an open instrument case.

"Now's the time," Stubb whispered. *"Now."*

CHAPTER
FIFTY-EIGHT

It was the gas mask in Schell's pocket that had, at first, puzzled Rebecca—but then, it had suddenly made absolute, and awful, sense.

Whatever their plan was, and however they were planning to execute it, there were only moments to avert it.

Seizing the mask and looping it around her neck, she falteringly made her way to the exit, and then, with both hands to steady herself against the stone walls, climbed, one laborious step after another, up from the crypt. The boy choristers were sweetly singing, in their high-pitched harmony, as she propped herself in the arched doorway, swaying on her blazing foot. Looking all around, she saw no sign of Wells, or Graf, or for that matter, anything amiss. Until she noticed a young sailor, in a wheelchair, glancing at her, for all the world as if he had been expecting her. He was pointing, and rather urgently, toward the door to the upper gallery. She knew that staircase—she'd gone there several times over the course of her life—and she knew that it was hundreds of steps high. Hundreds of steps that she would never be able to climb in her present condition.

But she also knew that it led to the balcony that overlooked the entire center of the church, and its congregation.

She looked up at the iron railing—black and gold—that surrounded the Whispering Gallery, and though she could not be sure from such a distance and at such a height, she thought she saw someone in a dark overcoat, sitting just behind it. Her eyes went from that commanding post to the congregation below, from that high ground to the mosaic medallion in the floor—a target as plain as any in the shooting range at the Fairyland arcade.

It all came together for her in one terrible flash. Careening toward the pulpit, she knew what she had to do—and knew that she might have only seconds to do it.

CHAPTER
FIFTY-NINE

Under most circumstances, Graf would have been transported by the organ music, carried away on the tide of Bach's genius. A countryman, of course, and in his view, the superior composer, even to Beethoven. Where Beethoven was all emotion, Bach was all intellect, his compositions so exquisitely calibrated in their harmonic and motivic organization that he might just as well have been a scientist. Graf felt that he and Bach, however different their occupations and aspirations, would have had a seamless meeting of the minds.

But now, he was simply waiting for the music to stop, waiting for the last chords to die out, so that in the ensuing silence he could shout out, in triumph and exultation, the kaiser's own war cry, "*der Sieg ist sicher!*"—"victory is assured!"—and hurl his bomb at the gleaming target below. That moment was coming, and soon, and in preparation now, he lifted the canister from his lap and shook it, just enough to hear the tinkle of the glass tubes cracking inside, their contents commingling with the gas, to make the lethal brew. The explosive charge was set, and there was nothing left to do but to don the gas mask hanging down around his neck. With gloved hands, he removed his eyeglasses—he always felt strangely naked without them on—and slipped them into the pocket of his baggy coat. Then he tightened the straps of the mask behind his ears and settled the device over his mouth and nose.

The air was suddenly stale, and he could hear his own breathing. His vision was obscured behind the thick goggles, and the gallery, dim to begin with, darkened further. He had to blink several times just to focus his vision, and then, once he felt accustomed to having the mask on, he stood up and approached the railing. He held the bomb like an offering, and as the last measures of the music played out, he lifted it high above his head, both hands damp with a nervous sweat, and waited. He was not a praying man, but now he did. He prayed for his attack to go off without a hitch, to rain down destruction upon his enemy, to instill fear in English hearts everywhere and shatter the nation's will to fight on. He was praying for all these things when he caught, out of the corner of his eye, a furtive movement.

At first, he considered it a mere shadow, but when he dared to turn his head and look away from the black-bordered sun that lay below, he saw it again, much closer, so close that before he could even react, he saw a murky form lunging straight at him. The sharp end of an iron rod prodded his breast, hard, knocking him backward and off of his feet.

The bomb slipped from his hands, traveling the length of his body like a rolling pin and then sliding onto the floor, where it butted up, unexploded, against the bottom of the rail . . .

CHAPTER SIXTY

Rebecca had scrambled halfway up the steps to the pulpit, waving her gas mask, before a member of the cathedral watch spotted her and vaulted up right behind her.

"Let go!" she cried, batting his hand away from her arm. The bishop, looking aghast, tried to push her back down, but she shoved past him, too, and trying desperately to make herself heard over the final measures of the music, shouted, "Get out! Get out!" And then to emphasize the reason, she waved the mask back and forth above her head. "A gas attack is coming! A gas attack!"

She saw the front rows of the congregation taking notice, stirring uncertainly in their seats—was this woman mad?—and a few people quickly rising. From the far quarter, the navy man in his wheelchair picked up the cry, "Evacuate the cathedral! Now!" Even the watchman who had tried to stop her fell silent, and the bishop, holding his Bible in confusion, let her go on.

"Get out!" she repeated. At a clatter in the gallery high above, she looked up. All that could be seen was a tussle of some sort. Was it Wells, grappling with Graf and holding him at bay? Pointing her arm up at the fracas, she shouted, "Get out!" again and again, until her own lungs gave out and the bishop, at last grasping the situation, picked up the cry.

"Go!" he cried, stepping in front of Rebecca to lend his own authority. "Go now!"

With that, the stunned worshippers leapt to their feet and in a frenzied rush made for the exits on either transept, or back through the great western portal where most of them had entered. Those who were elderly, infirm, or wheelchair bound were swept up in the tide and carried toward the doors, the St. Paul's watchmen trying to keep anyone from being trampled underfoot. The choristers, in their white gowns, flew from their choir stalls like a flock of startled doves. All was pandemonium, as the organ abruptly stopped and the cathedral was filled instead with the rumble of a thousand stamping feet and the roar of terrified cries.

Rebecca craned her head to see what was happening in the Whispering Gallery above, but from this pulpit, so far below, it was all like a shadow play, enacted behind the iron railings . . . angels and demons battling it out on the crenellated ramparts of heaven.

CHAPTER SIXTY-ONE

Graf had dropped his missile and fallen back with a thump against the bench, but Wells knew that the struggle had only just begun. With his gas mask still in place, the German rebounded, leaping up and batting at the iron poker that Wells was using like a rapier, thrusting and parrying to keep his enemy off-balance.

Oh, how Wells wished that he held a better weapon!

Graf, cursing under the mask, was struggling to grasp the poker that Wells suddenly swung in a wicked arc at his head. With his first swing, Wells missed entirely, but the second connected, and to his relief, he saw Graf slump to one side, the mask slipping askew. But then the German's hand dug into the pocket of his overcoat and fumbled around, before coming out with the revolver Wells had feared.

From a crouching position, he raised the gun and fired, an orange blaze erupting from the muzzle and the bullet ripping just under Wells's arm, so closely that the fabric of the sleeve was torn. If he left any distance between them, Wells knew that the next shot might hit home, so instead of retreating he lunged at his opponent, slashing at his arm with the poker so forcefully that the gun went off again, the bullet banging bright sparks off the filigree of the railing. With one more blow to his wrist, Wells knocked the gun entirely free from Graf's shaking fingers. It clattered to the floor, as the reverberation of the shots echoed around the chamber, a percussive accompaniment to the panicked cacophony far below.

In a rage, Graf ripped the mask off his face and snarled, "You damned fool! You damned old fool!"

Wells, exhausted, could barely stand, the hand holding the poker drooping at his side. *Again,* he thought, *hit him again.* Or better still, he should scramble for the gun.

"You can't win," Graf gasped, leaning back on the bench, breathing hard himself, and cradling his battered arm. "You've already lost!"

"Have I?"

"You and your whole bloody country."

Wells was not about to argue the point just now. He suspected Graf was just playing for time, a thought confirmed in the next instant when, sufficiently recovered, Graf bolted up and ducked toward the railing.

But it wasn't the gun he went for—it was the cylinder a few yards away.

Wells spun around, but Graf had already managed to pick it up. Holding it above his head with both arms—one of them broken and bent—he teetered to the railing, a wicked grin creasing his face. His glittering eyes were fixed directly below, on the gold roundel in the cathedral floor, and he was shouting something in German just as Wells leapt to tackle him. But the distance was too great, and all the tackle succeeded in doing was knocking the man over the rail, the bomb still clutched in his hands. Through the filigree, Wells watched in horror as Graf plummeted from the gallery, the tails of his overcoat flapping as wide as Satan's wings, and then, on impact, disintegrating in a blinding ball of white smoke, crimson flame . . . and green gas.

CHAPTER
SIXTY-TWO

Rebecca, perhaps the last one left on the cathedral floor, saw Graf fall.

Like a bat swooping down from a belfry, he plunged over the balcony rail, something gray and metallic in his hands. And then, before she could even comprehend what she had just seen, came the white-hot detonation, the blast so extreme it threw the raised pulpit off its base and sent it flying toward the south transept. She was thrown with it, and only when it crashed against the far wall, was she able to lift her head enough to see the cloud of green vapor, mottled with specks of what looked like tiny flitting moths, spreading in all directions.

The gas mask was still entwined in her fingers and with trembling hands she affixed it to her face, before crawling to her feet and stumbling from the wreckage. Fire and fumes were everywhere. The door to the crypt had been nearly blown off its hinges but she staggered toward it, shoving it back up against the door jamb the moment she had passed through, then clambering, half-blind behind the ill-fitting goggles, back down into the deepest recesses underground, as fast and as far as she could go from the creeping green tendrils of the gas. Her left foot felt as if it were a cake left baking in the oven.

But what about Wells? What had happened to him, up in that gallery? Had he survived the struggle with Graf, only to perish—God forbid—in the deadly fumes filling the cathedral?

The body of Schell lay where she'd left it, several yellow teeth and a hank of his hair swimming in the pool of blood. She slunk to the farthest end of the crypt, past the massive sarcophagus of Nelson, which rested directly beneath the gold medallion in the nave above, and then past the granite tomb of the Duke of Wellington, too, before collapsing atop a black marble slab that marked the grave of the cathedral's great builder himself.

She was tempted to remove the mask, but for fear of the gas somehow having penetrated even to these depths, she left it on, and instead closed her eyes and tried to regulate her breathing, slow the trip-hammer of her heart, and squeeze her leg to keep the agony in her foot from coursing up the rest of her body. It didn't bear to think of what might lie ahead; she had seen what had happened to Silas Drummond.

But at least, she reflected grimly, there was one mystery that had now been solved. Even if it was too late to do anything about it, she knew at long last what deadly cargo Graf had been carrying in that precious viola case.

CHAPTER SIXTY-THREE

From his time in the trenches, Wells knew the taint of gas, and sprang for the mask lying on the bench, yanking it on. But he still needed to get out of the way of the noxious cloud, billowing upward like some poisonous toadstool.

Picking up the gun, he staggered through the archway, then up another flight of stairs to the Stone Gallery, which surrounded the outer dome and cupola. A padlock secured the door, but a shot from the gun blew it to pieces, and then, with a swift kick to the frame, he was outside, the stars twinkling in a moonlit sky, the whole vast city of London, largely dark from the blackout, spread out around him on all sides. He risked lowering the mask, and gulped at the night air. From such a windy height, it was a miraculous, but knee-rattling, sight, the towers and steeples of the metropolis rising like black needles, the silver sash of the river Thames wending its way under the graceful bridges.

From far below, he could hear the clanging of the fire brigade's wagons, and though it was blood-chilling to look down, he could see crowds of people fleeing from the cathedral in all directions. Had they all escaped in time, or had the bomb claimed a host of lives?

Had it claimed Rebecca's? He prayed that she had remained below, in the crypt, where she might have been sheltered from the explosion. If only he had been able to stop it, if only he had figured out the plot sooner, and in time to avert it . . .

"You did well," he heard a voice, full of gravel, murmur at his elbow. He didn't even need to turn to see who it was.

"Not well enough." How long would it be before he could safely descend and go in search of Rebecca?

A lone cloud passed across the sky, but when it was gone and Wells did turn his head, he saw Sergeant Stubb etched in moonlight, silver and shimmering, leaning beside him at the stone parapet, as casually as if the two of them were simply observing the ducks from the bridge in St. James's Park.

"I'm not your charge anymore," Wells said, gently. "You can, if you wish, move on."

"Noted." His fingers were unwrapping a packet of Victory lozenges. "But have a look at that, will you?" he said, gesturing at the limitless expanse of night sky and distant stars, the silver moon hanging as if on an invisible chain.

"Yes."

"Hard to give up on all that, wouldn't you say?"

Wells couldn't imagine doing so. Even with all the horror he had seen, the death and destruction, it would be hard, when his own time came, to give up on all that. The very notion of such a renunciation was a thread that wound its way through some of his most famous books, stories in which all the quotidian joys and pleasures were judiciously weighed against the cosmic indifference and routine cruelties of life upon earth. After a pause, he asked, "What happens next?"

The soiled St. George's patch on Stubb's sleeve twitched with his shrug. "Give it time. You'll see soon enough."

Easier said than done. Wells had always been a man impatient for the future to unfold, a man who looked toward a world where mankind had learned to live in peace, where science served only to better the earth and the myriad creatures who inhabited it, where, one day, even the power of the atom had been mastered and its unlimited potential harnessed.

Like the baying of hounds, Wells heard the rising cry of air-raid alarms from the East End. In the distance, and by squinting, he could just make out a pair of zeppelins, the size of silver buttons, hovering high above the city. The wardens had been right—with the weather so clear, it was a likely night for a bombing raid. On the wind, he could hear the first concussive blows, and see the reddish glow from the fires that the bombs had ignited. That warm glow, he knew, denoted ruined buildings and slaughtered people . . . a vision conjured in one of his own stories. A veritable war of the worlds. Another instance of life imitating art, not the other way around. How tragic that his imagination should have prefigured such a grimly authentic scene.

When he looked to his left, Stubb was already half-gone, his body dissolving before Wells's very eyes. It was as if it had been composed of a million fireflies, all of them now dispersing in the night wind, winking out, one by one. Among the last things to go were the sergeant's eyes, dark and mournful.

Hard to give up on all that.

And then, the eyes vanished, too. He was now, truly, an invisible man. Another of Wells's own creations.

All that remained on the parapet was the lozenge packet. Wells reached for it—a last memento—but then it was snatched up by the wind, or perhaps an unseen hand, and whisked into the darkness like an albatross flying before a storm.

CHAPTER
SIXTY-FOUR

Although it was unlikely that Wells would have been anywhere near St. Paul's Cathedral—he was by no means a religious man—Jane had been frantic all the same after hearing the news of the catastrophe there. She had tried several times to contact Wells at the flat on St. James's Court, but with no success. The zeppelin raids had been known to interfere with communications not only between London and Easton, but to all parts of the country.

So it was with mixed emotions that she saw Slattery's familiar livery car proceeding up the rectory drive the next day. She had not had to face the man since he had wantonly killed young Kurt in the barn and she would have liked to keep things that way, but she also knew that he might be carrying a telegram from her husband. There was little reason for him to be coming there, otherwise.

She was already at the open door, bundling her sweater around her shoulders, as he approached with not one but two envelopes in hand. She could hardly bear to look him in the eye, as she ripped open the telegram first.

"FEAR NOT STOP I REMAIN INDESTRUCTIBLE," it began, and she had to smile. "BUT MUCH TO DO HERE STOP

DEBRIEFINGS WITH WINSTON ET AL STOP HOPE ALL IS WELL AT HOME STOP MISS YOU AND SEND MUCH LOVE. H. G."

What she missed were the long, discursive letters he used to send, years ago, from his far-flung lecture destinations or research trips, brimming with colorful anecdotes and amusing doodles. But she knew he was too busy for that now, and she resolved, on the spot, to go to London on the afternoon train. Why was she fretting and pining in the countryside, when there was no longer any need for her to be there? When, in fact, nothing would be more welcome than to get away from the scene of such a recent tragedy, even if it did mean subjecting herself to the zeppelin attacks on the city?

"Do you want me to wait for you to write out a reply?" Slattery asked, his tone a bit more curt than it had once been. He still suspected some collusion here, something amiss about the German boy in the barn, and he apparently wanted her to know it.

"No need," she said, "you can go."

"Not till you've opened that other one," he said. "It's from Doc Grover's wife."

"You know what's in it?" she said, though it was still sealed.

"She said I was to wait for you to answer something, and then return it to her."

Jane could guess what it would be, and she was right. Maude had written her a cursory note saying that she was to be relieved of her duties as deputy watch commander, and asking that she sign and date the note as a receipt for the official town records. "Wait here," she said, stepping into the foyer to find a pen. She'd never wanted the job in the first place, and would be glad to be rid of it. She folded the note into the envelope and gave it back to Slattery. He weighed it in his hand, as if wondering at its contents, and raised his eyes in a deliberately insolent manner. Jane figured he knew exactly what the envelope contained.

"That's it, then?" he said.

"That's it. And goodbye," she said, closing the door so quickly it might almost have caught his nose. Secretly, she wished that it had. Leaning against the back of the door, she took a breath, relieved not only that her husband was well—that was the paramount thing—but that she had been freed from an unwanted duty.

She missed H. G., even if it was only the sound of a scratching pen or pounding typewriter. The silence of the house oppressed her. And truth be told, she grieved for the young enemy soldier—how perverse was that?—who had become so much more than that to her; harboring him, despite the dangers, had given some structure, and higher purpose, to her days. She felt alone, and adrift, and was wondering where she should fetch up next. How many other women, she thought, were left in much the same quandary these days, caught between the life they had once led and the uncertainty of the one that now lay before them? She knew she should take some comfort from that camaraderie, but, as with most abstract concepts, in the last analysis it provided little actual help. Life was just something one stumbled through, as best one could, until even one's stumbling came to its inevitable end.

CHAPTER
SIXTY-FIVE

Wells was slumped in the chair when Nurse Chasubel put the cup of hot tea on the table at his elbow, then draped a scratchy wool blanket over him. He looked up, wearily, and thanked her.

"If you insist on staying the night again, we could probably find you a bed," she said, but Wells declined. The hospital was overcrowded as it was, and the last thing he wanted to do was occupy a cot that might be used for one of the war wounded.

"How is she?" he asked, and Emma said, "Much the same."

"No better at all? What about the fever?"

"It won't break any sooner just because you're here keeping vigil. You could go home, you know. I promise that I will send you word of any change in her condition."

But that was not good enough. He was not going to leave the Communicable Diseases Ward until he was sure that Rebecca was out of the woods and safely on the road to recovery. It was, he felt, the least he could do. If she had never met him, she would not be in the peril she was in right now.

When he'd come down from the cupola, gas mask firmly in place, and clawed his way through the wreckage left by the bomb and the gray-green miasma that hung in the air like a ghastly pall, he'd seen no sign of life in the cathedral. But no bodies either, thank God. The wardens must have had sufficient warning—had he heard Rebecca's voice, booming from the pulpit, or simply imagined it?—and herded everyone out the doors, which had been slammed shut after the last evacuee had made it out. He'd had to clamber over the shattered frame of the pulpit and a million shards of plaster and mosaic and stone, before coming to the door leading down to the crypts. It was closed—a lucky sign, as it might have provided some protection to Rebecca if she had remained down below—but when he shoved it with his shoulder, it fell from its hinges and crashed to the floor. A cloud of milky dust rose toward his mask. The winding stairs were dim, just enough light filtering up from the gas lamps below for him to see the crumpled body of the watchman Graf had shot. He stepped over it, and once in the crypt, he saw Schell, even bloodier and more battered than he recalled, sprawled out on the floor.

But Rebecca was nowhere to be seen.

Had she recovered enough to make it out alive? Had someone come along to help rescue her? His heart leapt at the thought. Even now, perhaps she was on her way to the hospital. He longed to lift the thick goggles to see the scene more clearly, but knew better than to try. Not yet.

There were scuff marks in the dust, even a spot or two of congealed blood, all leading away from the corpse. Moving cautiously through the gloom, he traced them back, past the monumental sarcophagi, and all the way to the grave site of Sir Christopher Wren himself. A black marble slab set into the floor . . . on which he found Rebecca, prostrate and unmoving.

His heart had seized up in his chest, as he dropped to his knees and gathered her to his breast. It was several seconds before he was able to detect a breath—faint and shallow—and then, lift her from the grave. He could barely recall how he managed to carry her all the way up and out of the cathedral, but once outside, he had collapsed from the exertion. Two of the St. Paul's watchmen had found him, with Rebecca still in his arms and his gas mask discarded on the pedestal of the statue to Queen Anne, and transferred them both to an ambulance.

"Guy's Hospital," Wells had croaked, but the drivers in the front seat had insisted, "There's closer than that."

Shaking his head, Wells said, "Must be Guy's." She had to be admitted to the Communicable Diseases Ward as quickly as possible.

"Who's he to tell us our job?" one muttered to the other.

Wells, having overheard them, piped up, "I'm H. G. Wells, that's who."

They stopped to look at him, and also at the unconscious girl, more closely, before the driver said, "Blimey. He may be right." Leaning on his horn repeatedly, he forged his way through the frantic crowds still milling about in the streets. "Guy's Hospital it is."

Driving into the central courtyard, horn still blaring—for once, Wells was happy to have been able to trade on his fame—Rebecca was moved to a gurney and wheeled to the upper floor, with Wells holding on to one of her own hot and damp hands. Nurse Emma Chasubel promptly rose from the entry desk, and then, seeing who it was, hurried toward them. "Were you at the cathedral?"

That news had traveled fast. Wells nodded. "She's burning up. But it's from a previous injury—in the German's lab." He and Emma exchanged a look, full of import.

"Then we'll put her in Room 6," she said. "It's just been vacated and sterilized."

It did not escape his notice that Room 6 was the same private cell in which Silas Drummond, late of the Horse Guards Parade, had been housed. Wells slumped into a chair at the table where he had once seen a copy of *Sons and Lovers*, while Emma and another nurse went about removing Rebecca's clothes and cleansing her body. When it was done,

Emma came to Wells and said, "The wound on her foot. How did that happen?"

He told her what he knew, then quickly followed up by asking when Dr. Phipps would be there to assess the situation.

"He's in surgery, and won't be out for another hour or so. In the meantime, we have started all the necessary and prescribed procedures."

Wells must not have looked sufficiently reassured.

"We are doing everything that can be done," she reiterated.

"But will it be enough?"

She didn't answer him, but how could she? No one could reliably foresee the outcome of something like this.

And that was how it had remained for two days now. Rebecca swam in and out of consciousness, her fever smoldering like a fire in an underground coal seam, her foot and leg swelling ominously, like a pink balloon about to burst. Every so often she would become lucid enough to recognize him and even speak a few words, but not everything she uttered was coherent. Mixed in with talk of horses and penny arcades were invocations to the patron St. George, which he took to be a reference to Machen's story. He only hoped that it was true, that some guardian angel was indeed watching over her, though most of the time it was her mother or one of her sisters, who, like Wells, waited anxiously for any sign of improvement.

Mrs. Fairfield, who had once been so deferential, was well past that now. She blamed Wells for having involved her daughter in such a terrible situation, and had quickly supplanted him as the one Dr. Phipps was to consult and keep informed. It was Emma who would then later relay the findings to Wells, out of the family's earshot.

This afternoon, Wells was fortunate enough to intercept the doctor on his rounds. The man was so overworked that he had come to resemble the pallid and sallow patients in his ward. Spotting Wells, who always delayed him with questions and entreaties, he had tried to scurry past, head down, but Wells was too quick for him.

"A word, Phipps!" he called, springing up from his chair.

"I am behind my time already, Mr. Wells."

"I quite understand, and apologize for this delay. But about Miss West—"

"The range of options is narrowing very fast."

"Meaning?"

"The leg will have to go. It should have gone yesterday." His tone indicated that he was past mincing words. The man, his white coat splotched with blood and God knows what else, was simply exhausted. "Only her age and sex have kept me from acting sooner."

Wells was stunned. Even though he had known all along that the situation was dire, he hadn't yet heard it so bluntly expressed from the physician in charge. "That is the only way?"

"Even so, it may be too late."

"For what?" he asked, though he knew perfectly well what the doctor was suggesting.

"The infection is so virulent, we cannot stop it. We cannot even specifically identify it."

"But if you could?"

Phipps sighed in exasperation. "At least then we might know better how to fight it. We would have a chance."

He shambled off, as Wells stood, transfixed, desperately wondering what he could do. Mrs. Fairfield and her daughters had gone home an hour or so before, clutching damp handkerchiefs and avoiding so much as any eye contact with Wells, which meant that he might have the small viewing window into her cell all to himself. While Nurse Chasubel was busy with the other patients in the main ward, he went back to the quarantine sector, hung with warning signs, and donned a fresh white gown and mask from the supply in the cabinet. Glancing through the crosshatched windows set in the steel doors, he saw in each room a single man, lying still, breathing tubes protruding from his mouth or nose, a white blanket with a blue stripe drawn across the ravaged shell of his body. At Room 6, he hesitated before looking in again. He was always afraid of what he might see.

But when he did step close enough to look in, he saw Rebecca, as usual, lying, swaddled in bandages and sheets, on the iron cot. Her head was propped up, as was her left leg. Her brown hair, usually so rich and lustrous, was matted and spread across the pillow; her eyes and mouth were closed, and angry black blisters marred her cheek and arm.

And then, oddly, he found his view obscured.

It was as if something had passed before the little window, though what he could not tell.

Thinking it must be a problem with his eyes, he rubbed them, and then looked again.

The view was unobstructed now, but something even stranger was happening. Portions of Rebecca's body and bed were omitted from his field of vision, as if something were standing in the way. Wells felt that familiar twinge at the bridge of his nose, and the faint odor of the trenches. And even as he watched, the faint outline of another person— a man, all in gray, a uniform—appeared at her bedside.

But this was no patron saint. This was a ghost.

A German ghost. Ministering to her.

Even after all he had already seen and been through, Wells was stunned.

Had Von Baden remained in this ward ever since Wells had first seen him standing forlornly behind his beloved Emma Chasubel?

Wells considered barging in, he had even taken hold of the door handle, when the apparition turned toward him, shaking its head slowly. Wells stopped short, and the ghost drifted toward the door, taking on definition as it came. When it was close to the little window, it looked steadfastly, even imploringly, into Wells's eyes, and through pallid lips uttered two words. *"Das Notizbuch."* A moment later, in English, "the notebook."

Wells's mind scrambled to make sense of that, then remembered the notebook—of course!—that Von Baden had entrusted to him in the underground lair. Wells had turned it over to Colonel Bryce at the Ministry, on the chance that, once translated, it might contain some information useful to the British war effort. Did it instead contain some information that might prove vital to Rebecca's salvation?

"Why?" Wells said. "What's in it? Can't you tell me now?"

Through the closed door, the ghost simply repeated, "the notebook."

Nodding vigorously to acknowledge that he understood, Wells was off like a shot, nearly bowling over Emma as he hurried through the main ward, still cloaked and wearing the gauze face mask. In fact, he did not remember to doff them at all until he had left the confines of the hospital and leapt into a passing cab. "Whitehall!" he tried to shout to the driver, who had to say, "What's that? Can't hear you behind that mask, Doctor."

Wells ripped the mask away, and shrugging off the gown, reiterated his destination, adding that haste was of the essence. "It's a matter of life and death!"

"These days," the driver said, turning on his headlamps in the gathering dusk and stepping on the gas pedal, "what isn't?"

CHAPTER
SIXTY-SIX

"What do you mean, you don't have it?" Wells said. "I gave it to you myself!"

"And I gave it to the Admiralty office," Colonel Bryce explained with maddening composure. "The best translators and code-breakers are all assigned to them."

"Code-breakers?"

"In case you have forgotten, Mr. Wells, even a cursory examination of the notebook revealed a number of equations, figures, and formulas. I thought it best to leave it in their hands."

"And they have it now?" Wells said, not rising from a chair as he had never even bothered to sit down.

"I presume so."

And Wells was off again, on foot, crossing the street to the Old Admiralty office, where he was fortunate enough to find his friend Winston still at his desk.

"What is it, Wells?" Churchill exclaimed at the sight of his frantic friend.

"The notebook," Wells said, dropping into a chair this time, "from the German deserter."

"One of the ghouls?"

"I do not choose to call them that," Wells said, bridling, "but yes—the notebook that Friedrich Von Baden gave me. I need to have it back, immediately."

"Calm yourself," Churchill said, buzzing a button on his desk. An adjutant, the same one that Wells had breezed right past, appeared in the doorway, was given his orders to retrieve the notebook forthwith, and then vanished.

"And now, may I ask why? What's so important about this notebook?"

"Rebecca West is at death's door. She has been infected with something, some bacterial strain, and that notebook may contain some medical notes, experimental protocols, crucial to her cure."

"I'm sorry, H. G., I was unaware. We have all had our hands full, as you can imagine, with the disaster in St. Paul's."

"Rebecca was there. So was I."

Churchill's ears perked up. "It wasn't Rebecca, was it, who manned the pulpit and warned everyone to leave?"

That confirmed it for Wells. The papers had carried stories of the anonymous but heroic young woman who had done so.

"She saved countless lives," Churchill said.

"All the more reason that we must save hers now."

"By all accounts, there was a struggle in the Whispering Gallery, too. Several people attested to seeing some commotion up there before they ran for their lives." He waited, but Wells said nothing. "May I assume, then, that the man who exploded the bomb—whose remains were atomized in the explosion—was the elusive Dr. Graf?"

"You may."

"And that he did not intend for the attack to be suicidal?"

Wells nodded.

"May I also assume that he had some *assistance*, then, in falling from that great height?"

Wells demurred, but that did not keep Churchill from rising from his chair to clasp his hand and shake it heartily. "Good job, old man, good job. For an ink-stained wretch, you do quite well in the field."

"Excuse me, sir," the adjutant interrupted from the doorway, "but I have a copy of the notebook's translation from the Linguistics and Codes departments."

Although he tried to hand it straight to Churchill, Wells was too fast and intercepted it. "What's this?" he said, as he scanned the twenty or thirty loosely bound pages. On many of them, he saw blank spaces and the letters "CSP" typed instead. "Winston, what on earth do these letters stand for?" he demanded, jabbing his finger at them.

"Censored for security purposes."

"But those may be the very parts crucial to me, and to Rebecca. Von Baden only said to get the notebook."

"The ghoul—excuse me, Von Baden—said to get it?" Churchill asked, confused. "When was that?"

"This afternoon," Wells said, defiantly.

"The one who was killed in the underground trench?"

"Yes. And don't think I miss your point. You think I've lost my mind. Well, maybe I have. We can argue about it later. Right now, I need that notebook—the original—and in its entirety."

Churchill looked at the adjutant, standing in the doorway for further orders. "Can you go back to Coding and retrieve the original?"

"I'm afraid it's no longer there, sir."

"Then where is it?"

"The bio-warfare department."

"Why?" Churchill asked, though Wells could easily guess.

"Apparently, the translators immediately deciphered enough of the text to determine that much of it had to do with bacterial agents and toxins."

"Where is that department quartered?" Wells barked. "Where?"

The adjutant started to explain that it was several buildings away, around a corner, when Wells grabbed him by the arm instead and said, "You are taking me there, right now!"

The adjutant threw a look at Churchill, who nodded his assent, and reaching for the phone, said, "I'll tell Professor Metzger that you are coming there on my authority."

Hustling the bewildered young man through the streets, Wells could think of only one thing—time. Would the notebook yield some lifesaving clue, and even if it did, would it be soon enough to save Rebecca?

It did not look promising at first. The adjutant drew Wells toward what appeared to be an old abandoned horse stable, several blocks behind the impressive structures of Whitehall. Its windows were boarded up, and its steel door, stenciled with the words "Ancillary Research Programs," was guarded by a sentry in a box.

But their arrival had plainly been anticipated, as the sentry immediately admitted them. A steep flight of steps led down to another set of steel doors—guarded again—and behind this, to Wells's surprise, an enormous cavern-like space, with circular lights overhead, the low susurration of fans, and long lab counters dotted with microscopes and all the other familiar lab equipment. Fifteen or twenty young men—and women, too—were seated on metal stools, bent over their work.

Professor Metzger, removing his rubber gloves, approached Wells and the adjutant, and introduced himself. An elderly man, and short to begin with, he was stooped over so badly he could barely raise his head high enough to look them in the eye.

"A pleasure to meet the man who wrote my favorite story, 'The Stolen Bacillus,'" he said to Wells, who thanked him, but wanted to waste no time on pleasantries. "I need your help, Professor. Urgently." In quick strokes, he outlined what had happened to Rebecca—the cut foot, Graf's lab, her present sickness and dangerous decline—as Metzger bobbed his head, taking it all in. When Wells paused, he said, "Come with me," and led the way, at a maddeningly slow pace, toward another room at the rear of the cavern, where a basket of face masks hung beside the sealed door.

"Protocol," he said, putting one on, and waiting for Wells to do the same. "No need for you to do so," he said to the adjutant. "You may wait out here."

Inside, the air became markedly cooler, and the light dimmer. Locked glass cases lined the walls, but no one else was present.

"The notebook, which I'm afraid has been utterly disassembled, described experiments with enteric diseases—cholera, dysentery, typhoid, things I hardly need to explain to you—but also a number of other animal diseases, such as swine fever, rinderpest, foot-and-mouth, anthrax, and glanders."

That last pair, the ultimate unholy coupling.

"It sounds to me as if your young friend has been infected with some variant or combination of the latter two."

"Regrettably," Wells acknowledged, "I agree."

Going to the most remote of the glass cases and unlocking it with a key from a long silver chain looped to his belt, Metzger removed two vials stoppered with red plugs, and labeled with a host of numbers and letters.

"Mark you," the professor said, "I cannot guarantee anything. I have not seen the patient myself, or the symptoms you have so carefully described, but from what you say of her grave condition, I can only urge her physician to administer one or both of these as promptly as possible."

"But how could you have cultured them so quickly?"

"We started the antitoxin formulation the moment we got the notebook, days ago. We were told it had come from an anonymous German source, one who had, based on some of the formulas, previously worked at their secret base in the Baltic Sea."

"And so it did."

"We were—and are—afraid that these deadly poisons are being manufactured on an industrial scale. We had no choice but to take immediate action."

Wells started to wrap the two vials in his handkerchief, when Metzger said, "Oh, we can do better than that," and instead placed them in a cotton-lined box the size of a cigar case.

"I can only wish you the best of luck," Metzger said, his pale eyes peering up just above the mask. "Perhaps the work of this monster may have yielded some small good in the end, after all."

"The man who wrote that notebook," Wells said, turning to go, "was no monster. No monster at all."

CHAPTER
SIXTY-SEVEN

She was only occasionally aware of her true surroundings, a narrow bed in a small cell. She would catch a partial glimpse of masked faces, of Dr. Phipps, or that kindly nurse Emma, and even snatch a few words of what they were saying to her—"Rebecca, can you tell us anything more about what you cut your foot on?"—or what they were saying to each other—"We can only drain the wound so often before something more drastic will have to be done." She knew she was in a very bad way, and only hoped that when the time came for her to die, she would not be in the middle of one of the nightmares in which, most of the time, she was now living.

In those foggy dream states, she was usually running, running from a host of enemies—Anton Graf, wielding a needle the size of a kitchen knife, or his brutal henchman, Schell, with half his head gone. Although she often envisioned roaring flames all around her, and even felt their heat scorching her skin, she simultaneously felt, deep down inside, nothing but a cold ache, as if a stubborn lump of ice were wedged there. However uncomfortable the ice made her feel, she didn't want it to melt, because when it did, she felt she would be gone.

The passage of time was meaningless; she did not know if she had been there for hours, or days, or even weeks. The only moments approaching some sort of solace were those when she heard the voice, muffled by a mask, of Wells, and even felt his gloved hand rest lightly on her shoulder, or, once, brush some hair from her cheek. She longed to reach up and touch him, but her arms were restrained—why?—and the only words she could utter came out, even to her own ear, as garbled and incoherent. He had lovingly whispered, "My Panther, come back to me," and she had so wanted to reply, "Jaguar, I am trying," but even something so simple as that had been beyond her.

But now, she had become vaguely cognizant of additional activity. The doctor and nurse were murmuring encouraging words, and she felt the sleeves of her gown being raised to receive inoculations. At first, she shuddered—needles made her think of Graf and his hideous experiments—but Graf was dead. With her own eyes, she had seen him plummet from the gallery at St. Paul's. Whatever the doctor and nurse were doing now was surely intended for her benefit. How could it not be?

When they were done, and another cold compress had been laid across her forehead and eyes, she lay still, alone again in the cell . . . except for that vague apprehension of another presence in the room. Not Wells. But something, or someone, benign and invisible. Was it an angel, like one of those in Machen's story? She had felt its touch, but could not touch back. She had spoken to it, but heard no reply. Still, she took some comfort from it. The spirit was an ally, willing her to fight for her life, and she was grateful for its ineffable protection.

CHAPTER
SIXTY-EIGHT

That night, even after Dr. Phipps had agreed to administer the antitoxins—
"At this point, we might just as well try anything," he said to Wells in a tone
that plainly suggested he thought the whole business a lost cause—the only
change was for the worse. Rebecca's fever seemed to rage, the sweat breaking
out on her brow and blistered limbs. Wind and rain battered the hospital
walls, as she twisted and turned in the soaked sheets, sometimes calling out
for Wells, and sometimes, to his puzzlement, speaking to someone who
seemed closer, in the cell, someone bending over the bed itself.

Could it be . . . Von Baden? He struggled to see him, but to no avail.
Were the two of them—the dying girl and the dead soldier—commun-
ing in some strange purgatory?

When he could not stand to watch through the little window in
the door, or linger in the ward where Emma Chasubel kept a tender eye
on him, he wandered the corridors of the hospital. Most of the patients
were asleep—blissfully so, given their injuries and agony—but enough
were awake that he was able to stop here and there and buck one or two
of them up. Meeting the famous H. G. Wells was an exciting event, and
he signed several plaster casts with a flourish. In the sunroom, dimly lit
and lashed by gusts of wind, he found a young soldier with a missing

right hand, struggling to write a letter with his left. The man laughed at the scribbles he'd left on the page.

"I never was very good with words," the soldier confessed, "but not so bad as this."

Wells, impressed as always with the resilience of these damaged young men, conceded that hieroglyphs might be more easily decipherable. "Would you like me to serve as your scribe?" he said, taking up the pen and paper.

"H. G. Wells, writing *my* letter?"

"The sentiments I will leave to you. I'll just handle the penmanship." And he did. Though reticent at first, the young soldier—a proud recruit of the First Edinburgh City Battalion—soon warmed to the endeavor, and before long he was rattling away to his family at such a clip that Wells had to ask him to slow down. When they were done, the soldier asked if Wells would include a postscript, saying who had actually written down the words. Adding a few lines of his own, praising them for having raised such a courageous and patriotic young man, Wells signed the letter, sealed it in its envelope, and blessed the boy with a hand on his head. It reminded him of his time in the subterranean lair of the so-called ghouls, when they had come to him with their own stories, as if in a confessional, and he had given them absolution simply by listening, without judgment.

By dawn, the rain had begun to let up, and Wells, who had drifted to sleep in a chair, was awakened by a gentle hand on his shoulder. He looked up, blearily, to see Emma holding a cup of tea, and he was instantly afraid of what she might tell him had happened while he'd slept. He pushed himself up in the chair, bracing himself, but she quickly put his fear to rest by smiling and saying, "The fever's broken."

He could hardly believe his ears.

"Mind you, she's not out of the woods yet," she said, placing the hot tea on the table at his side, "but I think she will come out all right."

He sat up even straighter, fully awake now, and said, "Thank you, Emma, thank you for letting me know. The antidotes are working, then?"

"Maybe so," she said. "Something is."

"Something?"

"She's got a spirit in her."

"That she does. No one more so."

"And something, or somebody, watching over her. A guardian angel, I'd say."

He knew that she was not referring to him. Indeed, he knew precisely what—and to whom—she was referring. Wells had returned Friedrich to her, and now the ghost was repaying the favor by returning Rebecca to Wells.

He went back to the quarantine area, put on the protective garb, and then watched through the little window as Dr. Phipps removed a cold compress from Rebecca's forehead, then took her pulse. She was lying still, but breathing steadily, her features for once untroubled. When the doctor saw Wells looking in, he nodded calmly, and though his face was concealed by the mask, the optimistic message was clear.

Wells turned away, bone-weary, and under his breath said, "Thank you, Friedrich." Then he set off for his flat on St. James's Court and the prospect of a hot bath, a boiled egg, and, at last, a soft bed for the night.

CHAPTER
SIXTY-NINE

Having sat up most of the night, Jane heard the taxi pull up outside the flat, and went quickly to the window. The morning sun beat down on the street, still glistening from last night's rain. Holding the curtain back, she saw the driver coming round to the back seat to help his passenger out. It was H. G., but looking as weak and fatigued as she had ever seen him. A few words were exchanged at the curb, the driver guffawed, and Wells, clutching the railing, mounted the steps slowly. By the time he'd entered the building, Jane was already waiting in the open door to the flat.

At the sight of her, his face lit up.

"Of all the surprises I might have wished for . . ." he said, moving to embrace her.

He felt frail in her arms, and his color was not good. Once inside, she was tempted to ask where he had been all night, but wasn't sure she would welcome the answer. To preempt it, she said, "I just couldn't stay at the rectory another minute. It was too sad there."

"I quite understand."

"And on top of that, Maude Grover has fired me as deputy watch commander."

"Now there's a blow," Wells said, and they shared a laugh. "Did you have to relinquish all the rights and privileges of that high office?"

"Right down to the crown and scepter."

Wells kissed her again, warmly, on the cheek, and collapsed into an armchair by the hearth. "I've been at the hospital all night," he said, addressing the question hovering in the air. "Guy's."

"Are you ill?" Jane asked urgently.

"No, but I'm afraid that Rebecca has been."

So, Jane thought, her guess wasn't entirely far off. She suspected that he might have been with Rebecca somewhere, though the hospital was not where she had imagined.

"It's a long story, which I am too exhausted to recount in detail, but she was infected with a deadly bacteria and she is being kept under close supervision and quarantine."

"And the prognosis?"

"This morning, the fever broke, and she appears to be on the mend. It's still a bit touch and go, but she will come through all right. I'm quite confident of that."

"Oh, what a relief." And, oddly enough, she meant every word. Her husband's passades had grown so old hat, they were hardly worth belaboring. And although she had known from the start that this Rebecca was something more serious than that, she had never doubted H. G.'s love and devotion to her, his loyal and cherished wife. Their marriage rested on some other, higher, and more durable ground . . . and always would.

"I need a blazing hot bath to get this hospital stink off of me," Wells said, and Jane replied, "I'll get it running while you undress."

"And would it be too much to hope that there is an egg or two in the house?"

"I brought a half dozen up from Easton with me."

"A hot bath, fresh eggs—perhaps a basket of scones, unless I miss my guess—"

"Don't forget the rasher of bacon."

"I'm not sure if I tell you this often enough," he said, laying a palm gently against her cheek, "but on the chance that I've been remiss, I love you, my dear, more than I can ever express. Words are supposed to be my stock in trade, but my life would utterly fall to pieces without you. I'd be Humpty-Dumpty."

But Jane already knew all that. "Go and get ready," she said. "Leave everything to me."

Muttering "all the king's horses, and all the king's men," he shuffled off down the hall, unbuttoning his coat, and disappeared into the bedroom. Upon her own arrival, Jane had scoured that room for any sign of a visitor, and been relieved to find none. Though Wells had always been open with her, he also exercised discretion.

When he came to the breakfast table, thoroughly scrubbed, his thinning brown hair slick on his head, he was wearing the silk dressing gown she had bought him for their previous anniversary. And although there were a thousand things warranting discussion, neither one of them did much talking. Wells seemed too drained, and she knew enough not to press him. He asked of course about their boys, but she assured him they were quite safe and doing well at school. He asked about the repercussions in Easton from the tragedy with Kurt, but she said everyone, apart from Slattery and Maude Grover, was behaving in a perfectly respectful manner. They then relapsed into eating their breakfast and reading the morning newspaper in a companionable hush, as they did most mornings at the rectory. For all his volubility in public, Wells could be quite subdued at home, comfortably quiet and relaxed. Jane liked these times with him best of all.

When he had finished mopping up the egg yolk from his plate, and turned over the last page of the newspaper, he said that he was due back at Winston's office that afternoon, "to go over this whole St. Paul's affair."

"Why you?" she asked, before tumbling to the next question. "You weren't there, were you?"

"I was," he admitted. "But that must go no further."

The look in his eye reinforced his admonition.

Jane nodded—Lord knows, she had kept a hundred other secrets for him—but wondered just exactly what part he had played. The newspaper accounts had been fairly mysterious—leading her to suspect the heavy hand of the military censors—but that there had been a major explosion in the main rotunda was undeniable. All access to St. Paul's Cathedral was forbidden until further notice, something that had never happened in London since the cathedral's construction hundreds of years before. Much as she loved him, Wells would always remain to some extent a man of mystery—to her, as much as to the rest of the world.

"But first I am going to need a nice long nap in a big soft bed," he said, laying a hand on top of her own and giving it a gentle squeeze. "I wonder if you might not need some rest, too?"

Jane, who had barely slept a wink the night before, could think of nothing more appealing. "Let me just clear up the table first," she said, but Wells shook his head.

"That can wait." Rising from his chair with her hand still in his, he led her down the hall, his slippers scuffling on the floor, and once in the bedroom, they lowered the blackout shades to keep out the morning sun.

EPILOGUE

December 12, 1940

The master of ceremonies, Sir Somebody-or-Other, had been droning on for so long, Wells could barely keep his eyes open. It didn't help that the dinner had been a heavy one—roast beef and potatoes—or that he'd drunk too much claret. Diabetic now, he knew that he should limit his drinking and watch his diet more carefully, but at seventy-four—with one world war behind him, and another one now well underway—he had adopted a far more cavalier attitude toward transitory pleasures.

"And then there are of course the famous scientific romances, as our honored guest has called them, with which he first made his name." Sir Somebody, not content to simply name a few, was listing them, and giving a précis of each plot, some of which even Wells had forgotten in all but their broadest outlines. Why, he wondered again, had he even accepted this honor from the Albion Society? Was it because one of his personal heroes, the Antarctic explorer Ernest Shackleton, a man whose epic defeats were more inspiring than other men's victories, had accepted the same prize years before? It wasn't as if the study of his new flat on Hanover Terrace, overlooking Regent's Park, lacked for awards. The walls were already overloaded with plaques and medals and ribbons. The only one he'd missed, though nominated for it four times, was the Nobel Prize in Literature. It would have been nice to add it to his collection, but no matter. His career had been a long and celebrated one, and he couldn't complain.

Looking out from the dais and toward the long, narrow windows that lined the dining hall, he saw the night sky illuminated by the criss-crossing of the searchlights, constantly on the alert for signs of another bombing raid by Hitler's vaunted Luftwaffe; he was reminded of the attacks, well over twenty years ago now, of the zeppelins. How deadly and menacing they had been at the time—the "baby-killers," as they'd been called—but how primitive and inefficient they seemed today by the standards of the Blitz. Of course, he'd foreseen it all in his work; his novel *The Shape of Things to Come*, written in 1933, had even predicted a second world war erupting in this very year, and had described in brutal detail the aerial bombardment of cities and civilian populations. It gave him no pleasure to have been proven right on so many sad scores.

By the time the speaker finally gave way at the lectern, Wells feared that the audience, enjoying their after-dinner liqueurs, would be half in their cups, or fast asleep, but there before him, at the front tables, awake and smiling up at him, were some old friends, among them an alarmingly decrepit Arthur Machen and a still comely Rebecca West. Jane, poor thing, had been lost to cancer thirteen years before, and Winston, of course, was too overburdened as prime minister to find time for a literary occasion like this. Wells took his prepared remarks from the inside pocket of his jacket, but he hardly needed to do so. He had attended so many of these events, and given similar addresses so many times, that he could speak extemporaneously and from the heart.

After a few casual remarks by way of thanks, Wells said, "I only wish that the grim forecasts in my books had remained there, unfulfilled. But instead, I have only to glance out these windows to see their realiza-tion. That I once believed mankind would come to its senses—after the slaughter at the Somme, after Verdun, after Ypres and Passchendaele and Belleau Wood, after an entire generation was offered up on the bloodiest altar ever erected—now strikes me as hopelessly naive. A war to end all wars? Like a hanging to put a stop to gallows. Can't be done."

Rebecca's rich dark hair was threaded with silver now, and her figure had grown stout. But she remained the one woman for whom he had felt not precisely the deepest devotion—that honor still fell to Jane— but the greatest and most enduring passion. Although their lives had taken many turns—they had even had a son together, and she was now married to a man he much respected—it was to Rebecca that his thoughts most often turned when he wished to bask in some pleasant reverie during these difficult days.

"In my books, I predicted many things that came to pass, such as armored tanks and aerial combat and a wider freedom for the female sex, along with some things that I fear may yet occur—I refer to the atomic bomb, whose potential for destruction is so great its creation could alter life, or end it, on this planet forever." The Germans had already mastered a bomb that could explode not on contact, but only after burrowing into the earth, where its targets might be taking refuge, in vain. "There is no doubt in my mind that such an atomic weapon is being feverishly sought in our adversaries' secret laboratories even now."

When alone in his study at night, his eyes too weary to read any-more and his hand too unsteady to write, he would recall happier times. The first time Rebecca had kissed him, for instance, the night before his fateful journey to the Front . . . the first time they had gone to bed, when he had dubbed her Panther and she had called him Jaguar . . . the fertile exchange of political opinions and literary critiques, and the amusing little doodles—the "picshuas"—that he had drawn for her whenever they were apart.

"The one thing that I missed was the submarine," he confessed. "I could never imagine an underwater vessel not foundering or suffocating its crew, but there I was wrong. Not a day goes by that we do not read in the papers another story of the U-boats making one more deadly attack on our navy."

Though it was hard to do otherwise these days, he was painting, he recognized, a very gloomy picture for the assembled guests, there simply to honor a literary lion in the winter of his career. But before he could change course, and as if to underscore the point, his pause was suddenly filled by the distant wail of an air-raid siren. It was a sound that began low but swiftly rose to a harrowing pitch that, like the ululations of the Martian invaders in *The War of the Worlds*, encompassed all of London.

No one leapt from a seat, but everyone promptly put down their cups or glasses, and took their coats from the back of their chairs. There was no point in going on with his speech. Wells quickly thanked them all for coming, "but more pressing matters are now before us." Sir Somebody stuck a plaque into his hand and advised everyone to take shelter in the tube station just around the corner.

After Wells stepped down from the dais, Rebecca helped him on with his coat and hat, and tucked his scarf tightly around his throat. Machen, bent over, a few scraps of white hair clinging to his scalp, took a moment to shake his hand, and praise a piece Wells had written for the *Times* that day. "I think your point about a world body that could adjudicate future issues was especially well conceived," he said, and would have gone on had Rebecca not interceded.

"Arthur, now is not the time. Let's make for the door."

Most of the others in the audience had already exited, and by the time the trio had emerged onto the blacked-out street, people were streaming toward the Underground station. But Wells resisted, turning instead in the other direction.

"H. G., where in the world do you think you are going?" Rebecca asked.

"Home." He was not about to let the Nazis win by keeping him from his own home.

"Are you mad?"

"The place hasn't been hit yet."

"The windows have been shattered, twice, and the door has been blown off."

"It was replaced, just last month, with a much sturdier one."

But Rebecca put a firm arm through his, and put an end to the debate by guiding him toward the station. He knew she was right—navigating the rubble-strewn streets in the dark would be impossible. But all the same, he felt a visceral reluctance.

At the entrance to the station, an air-raid warden was waving an electric torch back and forth, encouraging everyone to keep calm and proceed in an orderly fashion, but before Wells entered, he took one last look over his shoulder, scanning the night sky for any sign of the enemy bombers. But all he could see, in the direction of St. Paul's, was a squadron of British Spitfires heading off to encounter them. The bravest of boys, those pilots; Wells had met many of them after an address he'd given at the RAF air base in Croydon, and it grieved him now that for some, flying overhead at this very moment, this might well prove to be their last mission.

The stairs, narrow and steep, weren't easy at the best of times, but right now they were teeming with people, some carrying precious articles, others foodstuffs and pillows, and on the way down Machen was lost in the crowd, borne away on the seething tide. Wells himself felt the rising fear in his chest that he experienced whenever he was asked to descend into some subterranean space; it was a fear that had been growing ever since the events of 1915. His time below the earth, buried among the ghouls, had made a lasting impression, one that had only become stronger over time, like a stubborn weed that resisted any attempt at extirpation. Perhaps sensing it, Rebecca tightened her grip on his arm, and kept him shuffling down.

At the bottom, a civil defense volunteer was admonishing everyone by saying, "Don't congregate here, we need to make way for those behind you. Move on into the tunnel."

Although the lights were on overhead, the electric current to the tracks had been cut off. Still, the tunnel was oppressively hot from the trains that had been passing through all day, and from the heat of all the bodies now cramming the platforms. The smell, too, was well-nigh unbearable—hundreds of panicky people jostling for a few inches of space, and already spilling over the second white line painted on the floor—the one that marked the closest proximity permitted to the edge of the platform. Wells and Rebecca proceeded gingerly, stepping over and between the people sprawled every which way they could manage.

"Under that arch ahead," she said. "I think I see a bit of space against the wall."

Wells allowed himself to be led to a niche below a vaulted archway, and Rebecca laid claim to it. On one side, an old man was clutching an ornate clock, on the other a family had laid a blanket down and three small children were already spread out on it.

"I should never have accepted this damn award," Wells grumbled, propping the plaque against the dirty brown brick. "I'd be at home right now with a newspaper and a glass of whiskey." Unbuttoning his coat, he flapped it open. How on earth would he make it through the next several hours? He could barely breathe already.

"Let's just make the best of it," Rebecca said, sitting down with her back against the wall.

"And how do we do that?" he said, taking a place beside her. "A game of gin rummy?"

"Shh—listen," she said, and though it was muffled, he could hear the low drone of airplanes, dozens of them, and then the rattle of anti-aircraft fire. Everyone in the tunnel had fallen silent, listening to the battle high above. Wells knew what would be coming next, a sound that never failed to remind him of the story of Jack and the Beanstalk. It was the heavy plodding of a giant's feet, one after the other, as bomb after bomb landed somewhere in London, demolishing streets and homes, killing any living thing unlucky enough to be within range of its lethal blast.

He put an arm around Rebecca's shoulders and pulled her to him just as the giant stamped his foot, sending a shiver through the concrete platform. The train tracks zinged, a fine silt descended from the vaulted roof, and the lights flickered on and off.

"That was a close one," Rebecca murmured, and Wells nodded. Even here, he knew, they were not safe—in September, a bomb had landed smack on the Marble Arch Station and killed twenty; in October, six hundred had been killed or injured at Balham. It was all just a matter of luck—good or bad.

The old man was reciting the Lord's Prayer over his keepsake clock; the children on the blanket were sniffling and crying. Out of nowhere, a calico cat appeared, eyes wild with terror, racing headlong into the black depths of the tunnel.

As if things could not get worse, Wells felt that old tingling at the bridge of his nose, herald of the sharp pain that used to precede some of his attacks. The foul odor of the trenches came back to him.

Another of the giant's footfalls, even closer than before, thumped overhead; bolts shot up from the rails, pinging into the ceiling. He felt a strange pressure on his shoulder, as if someone had laid a hand there, and he heard a gruff voice whisper in his ear, "Move down!"

Wells turned his head, but no one was there. It didn't matter. "We have to move!" he said to Rebecca, before alerting the old man and the family on the blanket.

"Why?" Rebecca said.

"Just do it," he barked, as the family took his order and scrambled in confusion farther into the tunnel. The old man stayed put.

Seconds later, there was a greater explosion up above than ever, and a fiery cloud of dust and debris billowed from the stairs leading down into the station. Cries and screeches echoed off the walls, the reverberations from the blast shaking a whole section of brick loose and sending it crashing down onto the very spot where Wells and Rebecca had huddled . . . and where the old man, now fatally crushed beneath the wreckage, had remained. Wells pulled Rebecca into his embrace, shielding her face inside his open coat, as smoke and ash engulfed them. Just before the lights went out altogether, Wells glimpsed, in the reddish glow from the detonation, the faintly glimmering image of a stocky man, in a tattered khaki uniform with St. George on the sleeve.

Still on duty, Sergeant, he thought, *after all these years.*

For the next half hour or more—time passed strangely in the pitch-black of the tunnel—they held each other and waited for the giant to stomp away. Eventually, the all-clear was sounded, and Wells was able to check on the old man, whose heart had indeed stopped, but whose hands still clung to the shattered clock. Amid much shouting and shoving from all quarters, the wardens and constables, using electric torches and tin whistles, herded the survivors back up the rubble-strewn steps and into the street. On the opposite side, an immense black hole marked the spot where a grocery store and haberdasher had stood. Timbers burned and crackled, as the fire brigade, looking as if they were wrestling with immense black pythons, deployed their rubber hoses.

"I pray that no one was in there," Rebecca said.

It was a vision from his own celebrated book, but this destruction had not been inflicted by alien invaders from Mars. This was all humanity's own folly.

"Thank God you ordered us to move when you did," Rebecca said. "How did you know?"

"A hunch."

But he knew that she had long ago guessed at the source of his intuitions.

Squeezing his arm as they picked their way around the crater, she said, "Be sure to thank Sergeant Stubb for me."

"If I see him again," Wells assured her, as he directed their steps toward Hanover Terrace, where he hoped his home still stood, "I shall."

AUTHOR'S NOTE

Since I so freely mix fact and fiction in my books, it has become my custom to add a few notes straightening things out in the end. Most of what you've just read is grounded in historical fact, but I'm afraid I have taken my usual liberties, compressing time and events somewhat in order to make a more coherent tale.

For instance, the short story by Arthur Machen (a popular Welsh writer and mystic in his day) that launches this narrative is real—it was called "The Bowmen," and it was published in the *Evening News* on September 29, 1914. But I have made my own rendition of it— much abbreviated and more accessible in respect to its language—for the opening chapter of this book. If you want to read the original, and in its entirety (which I highly recommend), it is available online for free at several sites.

The affair between the young Rebecca West and H. G. Wells is also quite real—and they really did call each other, respectively, Panther and Jaguar (that was a fact just too good to pass up)—though their relationship actually began a couple of years earlier than presented here. Rebecca went on to a long and illustrious career as a journalist and author, until her death at the age of ninety on March 15, 1983. Rebecca's two older sisters, only sketchily presented in this book, were accomplished in their own right: Winifred (Winnie) trained as a teacher, and Letitia (Lettie) as a physician and later barrister.

Although Aleister Crowley, the magus, did indeed exist, and pursued all the deviant and occult practices herein described (and then some), he didn't play the particular role I have assigned him in this story. (Nor did I burn his house down gratuitously; that really did happen.) The Earl of Boleskine was one of his many monikers, and "Do What Thou Wilt" was the slogan he lived by—and died by, in the Netherwood boarding house in Hastings, Sussex, on December 1, 1947. He was seventy-two. The funeral—sparsely attended, and held at a Brighton crematorium—was dubbed a "Black Mass" by the tabloid press.

His accomplice in this story, Dr. Anton Graf, is *not* a real person, though he was inspired by Anton Dilger, a German bacteriologist and saboteur who did indeed work on nefarious schemes, some of them successful, to poison British and American livestock during the First World War. That full and true story is powerfully presented in *The Fourth Horseman* by Robert L. Koenig (Public Affairs, 2006). Mr. Koenig had nothing to do with this novel, so don't blame him for any of my mistakes, etc., but do be forewarned—his harrowing book is not for the faint of heart, or animal lovers (like me).

As for Wells, he died several years after the close of this story—on August 13, 1946, at the age of seventy-nine, of unspecified causes. But he had been in declining health for years. He was cremated at Golders Green Crematorium in London (as, so it happens, was Bram Stoker, the subject of my previous novel, *The Night Crossing*), and his ashes were scattered to the four winds above the English Channel. By way of epitaph, Wells had provided his own. When one of his old novels, *The War in the Air* (first published in 1908), was reissued in 1941, he wrote a new preface for it. In this updated introduction to the book, a novel which had been written long before anyone had ever heard of anything like the Luftwaffe or the Blitz, or seen so many of its author's dire predictions come true, Wells declared that the only proper words on his tombstone should be, "I told you so. You damned fools."

ACKNOWLEDGMENTS

It may not take a village to *write* a book, but it does take a village to *publish* one.

First and foremost, there's my indefatigable literary agent, Cynthia Manson, who has seen me through the long and arduous publication of this and many another book.

Then there's my editor, Caitlin Alexander, who never fails to encourage and challenge me at the same time.

And finally, my astute haiku master and publisher, Jason Kirk, who has enthusiastically shepherded my last three books into print—along with the help of all the unsung heroes on the 47North marketing and publicity team.

To all of them, I extend my deepest gratitude. Truly, I couldn't have done it without you.

ABOUT THE AUTHOR

Robert Masello is an award-winning journalist, television writer, and bestselling author of many novels and nonfiction books. His historical thrillers with a supernatural bent have been published in seventeen languages and include *The Night Crossing*, *The Jekyll Revelation*, *The Romanov Cross*, *The Medusa Amulet*, *Blood and Ice*, and the Amazon Charts bestseller *The Einstein Prophecy*. His articles and essays have appeared in such prominent publications as the *Los Angeles Times*, the *Washington Post*, *New York* magazine, *People*, *Newsday*, *Parade*, *Glamour*, *Town & Country*, *Travel + Leisure*, and the *Wilson Quarterly*. An honors graduate of Princeton University, Masello has also taught and lectured nationwide, from the Columbia University Graduate School of Journalism to Claremont McKenna College, where he served as visiting lecturer in literature for six years. A long-standing member of the Writers Guild of America, he now lives in Santa Monica, California. You may visit him at www.robertmasello.com.